Lisa Dierbeck was raised in New York City. She has worked in a homeless shelter in London, in fashion in Milan and in a Manhattan art gallery. She contributes to *Elle*, *Glamour* and the *New York Times* and lives in Brooklyn, NYC.

One Pill Makes You Smaller

Lisa Dierbeck

CANONGATE

Edinburgh · New York · Melbourne

For V.J.R.

First published in 2005 in Great Britain by
Canongate Books Ltd,
14 High Street,
Edinburgh EH1 1TE

Originally published in 2003 in the USA by
Farrar, Straus and Giroux

10   9   8   7   6   5   4   3   2   1

British Library Cataloguing-in-Publication Data
A catalogue record for this book is available
on request from the British Library

ISBN 1 84195 628 7

Designed by Abby Kagan

Printed and bound in Great Britain by CPD Wales

www.canongate.co.uk

Child of the pure unclouded brow
And dreaming eyes of wonder!
Though time be fleet, and I and thou
Are half a life asunder,
Thy loving smile will surely hail
The love-gift of a fairy-tale.

—Lewis Carroll

One Pill Makes You Smaller

Of Love and Squalor

You're so fucking pretty, Alice," said Rabbit. "Why are you so completely gorgeous? Huh?"

Alice didn't answer him. Silence, she'd found, was the best response. Rabbit was lying on Aunt Esmé's bed with his dirty motorcycle boots propped up against the wall. His narrow pointy face was upside down: his head was hanging off the end of the mattress where his feet were supposed to be. His long hair fanned out underneath him, spilling over the bedspread until the ragged ends brushed the shag carpeting on the floor. Rabbit was high, as usual. Alice had seen him take one of the yellow pills that resembled her daily vitamins as soon he'd walked into the Dollhouse. That was what Aunt Esmé's friends called the cramped attic room. It had a sloping ceiling covered with tinfoil, and a glass cabinet filled with antique porcelain dolls that no one—except for Rabbit—played with anymore. Rabbit held the small Zeit bisque doll in his arms. Repeatedly, Aunt Esmé had told him not to take it out of the cabinet, because soon the Duncan estate would be auctioned—Dean Duncan had gone broke—and the bisque dolls were worth money. They had soft cotton bodies and hard ceramic heads. Their shoes were made of white kid leather. Their faces had been hand-painted in Switzerland, at the Zeit toy factory, in the 1860s. Rabbit had already chipped one of the doll's pink ears. When told not to do something, he didn't listen.

Rabbit kicked the light switch with his heel, turning on the black light—a slender tube of glass above the headboard. All the white objects in the room—the rocking chair, the rug, the bedspread—were transformed into an electric shade of violet. The whites of Rabbit's eyes and his big buckteeth turned violet, too. The curtains had been drawn against the daylight. Everything in the Dollhouse glowed in the dark. Alice wondered if the color white would vanish, even after Rabbit opened the curtains up and let the sun back in. Maybe whatever had turned to violet would stay that way.

"You destroy me, Alice," said Rabbit. "Do you realize that? You kill me. You ravage me. You really do."

"Shut up, Rabbit," said Alice.

"I just paid homage to your beauty, you fool. Were you raised in a barn? You're supposed to thank me."

"Thank you and shut up," Alice said.

Rabbit sighed. "Women. You're so cruel."

Alice was sitting on the beanbag chair in the corner of Aunt Esmé's room, right near the door. Behind her, low to the ground, was an autographed poster of Crash Omaha. Crash sang once a year with his band, the Idiots, at CBGB's. He'd met Aunt Esmé at Max's Kansas City when she was a high school freshman.

"For Esmé, with love and squalor," read the autograph in scrawling, jagged handwriting. "Yours eternally, Crash."

Alice thought Crash Omaha would have gotten an F in penmanship, an F in personal hygiene, and an F in organizational skills. Once, he'd come over to their house to see Aunt Esmé. While he was in the kitchen foraging in their refrigerator, he'd asked Alice to tell him her view of life. She'd said she wasn't sure what life was (maybe stones were alive, maybe snow was) and he'd burst into raucous laughter as if Alice were hilarious. His real name wasn't Crash Omaha, but Joey Pots. He didn't look as bad in person. In the poster, his mascara was running and his face was skeletal and haggard. He had red blood dripping down from the corner of his mouth. His stage show, he'd explained to Alice, was billed as "a bacchanalia of self-destruction." He was supposed to chew on broken glass. He'd told Alice that the glass was manufactured specially for the Idiots as a stage prop. It was made out of sugar and water and, if the Idiots were successful, it would be packaged with their photo on it as a "novelty item." He'd taken a piece of the fake glass out of the pocket of his leather jacket and displayed it to her proudly. Rock candy, he'd called it. It had been transparent. He'd offered Alice a bite, but it had been so brittle that when she tried to chew it, she'd nearly cracked a tooth. He'd laughed at that, too. His hands, with their black nail polish, had reminded her of Rabbit's.

Alice had her back turned to the Crash Omaha poster. She was making a collage from pictures that she'd cut out of Aunt Esmé's magazines. She took the eyes out of the rock stars' faces in the photographs from *Creem* and improved them. She pasted lovely new images inside them—tiny pastel-colored scenes from travel ads of leafy palm trees and lemon groves, and sandy beaches on serene, solitary islands surrounded by blue seas. She tried to work on her collage without looking up. Whenever Rabbit announced that he was being ravaged and destroyed by Alice, she ignored him. He had a thin black mustache that drooped down his cheeks, past his jawbone, forming two spindly long whiskers. He had beady dark eyes that sought Alice out when he saw her in the hallway, in the kitchen, on the stairs, in the library on the second floor, in the front garden, and in the backyard. She'd known Rabbit since she was in the fourth grade. That was when she'd undergone the first of her alarming rapid-growth spurts, like the Grow-Me Barbie doll whose torso lengthened when Alice pulled her hair in one direction and her legs in the other. Rabbit knew that despite Alice's unusual height, she was eleven. He'd even attended her eleventh-birthday party. Still, he raved on and on about her gorgeous this and her gorgeous that. Every time he did it, Aunt Esmé had to interrupt him.

"May I remind you that Alice is under twelve?" she would say from her usual spot beneath the window.

She didn't say that now. She was down on the floor with Stuart Applebaum, her slender fingers entwined with his. Stuart was taking premed classes over the summer, preparing to study psychology at Columbia University in the fall. His head rested on Aunt Esmé's stomach. She was wearing her midriff peasant blouse. Alice could see the five petals of the daisy that Stuart had drawn, with a ballpoint pen, around her belly button. Her fine straight hair, parted far to one side, flowed all the way down to her hips. Stuart said Aunt Esmé looked like Lauren Bacall, yet she claimed to be obese. She didn't smile often, but she had a pert snub nose and jolly, chubby cheeks.

"Alice, angel face, why don't you come over here and give your Rabbit a nice kiss?" said Rabbit. He waved his hands, beckoning to her. He wore a Mickey Mouse watch and a studded leather wristband.

Persephone raised her head and growled at him. The dog sat by the stairs, where it was cooler, in the hallway. Persephone was suspicious of Rabbit. Whenever he moved, she growled. His motorcycle boots clattered when he walked up and down the stairs. Persephone was disturbed by boots and by loud noises. Alice figured a loud man in boots must have beaten Persephone with a stick when she was a puppy or something. Alice and her mom had found the dog long before Dean and Rain had divorced—when Alice had been in kindergarten. The fluffy gray mutt had been shivering in an alley behind the school yard, half starving, her rib cage visible. She was a mongrel, part terrier and part Lab.

"Persephone, Persephone," said Rabbit now, as Persephone began to bark. "What did I ever do to you? Why can't we be friends, girl? Why do you dislike me?"

Persephone nestled her chin against her front paws, eyeing Rabbit balefully. She continued to growl, a low rumbling that sounded like approaching thunder.

"You should feed her, Rabbit," Stuart suggested. "That would give her some positive reinforcement. She'd come to associate you with nourishment and food."

"That's not a bad idea," Rabbit said. "But I don't want Persephone to kiss me. The gal I'm after is Alice."

"Quit hassling her," said Aunt Esmé. "Alice, if Rabbit is bugging you, feel free to leave. He's perfectly annoying and disgusting."

"Alice is devoted to me," Rabbit said. "We're great pals. Aren't we, Alice?"

"I guess," Alice said. She opened the jar of rubber cement. She took the brush out and daubed some glue on the picture she'd cut out. It was a chrysanthemum. Its intricate shape required intense concentration and advanced cutting skills. She was going to improve the paper rock star. She didn't know his name. She covered his left eye with her chrysanthemum.

"If you won't kiss me, at least bring that great glue over here," said Rabbit.

"It causes brain damage you know, you moron," said Aunt Esmé. "We've got better shit than that anyway. Take a look in the toy chest. Glue is crap."

"I like the rush. Give it here, hot stuff," said Rabbit.

"Do *not* call my niece hot stuff. Okay? You can't come on to her all day long, Rabbit. There's got to be some limit."

"I'm not coming on," Rabbit said. "Am I bothering you, Alice?"

Alice shrugged. If she was quiet, maybe he'd stop his constant jabbering about how quickly she was growing, what a big girl she was already, and so on. It was murder to sit through, to listen to. Alice held herself responsible. She blamed her own physical condition. It was "the premature onset of pubescence," said Dr. Fineman. Ever since it had struck, Alice had become a circus act, a one-girl freak show: the kid with tits. She wanted to get a tattoo on her forehead that declared what Aunt Esmé always said to Rabbit: Please don't bother Alice. She's eleven.

Even then, she wasn't sure he'd pay attention to the sign. She didn't look her age, according to Rabbit. She looked three to five years older. It was like a prison sentence: three to five. A period of vigilance and waiting. She hoped to be left alone for a few more years, until she became the age she already seemed to be. In the meantime, she regarded her womanly figure as a deformity. She had to go to the doctor every six months to be measured, and examined, and monitored. Dr. Fineman hit her on the knee with his little silver hammer and looked down her throat with his little flashlight. He recorded her height and weight on the chart he kept over his desk, next to a map of the United States. The map was covered with colored pins. He told Alice she was part of the Fineman Study, a national research project. He was collecting data on Alice—and on twenty-two other girls in New York City—whose "growth rate and maturation process" had "exceeded current statistical norms." Dr. Fineman had a theory that the average age most girls entered puberty was lower, in 1976, than it had ever been. The Fineman Study girls were just the tip of the iceberg, he assured Alice. It was the printed statistics that were misleading, and he wanted them to change. The old data made doctors think that ordinary girls didn't "develop" until they were fourteen. But "under certain environmental circumstances," they did, he said. Alice didn't like having developed under certain environmental circumstances. She didn't like being fussed over. She'd been singled out as rare, odd, and unique. She was the tallest girl in her grade; kids made fun of her; male teachers took her aside for quiet personal chats. During recess, her gray-haired gym instructor, Mr. Ridley, sat next to Alice on the wooden bench in the school yard. He kept asking Alice for her advice about his divorce, as if she were an adult. Everyone was divorcing nowadays, Alice told him. Her parents had. He thanked her profusely for listening. And again, Alice had yearned to say: But what do I know? I'm eleven. There was something about her, Aunt Esmé said, that made people want to approach her. Aunt Esmé said it was a pink aura full of positive energy that attracted them. Boys Alice had never met before came up to her in the street and, out of the blue, offered to buy her stuff. They suggested drinks, lunch, picnics, hot dogs. Alice had linked this phenomenon to her participation in the Fineman Study. It had to do with how she looked. Presumably, all across America, other Fineman Study girls were fending off these sorts of offers at the same time that Alice was. They were watching their teachers blush at them, and turning away resolutely when the teenage guy on Fifth Avenue called out to say, "Where you going, beautiful? When will you marry me?"

Alice had seen the other Fineman Study girls' names typed on a sheet of pale green graph paper. The first three had remained lodged in her memory: Irene Abrams; Hilary Anderson; Rebecca Burns. Alice's last name, Duncan, had appeared sixth on the list. Each name had been followed by hieroglyphics: symbols, initials, indecipherable scribbles, and a row of numbers. More than once, Alice had wished she could meet these other rapidly developing young giantesses, but she found this difficult to explain to Dr. Fineman. She hadn't ever worked up the courage to ask him if she could. She was growing at a breathtaking pace, like the beanstalk that had sprouted overnight in the children's story. She'd begun to develop breasts when she was eight. She got her period when she was nine. At eleven, Aunt Esmé said she was "baby-faced." Yet Alice stood a staggering five feet seven inches in her bare feet. She'd already had to buy new clothes three times that year. She couldn't keep up with it. Her skirts were always a half an inch too short and her shirts were always a half an inch too tight. Her legs continued to elongate, her bosom continued to mushroom. In the hallway at the Fieldwood School, children had mistaken the Giant Alice for a teacher. Her friends asked her to sneak them into *The Exorcist*, which was rated R. Alice, in high heels and lipstick, had done it, pretending to be seventeen. The woman in the ticket booth never even asked her for ID. She just said, "Enjoy the movie."

Though Rabbit's advances disturbed her, she felt the real trouble wasn't Rabbit. It was Alice. She was two contradictory things at once. She had a kid's head grafted on a woman's body. It embarrassed and upset her. It wasn't only Rabbit who reacted to her strangely. Lately people had been staring, not so much at Alice as at THE BREASTS. THE BREASTS were larger than before. "Lookin' good," one man had said while gazing, fixedly, at her chest. Alice, who had been taking Persephone out for a walk on Seventy-second Street, had recognized him. He was Mr. Mann, Felicia Mann's dad. Felicia was in Alice's sixth-grade class at the Fieldwood School. Mr. Mann had been standing in the doorway of his office. It was on the ground floor of a brownstone. He was a professional masseur who gave back rubs. He had a beard, an earring, and pink eyes.

"Hi, Mr. Mann," Alice had said.

"Hi there."

THE BREASTS, apparently, operated upon him like two tractor beams, magnetizing his eyes. She felt terrible. She felt she had exposed Superman to kryptonite. Mr. Mann was unable to see her face. He was weakened, hypnotized. He had no idea that she was his daughter's school friend, Alice thought. After a second, he managed to break away from the unholy pull of her deformation. He looked at the rest of Alice.

"Mr. Mann?" she said.

But his glance had returned to her chest.

"Would you like to come inside for a glass of wine?" he said with a leer.

"Mr. Mann, I'm Alice," she'd said. "Alice. Felicia's friend."

"Hello, Alice," he said. "Come on in and have some wine with me."

"I'm Alice Duncan," Alice had said. "Alice Duncan," she repeated. "Alice? From the Fieldwood School? The sixth grade." Alice looked at him for a long moment.

"The. Sixth. Grade," she said more loudly, as if he were deaf.

He smiled fondly at THE BREASTS.

She couldn't tell if he'd heard her. She hoped he hadn't, but she thought he had. He was probably high, like Rabbit usually was when Rabbit did that. As soon as Persephone began to snarl at Mr. Mann, Alice had tugged on the leash and they'd walked away.

"It was Mr. Mann," Alice had whispered to Persephone as they passed the entrance to the Whitney Museum on Madison Avenue. "That was Mr. Thomas Mann, my friend Felicia's dad. Her *dad*."

Persephone had gazed up at Alice, her tufted eyebrows trembling, as if she understood.

And Rabbit said that age was just a number. That what counted was how Alice felt inside. Inside, Alice felt like a monster, a shy weird one of whom no one was afraid. A well-liked monster whom grown men greeted with a friendly "Well, *hello* there, babe!" In school, with kids her own age, she was ridiculed. They called her Gigantor. They called her Stacked. They made noises behind her back. But on the sidewalks of New York, Alice was approved of. She was popular. Everyone was popular on the sidewalks of New York at this precise point in time. Strangers winked at one another on the steps of the Metropolitan, sidled close, lit each other's cigarettes, swapped phone numbers. They struck up conversations by the lake in Central Park, stripped their clothes off, and streaked across Sheep's Meadow. They tossed dandelions in the windows of police cars as they passed. Alice had seen all this, and she'd seen the great blue haze, the clouds of dope that hung heavy in the gardens behind the Central Park band shell, where Aunt Esmé scored her boyfriends, her musicians, and her drugs. It didn't matter just then that Alice was eleven. It began with Rabbit, and it ended with J.D., but it could just as easily have been anyone.

———

Stuart reached across Aunt Esmé's torso and picked up the plastic baggie filled with pot that was on the floor next to her hipbone. "Should we kill this?" he said. "Or save it for next time?"

"I'm wasted," said Rabbit, from the bed.

"What d'ya say? Should we finish off this dime of gold, you and me?" said Stuart.

"In a sec," Aunt Esmé told him, patting his head.

He lay back on her stomach. "You feel good," he said. "Like a firm pillow."

"Don't get too comfortable," said Aunt Esmé. "In about six seconds, I'm going to go downstairs to get something to eat."

Stuart let the baggie drop from his hand. Some of the buds spilled out onto the carpet. He left it lying there. This was atypical. Usually, Alice had noticed, Aunt Esmé and her boyfriends took meticulously good care of their drugs. The pills, powders, and weeds came inside rolled-up plastic bags, and each one was treated like a cherished toy. Aunt Esmé called the wooden cigar box she kept her stash in the "toy chest." Like good children, they always put their toys away. There was a test tube inside the toy chest filled with white powder and sealed with a cork stopper. There was an envelope that contained a dozen tiny squares of paper, each one smaller than a postage stamp, printed with abstract patterns. There was a disposable lighter, and a pipe. All these items were neatly arranged inside the toy chest, lined up in tidy rows. Alice wasn't allowed to take the drugs. But because she was "really very mature" she was welcome to sit in Aunt Esmé's room, and unless the door was locked, she could go in whenever she wanted to.

The presence of the drugs made Alice feel left out. Some of the stuff Aunt Esmé had started taking slowed her speech down and gave her eyes a blank, deadened quality, like a shark's. That dead look intensified the bad feeling Alice often had. The bad feeling had been born around the time Rain had filled a suitcase with clothes, hugged Alice goodbye, and left, promising to send for Alice one day. Alice had always known, in her heart of hearts, that Rain might leave. Her presence in the house had felt uncertain, temporary. When Aunt Esmé and her friends were high, Alice felt as if they'd gone away, too. Alice, wanting to participate, had asked if she could make a collage for the toy chest, gluing her cutouts onto it. So now the toy chest bore one of Alice's surreal collages, made of words and eyes. Aunt Esmé, Stuart, and Rabbit had all admired it. It was a great relief to Alice that people enjoyed something she had made for them, and could look at with interest, rather than gawking at Giant Alice and THE BREASTS. She kept them hidden behind thick sweatshirts, contained by large white cotton bras that looked like bandages. Though THE BREASTS were round and symmetrical, she didn't feel they belonged there, on her chest. She would have liked to detach them and put them away for use at a later date. Ideally, she would have stored them in a toy box of her own—a package marked Do Not Open Until Christmas 1981. It was better to have attracted notice for the collages, she felt, than for THE BREASTS. THE BREASTS were a phenomenon she'd had no part in. Alice hadn't created them. They'd spawned themselves. Good or bad, "gorgeous" or not, Alice couldn't take credit for them. The collages, on the other hand, were the product of her industry. She'd worked hard at them. She could make collages for hours, creating whole landscapes of cutout castles and cutout forests, cutout animals, cutout spaceships, cutout aliens, cutout couples, and cutout parties. Aunt Esmé had said that Alice might be an artist like Dean when she grew up. Alice thought she might like to be an artist, but she wouldn't want to be like Dean. He was a schiz. Alice had overheard Aunt Esmé talking about him on the telephone. She'd said that Dean was "gonzo on lithium" and "way mentally unstable," because "no one likes the type of paintings he does nowadays."

Alice didn't like Dean's paintings, either. He always painted the same thing: adults wearing baby clothes. It was boring. She'd told this to him frankly, not to be mean, but in the hope that he might do something new, that he'd feel better, that he'd change. She'd wanted to inspire Dean. He often paced the floors of his studio muttering, loudly—as if wanting them to hear—"It's inspiration, damn it. It's inspiration that I lack!" But when Alice had said the adults-in-baby-clothes theme was tired (she'd learned to talk this way from him, about themes being tiring), Dean hadn't been inspired at all. He'd just agreed.

"Ah, my palette," Dean had said, sucking on his pipe in the high-ceilinged, dilapidated rooms he painted in. "It's bleak, Alice. It's relentless and depressing. It reflects the dark inside my heart and the dark inside my mind."

As she often was inside Dean's studio, Alice had felt frightened.

"I can't imagine why a collector, or anyone else for that matter, would want to spend three grand to have all this black murk of mine hanging in their living room," he had continued. Then he'd hung his head in his hands, his usual signal for wanting to be alone.

Unfortunately, the art collectors agreed with him about the murk and bleakness. "Portraiture is out. Conceptual is in," Dean's agent had said to Aunt Esmé at one of Dean's poorly attended cocktail parties. (Alice had been standing next to the buffet table, in the backyard, eating canapés. Dean himself hadn't been there. He never came to his own parties.) Though Dean's work had once been fashionable, it had become, the agent said, "passé." Art collectors had gradually stopped buying. Dean's faltering career had precipitated his first major breakdown. He separated them into Majors and Minors, like baseball leagues. He had a second Major after Rain left. When Alice was nine, her mother had moved to Rome with a man named Knut and had begun designing shoes. She was rediscovering joy. That's what her postcard said. Rain had been twenty-six when she left them. She'd been seventeen when Dean had married her. He was sixty now—an old, old man, Alice thought. And, Alice thought, old men might die. The only dead person she had ever known was Edgar Allan Poe, who wasn't a person at all, but an aquatic salamander. She'd buried Edgar Allan Poe underneath the azalea bush in the front yard. Dean had painted flowers on Edgar's little tombstone in acrylics. He wrote, in calligraphy, "E.P. 1975–1976." He had explained to Alice that for an aquatic salamander, a year is a full lifetime. But now there was a new blue sign next to Edgar Allan Poe's tombstone. The white letters on it said: Corcoran Real Estate. FOR SALE.

Alice put the finishing touches on her collage. Aunt Esmé, Stuart, and Rabbit all had their eyes closed, as they always did when listening to the slow, spooky record. It was by Pink Floyd. Even the name struck Alice as improbable. What was a floyd, anyway? And how could it be pink? Everyone in Aunt Esmé's circle talked about Pink Floyd with reverence, but the music was meaningless to Alice. She liked cheerful music with lucid, pleasant lyrics that made sense. She liked the early, and not the late, Beatles. She preferred them when they'd been clean-cut and chipper. She'd wanted the music to stay perky and upbeat—but when the Beatles grew their hair down to their shoulders and began wearing necklaces, it had gotten more complicated and sad. The messy hairstyles had led to messy music, messy clothes, messy lives. While Alice kept her own room neat, Aunt Esmé's room was littered with laundry, records and cassette tapes, and the residue of late-night snacks. Her friends sat around and listened to the caterwaul of Robert Plant, or to the weepy guitar of *The White Album* and the babble of "number nine, number nine, number nine." Now school had ended for the summer, and they spent all day hanging out by the boathouse in the park, returning in the late afternoon to loaf around. They were dreary. They were decadent. They had the arrogant superiority of teenagers. But they were the only friends Alice had. Everyone else she knew called her Gigantor, except for Veronica Dreyfuss and Skye Winston, who—like many of the neighborhood children on the Upper East Side—had gone away to summer camp.

"Alice," said Aunt Esmé. "Would you mind going to the kitchen and getting us some snacks? I've got the munchies."

"Okay," said Alice. "What should I get?"

"How about some of those chocolate chips?" she said. "Those are good."

"I vote for Oreos," said Rabbit.

"Chocolate chips and Oreos, both," said Stuart.

"All right," said Alice. In Dean's absence, they survived on cookies, pizza, and spaghetti with miniature meatballs that they ate cold, straight from the can. They sent Alice downstairs like a waitress. She didn't mind being sent on errands. Aunt Esmé was much nicer to her than other people's big sisters were. Aunt Esmé was actually Alice's half sister, from Dean's first marriage. She was supposed to take care of Alice, and to stay in the house every night. She didn't. Often she went out in the evening and didn't come back until the next morning. Now she had a new "connection"—someone called J.D.—who came from North Carolina. He was spending the summer there, in a town called Dodgson, where Aunt Esmé said he owned a house. J.D. had only been in North Carolina since late May, but Aunt Esmé had already driven eight hours there and back to see him, twice, leaving Alice to spend two long weekends in the house on Sixty-seventh Street alone. Aunt Esmé had pleaded with Alice not to ever say anything to Dean about her disappearances.

"I've got to go make a drug run," she said. "J.D. has *the* best blow."

Alice wasn't sure what the best blow was, and she didn't ask. She figured it was the white powder that Aunt Esmé sometimes carried with her inside her fringed handbag. It didn't matter that Aunt Esmé took drugs right out in the open. She'd stop anywhere—on the street, or in a department store—to take a pinch of the powder from her bag, lift it to one nostril, throw back her head, and snort it. It didn't matter that she left Alice alone for days or hours at a time. It was just that Alice didn't like being by herself in the house at night. The floorboards creaked in the room where Rain used to be, and the branches of the cherry tree in the front yard near Edgar Allan Poe's grave swayed in the wind. They scratched against the glass with a soft tap, tap, tap. It sounded like a lizard's paws. Then it sounded like a serpent's tongue. Then it sounded like five weak fingers rapping on the windowpane, the same gentle fingers that used to comb and braid Alice's hair. Alice would run upstairs and call out "Rain? Is that you? Are you here?" Rain had asked Alice not to call her "Mom" or "Mama" or "Mommy," like other children called their mothers. The house was haunted, Alice thought, by the woman Dean had called a free spirit, her young mother's ghost.

When she got back from the kitchen, carrying a plate filled with cookies, Aunt Esmé's door was closed. Alice tried it tentatively. It was locked, as it often was. Alice set the plate of cookies down, like a bellhop delivering room service in a hotel. As she passed the mirror in the hallway, she paused to look at her reflection. Sometimes, when the two girls were by themselves, they'd stand here. Aunt Esmé would try new hairstyles out on Alice. Then, feature by feature, she'd analyze their looks. She said Alice had liquid brown eyes like a doe's. But Alice only saw her flaws: a pinched, ashen face, droopy mouth, big lips. The skin under her eyes was puffy, and permanently discolored. Aunt Esmé said a little makeup would correct that—though she deplored Alice's prissy taste in clothes.

Alice returned to her own room, two flights below, on the third floor. She listened to Simon and Garfunkel sing "Bridge over Troubled Water," one of the melodic songs that she liked. She was flipping through all of Aunt Esmé's old copies of *Sixteen* and *Seventeen* and Dean's *Artforum*s and *Architectural Digest*s, and Rain's ancient *Vogue*s and *Harper's Bazaar*s. She was looking for tiny pictures that she could paste inside of rock stars' eyes.

"Alice! Where are you?"

It was Aunt Esmé calling for her. Alice set the magazines down and went back upstairs. They'd lock the door when they didn't want her with them, and then when they were done, they'd call her back in.

"Hey, girlfriend," said Aunt Esmé as Alice padded, barefoot, up the stairs. "Thanks for the cookies."

"Did you eat them all?" Alice asked incredulously.

"Yeah. They were excellent."

"You didn't save any for me?"

"I thought you had some," said Aunt Esmé.

"No," said Alice.

"Silly. Next time help yourself."

"I was waiting for you."

"Well, don't. Two boys are a handful. Trust me."

Alice hesitated on the landing. Twice, she'd gone in too early and had seen Rabbit naked. He'd been lying on his side, curled in the shape of the letter S. Aunt Esmé had been curled in the same shape, right behind him. Stuart had been behind her, huddled close. They'd reminded Alice of newborn puppies in a heap. They'd looked helpless. They'd been asleep.

"Come listen," called Rabbit from inside the room. "We've got the new Zeppelin bootleg."

"I don't like Led Zeppelin," Alice said from the hallway. She could only see the top of Rabbit's head and a corner of the mattress.

"It's an acquired taste," he said. "You have to like them, Alice. And you will."

Led Zeppelin was along the same lines as Pink Floyd, Alice believed. They, too, had a nonsense name and bathed people's brains in their eerie, otherwordly twilight that descended every time the music played. As she listened, Alice imagined she was an insect who had been washed down the drain and left to wander around forever in a subterranean maze.

Aunt Esmé propped the door open with an old sneaker, and Alice walked in. Stuart was lying on the bed with an inflatable pillow under his neck. The pillow belonged to Alice. They often took things from her room. She used the pillow as a flotation device when she went to the swimming pool.

"You're lying on my float," Alice said to him.

"Am I?" Stuart listened to her. He was not like Rabbit. He cooperated.

"Yes, you are," said Alice. "And I can't swim without it. I need it."

Stuart lifted his head so Alice could take her float away from him.

"Don't you know how to swim yet?" he said, resettling himself against the headboard. "I thought you learned."

"I'm too heavy," Alice said. "I sink."

"She's too heavy, she's too heavy." Rabbit began to sing the Beatles song. It was not among Alice's favorites.

"Alice Duncan," said Aunt Esmé. "You don't weigh more than a hundred pounds. Don't be like Dean, who's so paranoid. Don't be irrational and crazy."

Alice wanted to tell them that THE BREASTS felt heavy. But then they would all begin remarking on what a nice figure she already had, and what a weird trip it was, and that she was going to be a heartbreaker any day, and they would stare at her. Because of THE BREASTS, Alice couldn't swim. She only paddled cautiously in the shallow end. She thought continuously of a great white shark, headed for her, its red maw open, its crooked teeth like saws, unfeeling, disinterested, mechanical—ready to devour her. Obviously, there were no sharks in pools. Alice told herself that, without effect. She'd been able to swim before the arrival of THE BREASTS. She'd liked swimming, and had been very good at it, when she was seven.

But once she began "developing prematurely" (how she hated the term Dr. Fineman used, while giving her an ominous smile) Alice thought of sharks whenever she went to the Y for the swimming hour. She would clutch the inflatable pillow to her stomach and stay close to the edges of the pool. The swimming hour was every day from four to five o'clock, except that this year Ethyl hadn't renewed the Duncan Family Membership. Ethyl was their housekeeper. Alice loved her. She didn't work for them anymore.

"We'll get Ethyl back," Dean had said before he committed himself to Saint Joseph's Hospital. He'd been staring and staring out the window at the cherry tree. "We'll hire Ethyl, at least part-time, when I'm mended and back on my feet again."

Dean always said "mended," that he needed "to mend." Though, when "sick," he lay on the couch in his studio and wept, though he slashed his canvases with the Thanksgiving turkey knife, though he walked up to the roof one night and said the next morning that he'd contemplated "an ending"—Alice harbored a suspicion that there was nothing wrong with Dean. She doubted him. Her doubt made her feel worse than his mental illness did. It made her think she was a bad person.

Rabbit was just where he had been, on his back. He'd moved further down on the bed so his head wasn't hanging off the end of the mattress anymore. His feet were propped up on the wall, only now he'd taken his boots off and was just wearing bright red socks. Alice could see the dusty outline of the scuff marks Rabbit's bootheels had left on the wall. They were open semicircles, like the letter U. Aunt Esmé allowed her friends to mark her walls up. They were entirely covered with doodles, stickers, and graffiti. There was only one spot in Aunt Esmé's room that no one was allowed to interfere with. This was a small blue heart that she'd drawn in eyeliner immediately above the bed. It was no bigger than a thumbnail. Inside the heart was a wispy blond pubic hair that Aunt Esmé claimed belonged to Crash Omaha. She'd borrowed Alice's rubber cement glue to attach it to the wall.

"Crash wuz here," read the long, spindly letters underneath it. An arrow pointed downward, toward the bed. He'd signed and dated it January 16, 1974. It had been Aunt Esmé's fourteenth birthday. Now Rabbit's feet were moving unacceptably close to this sacred souvenir.

"Rabbit, you pig! Get your feet away from Crash," Aunt Esmé said.

Rabbit put his feet down on the pillow. He was reading a copy of *Natural History* magazine, one of the old ones Alice had found in the dumpsters behind the building next door. She often used discarded magazines to make her collages. He peered at Alice from over the top of the magazine. "Alice," he said, "check this out. This is cool." He turned the magazine around so that Alice could see it.

Alice took a look. It was a photograph of a black-and-yellow bee.

"It looks like a bee, doesn't it?" said Rabbit.

Alice nodded.

"Aha," said Rabbit. "You've been deceived. Things, my dear, aren't what they seem to be. It's not a bee, Alice. It's a fly. It's a trick of nature. A disguise."

"So?" said Alice.

Rabbit reached out toward her leg and clamped his hand around her ankle. "So," he said. "Nothing. I got ya."

"Let go of me," said Alice, "or I'll kick your teeth in."

"That's enough, you two," said Aunt Esmé, who was busy by the stereo rearranging her records. She'd sort them alphabetically until she got to H or J, and then she'd ask Alice to do the rest of them. "The next person who behaves like an animal in this room will be kicked out of here," she said, yawning. "Permanently."

Rabbit released Alice from his grip. "Camouflaged as a stinging insect, the rat-tailed maggot deters attacks from frogs and reptiles," he read aloud. "Though defenseless, it cleverly mimics the honeybee to fool its natural predators."

Alice took the magazine. "That's mine," she said. "Give it back to me, please." She began to gather her posterboard, her scissors, and her glue.

Aunt Esmé crossed the room holding an album in her hands. She threw herself down across the bed.

"Ugh!" Stuart said as she landed on him with a thud. "Esmé, you're not exactly a feather." There was a brief scuffle during which Alice retrieved her collage from the floor. It had gotten bent and torn.

"Who did this?" Alice said accusingly, brandishing her dented collage.

"Hush. The queen bee speaks," said Rabbit.

"Who messed up my collage?" Alice said.

"No one," said Aunt Esmé.

"Can't you take care of anything except your stupid drugs?" said Alice. She set the collage down on the table and tried to smooth it with her hand. The glue hadn't set. She'd carefully traced the outline of the images with a black Magic Marker. Now the ink had been smudged.

"We didn't mean to, Al," called Aunt Esmé. Evicted from her bed, where Stuart and Rabbit had rearranged themselves more comfortably without her, Aunt Esmé opened the steamer trunk she kept by the bookshelves near the window. She'd arrived in America with that trunk, she said, from Vienna, when she was small. Dean's first wife was a dance therapist who grew up in Austria and was living in New Mexico.

"Let's do some hits with this," said Aunt Esmé. She took a hookah out of the trunk. It looked like a six-headed serpent, with six long winding necks and a potbelly made of brass. Rain had sent it to them one Christmas, from Tangier. The package had arrived, wrapped in brown paper, with a dozen exotic stamps on it, printed in pale earth tones of rust and green.

Aunt Esmé set the hookah down in the center of the bed. It wobbled from side to side. Rabbit put a trigonometry textbook under it to steady it. When that didn't work, the three of them got up off the bed and settled themselves around the hookah on the floor.

"My collage is ruined," Alice said.

"Don't be sore at us," said Rabbit. "We're stoners. We're dead-beat pillheads."

"We're adolescents," chimed in Aunt Esmé.

"We're not responsible for our actions," Rabbit continued. "We can't help ourselves."

"Would somebody be kind enough to shut their face and play some Zeppelin?" said Stuart.

"Alice, would you be a super generous considerate kind of girl?" Aunt Esmé asked.

Alice sighed and retrieved the albums Aunt Esmé had scattered across the quilt on her bed. She lifted up the one called *Houses of the Holy* and studied it. The album cover showed six little girls climbing up the side of a cliff. They were as identical as paper dolls. They had coiled platinum blond hair, like Alice. They were naked.

From across the room, Stuart was gesticulating at her, frantically. He was in the middle of inhaling, holding his breath, so he couldn't speak. "Forget the bootleg," he said, exhaling a puff of swirling smoke. "Would you put that one on? It's among the best ten albums in the known universe. Jimmy Page is God."

"Top five," corrected Aunt Esmé. "God is Robert Plant."

Gingerly, Alice took the shining black disc out of its jacket, holding it suspended between her hands, the way Aunt Esmé had taught her, so she wouldn't scratch or damage it. She set it down on the turntable. The jangling, clashing sounds began to fill the room. Soon it was interrupted by Persephone, howling.

"Oh, Persephone, you idiot," said Aunt Esmé. "Alice, this is a sublime album, and Persephone is making a racket. Can't you quiet your dog down?"

"Be good, Persephone," said Alice.

Persephone knitted her eyebrows together and looked worried. She gave one short whine, lifted her paw off the floor, and set it down again for emphasis. Persephone didn't care for Led Zeppelin, either. "I'll be right there," Alice told her. She wanted to see what it was that Aunt Esmé, Rabbit, and Stuart heard in this weird music. She tried to listen to it, to keep an open mind. She pored over the lyrics and scrutinized the cover of *Houses of the Holy*. The colors were harsh and glaring, just like the songs themselves. The yellow of the girls' hair was too bright, the sky too orange. Chemically altered. Artificial. A mysterious purple light emanated from a distant source that couldn't be identified. Alice found the image shocking. The naked children, she felt, should have been clothed.

The little girls looked as if they were intent on getting someplace, Alice thought. But they'd embarked on a dangerous mission. One of the rocks had a circular hole in it, big enough for a child to slip through. She wondered what fate awaited them when they got to the top of the rocks. They might find the "houses of the holy," or they might drop off the cliff, one by one, like lemmings. They appeared to be under a spell—sleepwalking, drugged, or hypnotized.

"Aunt Esmé, can I please make dresses for the children?" Alice asked.

"Huh?" said Aunt Esmé.

"Can I glue paper clothing onto the girls here, on the *Houses of the Holy* album?"

"Oh my God," said Aunt Esmé. "That would be sacrilege. Are you out of your fucking mind? You can't do *that*. Absolutely, positively, not."

Alice contemplated the picture. She wished that she could put herself into it, not small and naked but tall and dressed—armed and armored in a coat of steel. She'd be the giant bronze statue of Alice in Wonderland in Central Park. She'd sit on a toadstool ten feet wide and five feet high. Playing safely, they could climb on her, and she would clothe them in dresses made of flowers. Oh, she'd have her arms open wide, like the boy in the book, to catch the girls when they fell. Because the naked children would fall. Alice wished they wouldn't, but they always did fall, they'd been falling forever, and they always would.

Cell B

lice was waiting for Dean in Cell B. He'd called it Cell B on the day he was admitted, and the name had stuck. It was, in fact, Room 210B in Saint Joseph's Hospital in New Milford, Connecticut. Standing at the windows, which had wire mesh inside them, Alice looked around the room. It was only slighter larger than Persephone's doghouse underneath the deck in their backyard. Pushed against one wall of Cell B was a single bed, neatly made, with crisp white sheets and a navy blue blanket. One flat pillow lay on top of it. The covers were pulled tight. Alice compared the spare, cold look of Cell B with Dean's two-room suite on the third floor of their house in Manhattan. At home, he owned a vase that had been painted by Picasso set up on a special table. At home, he had a desk with pigeonholes, and a pen that came inside a box lined with something like blue velvet, and stacks of thick ivory writing paper, and envelopes with his name on them. He had a rectangular leather blotter, and on it he kept an ancient copy of a brown hardcover book. It was called *Lives of the Artists*. He would read that, sitting at his desk, sipping from a glass no bigger than a thimble. He kept his wire-rimmed reading spectacles on top of the book, and beside it, a pad of paper to take notes on. Above his desk, Dean had a reproduction of a painting by a man named Lippi inside a heavy frame. It was called *The Annunciation*. It showed an angel kneeling while a woman cradled her arms against her chest, as if she imagined herself rocking a baby. Across from his desk, he had a sleigh bed made of polished maple, and a handmade quilt filled with goose feathers. At Sixty-seventh Street, Dean still had all those things. They were all there, untouched, awaiting him. But he liked it better in Cell B, in Connecticut, at the Bin, safely away from Alice and her deformity.

Obviously, he was running away from her. Rain had left Alice, and now Dean was leaving. Alice was repulsive due to her premature maturation process; her grotesque but mesmerizing body parts; her bizarre height. She was attractive to certain individuals such as Rabbit; her gym teacher; Mr. Mann. Strangers also liked her. But she was repellent to her parents. Alice didn't articulate this theory to anyone. She sensed it in her bones, the way a dog knows things—by instinct. She knew it because Dean had stopped hugging her when her body had begun to change. Rather than stay in the house with Alice, he preferred this miserable chamber with its puce linoleum floors and fluorescent lighting. It was hideous. The only appealing thing about Saint Joseph's was the fountain by the front entrance. Deck chairs with built-in umbrellas were lined up on the lawn. But inside it was a hospital, spare and antiseptic. Dean wanted shock treatments. He wanted to mend. He wanted blood tests to regulate the medication. He wanted seclusion, which was easier to find in Connecticut, in a hospital, locked up. In Manhattan it was "hard to get any peace or solitude." He'd come to live here, Alice thought, by choice.

Aunt Esmé had gone down the hall to the Living Room in order to find him. On their monthly visits, Alice avoided the Living Room as much as possible. It was filled with gray-faced men in their slippers and bathrobes staring vacantly at a huge color television set. The only time she'd seen them animated was when they were watching football. Usually, they just sat there on the cracked vinyl sofa. It had a tear on its arm. Yellow stuffing was coming out. In the first few weeks of Dean's stay there, when she'd been able to tolerate the sight of the Living Room, Alice would check the arm of the couch each time she visited, just to see if anyone had fixed it. They never had. Soon enough, Alice concluded that—whether a patient's disorders were Major or Minor—things at the Bin would not be mended. They would remain permanently broken.

Dean said that his paintings had drained him of his vitality. Every time he made one, it cost him something. Each brush-stroke sapped him of strength. Alice hadn't believed him. But as he entered Cell B with Aunt Esmé behind him, this seemed to Alice to be true. With every passing month, he was shrinking—wasting away. His skin clung to his cheekbones, as if his skull were ready to emerge. His cheeks were sunken. As the rest of him diminished, his dark eyes seemed to grow. They were almost black. Even before the Bin, they'd appeared too large for his thin face. Searching eyes of endless depth, inward-looking, filled with self-pity, fear, and sorrow. He shuffled inside the room in the fleece-lined slippers he ordered from Bergdorf Goodman's men's department every year. His movements reminded Alice of Aunt Esmé's when she was high. They were careful and slow. He felt nothing anymore, he'd said. The blessing and the curse, he said, of lithium.

"Hello, Alice," said Dean, "how good to see you." But he didn't seem especially happy. Alice put her arms around him and squeezed him tight. She knew he didn't want her to. He didn't like her to "cling." He patted her shoulder and drew back.

"Let's see if we can find ourselves an extra chair," said Dean. He peered out into the hallway uncertainly. He'd been living at the Bin for months, but he didn't ever seem to feel at ease there. This, too, Alice found depressing. She could envision him vanishing and someone else's father walking into Cell B and replacing him.

The three of them stood around awkwardly. It had become difficult for Alice to figure out, when she was in Cell B, what to say. Often she asked Dean for things she didn't especially need or want, just to fill the blank space that hovered between them, just to warm the cold, cold air. The blankness and cold emanated from the Bin's hallways and floorboards, seeping out of the walls and ceilings. Alice had to talk loudly to dispel it.

"Dean?" she said. She always addressed him as Dean; he was dismayed by "Dad" or "Daddy."

"Alice?" His face was blank. He rarely smiled at her.

"Aunt Esmé said I can go to camp this summer," she said.

Dean looked over at Aunt Esmé. "I'm afraid we can only afford to send one member of the family to camp this year. And this summer, dear, it's me."

"*You're* going to camp?" asked Alice.

"No, Alice. This is my camp. Right here. A camp for adults who feel troubled."

Dean was troubled. There was nothing wrong with him, really, Alice thought. But her love wasn't helping him. It even, possibly, was harmful. She was powerless to cure him, to bring him back—there was nothing she could do.

"You've been here longer than camp is supposed to go," she

said angrily. "You've been here for eighteen weeks, Dean. Eighteen! Camp only lasts for eight. You've been on summer vacation for twice as long as you're supposed to be. You've been inside this camp forever."

"Alice," said Aunt Esmé. "Be more considerate of Father."

Dean shifted from one foot to the other. Aunt Esmé always called him Father. For some reason, as far as Dean was concerned, "Father" was okay. Alice had tried calling him Father once, but it had sounded false—stuffy, old-fashioned, British.

Dean looked down at the floor. "No," he said, looking very sad and very sorry for himself. "Alice is right. It's a long summer vacation for me, in a sense." He sighed piteously. "It isn't fair to either of you. To be called upon to make these painful sacrifices for me. But if things go well when I get out, if I can mend, then you can certainly go to camp next year. And I hope, for both your sakes, that the sale of the house will help you, when the time comes to go to college."

The subject of their finances and schooling was a difficult one. For the two years that Aunt Esmé had been living on Sixty-seventh Street, Alice had attended private school while Esmé had gone to an alternative public school called Learning City. Aunt Esmé's mom had once sued Dean for child support. Shortly after that, Aunt Esmé had moved in with them. It was such a taboo topic that Alice didn't know what the outcome had been. Dean was supposed to pay for something, but no longer could. He had filed for bankruptcy. In the fall, Alice wouldn't be returning to the Fieldwood School. She'd be going to public school like Aunt Esmé.

"You could enroll Alice at the free summer day camp on Eighty-second Street, at P.S. 6," said Dean.

"I want to go *away* to camp," insisted Alice—dangerously—without knowing why. "I want to take acting lessons, like I did last year at Camp Monaghan. I want to make pottery and jewelry. I want to ride on horseback and go hiking."

Dean hung his head.

Alice was ashamed of herself. No one said: Dean was rich and now he's poor. No one said: You were spoiled and now you won't be. No one said: The Duncans' accountant had filed for bankruptcy because Dean is a manic-depressive and he has no money.

Dean examined the frayed cuff of his shirt. He didn't look at either of them.

"I tell you what, Al," said Dean. "If you two can find someplace for Alice that's reasonably priced, we'll look into it."

"Thank you," said Alice. What had she done? She would destroy the family. She felt ill.

"What about the Balthus Institute, Father?" said Aunt Esmé.

"What about it?" Dean said.

"Remember that arts program I went to in Dodgson?" said Aunt Esmé. "When I was a kid? Before I moved in with you?" Alice had noticed that over the years, Aunt Esmé's voice had changed. It shifted upward at the end of statements. She never said anything. She only asked questions.

"The arts program. Yes," said Dean absently. His face had slackened. He looked sadder than he had when they'd walked in. Alice had done this. She'd depressed him.

"It's an experimental course in creativity," said Aunt Esmé. "A real good friend of mine has a summer house up there. In North Carolina."

"I'm aware of what the institute is, Esmé," snapped Dean. "Hans Balthus is a neglected master, a superb artist who is no longer appreciated. He's a dear old friend of mine. I was lucky enough to study with him in Paris. But you didn't think much of the place. Did you?"

"No," said Aunt Esmé, looking down at her shirt and untangling her necklaces. She wore ten necklaces at a time. "But I haven't got Alice's visual gift. Her talent."

"Fine," said Dean. "Give them a call, for Alice, if you like. Find out if the price is right."

"If you have no money, they give scholarships," said Aunt Esmé. "Because . . . remember? Mom and I couldn't pay our rent that summer. She had to get food stamps. The child support. You weren't—"

"Hmm," said Dean.

Alice was horrified. She couldn't believe Aunt Esmé had blundered into the forbidden topic.

Aunt Esmé knew she had erred. She tied a knot in one of her beaded necklaces. Then she untied it again. "Mom sued you," she continued, inexplicably. "And took you to court. And you didn't show up? Father?"

"Hmm, hmm," said Dean again. He said that when he didn't want to talk about it—a kind of humming noise.

Aunt Esmé dropped it.

In the pit of her stomach, Alice felt a deepening sense of doom.

"I brought you a present, Dean," Alice said, to lighten the mood. She grabbed the manila envelope from under Aunt Esmé's arm and handed it to him.

"That was thoughtful of you, Alice," he said. He sounded surprised that she could be thoughtful.

Alice watched him open it.

"Get well soon, Daddy," he read out loud, nearly choking on the final word. "Hurry up. Love, Alice, Esmé, and Persephone, your offspring." Each of the letters was a different size and typeface. She'd cut them out individually from magazines and newspapers. The collage was in the style of a kidnapper's ransom note.

"Interesting," said Dean. He held the collage at arm's length.

The message was surrounded by angels that Alice had made by attaching birds' wings from the *National Geographic* magazines to photographs of herself at different ages. For a brief, exhilarating instant, Alice thought that he admired it.

"Oh, Alice," he said. "You didn't use the photos that I hired Lucille Prescott to take of you on each of your birthdays, did you?"

"Kind of," Alice admitted. "You said Lucille Prescott has a maudlin eye."

"Did I say that?" said Dean. "How perceptive of me."

"Yes, you did say that, actually," said Aunt Esmé. "I remember."

Alice looked at Aunt Esmé gratefully.

"That may well be true, but maudlin or not, she's the most expensive portraitist. Which is not to say that she's the best. Prescott charges a fortune nonetheless. You shouldn't take a scissors, recklessly, to our family belongings."

He was angry, as Alice had known he would be. What had she done it for? She wasn't sure. "But I didn't do it recklessly," Alice said. "I did it on purpose."

Dean chewed on a hangnail. "I see," he said.

"I *reappropriated* them," said Alice, carefully articulating the big word. "Like you did when you made the assemblages of '64."

Dean had said the assemblages of '64 were his masterpieces. A series of three abstract paintings, they had household objects—a toothbrush, a coat hanger, a bar of soap—attached to them. But he'd done them more than a decade ago, when Rain had been pregnant, and he couldn't do them now. The muse for the assemblages had been Alice's mother, who was gone.

"My assemblages," he repeated.

Aunt Esmé coughed. "You know, Father, Alice's collages are a blast. My friends and I dig them. We groove on them. Real wildly." Aunt Esmé only used that kind of slang when she was scared. There was something scary about Dean and his mood swings.

"The last collage Alice made was totally psychedelic," Aunt Esmé burbled on, seeming to wish to distract them all. "It had this far-out pattern that kept repeating. We titled it *Infinity*. I taped it over the toaster on the kitchen wall."

"Infinity," said Dean, still staring at the get-well card.

"I made it by folding the page up like a fan, Dean," Alice said with pride. "I folded it a hundred times. And then I cut the design along the side of the fold. The way you make paper dolls."

"Man, I stared at *Infinity* for, like, an hour and a half," Aunt Esmé said.

"At least we still have the Prescott negatives, I suppose," Dean said. "Unless you cut those up, too. Did you, Alice?"

"No," Alice said. Her collages were better. Was that it? Her collages were better than his adults-in-baby-clothing paintings were. Her collages were so much better than his paintings that he'd never forgive her for it. She'd known cutting up the Prescott photographs would annoy him. Yet she'd wanted him to like the card.

"It's not important," said Dean. He set her collage down on his metal table, staring at a space a few inches above Alice's shoulder. His expression reminded her of the one on Charlie Chaplin's face. Charlie Chaplin was Alice's pet hamster. His bright dark eyes were alert, but remote. Charlie Chaplin would glance up when Alice lifted the Lucite covering over his glass tank. But he'd stopped looking at things in the distance. He was accustomed to living in a small space. Alice's father had acquired that look, of a creature in a cage.

"Alice?" he asked.

"Yeah?"

"Do you ever make collages with photographs of your own?"

"No."

"Give Alice my Polaroid when you get home," he told Aunt Esmé.

Alice's heart leapt for joy. Would he say anything more? But that was it—the Polaroid. End of discussion. It was over.

"Shall we go play a match of Ping-Pong, girls?" he said.

"Let's!" said Aunt Esmé with elaborate enthusiasm.

"I wrote the score down somewhere," said Dean. "I believe I'm winning by twenty-six points. Or was it twenty-four?"

"It was twenty-one," said Alice, who remembered things.

And off they went, down a gleaming white hallway, to a room which had no windows.

The Swimming Hour

See you next month, girls!" Dean called out behind them. Aunt Esmé and Alice walked down the corridor that led away from the cafeteria, where the three of them had eaten dinner. Dean seemed cheered by the fact that they were leaving. The way he said "See you next month" made Alice think he was reminding them not to come next week, or the week after, or the week after that. When Dean had first gone to Connecticut, Dr. Oppenheim—his psychiatrist—had called Aunt Esmé at home. He'd suggested that they limit their visits to once a month because Dean needed rest. "As hard as this might be for you to understand," said Dr. Oppenheim, "frequent contact with the family might throw off his equilibrium. Let's not overdo it."

Alice had stood in Rain's old room and listened in on the telephone call, on the extension.

The night air was brisk and damp as they wound their way past the cars in the parking lot and headed toward Dean's old Volvo.

"I'm never going to make it to CBGB's by midnight," Aunt Esmé said, glancing at her watch. Visiting hours ended at 9 p.m. "We're going to have to crank it." She glanced at Alice. "Are you okay?"

Alice nodded. She was looking around, feeling peculiar, as if she'd never noticed her surroundings before. This often happened to her when she said goodbye to Dean at Saint Joseph's: a noticing, a heightened sense of reality. It was because there was so little to look at inside the building. Now she studied her immediate environment in detail. A streetlamp cast an orb of light against the sky. A row of peach trees threw shadows on the asphalt. The gray statue inside the fountain stood with a hand on its hip, one stone arm outstretched. The arc of water above the statue's head was gone; a guard must have turned the fountain off. Cars were pulling out of the driveway. Alice watched as one by one, the visitors to Saint Joseph's sped away to their homes, each one departing with a roar and a flash of headlights down the black road.

Alice glanced at the interior of the Volvo. When Dean had had the car—before undergoing his treatment—it had been clean. Now that Aunt Esmé was driving it, it was filled with trash. The floor was heaped with stacks of papers from her classes at Learning City, which allowed students to get high school credit for doing internships and volunteer work in New York. Aunt Esmé was an intern at Foxglove Sound, a record studio on Eighth Street. Her ambition was to be a sound engineer, but she said she spent most of her time making coffee and "dispensing pharmaceuticals" to "the candidates." The candidates were hopeful young men who were not yet, and probably never would be, rock stars. The seats of the car were littered with dented cartons of fried rice (as part of her job, Aunt Esmé fed the candidates takeout Chinese food); old bottles of Tylenol (the candidates got headaches from their own music, which was loud); empty beer cans (the candidates drank beer); crumpled packs of clove cigarettes; half-eaten bags of potato chips; and articles of clothing discarded by musicians that Aunt Esmé had driven home at the end of their recording session. Aunt Esmé had gone through a lead singer stage, but had decided they were "narcissists." Lead guitar players, she declared, "had too much ego." Bass players were "easygoing," but self-absorbed and uncommunicative. With the exception of Crash Omaha, she preferred drummers. She claimed they were in touch with their "primitive instincts" and were "electrifying" to be around. Aunt Esmé was always being electrified by one thing or another.

"Look, Alice," she said in the parking lot. "There's a rumor that Crash's going to make a guest appearance at the gig tonight. Do you mind if I fly?"

Alice shrugged her approval. Aunt Esmé liked to drive at top speed. Alice had found that even if she objected, Aunt Esmé didn't slow down.

Casting a quick glance over her shoulder to see if there was anyone left in the parking lot, Aunt Esmé pulled out her evening purse. It was made of red-and-yellow silk, and it had a braided shoulder strap with a row of red fringe along the bottom. She'd shoplifted it from the Blue Angel, her favorite boutique, in Greenwich Village. For a while, Aunt Esmé had carried it only on special occasions, when she went out at night. But after one of the candidates had spilled beer on it, it became her everyday bag. It was filled with cocaine. She said her dealer, J.D., had given her the coke as a thank-you present. Alice had never met this dealer. Aunt Esmé never referred to him by name, but only by his initials. He'd left New York for the summer and wouldn't officially be open for business again until the fall. The coke had been his parting gift to a regular customer. When Alice had first seen it, two weeks earlier, it had been wrapped inside a square of tinfoil and tied with a red ribbon. Aunt Esmé had opened it up, revealing two white blocks. Each one was the size of an ice cube. One side of each block was slanted at an angle. Alice had learned about the shape in her fifth-grade introduction to geometry. It was a trapezoid. Aunt Esmé had broken the trapezoid apart using a razor blade and had sealed it in a zip-lock baggie before she slipped it inside the Blue Angel handbag. At some point, the baggie had opened, spilling the contents into the bottom of Aunt Esmé's purse. Because there was so very much of it, she hadn't bothered to gather it back up again. She'd just let the loose white powder lie there.

In the past, Aunt Esmé had been more cautious and more responsible about her coke—keeping it in the toy chest, with the other intoxicants that were lined up in their rows, nicely. Once, when Aunt Esmé had had some friends from the record studio over, Alice had watched while she painstakingly cut the cocaine up with a razor blade on top of a glass mirror, creating six neat white tidy piles. But all of that had ended in the wake of J.D.'s overly generous gift. In the parking lot of Saint Joseph's Hospital, Aunt Esmé didn't go through any of these preparations. She just took a pinch of the coke from out of her purse and lifted it to her left nostril, tilting her head back slightly and inhaling, hard. She made a loud snorting sound. She snorted again. Then she took a second pinch and put it up her right nostril. Since J.D. had gone to North Carolina in May, Alice had witnessed this public ritual several times.

"Couldn't they arrest you?" Alice asked while Aunt Esmé snapped the handbag closed.

"The cops, you mean? I doubt it. I'm sure they like good

blow as much as I do. I'd just share it with them, Alice. That's what's so nice about having plenty to go around." She didn't take any more of the coke from her bag, but lay back in the driver's seat and rested from the exertion, snorting contentedly.

"Ah, man," she said. "Now I'm energized."

Alice studied her face. She was paler than ever. Her hair had grown longer in the last few weeks, and it looked lank and mangy. It had darkened and flattened. She didn't look energized. How sad everyone was, Alice thought, and wondered why.

"Now I'll race us home," said Aunt Esmé, "and I'll be downtown in time for the first set. Roll down the windows all the way, Alice! Let the wind in! We're ready for takeoff!"

Alice buckled her seat belt and hung on to the handle above the door. She held on so tightly that she could feel her nails digging into her palm. The speedometer said the car was driving sixty miles an hour. Alice watched the arrow edge upward a notch, another notch, and another. Then she didn't watch the speedometer anymore.

At midnight, Alice was alone in the house making a tunnel for Charlie Chaplin. She'd found six packages of paper towels in a closet in the basement, where Ethyl used to store supplies. She'd unrolled them all to get the cardboard tubes out. She'd filled the dining room with the winding, curling trail of paper, longer than a bridal gown's train. Alice had wadded it up and had taken it outside, stuffing it into Persephone's doghouse. Persephone had welcomed the addition to her abode, and had been digging happily in the paper for an hour, rearranging her new nest.

Alice placed the cardboard rolls end to end on the dining room table, and Charlie Chaplin explored each of them. This was one of the things that Alice wasn't supposed to do: let Charlie Chaplin on the table. It, too, would be sold, like the Zeit bisque dolls and the silverware. It, too, was worth money. Alice rarely broke the rules, but she needed to keep her mind off the possibility that she was by herself in a haunted house.

She broke off a bit of a Fig Newton and offered it to Charlie Chaplin. He took it between his paws and squatted on his haunches, perched at the opening of his cardboard tunnel as if it were his home. He ate some of the Fig Newton, and stuffed the rest inside his cheek pouches when Alice offered him some more. He looked intently at the food in front of him, gazing vacantly at Alice—the huge, unknowable Goddess Alice who provided him with food, Alice thought, the She who sheltered him but who, to Charlie Chaplin, must seem a thousand miles high, like a great mountain, a thousand miles away. He nibbled on his cookie, squinting in the direction of the great, giant deity who provided for him; who ordained when he would enter and exit his glass cage; who gave him cardboard tunnels to run through; who took those tunnels away. Alice ate some cookie, too. Together, she and Charlie Chaplin finished one stack of Fig Newtons, along with a container of ice cream. That was dinner.

The house was vast and empty. Alice slipped Charlie Chaplin into the breast pocket of her denim shirt with his paws sticking out over the top, like one of the pocket protectors the nerds wore at school. He blinked, his whiskers quivering. He was going somewhere, that was all he knew. He didn't know he was in the pocket of a goddess. She went from room to room, turning on every single light, and every radio and television. It was too still, too dark, too quiet. Alice turned on the ultraviolet light and the lava lamp inside the Dollhouse. She switched on Aunt Esmé's radio, and it started playing Deep Purple. In Rain's old room— she'd had her own bedroom, separate from Dean's—Alice turned on the lights over the big bed up on its platform, like a stage.

There were Art Deco lamps shaped like leaves. Beside the vanity table, with its folding mirror and its three-legged upholstered chair, Alice paused to turn on both of the bronze wall sconces. Though she had been gone for two years, Rain's radio alarm clock was still set on the old jazz station she'd liked. Alice turned up the volume. Billie Holiday was singing.

"Good morning heartache," sang the sweet voice that was at once weak and strong. It was full of painful beauty, a sense of grief. Alice stood, in reverence, and listened. Charlie Chaplin listened. But the whispering emptiness remained, and filled the house with gloom.

The door to Dean's studio, which had his bed in one room and his working space with his canvases and easel in another, was shut. Alice opened it and turned on the overhead fluorescent light. It buzzed and flashed twice before the light came on and Alice saw the dull greenish faces that surrounded her. Propped against the wall, unframed and on every surface, were the portraits of politicians and celebrities that Dean had done. The figures were shriveled. He'd shrunken them all down to the size of infants. They were sitting in their carriages and playpens, dressed in white lace bonnets, lace-up boots, and christening clothes. Dean painted them from photographs and baby pictures now, but when he'd been in vogue the "muckety-mucks"— philanthropists and socialites—had posed for him in person. The colors were dull browns, coal black, and subdued gray. Dean covered his paintings with a sepia glaze. The compositions were jarring and off-balance. The arms and legs were too long, like Alice's. The fingers were bony, like Rain's. The fingernails were as shapely and pointed as a woman's. The cheekbones were sharp and prominent. The faces didn't look soft and round, like real babies'. They had Dean's mournful, watchful eyes. Alice switched the lights off and closed the door, shutting out the hopeless people. She didn't want them in the house.

Slipping Charlie Chaplin back into his cage in her room, Alice went downstairs and turned on the small black-and-white television in the kitchen, and the color TV in the den. Both were airing an endless commercial about a Ginzu, a "versatile knife."

Tap tap. Tap tap tap.

Alice heard it on the windowpane, the sound of flesh against glass.

Tap. Tap tap. Tap.

She sat very still for a moment. Then she walked toward the front window, the one that faced the garden and the street. She could see him by the cherry tree, leaning against the fence and looking in. She could tell from his stooped shoulders and his drooping head that Rabbit was stoned.

Tap. Tap tap.

Alice shook her head no.

He pointed at the door. "Can I come in?" he mouthed.

Alice gave him the finger.

He pressed his hands together, praying. He shook his clasped hands at her. "Come on, Alice," he said. "Be a pal. Let me in."

She closed the shutters and walked away.

Rap. Rap rap. Rap rap.

He was knocking at the front door now. Alice drifted into the living room, on the opposite side of the house, as far away from Rabbit as possible. She walked into the vestibule by the garden door. She opened the door, got down on her hands and knees, and climbed into Persephone's doghouse.

Persephone had been sleeping soundly. She raised her head, startled. Alice threw her arms around the furry neck and nestled against her flanks.

Buh-boom, buh-boom, went the front door. Boom-bah boom boom-bah. He was pounding and pounding. He kept at it.

Alice got up.

Persephone got up.

"No," Alice said. "Stay." She ran to the front door and threw it open.

"Fuck you," she said to Rabbit's face.

"Oh for God's sake, Alice," he said, shoving her aside and waltzing in. "You're such a drama queen. Have you got anything to eat?"

"I'm not doing it," said Alice. "I'm not giving you a drub again."

"Fine. Your loss. Okay?"

She had rubbed it for him twice. Each time, he had paid her ten dollars. She had tried to piece these incidents together, step by step, but she still couldn't figure out exactly how and why she'd allowed this indignity to happen. She didn't want his money. She didn't want anything to do with him. And yet she had relented.

"What is with you?" Rabbit said, glancing around the house. "Have you got a hundred different radios and televisions playing in here or something?"

Alice said nothing.

"Come on, Alice," he said. He punched her on the arm. "Will you forget it? I forgot all about it by now."

Alice bit her lips.

"Can we kiss and make up at least?" said Rabbit. He had taken his hair out of the rubber band he usually bound it in. It fell about his shoulders and his face. It was softer than silk, Alice remembered.

"I don't have anything for you," Alice said. "I finished the Fig Newtons."

"Your kiss is sweet."

Alice returned to her post by the back window, facing the yard. Oh, she'd done it now. She'd let him in. She couldn't stay still. She couldn't get comfortable. Stupid Alice, she thought. You're a great big stupid girl.

Rabbit followed her.

Alice could see Persephone out on the garden path. She scratched the door with her paw. Everyone wanted to get in. If Alice had let Persephone in the house, she would have attacked Rabbit. If Alice had let Persephone in the house, she would have protected Alice.

Alice scrunched herself up against the door, leaning her forehead on the small round window.

"What do you see?" said Rabbit when he got there. He came up behind her and pressed himself against her.

"Nothing," said Alice.

He put his hands over her eyes.

"Now what?" he said.

"I see stars," said Alice. A thousand twinkling lights had appeared.

"Those are in your head," said Rabbit.

She could feel his hard-arm pressing up against her, just as she'd felt it before. His hands moved from her eyes to THE BREASTS. He held them there.

"Don't touch me," said Alice. "Don't take my clothes off."

"What are you now, a nun?"

"I'm a nun now," Alice agreed. She had left most of her clothes on the last time, though Rabbit had managed to remove her shirt. He seemed to have a monkey's hands, quick and grabby.

He hitched his thumbs around the belt loops on the front of her pleated skirt, pulling her toward him. "Lighten up, for Pete's sake," he said. "You'd think I was Richard Nixon or something. Am I so bad as that?"

"Yes," Alice said, after giving it some thought.

"Ouch. You hurt my feelings. What a bitch." He kissed the back of her neck. "Are you sure I can't take this off you?" he asked her, tugging at her shirt.

"I want to stay like this," said Alice, to the window. And that was true—to remain as she was, not to be told she was ravaging or destroying anybody, to linger forever on the threshold of an invisible door marked For Adults.

"Will you touch me then, if I can't touch you?" Rabbit asked.

It always ended this way. Alice nodded her consent. She began the drub for him, reaching back to hold it.

"You still don't know how to do it right," he said. "If you would turn around and take a look at the patient, Nurse, that would help."

"I don't want to," Alice said to the moon. "I don't want to see."

"All right, Alice. I don't know why I put up with you. But I do. Because you're just a baby." He moved it around near her bottom.

"This time, don't get it on me," Alice said.

"Yes ma'am, Nurse Ratched," he said. He was quiet for a while. He finished the drub himself.

Alice folded her arms against the windowpane. She didn't turn around.

"This is for you, Alice."

It was 1:30 a.m. They were watching the Late Late Show—an old movie with Marilyn Monroe and Bob Hope. Alice was half asleep, leaning against Rabbit. They had a woolen blanket draped over their legs. He was eating Froot Loops by the handful, without milk, from out of the box. They were sitting on the couch.

"What is for me?" Alice asked, opening her eyes.

"This," he said, kissing her on the mouth. "And this." He had something in his hand. It was the Mickey Mouse watch.

"Why does everyone try to give me things?" said Alice. She didn't want to take it.

"Two reasons. One, you're hot. Two, so you don't ever tell Aunt Esmé. Hear me? Don't ever tell."

"Okay," said Alice, stifling a yawn. She let him strap the watch on. It was too wide for her thin wrist.

"There's only five years between us, pal," he said. "But it's enough to screw me. To say nothing of the damage to my reputation. If this thing got out. Alice, I'm a ladies' man. All my other girlfriends are in high school. What would people think?"

"I don't know," said Alice. "What would they?"

"Let's not find out," said Rabbit. "Jeez, it's late. I'd better split."

"See you around."

"See you."

He ambled out. After she heard the door slam, she went into the hallway and locked the door behind him. She looked down at Rabbit's wristwatch.

Tick. Tick tick.

Alice held it in her palm. Mickey Mouse was standing in the center, smiling shyly. He was, Alice saw, a circus freak—just like she was. His head and ears were enormous, but his torso and limbs were scrawny. Alice felt a surge of sympathy and affection for the mutant mouse, dressed in his baggy shorts and white gloves—part clown, part boy, half mouse, half human. At the end of his sticklike arms, his fingers were fat and swollen, like inflated balloons. His hands were oversized and bulbous, sheathed in a pair of puffy white boxing gloves. One huge index finger pointed to the number 1. The other crossed over his waist, in a twisted contortion. He was pointing the way up to heaven, Alice thought, and down to hell.

Tick tick. Tick.

"This is where you're going," said Aunt Esmé, handing a piece of paper to Alice. She was alert and businesslike, as if it were the middle of the day.

Alice stretched and yawned. She'd been sleeping on the couch in front of the television. The lights were on. Through the window, she could see the dark night sky outside. Alice looked down at the dusty black-and-white brochure Aunt Esmé had placed inside her hand. "The Balthus Institute," Alice read.

"It's that arts camp in North Carolina," Aunt Esmé said. "It looks cool, no?

"Sure," said Alice sleepily. "I guess so."

"You're leaving tomorrow morning. I signed you up for a short stay."

"Tomorrow?" asked Alice.

"First thing. You'd better head upstairs and get your shit together. Departure time is coming. It's about four hours away."

"What do you mean?"

"I'm going to put you on a Greyhound bus, girl. You leave at nine. You'll be back before you know it."

"When?"

"In twenty-three days."

"You're sending me to camp tomorrow? For three weeks?" It was too sudden.

"Best I could do on short notice, Alice," said Aunt Esmé. She took the brochure back and read aloud. "Printmaking, sketching, still life, landscapes, watercolors. Great, right? All the great crap that you're good at, all the great crap that you like."

Aunt Esmé had sat down on the arm of Alice's chair. Alice read the brochure over her shoulder. The photographs looked as if they'd been taken long ago. They showed a kidney-shaped swimming pool, wrought iron lawn furniture, café tables beneath tall white umbrellas, and a rose garden. It looked inviting and quaint. On the back of the brochure was a picture of a pottery wheel, a set of paints and brushes, and a loom. Underneath it, in handwriting Alice had never seen before, were the letters J.D., followed by ten numbers.

"How did you find out about this?" said Alice, suddenly suspicious.

"I told you, Alice. When I was younger—before I moved in with you and Dean—I went there."

"How many years ago?" said Alice.

"I don't remember. Three? Five?"

"Where did you get this brochure, though?" Alice asked.

"A friend of mine has a summer house up there."

"And?"

"And what?" said Aunt Esmé.

"Did you call the camp and ask them to send this to you? Or . . ."

"He happened to have it lying around. So what?"

"Lying around where?" said Alice.

"What are you? The Grand Inquisitor?"

"Where did he have this brochure?" said Alice.

"In his car."

Alice glanced, reflectively, at the Mickey Mouse watch. "How long had it been there?" she asked.

"Oh, Alice, what difference does it make?" Aunt Esmé stood up.

"Where did the brochure come from?" Alice asked again. She found she was horribly frightened. She wanted to scream: Don't make me go.

"I don't know," Aunt Esmé said. "But it's the camp I went to. All right? Same place. Same people. Same cheap cool artsy camp. I'm sure it hasn't changed since the summer of '70."

"Nineteen-seventy was six years ago," said Alice. "You haven't been there since you were ten."

"I told you, I don't remember everything exactly. What's your problem, anyway? I thought you wanted to go away. Don't be a pain."

"It doesn't look anything like Camp Monaghan," Alice said.

"It's more rustic," said Aunt Esmé.

"There aren't any tennis lessons," Alice said, looking at the brochure. "Or ponies. There's no auditorium with a movie projector. I don't think there's even a theater."

"Of course there isn't," said Aunt Esmé. "I didn't have ponies and tennis and all that bullshit when I was your age."

Alice heard bitterness in Aunt Esmé's voice. "You had it better than me," she continued. "Now we're equal, Alice. I'm the same as you."

Alice shivered. Moving the band of her watch, she pressed her index and middle fingers against her wrist.

"What are you doing?" said Aunt Esmé.

"I'm checking my pulse," said Alice.

Aunt Esmé laughed. "What for?"

"Something's the matter with my heart. I can hear it ticking."

"It's just that watch you're wearing, stupid. Here. Let me see."
She took Alice's hand in hers.

"Did you shoplift this?" asked Aunt Esmé.

"Yeah," Alice lied.

"From which store?"

"From Gimbel's."

"Good choice. That's one of the best places for shoplifting.
The store detective doesn't give a shit. He'd rather read the *National Enquirer*. Right?"

"Right," said Alice. She heard the loud pulse, the rhythmic
pattern, beating in her head. She kept her fingers clamped down
on her wrist. She couldn't find her heartbeat. She was counting.
She had to count from one to one hundred, slowly, steadily. She
didn't know why.

"Would you let go?" said Aunt Esmé, prying Alice's fingers
off. "Let me see it."

Alice kept it hidden.

"What's gotten into you?" said Aunt Esmé.

I don't want to go, Alice said. But the words didn't come out.
They stayed in her body, trapped. Over and over again—Don't
make me go, I'm scared, I'll die—bah-boom, bah-boom, like a
heartbeat, but in her head.

"Don't get that look, Alice," said Aunt Esmé, staring at her.

What look? Alice thought. Again, the pattern started—an
endless echo—whatlookwhatlookAuntEsméwhat.

"You look weird. Like Dean before he cracks up."

"I'm not weird." Alice's voice came back again. "I just don't
want to go there," she said. "And if I don't want to, you can't
make me."

"Of course I won't *make* you. But I'll ask you, Alice.
Please?"

Alice tried to determine the difference between making her

and asking her. Asking was better. But it was only asking if she could say no. Otherwise it wasn't a question.

"Why should I?" said Alice.

"As a major, major personal favor. To me, Al. To your Aunt Esmé. To your half sister. Your big buddy."

"I'm not going," Alice declared.

"You said you wanted to," said Aunt Esmé.

"I changed my mind," said Alice.

"It's just three weeks. I promise. Just from tomorrow until August 2nd. I'll definitely be back by then," said Aunt Esmé.

"Back from where?"

"I'm going to L.A. for a few days."

"What's in L.A.?" Alice said. She looked at Aunt Esmé, who was smirking. "No," said Alice, "don't even tell me."

"It's important to me," said Aunt Esmé.

"It's Crash."

"Yes. Crash's back from London. He needs me, Alice. He's not doing well."

"Why can't he come here if it's so important and he needs you so much? Why do you have to go there? It's around twenty million miles away," said Alice.

"It's three thousand miles, Alice. He invited me."

"Does he actually remember who you are?" Alice asked meanly.

Aunt Esmé wasn't bothered. "I *think* so," she said. "I found out where he was staying and I called him. I invited myself, in a sense."

"In a sense?" Alice repeated.

"Okay, I invited myself. Really. Is that a crime?"

"It's dumb. What are you going to do in Los Angeles?" Alice said.

"Same thing I always do, I guess. I'll hang out with Crash in his room, instead of hanging out with Stuart and Rabbit in mine."

"That sounds worth it," said Alice.

"It will be."

"What about Persephone? What about Charlie Chaplin? You can't just leave them."

"I'll take her with me. Rabbit will stop by and feed the hamster."

"You'll take her, how? In Dean's car?"

"On the plane. Crash's flying me."

"How will you carry her? Who's going to take her out for walks?"

"I'll handle it, Alice. I'm sixteen years old. I know how to take care of a dog. Okay?"

"Last year, you took her leash off in the park. You let her get away. She was missing for half a day."

"Forget last year."

"You have to be careful, Aunt Esmé."

"With Persephone?"

"With Crash. He chews fake glass. He does hard drugs. He's a total weirdo."

"You're such a worrier. He's harmless. He's the most adorable guy on the planet. You don't know him, that's all."

"Oh yes I do."

"What's that supposed to mean?"

"Nothing." She knew Crash like she knew Rabbit. From a brief encounter in the shower stall. Alice had been getting out. And Crash—who at least wasn't as ugly as in the poster—had been getting in. He had a greenish tattoo of a cockroach on his thigh.

"Aunt Esmé," said Alice. "Don't go."

"Oh shit, Alice. Stop talking like that. In that whining quavering voice. You're not a baby. You can go to camp by yourself for a couple weeks. You're acting like a child."

The bad feeling was exploding in her guts. She didn't want to go to camp now. Everything was going to go wrong. Everyone was in peril—Dean, Alice, Persephone, Aunt Esmé, Stuart, even Rabbit. Only if Aunt Esmé stayed in New York City, with Alice, could they stop it.

"Please don't go to Los Angeles for Crash Omaha," said Alice. She didn't say the other part: Please stay in New York, for me.

"I have to," said Aunt Esmé. "It's a once-in-a-lifetime opportunity. Crash's going to be a star someday, Alice. Then you'll see."

"What if he is? What will I see?"

Aunt Esmé didn't respond. "Alice?" she asked instead.

"What?"

"This trip of mine to L.A.? This bus ride of yours down to North Carolina?"

"Yeah?" said Alice.

"It's just between you and me. I'd appreciate it if you wouldn't mention it to Dean."

"I won't tell anyone," said Alice. She drank a cup of cold left-over coffee to wake herself up, and did a load of laundry. By the time the washing machine had finished, Aunt Esmé had gone to bed. Alice went upstairs and stuffed her backpack full of clean clothes, not even bothering to fold them. Then she went into Rain's old room and opened the walk-in closet. She ran her hand over Rain's dresses. She took a handful of them, bunched them together, and lifted them to her nose. The cool silks and gossamer chiffons smelled faintly of a perfume that she remembered, a scent of lipstick and powder. When she let go, they swung through the air for a second, fluttered, and went still.

Without looking, Alice's hands found the sundress Rain had worn that distant Saturday when she'd taken Alice to the playground. When they'd returned to the house that afternoon, Alice had broken a vase. It had been gold and turquoise, shaped like a tulip. It had come from Venice, and had been important to her mother in some way. Alice had long assumed that it was, in part, because she'd shattered this tulip vase that her mother had left the next day. Alice remembered the feel of the vase slipping from her hands—the long, long moment of realizing that the vase would fall now; the inability to stop it; the inevitable crash. Alice remembered the feel of the dress, with her tall, muscular mother in it. It was worn and soft from many washings. Not a dress-up dress. A dress in which to play with Alice, a dress to be a mother in. Some things were valuable, like chiffon evening gowns and vases made of glass. Those things might be destroyed—ravaged, Rabbit had said—by pretty children. Some things were cheap, like sundresses and third-rate summer camps. If they were lost or damaged, they could be replaced.

Her thoughts spun around senselessly. It was Alice's fault. Her own fault, it was. She broke the vase. THE BREASTS appeared. They cast her mother out, drove Dean crazy, made Rabbit whisper, made Crash laugh, brought shame and ruin upon them all, made a girl into a giant. She was being sent into exile for her sins, to a penal colony. The Balthus Institute was a prison camp.

"Stop," Alice whispered to her brain, with its thoughts in spirals. The dress was made of calico, with a red-and-white-checked ruffle at the hem. She gathered it in her hands but it was empty, like the shells left behind by hermit crabs. After a long moment, Alice packed Rain's sundress in her bag.

Alice on the Road

Early the next morning, in the Dollhouse, Alice woke up Aunt Esmé but she wouldn't get out of bed. She looked at Alice and pointed at the alarm clock. "You've got to catch the 9:20 bus to Dodgson," was all she said. "I left some money for you downstairs, in the kitchen drawer. Don't be late." She pulled the covers up over her head.

Alice walked down the hall, into Aunt Esmé's bathroom. She began to steal things, taking them randomly, putting them all into her backpack. She took Aunt Esmé's blue nail polish, her glitter eye shadow, her pale peach lipstick. Underneath the sink, in a heap of straps and buckles, she found Aunt Esmé's four-inch platform shoes. She put those in her bag, too, and walked downstairs to Dean's studio. She found his camera, inside a case, on the storage shelf. It felt heavy when she put the strap around her neck. It bounced against her as she walked downstairs. It looked to Alice as if she were carrying a wolf's head, sheathed in a black mask. The lens was its snout. It had a zipper for a mouth.

In the kitchen, Alice took a stack of twenty-dollar bills from out of the silverware drawer. She counted them. There were ten. She slipped them into the outer pocket of her backpack. Before she left the house, Alice filled Charlie Chaplin's bowl with hamster feed. She gave him an extra water bottle, tipping it upside down and attaching it to the lid of his cage so that he could reach the spout. After that, she opened the back door and let Persephone in. She fed her and patted her.

"Bye, Persephone," said Alice. "Be good."

Persephone stared up at her mournfully.

Outside, the street was quiet. It was a Saturday morning in July, already warm and humid. On Second Avenue, the mica chips inside the sidewalk flickered in the sun. Down the block, a uniformed doorman was eating a bagel. Alice didn't know where she was going. She'd never been to Port Authority. But she stuck out her hand and hailed a cab.

"Which is Port Authority?" she asked the driver when they arrived at the confusing tangle of buildings, pedestrians, street vendors, and yellow cabs.

"You're looking at it," said the driver, as if Alice were mentally retarded. She handed him a twenty and forgot to ask for change. The street was filled with people. Alice walked inside a cavernous building that was supposedly the bus station. In the lobby, a man was dealing cards on an upside-down cardboard box. A crowd had gathered to watch. Alice stood, for a few minutes, by the wall. She lifted her watch to her ear and listened to its ticking. She checked her pulse to see if her heart was beating.

In the bathroom of the bus station, she changed out of her shorts and T-shirt and put on Rain's halter dress. She daubed some of the peach gloss on her lips and, above her eyes, brushed on the pale glittering eye shadow that Aunt Esmé wore when she went out to Max's Kansas City and CBGB's. She traded her basketball sneakers for the platforms. When she looked at herself in the mirror, she felt calm. She was a grown-up now. The transformation was complete. She pointed the camera at her reflection and snapped the shutter. The photograph popped out. The black part turned light as she waved it in the air, holding it between the fingers of one hand while it was developing. Alice's self-portrait appeared from out of the darkness. She studied the image for a second, measuring the distance between how she looked and how she felt. Then she slipped the photo inside a zippered compartment of her bag and went back out into the wild.

The station was a zoo. There was no order to it. It was chaos, yet everything was perfectly obvious. A sign told you what to do. INFORMATION meant ask a question. Alice went over to the man behind the booth that said that.

"Good morning!" he said. Evidently, he was glad to see her. He smiled broadly. He stole a look at her breasts.

This would happen, Alice explained to herself. This was the way, in exile. This was what adults would do.

"Hi," said Alice. "I'm trying to catch a bus that goes to some town called Dodgson. I think it's in North Carolina or something."

"Well, let's see," said Mr. Information. He had a haircut that made his scalp look flat, like Frankenstein's monster, a broken nose, and a broad face with even teeth. A booklet on his desktop had a long list of words and numbers printed on it. He ran his finger down the column. His nails, Alice noticed, were nicely manicured. This meant he could be trusted when it came to times and places, she thought. She was on her own now. She would assess each puzzle of human nature as it presented itself.

She was in charge of her own decisions. She would confront each problem head on and, like Sherlock Holmes, she would solve it.

"You can still make the 9:20 if you hurry," said Mr. Information. "It's a Trailways. Number 395. It leaves from Platform 2." He'd torn a sheet of paper off from a pad beside his elbow. "Let me write that down for you," he said, and handed it to her.

"Thanks," said Alice.

"You need to buy a ticket over there," he said, scanning her face and seeming to notice that she didn't quite know what she was doing at Port Authority. "See where it says Trailways, miss?"

Alice looked around the high-ceilinged space.

"That big sign. Red and white," he added.

"Over there?" asked Alice.

"Right over there."

Twelve minutes and four seconds later, according to Mickey Mouse, Alice had her ticket. Another eight minutes later, she was on the bus, in a seat by herself. When the woman at the ticket booth had said "Round-trip or one-way?" Alice had said, "One-way."

Hours passed, during which Alice took blurry photographs of the highway. She used up almost all her film. She spent six more dollars of Aunt Esmé's money when the bus stopped at Howard Johnson's. She sat on a swiveling stool at a Formica counter and ate a grilled cheese sandwich. She got back on the Trailways bus, lay down on the last seat, and sang quietly to herself.

"Like a bridge over troubled water/I will lay me down."

It was such a soothing, peaceful melody. Alice wasn't sure why the singer was lying down, or what the song was about. She sang it a little louder, though.

An old man at the front of the bus began clapping. He clapped slowly, but hard. One. Two. Three. Four times. It was not applause, Alice could hear that.

"Thank you," said the hoarse old voice. "For shutting the fuck up."

Alice continued to sing, soundlessly.

The bus climbed up into the hills, winding its way through a forest. It rose higher, and the malls, towns, and chapels dwindled away behind them, like a store window's holiday display. Little motels and highways were laid out in a valley far below. Above the bus, steep mountains pressed together, shoulder to shoulder, their peaks fading into a blue mist. Finally, the bus driver pulled up at a small rural station and said "Dodgson." It was 5:10 p.m. Alice was the only passenger to get off the bus. She found herself standing at the intersection of two country roads shaped like a cross. Each was a strip of black with a white stripe on either side, and a double yellow stripe down the center. Both roads cut through a wide expanse of trees. There was nothing but the forest—brown wood and green leaves—and the black road, in either direction, as far as she could see. Outside the bus station was a phone booth, three wooden benches, a planter containing wilted yellow daisies, and a soda machine. A blue sedan nosed up to her. The words Carnival Limousines were printed, by hand, on a cardboard sign held in place by the windshield wiper. The driver's hairy arm was propped on the car's open window.

"Need a ride?" he said. He had frizzy, uncombed hair. A pair of tinted sunglasses covered most of his face. They formed a dark band across the bridge of his nose, like a raccoon's. The lenses were striped: deep brown at the top, and pale amber toward the bottom, over his round cheeks.

"Are you a taxi?" asked Alice, who had assumed that all cabs were yellow.

"*I'm* not a taxi, no. I'm driving one," he said.

"Oh," said Alice. She looked at his face for a minute before climbing in.

He let the engine idle. "I was just trying to make a point. I'm in the doctoral program in linguistics at UNC."

"That's nice," Alice said.

He swung around and looked at her. "People make that mistake, the one that you did, all the time. I'm a person. A human being. Not a taxi. Do you know?"

"You're a person," said Alice. "Sure." She tried to sound sympathetic and conciliatory. He seemed irritable. She opened her backpack and began hunting for the address of the camp.

"I don't think folks should be equated with what they do," he said. "I want to be recognized for who I am. As an individual. A man."

"I was trying to find out if you were a driver," said Alice. "Or just some guy hanging around a bus station in his own car. I didn't think that *you* were a taxi. Okay?"

"This *is* my car," said the guy. "I *own* this limo service. I don't *hang around* at the station. This is my job."

Alice had found the brochure. She fanned herself with it. The air was cooler than it had been in the city, but close and still.

"I go to the station at particular times," the driver was explaining. "Arrival times. Times, as it were, when the bus is expected to arrive. At these times, I wait. I pick up passengers to get the fare. I run Carnival Limousines. I drive a car for a living. And I'm working on my Ph.D. Now. Do you have a better idea of what I do here? Are we clear?"

"Uh-huh," said Alice. She concluded, from something impatient in his voice—and from the way he looked at her in his rearview mirror—that the eleven-year-old Alice was vanishing.

"Would you take me to the Balthus Institute, please?" asked Alice, throwing her backpack on the floor and moving further back on the seat.

"Is it that old resort by Clayton Farms? About two miles east of here?"

"I have no idea," said Alice, trying to decipher the printing on the paper. "This says the number 1200. The letters SI. And the number 270. Does that tell you?"

"State Intersection 270, sure. I can find that. I've seen the place, I think."

"It's a summer camp," Alice told him. "A kind of art school. For kids."

He drove straight ahead. Far off on the horizon Alice could see some hulking blue shapes and some fog. She concluded these were mountains.

"Summer job, huh?" said the driver. "You're a counselor?"

Alice opened her mouth and began to say no. Her lips formed the word "yes" instead.

"What do you teach?"

"Swimming," Alice said. "And, um, pottery. And how to make collages. And how to fly airplanes. And how to dance."

"Airplanes?"

"Small ones."

"You can fly a plane?" he said. Again, he tipped his chin back and regarded Alice in the mirror.

"Not exactly," said Alice. "What I do is, I hold the kids up-side down. I shake them around. And I try to get them dizzy."

"Nice work if you can get it. How about we trade places? I'd rather shake kids up than drive a cab. Sounds easy."

"It's not easy at *all*," Alice told him sharply.

"No?"

"Of course not. It's serious. They have to be prepared. It's a preparation course for pilots. The, um, the airlines pay for it. But flying isn't for kids, usually. So it's not easy. Not at all. For kids, it's much more dangerous and difficult."

"Huh," said the driver, frowning. "I wouldn't think there'd be a big demand for child pilots. People. They get their kids into everything these days."

"Uh-huh. That's why I spin them around and around," said Alice. "That's my job. Sometimes they get sick from spinning. They probably hate me."

"Is that to get them accustomed to landing and takeoff?" asked the driver. "Like the astronauts?"

"Right," said Alice. "Like the astronauts. Yes."

"But *you* can't fly a plane. Can you?"

"Not yet. I will soon. I'll be learning. But, um, my summer job is just teaching the campers to spin without getting dizzy from it. And, uh, I teach basket weaving. And costume making. And photography."

He peered at her, critically, from over the frames of his sunglasses. He looked skeptical. Alice felt herself turning into a kid again. "You said it was pottery and swimming a minute ago," he said. He raised his eyebrows.

"Those too," said Alice.

"That sounds like a lot. I thought they just had sketching and watercolor classes."

"Yeah, well, you know. I do a little bit of everything," Alice said, trying to sound breezy and grown-up.

"I used to see those Balthus campers taking their class trips over to Sturgeon Lake sometimes," he said, "and carrying portable easels around with them. They'd be walking single file through a field someplace, or all sitting down together with their sketchbooks. They'd pile onto that old school bus. I haven't seen it lately. I haven't driven any passengers over to the Balthus place in years."

"Really?" said Alice with feigned disinterest. She fidgeted with her camera. They drove by a series of brick buildings shaped like an L. Alice saw a pizza shop, a drugstore, a hardware store, and a liquor shop.

"What's your name?" asked the driver.

"Rain," Alice said.

"That's pretty. Unusual. Did someone give you that name? It suits you."

"Oh, no. Absolutely not," said Alice. "No one gave me anything. I picked it out myself. I pick everything. Everything that has to do with me." Alice stared out the window. They passed a field of corn, great tall stalks planted in rows.

"So you're into choosing your own destiny?" asked the driver.

"Oh," said Alice, surprised by a question she didn't understand. "I don't know."

"I just thought, if you picked out your own name, maybe you were interested in the notion of self-invention."

"Self-invention?" said Alice.

"Yeah. Like, right now, I'm a taxi driver named Elvis. But when I complete my degree, I'll be Professor Elvis Darrow, Ph.D. That'll affect how people see me, what they think about me. Your name's a part of your identity."

"A part," Alice agreed. "Yeah."

"Do you have a last name, Rain?"

"No, I don't," she told him. "Not anymore. I got rid of it."

"How'd you manage that?"

"When I divorced my husband."

"*Husband?* Get out of here. You're joking."

"We married young. He knocked me up," said Alice, repeating the phrase she'd heard her mother use when she was talking to a friend. Alice had been eavesdropping. Rain's door had been closed. "It wasn't love," Alice said. "I wasn't old enough. I wasn't ready."

"Gee, that's too bad. I'm sorry to hear that, Rain."

"One name is better on its own, anyway," said Alice. The words came out quickly, like the lyrics from a song played over and over, and memorized. "One name by itself is strong. I'm learning to be myself. I'm in fashion design now. I used to be an artist's model, when I was just a child. It's like being a piece of furniture. The interesting job is to create things." She repeated this, word for word, from the conversation she'd heard Rain have, three years earlier, on the telephone.

"You got an early start, miss," said the driver. "Shit, I'm twenty-two and all I've done is drive a cab."

"I have a lot of responsibilities," Alice agreed. She sounded burdened, as grown-ups did. "And the sad thing is, I have no time left for my little girl."

In the rearview mirror, the driver was frowning. "You have a *kid*?" He didn't believe her. Alice could tell.

"Oh yes," she insisted. "Little Alice. She's the most important part of my life. She's everything to me. If it weren't for my Little Alice, I don't know what I'd do."

"Wow. How old is she?"

"She's two."

"Where is she now?"

"She's at the camp," said Alice. "Taking swimming lessons."

"Is that right? I didn't know they have swimming for babies up there." He let out a snort, an abortive laugh. He half turned around, then turned back to face the road. It was obvious that he thought Alice was lying. She didn't blame him. She'd been lying badly. She'd have to improve her lying skills or her attempt to become an adult would be a failure.

"Oh they do now," Alice insisted. "That camp has absolutely everything. You'd be amazed."

"I'd heard something like that. That's what they said. But that was a while ago. Well, miss, here we are." He'd pulled up beside a gray boulder. A bronze plaque, blackened with age, said BALTHUS INSTITUTE, EST. 1952. Immediately ahead was a narrow dirt path that undulated across a field. At the very end of it, no bigger than a deck of cards, were two low buildings, one behind the other, each lined with a row of doors. Trees and plants surrounded them, as if the woods were slowly closing in.

Alice's pulse quickened with foreboding. She covered her watch with her palm and felt Mickey Mouse leaping against her skin.

"Ordinarily, I'd be glad to drive you," said the driver. "But I'd get stuck. It's all up- and downhill. Too many steep inclines."

Alice picked up her bag and got out of the cab. "That's okay," she said, shutting the door with a decisive slam. "Goodbye. Thanks."

"Aren't you forgetting something?" he said.

"What?" asked Alice nervously. She felt her costume slipping.

"We generally pay for taxi rides," he said, "in the United States."

"How much is it?"

"Haven't you got any money, kid?"

"Of course I do," said Alice, still trying to be an adult.

"It's fifteen bucks. For you."

Alice dug out fifteen crumpled single dollar bills, together with an uncounted pile of small change. She didn't know whether he'd charged her more or less than he was supposed to. Either he'd ripped her off or else he'd given her a deal.

He was looking at her more closely now, Alice saw. "You've been shitting me this whole time, kid," he said. "Am I right? Haven't you?"

"Sort of," she confessed, keeping her eyes downcast as she placed the wad of bills in his hand.

He pushed his sunglasses down on the bridge of his nose. "Are you supposed to be here?" he said.

"Yes," said Alice.

"Are you absolutely sure?"

"Yeah."

"Someone knows where you are, kid? You didn't run away from home?"

"Someone knows," said Alice.

"Are you lying again now? Or, this time, are you telling me the truth?"

"The truth," she whispered. She was mortified that she'd been so transparent. She'd thought she'd glided effortlessly into adulthood, that her trick had worked. But he'd seen right through her. He'd played along with it, but he'd known she'd just been putting on an act.

The driver was shuffling through the loose papers on the dashboard. He handed Alice a card. It said Carnival Limousines, and it had a name and address on it. "This is where you can reach me," he said. "Okay?"

"Okay," said Alice. A lump was forming in her throat. As the blue car spun off down the road in a cloud of dust, Alice slipped her camera out of its case and photographed it. The Polaroid negative developed as she trudged along the path. On the shiny black square of cardboard was a shot of a license plate.

A Wonderland

From where Alice stood, on a dirt road that was sprinkled with rocks, the mountains appeared as a herd of camels. Their humped backs were visible against the purple haze of the late-afternoon sky. Alice looked down at her feet. Aunt Esmé's platform shoes were uncomfortable. She'd already developed a blister, just from wearing the shoes in the station and on the bus. As she grew closer to the blue buildings, she gave up trying to walk on stilts. She sat down in the dry grass by the side of the path and took them off.

The Balthus compound looked nothing like the photographs in the brochure. There was no pool. There was no lawn furniture, except for a weathered Adirondack chair. There were no café tables or umbrellas. There were no roses, just a straggling garden. The paint on the houses was peeling. The grass was bare in places, and the ground was cracked. The dirt path took a sharp turn here, to the right, and led to an old barn. It looked abandoned. The sign over the double doors had been obliterated. The letters BA, T, and S were all that remained of BALTHUS, with a streaky gap between them where the paint had worn away. Half a mile past that was a big white house with green trim, fronted by six columns. Broad, flat steps led up to its front porch, a small portion of which had collapsed. Behind the house was a hill, high and wide, dotted with eccentric metal forms that reminded Alice of a circus or a jungle gym. The thin strip of dirt path continued up the green embankment, stopping finally at a plateau at the top, where there was a log cabin. No one was in sight. Alice heard a dog barking someplace. She listened to the murmuring of leaves. For a brief moment, she considered running back down the dirt path and waving the taxi driver down. She'd tell him she'd made a mistake, and that she wanted to go home. But she'd been walking for almost twenty minutes. He was long gone.

Beside her was a cluster of bright bluebells and pale orange tiger lilies. Their stems seemed abnormally tall. When she stood up, barefoot, the blossoms were as high as the top of her head. Some of the petals had fallen off. The path felt hot against the soles of her feet, and the rocks were sharp. The two squat blue clapboard buildings in front of her were lined with doors and windows. As she surveyed her surroundings, it took her a minute to recognize that the huge dusty green sheet of plastic in front of the barn might once have been a swimming pool.

A man appeared from behind the barn, walking away from her, with slow deliberation, toward the hill. He ascended the steps to the front porch, opened the door, and disappeared inside. A lump formed in Alice's throat, and at the pit of her stomach she felt a knot of anxiety. She began to feel as if she were shrinking now, growing smaller and smaller, getting younger and younger—turning into a kindergarten kid who had gotten lost, who cried. She tried to stand up straight and be in command of herself again. But a small sound escaped her. She bit her lip so she wouldn't whimper. She huddled near the doorway of the barn, feeling that no one wanted her, that she belonged no place, that she had no home. Her great confidence had disappeared. She stood in the path, awkwardly, not knowing what to do. She was overcome by self-consciousness. It had become impossible to enter any of the buildings, to introduce herself, or to ask for help. She sat down on the decrepit Adirondack chair and took Aunt Esmé's blue nail polish out of her bag. With a shaking hand, trying to appear at ease, she began to paint her toenails.

She'd given two coats to all ten toenails when the man with the shag haircut reappeared. He made his way down the stairs and across the lawn, just as slowly and deliberately as before. He was in no rush, it seemed. But he was heading steadily toward Alice. His gait was loose and languid. His hips swayed from side to side. When he was a few feet away, he leaned against the trunk of a tree. "I thought I heard you crying," he said in a lilting Southern drawl. "I can hear a damsel in distress for miles. I've got good ears." He spoke without surprise, as if he and Alice were old acquaintances who'd been in the middle of a conversation that had been interrupted.

"I wasn't crying," said Alice. She put the brush back inside the bottle of nail polish and twisted the cap closed.

"I thought I heard you."

"No," said Alice. "Do you work here?"

"Me? Come on. You ought to know me better than that."

Alice studied him. He had a long oval face and a space between his two front teeth. His hair was tucked behind his large, prominent ears. They stuck out from either side of his head. He was wearing mirrored aviator glasses. Alice could see herself reflected back in them. Inside the silver lenses, she appeared distorted—a huge forehead, a face shaped like an eggplant, and a pointed miniature chin. She couldn't see the man's eyes, only this fun-house image of herself.

"I don't know you at all," she said.

"How quickly we forget," he said. "Correct me if I'm wrong. But I believe I got you high the other night. On the house. Not that you owe me."

"Not really," said Alice.

"You must have a high tolerance. Let me guess," he said. "Did the shithead dump you?"

"What shithead?" asked Alice.

"The one at Brewster's. When I met you a couple weeks back. Guy you were with."

He seemed not to know who she was. He'd mistaken her for someone else.

"I wasn't with a guy," said Alice.

"That's a good one. Don't I wish. His name is Jason Carlson, by the way. I've done business with him."

"I just got here," said Alice. "Five seconds ago."

"Well, I don't happen to know where your little friends are. As if I ever do. Faith and Hope are around here someplace, I think. I saw them about half an hour ago."

Alice was entirely disoriented by the nonsensical conversation. She felt she'd arrived in the middle of a play and didn't know her lines.

"If you want to chase the dragon while you're waiting, come on in back," said the man. He nodded toward the barn.

"I'll just wait here, thank you."

"Up to you. It's mighty fine shit, though."

"Are Hope and Faith the counselors here?"

"No. They're students. Classes haven't started yet, but they come and go as they please. They live here. When they want to."

"Do you live here, too?"

"Me? Nah. I got a summer place, over by Peter's Kill. And you? Still living with your ma and pa up in Seymour County, I thought you told me?"

"No," said Alice. "I didn't say that. I'm not from Seymour County. My dad's in the nuthouse and my mom split."

He took his sunglasses off. "No shit," he said. "You're *not* from Seymour County, and you *don't* live at home, and your name's not Clare. Is it?"

"No."

"I put my foot in my mouth again, didn't I?"

"I don't think so," said Alice, who wasn't familiar with the expression.

"Christ," he said. "I'm sorry. I feel very foolish. You must think I'm an idiot."

"Not really," said Alice, though she did think he was an idiot.

"I thought you were Clare Reynolds. What a pinhead I am. Forgive me." He extended his hand.

Alice took it.

He clasped her hand in his and held it for a long time, stroking her knuckles with his fingers.

"It's incredibly nice to meet you," he said. "Even if you're not Clare, and even if I'm a complete and total asshole." He pointed to his forehead. "My mind is blown," he said. "Over the years, I've destroyed most of the ol' brain cells."

He had still not let go of her hand. For some reason, Alice didn't know how to get her hand back. His friendliness was unsettling but contagious. She felt a strange desire not to disrupt him, or disturb the way he was: his need to hold hands, his problems with his brain cells, his confusion between her and other girls, the uneven cadence of his voice, his odd worldview.

"I'm holding on to you too long," he said, looking her in the eye. "Aren't I?"

"Kind of," Alice admitted.

"I do that sometimes. Sorry." He continued to grip her hand.

"I think you should let go now," Alice said.

"Okay." He gave her hand one last squeeze before he released it. She cast an appraising glance at him. He was barefoot, as she was, but unlike hers, his feet were dirty. He looked as if he'd been walking in mud. He was wearing a pair of jeans, hip-huggers, with a low-slung belt. Above this, incongruously, was a conservative white shirt of the sort that Dean's agent would wear with a tie and jacket. The shirt was wrinkled. One of the shirttails was untucked, and it was half unbuttoned, as if he'd been in the middle of getting dressed. He wore a leather cord around his neck. A silver amulet dangled from it. It was a round sphere with an eyeball in the center, like the kind that Veronica Dreyfuss had brought to show-and-tell, in the fifth grade, from a trip to Greece.

She was aware, as she stared at his jewelry and his clothes, that he was watching her—watching him. She knew she was being rude, studying him so obviously, but she couldn't help it.

"How tall are you?" she said.

"I don't know, man. Six foot four, around. How tall are you?"

"I'm five feet and seven inches," said Alice. She almost added: And I'm eleven years old. But, determined to continue her adult charade, she didn't.

"You're a shrimp," he said. He reached out and touched a strand of Alice's hair which had escaped from the headband she wore it in. He tucked it behind her ear, as if he were entitled to make close contact with her. "You're a shorty."

"I'm *not* a shorty," said Alice, drawn in, instantly, to the childish competition. "I'm the tallest girl in my class. I'm one of the tallest girls at the Fieldwood School."

"But compared to me, you're a shrimp, aren't you?" he said.

"No, I'm not," said Alice. She found herself staring at his face with an uneasy—a reluctant—fascination.

"Are too. Hello down there, Shorty," he said. He lifted his hand, wiggled his fingers, and waved at Alice. It was a dopey, comical gesture—as if he were dressed up for Halloween, a life-size version of the Mickey Mouse on her watch, a character at Disneyland. On almost every finger, he wore a silver ring. One had a black-and-white symbol on it. Another was shaped like a skull, with gaping eye sockets.

"Hello," said Alice.

"We meet again," he said.

Alice frowned, confused.

Just as he'd held her hand for too long, now he waved at her too much. He did it for several absurd seconds. Alice knew from her observations of Aunt Esmé that this sort of behavior meant a person was drugged out. Now he was tipping his head from one side to the other, making faces at her. She couldn't tell if he was sticking out his tongue and rolling his eyes to amuse her, or himself.

To be polite, she laughed a little.

"That's better," he said. "I wanted to see you smile. When you're happy, you're much prettier."

Alice stopped smiling. She found him a bit frightening. He wasn't like a regular person at all. And yet his face, she thought, was open, affable, and kind. It wasn't a handsome face, but an arresting one. He had a low, bulbous forehead, like the picture of Neanderthals in her sixth-grade science textbook, and a pronounced jawbone. His cheeks were shadowed with beard stubble. His brown hair was wavy. Above the aviator sunglasses, Alice could see thick eyebrows. His face was sunburned. The shape of his mouth was noticeably defined, as if someone had taken a pen and drawn it. Even when he wasn't smiling, the outer edges of his mouth turned upward, mischievously. The long curve of his thin lips reminded Alice of a lizard.

While she was looking at him, he pushed his sunglasses up on his forehead, sweeping his hair back up off his face. He met Alice's gaze and held it. There was something very strange about his slate gray eyes. The lids were heavy, as if he were sleepy. The lashes were thick and black, contrasting sharply with the pale, cool ice gray of his irises. As she studied his eyes more closely, she saw they were multicolored. Alice caught a trace of yellow and green, as if his eyes could capture the sun and the grass and reflect back anything that drifted past him. These were eyes that didn't pull Alice in, with a tug of sympathetic warmth, the way Rabbit's deep dark brown eyes did. They did something else. Alice didn't know what it was they did. That's why she looked and looked, far into them, trying to figure it out, searching.

"I don't know where to go," she said, finally.

"Why should you?" he said. "This place is a wreck." He paused. "It's a shame the Great Man retired. He's a big customer of mine."

"The great man?"

"Hans Balthus. The old camp director. He quit the job. It's been a different place around here since then."

"How come?" asked Alice.

The man pointed to his arm.

Alice looked, uncomprehendingly.

He put his thumb between his index and ring fingers and poked it through—so that just the fingertip was visible. It was something Alice's mother used to do, so long ago, when Alice had been little. Rain would pretend that her thumb was Alice's nose. She'd say, "I've got your nose, Alice." It was a game they'd played, in that other life, before. But the man didn't do that now. He pushed his thumb up against the inside of his arm, pressing it to a thick blue vein in his forearm.

Alice waited for the man to explain.

"Horse," he said.

"Horse?" Alice repeated.

"Almost killed him. He scored after that nasty business in the press. Poor fucker had a stroke. He's been feeding a serious habit most of his life. Not that I'm complaining."

"Oh," said Alice.

"Hans Balthus is brilliant. A brilliant artist, and a brilliant addict. Many talents. Spread himself too thin, I guess. Sculpture, photography, and illustration. Landscaping. Horticulture. He designed the Butterfly and Sculpture Garden over there." He gestured toward the hill. Alice saw, now, that it was dotted with sculptures of every size and shape.

"Who are you, anyway?" he said.

"I'm Alice."

"Alice? I know an Alice. Don't I? Wait, wait." He snapped his fingers. "I'll get this. Don't remind me. Alice is . . . Alice was . . . Alice is the baby sister."

"Are you J.D.?" she said, remembering the initials on the brochure.

"Ah, so we *have* met, after all! You know me?"

"My aunt might. I think."

"Hah. Yipes. I know too many chicks on the East Coast. Time for me to move west."

"I guess," said Alice.

"Wait a minute. Now I remember. You're one of the Cale sisters, aren't you?"

"Well, I . . ."

"See? I told you I'd get it. I never forget a face. You're Alice

Cale! God, it's been a long time. Last time I saw you, you were yea high. And now look at you. You must be in your teens by now. All grown-up and even more lovely than Virginia, your older sister."

"My sister," said Alice, "isn't named Virginia."

"Oh my God. Here we go again. But you *are* Alice, aren't you?"

"I'm Alice, yes." She hated to break it to him that he was wrong about her last name. She was going to say: I'm not Alice Cale. I'm Alice Duncan. I'm the daughter of Dean and Rain Duncan and Esmé is my half sister, five years older than I am, the daughter of my father's first wife, who came to East Sixty-seventh Street to take care of me after my mother left, and who I refer to as my Aunt Esmé. But that was much too complicated. It would only confuse J.D. He was already baffled, Alice felt. She shouldn't perplex him further.

"I'm Alice," she said again.

"Alice!" He looked pleased. "You're not quite up to dragon-chasing, are you?"

"No," said Alice. Poor thing, she thought, talking about imaginary dragons and murderous horses.

"You look a little young for the hard stuff," he said. "No offense, but you look—well. Square. Am I being rude? By saying that to you, Alice?"

Alice shrugged. "It's okay," she said. "Rabbit says the same thing."

"Who's he?"

"This guy."

"Well, he's an honest man. Because, see, some people will get really pissed off at you if you go up to them and you say: Why, hello there. You're a square."

"Uh-huh," said Alice.

"I don't believe in censorship. You know, Alice?"

"Sure."

"Do *you* believe in censorship?"

"I don't think so."

"I don't. In fact, I can't. With me, it all pours right out of my mouth. I just say the first thing that pops into my head, even if it's a very fucked-up thing to say, see. I can't stop myself, Alice. I call it out. I go ahead. I say it—anything at all. Nice things. Mean things. Whatever it is. I say it anyway."

"Uh-huh," said Alice, nodding her head.

"Something that I say could annoy you, man. Upset you, even. Or distress you. But then, Alice, you can say to *me*: You're annoying me, man. And then we're cool."

"You're annoying me, man," said Alice.

"Oh God. Really?"

"No," said Alice. "I was just kidding."

"That's *totally* cool. See, this is what it's all about, Alice. Communicating."

"Okay," said Alice.

"Baby Alice Cale," he said, shaking his head. "I'll be darned. It's incredible. You look great, if I may say so."

"Thanks," said Alice curtly. "Who should I talk to about the art classes?"

"I'm not sure there will be any, honey. They only managed to get one or two kids this year."

"Only one or two kids are here to study art this summer?" said Alice.

"As far as I know. The institute's about to close."

"What will happen to me?" said Alice tremulously.

"Why, anything you like. What would you *like* to happen to you? As you stand there. In that innocent. Flowered. Sundress."

Alice, embarrassed, took a sudden interest in her wristwatch.

"But enough about me, Fair Alice," he said. "We were discussing your likes and dislikes."

"I'm supposed to stay at camp until August 2nd," said Alice. "But now there isn't any camp here, you said. So I don't know what will happen. And I don't know where to go."

"There's a camp. It's just not overpopulated. I'm sure you're more than welcome. Odette will be thrilled to see a new student in her seminar."

"I have to think about it," said Alice. "Maybe there's a bus that leaves soon. A bus to take me back."

"Don't think, sweetheart. Just act. Thinking gums up the works. Trust your instincts, Alice. Go with the flow. Be spontaneous. Follow the impulse. First feel. Then do."

Alice bit her lip.

"But don't listen to *me*," he said. "That's just how I live. You don't have to be like *me*. You have to be like *you*."

Everything he said made her feel rattled. She was homesick. Her eyes filled with unexpected tears. She felt herself begin to crumble inward—to give up some internal battle. She covered her face with her hand, pretending she had something in her eye.

"You *are* crying," he said softly. "I can always tell when something's wrong. It's like this sixth sense I have." He put his hand on the back of her neck and left it there, a stranger's hand, an adult man's hand, uninvited but not unwelcome. It was warm and soothing. "There's nothing to cry about," he said. "Whatever the problem is, I'll try to fix it for you."

Alice thought this was charming and considerate. She pressed her fingers against her eyelids, to make the crying stop.

"Here," he said, lifting up the hem of his T-shirt and drawing close to her. "Allow me."

Alice looked up at him while he dried her cheeks. "This eye makeup you're wearing," he said, "is rubbing off on me." His voice was intimate and low. He'd bunched a portion of his shirt up in his hand and was using it, on Alice, like a washcloth. The cotton began absorbing all of Aunt Esmé's eyeliner and eye shadow. The tail of his shirt turned black and blue.

"I'm sorry I got your shirt dirty, J.D.," said Alice.

"Don't worry about it. He stepped back. "Now I can see you."

She could see, when J.D. tilted his head to one side, that he was doing the thing that Rabbit did: making Alice a contestant in the beauty pageant, the one she'd never wanted to enter but was always in. She'd been signed up automatically, at birth, she guessed—maybe by God, before His untimely death. Rabbit had read a book about it, and he said good and evil were the same, because God was dead. There was no wrong or right, he said. But there was still beauty and ugliness, apparently. And there was still quite a large panel of judges, Alice felt. She herself was not on the jury. She was being tried. She didn't know who made these assignments, or if it was possible to change the one that she received. She waited for the verdict from J.D.

"You're not as old as you were a minute ago," was all he said. "You look younger without that crap. You don't need that. Leave it off. What made you put it on? Did you want to grow up real fast?"

Alice had the same sinking sensation she'd had with the taxi driver: that her disguise had slipped. Her disguise of adulthood, she thought, was falling away. She couldn't decide whether to let it. "I stole the makeup from my aunt," she said uncertainly.

"I think you're right," he said, narrowing his eyes. "I think you probably ought to leave."

It was what he didn't say that made Alice think of Rabbit again. She recognized the warning signals in his voice, his crooked lips, his eyes. But it wasn't the same exactly. She didn't know why.

"I'll call the taxi man," she said. "And I'll go back."

"Go," said J.D. without a lot of conviction. "You go on, girl. You do that."

She'd put the limousine service's business card in the pocket of her dress. She could feel the corner of the cardboard with her thumb. "Is there a phone here?" she asked.

J.D. didn't answer her. His eyes traveled all over her, crawling up and down, like ants.

"Could you just tell me where the telephone is, please?" Alice repeated more loudly.

"There's something about a young girl crying that always does this to me," he said. "I'm sorry."

Alice didn't ask what the crying did, or why he was apologizing. She turned her back on him. She shielded her eyes with her hand, scouting out the possible location of the basic necessities she thought she might need: a bathroom, a police station, a gun, a knife, a phone.

"I'm not saying it's right, Alice. I'm not saying it's good or bad. I'm just telling you, darlin'. I'm just telling you what's true."

Alice didn't ask: what wasn't right, but what was true. His voice was hushed, and she had the crazy feeling that he hadn't spoken aloud—that she'd been able to read his mind somehow. She stared down at the Carnival Limousine card. She folded it in half, and then in quarters. She thought there must be a telephone in one of the blue houses toward the back of the field. But she wasn't sure that going indoors, where she might be followed by J.D., was the wisest move. She stood in the grass like a stork, balancing on one foot, and stared across the lawn at an open window.

"There's a phone in the hallway," he said. "You can go over and use it. I won't follow you."

Could he read her thoughts, too? Alice didn't move.

"Unless of course you want me to," he added. He smiled faintly. It was a lopsided half-smile, almost a snarl. It involved only the right side of his mouth.

Alice shook her head no.

"You're a good girl, aren't you?" he said, in a voice full of innuendo.

Alice didn't know how to respond. Her face was hot.

"You're blushing," he noticed.

Alice looked over at the window again—a little desperately. She looked around the deserted grounds, wishing someone would show up. The taxi driver, a guard, an ambulance, a police officer. Someone needed to be there. To patrol. She wanted to be rescued.

A grin had appeared on his face. It was dazzling. J.D.'s grin was a ten-thousand-watt smile with a deep dimple on either side. J.D. knew he had it, and he used it expertly, like a weapon.

"That's really cute," he said. "When you do that. I haven't seen a girl blush for me that way since the Paleozoic era. A few billion years ago."

Alice didn't say a word. She felt trapped and cornered. She was blushing: she liked him. He knew it. She'd told him. It wasn't her but her body which had spoken. She didn't especially agree with what it was saying, and she wasn't even sure she understood. But J.D. spoke this language of her body. He'd heard it.

Alice took a quick look at her watch. A conversation had been conducted, without words. It had taken about ten seconds.

"Now what?" said J.D. Apparently, he'd entered into her brain, where her most private thoughts were, and he was thinking along with her, wondering the same things.

Alice thought she might possibly start to cry again. She sensed this would be disastrous, giving him an opportunity to put his arms around her, to comfort her. She didn't cry. She resisted. She was eleven; J.D. might have been twenty-five, or thirty. The numbers didn't matter a whole lot just then.

"Do you go your way?" he asked. "And I go mine? Or what, babe? How do we play this thing?"

How do we play this thing. Alice would always remember these words, with their four hard truths, and their four ugly implications. (1) *How*: They had to make decisions. (2) *Do*: They had to act. (3) *We*: They were in it together. (4) *Play*: It was a game, and it would begin and it would end.

"I want to go home," Alice said. She didn't recognize her voice anymore. It was high, wavering, and hoarse. There was a question mark at the end of her sentence that had never been there before. She wasn't telling J.D. anything. She was seeking his permission. She was asking for his help.

"Okay," he said. "That's what we'll do. So long, Fair Alice."

"So long," said Alice.

She watched him stroll away, down the dirt path. She could see the bottoms of his feet, first the right one, then the left, then the right again. They were black, as if he hadn't washed them for a while. His faded jeans were torn at the back. Across his rear end, a thin line of tanned skin peeked through.

She picked up her backpack and walked toward the blue house. As she crossed the field, she thought she could feel him watching. When she reached the other side of the compound, she turned around. He was gone.

The Twins

Alice was searching for a telephone inside the blue building. A sign over the entrance said it was the girls' dormitory. Chinese lanterns, shaped like umbrellas, covered the fluorescent bulbs, bathing the shadowy hallway in a dull pink light. It was painted with murals from floor to ceiling. On the wall, a painted snail the size of Alice's head crept under a painted mushroom. A painted moth, its wings as wide as Alice's arms, flew over an arbor of grapevines. The air smelled of mildew, and the threadbare carpeting had been worn away in places. It felt cool and damp on Alice's bare feet. A dusty bulletin board displayed two dragons. They had cardboard heads and paws. Their forked tongues were made of felt. Origami ducks, toads, and parrots were pinned to paper fields, paper trees, and paper ponds.

On the other side of the bulletin board was a small door. No higher than a cupboard, it came up to Alice's rib cage. A garland of leaves was painted across the top and bottom. The words Studio J were written in a flowery script in purple paint.

Alice put her ear against the door and listened. Kneeling down on the thin brown carpet, she peeked in through the keyhole. Inside, she glimpsed a plain room with a bunk bed, a little drawing table, a little easel, and a little chair.

"Hello?" Alice called, standing up. "Is anybody there?"

No one answered. The corridor was lined with other half-size doors, each made of wood, each decorated with a garland, just like this one. Alice passed Studio I, Studio H, and Studio G. Halfway down the corridor, the doors began to grow. They came up to Alice's shoulder. At the end of the hallway, where there were four full-size doors, Alice found a flight of stairs. She was about to walk up it when she heard a telephone ringing nearby. She followed the sound until she came to a large door marked Studio E. Behind it, voices rose and fell. Music played softly. She knocked.

"Just a sec!" called a girl's voice. She spoke, Alice thought, in the same strangled way Aunt Esmé did when she'd inhaled dope and was trying to prevent the smoke in her lungs from escaping. Alice leaned against the wall. A collection of tattered posters had been taped over the mural. With a shock of recognition, Alice saw the Crash Omaha poster Aunt Esmé had at home.

"To the twins," said the autograph. "Eternally yours, Crash Omaha."

Maybe Aunt Esmé had been right about Crash, Alice thought. Maybe he actually would become a rock star. Or maybe, at some point in the past, he'd already been one. Alice looked at the other faces on the posters. She knew them, too. They were the singers from the pages of *Creem* magazine, the same ones whose records Aunt Esmé and Rabbit often played. In her room, Alice had cut apart their photographs. She'd cut out flowers for them, and had glued them over the musicians' eyes. There on the wall, Janis Joplin opened her mouth wide, like a yowling cat. Mick Jagger sprang from a panther's crouch, pointing an accusatory finger at the audience. Grace Slick cavorted with the members of Jefferson Airplane. Bob Dylan scowled over his guitar, his narrow face covered with beard stubble. Joni Mitchell, unsmiling and aloof, materialized from out of the blackness, her long fair hair blowing out behind her. Written on the wall beneath them, someone had spray-painted their names in garish, bubble-shaped letters: Janis, Joni, Gracie, Bobby, Mick.

Alice had the feeling that the posters were part of a religion. But they were ragged and torn, and the pieces of tape that affixed them to the wall had turned yellow. Alice touched the Crash Omaha poster distractedly. As she fiddled with a corner of the paper, a triangular piece of poster crumbled in her hands. The shred of paper floated slowly to the carpet, where a crack had formed in the baseboard. A plant had begun to germinate there, pushing two green shoots out of the gap in the plaster.

Just as Alice was about to give up on ever being able to talk to anyone in the dorm, the door opened to Studio E. Two teenage girls appeared inside a fragrant cloud of smoke.

"What's up?" said the taller, thinner one. She waved her hand in front of her face to clear the smoke away.

"How's it going?" said the shorter, plumper one. She cleared her throat.

"Not much. How's it going with you?" said Alice. The taller girl had the proud bearing of an empress. The shorter girl had the boxy build of a gymnast. With their sun-burnished faces, freckles, and wide-set blue eyes, they exuded health and competence. They had feathered, chin-length hair and spiky bangs. The taller girl's hair was striped like a skunk's, black with a streak of platinum. The shorter girl's hair was auburn and wavy. They wore copious amounts of jet black eyeliner. Their jet black mascara turned their eyelashes into furry, jet black caterpillars. Alice loved them instantaneously.

"This is Faith," said the bewitching skunk-haired girl, punching her sister on the shoulder.

"And this is Hope," said Faith, punching back.

"We're twins," Hope said. "I'm the little sister."

"And I'm the big one."

"Faith was born at 11:21 p.m. on May 16th, 1960," said Hope.

"And Hope was born two minutes after midnight on May 17th, so she's younger by a day," said Faith.

The twins were dressed in tank tops and skirts sewn from old pairs of jeans. Hope wore a glittering belt that said SHIT on the buckle. Faith had her hair tied back in a bandanna. They wore black motorcycle boots like Rabbit's.

"You're Alice, right?" said Faith.

Alice felt alarmed. "Yes," she said. "How did you know my name?"

"J.D. called just now," said Hope. "He said you'd be here."

"Oh!" said Alice. Hearing the two initials sent a shiver down the backs of her legs, as had once happened when she'd unplugged the hair dryer in Aunt Esmé's bathroom with wet hands. Alice looked at Hope expectantly, wanting to hear what else he'd said. But Hope had taken a comb from out of her back pocket and had begun to comb her glamorous, two-toned bangs.

"We haven't seen a new girl here for a while," she said, suppressing a yawn. "Not since the incident. Most of the instructors resigned."

"Me and Hope are the only students who come back every

summer," said Faith. "Our rents said we ought to show our gratitude to the Great Man. He discovered us. Our rents are in the South of France."

"What are rents?" Alice asked.

"Our parents," Faith explained.

"Me and Faith are child prodigies," said Hope, effortlessly arranging her hair in a stylish upsweep. "When I was twelve, I won first prize for visual arts at TCE. I had my first solo exhibition, in downtown Baltimore, while I was in the eighth grade. *Art Now* did a cover story. And Faith is the first American artist under eighteen to have a work acquired by the Museum of Contemporary Art in San Diego."

"Is that where you're from, Detroit?" Alice asked, admiring the way Hope was now clipping her hair, so perfectly, with a zebra-striped clasp. The silver bangles on her slender arms ran from her glorious wrists up to her glorious elbows. Her hairless armpit was as white as eiderdown.

"Chevy Chase," said Hope.

"The guy who falls down on *Saturday Night Live*?" Alice asked.

"No, dummy," said Faith. "It's a place in Maryland."

"Not to brag or anything," said Faith, bending down to polish her boots with a pink paper tissue, "but our combined IQ is 320. That puts us *well* above the genius range. Right now Hope and I are exploding middle-class attitudes toward war and death, as mediated by consumerism. You're not an advocate of virtuosity. Are you?"

"I don't think so," said Alice, bewildered and impressed.

"Neither are we," said Faith. "Hope and I resent craftsmanship with a passion. We reject the myth of quality."

"Hmm," said Alice, frowning and nodding. "Interesting."

"And you?" said Faith. "What's your approach?"

"I cut up magazines, give haircuts to rock stars, cut out paper clothes for naked people, and I make collages," Alice said.

"Collage," Faith said, sucking in her breath. "Oh no. No no."

"I do make them," Alice said.

"You can't," said Faith. She turned to Hope. "Can she revive collage, sis?"

"She can do whatever she likes," said Hope, studying Alice almost coldly. "If she doesn't mind being out of step with the rest of the contemporary art world."

"What's your full name, Alice?" Faith said. "Would we have heard of you?

"I'm Alice Duncan," she said.

"Duncan!" the girls repeated in unison.

If her friends Skye and Veronica had done that in the school yard at Fieldwood, Alice would have said "Jinx." The two girls would have linked their pinkie fingers. But now, that wouldn't do. Alice didn't know how to act. She crossed one leg over the other and lounged against the bulletin board, flinging her backpack to the floor. She tried to imitate the twins' aplomb.

"No relation to Dean Duncan, is there?" said Faith.

"He's my dad," said Alice. "Why?"

"Ugh," said Hope. "We abhor the Abstract Expressionists on principle."

"Painterly," said Faith. "Paint-er-leee! It's all about their *brushmanship*. Their internal *conflicts*."

"Their individualism," said Hope. "Their emotions, their angst, and their machismo."

"AE is hopelessly smug," said Faith. "It's hopelessly self-congratulatory."

"I'd rather see a gallery floor covered with vomit," said Hope.

"Me, too. Given the choice between a Rothko and a pile of puke, I'd definitely take the puke," said Faith.

"I'd give old Duncan senior a point or two," said Hope, "for dropping out of that revolting movement. Your daddy was a hero."

"Was he?" Alice asked, wishing she had never mentioned him.

"No," said Hope. "But he could have been. He didn't rise to the challenge. Like most of the AEs, he was lily-livered. Not to romanticize our role in society, but artists are outlaws. Dean Duncan chickened out. He caved."

"He did?" said Alice.

"Oh, come on. Portraiture?" said Hope, in a tone of disdain. "Give me a break. Bug-eyed caricatures of the rich? *Please*. It's just a poor man's Kokoschka in a muddy shade."

"It's not bold or brutal," said Faith. "It's not young or real or new."

"Dean can't paint because he's sad," Alice said, trying to make excuses for him.

"*Duh,*" said Hope. "That's abundantly clear. Sturm und Drang, doom and gloom. Brown and gray. I'd be bummed out, too, if I had *my* head stuck in the black paint bucket all day."

"What an oppressive legacy," said Faith to Alice. "You'll have to throw off the shackles."

"You really will," said Hope. "Well, Duncan junior. Welcome to the institute. Can we show you to your room?"

"Thank you, but I'm not sure I can stay," Alice said, intending to sound gracious and poised. "I came from New York City, because of a . . . slight misunderstanding." She pulled the phrase, neatly, from the air. Checking her watch, she added importantly, "I've got to be getting back now. I'll be late. It's a busy time of year." She was as self-assured as the twins. She was someone entirely unlike Alice. Quite a bit like Rain. She was worldly and elegant, as her mother had been. She wore black turtlenecks, white slacks that tapered at the ankles, and alligator loafers without socks. She had a boyfriend with an exotic name who sent flowers with a card. She sat in the backyard for long periods, draped across the chaise lounge, reading from the paperbacks she bought from the used book store. Beside her was a pile of sketches, pictures of shoes. A stone was placed on them so they wouldn't blow away. She held a cigarette. Her hands dangled loosely, with easy grace and languor, from her wrists. We're each the sovereign ruler of ourselves, she'd said, setting the book down with a thump. We must be who we are, and do as we please. She swept noiselessly out of the garden, and she swept noiselessly out of the house. She moved fluidly, like a dancer, like someone without limits, without bones. Rain left, but she could come back. She followed her own star, she said. She did just what she wanted to.

"How long did it take you to get here?" Faith asked.

"Eight hours," said Alice.

"And you're going to go *back*?" said Faith. "Drag."

"Big drag," said Hope.

"Super big drag," said Faith.

"Yeah," said Alice, "it is." She started thinking about the endless bus ride, and the empty house she'd find on East Sixty-seventh Street when she arrived. She'd never stayed there by herself for longer than a weekend. She tried to picture what it would be like to fend for herself for days and days. The house would creak and moan every night. She'd have to turn on the radios and televisions. Rabbit would have the key. Aunt Esmé would have given it to him. He'd stop by to water the plants and give hamster kibble to Charlie Chaplin. Persephone's doghouse would be there, but Persephone wouldn't be inside.

"Why did you even come here if you're just going to turn around?" Hope said with a sneer.

"My aunt got mixed up," said Alice. "I'm sure she didn't know there were hardly any students at the institute when she sent me here."

"There never *have* been any students at the institute, really," said Hope. "The Balthus philosophy is to treat everyone equally. We're learning from each other. We're encouraged to forge our own vision."

"It's a unique experiment in education," said Faith. "To quote from the mission statement."

"It's been an efficacious training ground for me and Faith," said Hope. "I'll pay my own college tuition with all the money I made selling photographs. I'm financially independent. No need for rents. No need for handouts."

Alice began to imagine selling her collages, the way Dean had once sold his paintings. Now she could stay at Fieldwood, and take drama class with Mrs. Lana du Maurier in the fall. She'd never have to go to public school. They'd never have to move out of the house on Sixty-seventh Street. Alice would take down the FOR SALE sign. She would rescue the entire Duncan family. Persephone would move inside, with Alice. Charlie Chaplin would have his own room. Persephone would have her own entire floor. Alice would take over Dean's studio. Rain, hearing that her daughter was a child prodigy, would come home, play Billie Holiday at top volume, chain-smoke, and move back into her bedroom. Dean would sleep there, too, the way parents were supposed to. Alice would be the boss, because she would be famous and she'd have a job. She'd tell everyone how to be and what to do. She'd hire Ethyl to cook dinner, with mashed potatoes and carrots and stuffing every night. She'd make Aunt Esmé stop cutting classes and put her clothes away.

"The two of you are the only people here?" she asked, suspecting that—no matter how tempting it was—she shouldn't stay alone in a school that was run by teenagers.

"There are a couple of other kids, and some good artists," said Hope. "Like Odette Noko, the celebrated sculptor. She's here from Paris."

"Don't go back," said Faith. "You ought to stay. You might evolve."

Alice was flattered.

"We could use your company," said Hope. "It's been boring around here since the Great Man retired."

"The Great Man," said Alice. "Why do they call him that?"

Faith and Hope looked at one another and shrugged. "Beats me," said Faith. "He's sort of an asshole."

The three of them stood in the hallway, looking puzzled.

"Well, Duncan," said Hope, "what do you say? Do you want to settle in? We'll set you up across the hall from us, in your own studio."

The thought of a bed to lie down in made Alice yawn. "Maybe I'll just stay for an hour or two," she said.

"Sure, Duncan," said Hope, walking a few feet down the hallway, "you can do that." She opened a metal cabinet next to a fire extinguisher. A row of keys was kept inside, each one hanging from a hook. Hope handed one of the keys to Alice. Attached to it was a circular white piece of cardboard with the letter A printed neatly in Magic Marker.

"A is for Alice," said Hope. "So A is your room—for however long you want to stay. And this is your key."

"Thanks," Alice said. The key marked A wasn't anything like the one she'd used to get into the front door of her own house. That one had ridges like those on a saw, and the inscription MEDECO in the center. This one, antique, was tarnished silver. There were two square pieces of metal at the end of the key. They looked like two steps, Alice thought, or two front teeth.

Accompanied by Hope and Faith, Alice opened the door

marked Studio A and looked inside. It really was like a motel, she saw, remembering a bygone family vacation to the Adirondacks. A sliding glass door led out onto the soccer field. A brass curtain rod was suspended over it, but the curtains were missing. The walls were covered with wainscoting. A chair made of bright orange plastic faced a metal desk. Above it hung a black-and-white framed photograph of a marionette, dancing. It had long hair tied in a big bow. It was wearing a lace dress, white anklets, and black patent leather Mary Janes. There was red-and-blue-striped ticking on the bare mattress on the bed, and no pillowcases on the pillow. Alice yawned.

"I think Duncan here needs sheets," said Hope. "Go find some for her, sis, and get her some towels, too."

"Thanks," said Alice sleepily.

"If you're hungry, the cafeteria's just a few minutes' walk down the path," said Hope. "It's on the first floor of the White House. Mary, the cook, sets dinner out at six. If you're famished, walk into the kitchen anytime and shout: Mary, feed me! She's got a hearing aid."

"The food is vile," said Faith, returning from the linen closet. "We prefer crackers." She handed Alice a folded set of matching towels, sheets, and pillowcases. They were pale blue, decorated with butterflies. Under the washcloth, Alice found a box of Ritz crackers and a tiny jar of grape jam.

"If you need anything else," said Hope, "ask Mrs. Hanson. She's the resident adviser in our dorm. She gets to stay here for free all year and watch TV. She keeps a gallon of ice cream for us in her freezer, and her door is always open. She used to be an art critic but she got fired a long time ago. She drinks."

Alice absorbed this information silently.

"Mr. Spencer's in the adjacent building," she continued.

"That's the boys' dorm, but this year, so far, we only have two guys. Mr. Spencer's an artist-in-residence. He's cool."

Alice was relieved to hear that some adults, at least, were present.

"What gallery did you say you were with again, Duncan?" said Faith.

"I'm not from a gallery," said Alice.

"No? How old are you?" said Hope.

"I'm sixteen and a half," Alice said. She needed to be older than Faith and Hope, at least by a small margin.

"Where have you shown?" said Faith.

"Shown?" asked Alice.

"What art exhibitions have you been in?" Hope said.

"Just the ones in my house," said Alice. "My aunt hangs my collages on the wall."

Faith and Hope exchanged a glance.

"I'd better get going," said Hope. "If I'm going to get any good shots in today, I've got to catch the light."

"I'll ride over to the photo studio with you," said Faith. "Do you want to take the Great Man's truck?"

"I think his nurse is driving him to town today," said Hope. "We'll take the bikes."

"See you around, Duncan," Faith said.

With a rustle of denim, a clink of metallic biker jewelry, and the patter of two pairs of motorcycle boots on the thin worn carpeting, the twins left. Locking her door, Alice stuffed her mouth full of crackers and swallowed them, barely bothering to chew. She threw the sheet over the bed and lay down. She could hear the drone of motorcycles. Tucking the pillow under her head, she looked at Mickey Mouse. It was 6:16 in the evening, and still light out. As she closed her eyes, a vision came to mind, unbidden, of J.D. without any clothes on. He was lying on top of a mountain, in the dark. He was smoking from a hookah. He was looking at the stars. Alice lay beside him, holding his hand.

Perturbed by the thought, she pressed her hand against her mouth. The image felt like something she needed to conceal from polite company. Even in private. Even from herself. It had to be kept in, like a belch. It had to be kept out, like a poison. She didn't know if the vision of J.D., naked, came from outside, an ether floating in the atmosphere, or from within.

Long Distance

everly Hills Hotel," said a woman's voice on the other end of the receiver. "This is Marsha. Can I help you?"

Through the window of the telephone booth, Alice could see the colorfully painted walls on the second floor of the girls' dormitory. She'd found the telephone after waking up. Spread out on the shelf underneath the phone were stacks of dimes and a spiral notebook. In it, Alice had written a list of names, addresses, and telephone numbers. The soft morning sunlight played over the textured ivory drawing paper.

"Can I help you?" said the voice again.

"Yes," said Alice, "I'd like to speak to my Aunt Esmé in Crash Omaha's room, please."

"What room number would that be, ma'am?"

"I'm not sure," Alice said.

"Hold one moment. I'll check for you." There was silence on the line. Alice checked her watch. It was 8:19 a.m. on Sunday.

"Ma'am?" said the voice.

"Yes?"

"There's no one by the name Omaha registered here. How are you spelling that, please?"

"Omaha," said Alice. "O-M-A-H-A. His real name is Joey Pots. He eats fake glass. He has a tattoo of a cockroach on his leg. He wears black nail polish."

"I'll be right with you."

Alice looked at the bus schedule that was tacked to a bulletin board near the phone. She picked up a pencil which was tied to a length of dirty string and attached to the bulletin board with a pushpin. Alice drew a circle around the number 9:41. That was the time of the next bus leaving Dodgson. It would arrive in Port Authority at 7:05 p.m.

"Wha?" said a man's voice, on the phone, in a deep baritone.

"Hi," Alice said. "I'm looking for my Aunt Esmé. She was staying with Crash Omaha."

There was a pause. Alice heard a thump: something heavy being picked up and put down. "Who's this?" said the voice, slurring the words.

"This is Alice."

There was a pause. A rattling. The sound of a nose blowing. Alice waited six more seconds. A throat was being cleared. "Listen, whoever you are," said the voice more crisply, "is there some reason that you're calling here at five o'-fucking-clock in the fucking morning?"

"Yes, there is," said Alice angrily. "Is this Crash Omaha?" Her chest felt tight, as if she were caught inside a vise.

"This is Crash."

"I know you," Alice said. "You have a green cockroach on your thigh and—" She didn't finish the rest of her description.

"And who the *fuck* are you?" he said.

"I just told you. My name is Alice, and I live with my Aunt Esmé," Alice said. "Is she there with you?" Her heart was pounding. She wanted to pummel the side of the phone booth with her fists and break it. It was just as it had been the time he came over to Sixty-seventh Street. Nice, in the evening, with his rock candy, his easy chuckle, and his earnest questions about Alice and her life. And in the morning, in the shower, with his stringy hair and wet kisses, horrible. Aunt Esmé said musicians were all like that, two-sided, two-faced, like Mr. Hyde and Dr. Jekyll.

"I don't know any Alice," he said.

"Yes you do," said Alice. "But I wasn't calling to talk to you." She couldn't see what Aunt Esmé wanted with him. He was a cretin.

"Just a fucking sec." Alice heard a rustling sound. "Esmé? Wake the fuck up. Could you tell your fucking girlfriends not to call here at the break of fucking dawn please? It's for you."

Seven seconds passed, according to Mickey. His big white finger dashed forward, hopping from one fine black line to the next, counting seconds. Each time his hand moved, Alice heard a click.

"Huh?" said Aunt Esmé.

"Hi," said Alice. "It's me."

Aunt Esmé snuffled. She sounded as if she'd caught a cold. "Alice, girl. How are you?"

"I'm okay," said Alice.

"How did you find me? I don't remember giving you the number."

"I called a few hotels," said Alice. "In Los Angeles." She had called nine of them.

"Is everything all right?" said Aunt Esmé. "How's camp?"

A curious thing happened. Alice had called to tell Aunt Esmé that there *was* no camp, that there were only a few students left

101

in a program that was about to close—and that she was thinking of going home, by herself, on another dismal Trailways bus. But she found she was unable to say any of that. The words wouldn't form themselves. Instead, loudly, Alice said, "It's fine."

"What's it like there?" Aunt Esmé asked. "Still the way I remember it? Still pretty? Still fun? Still nice?" Her voice sounded blurry and indistinct, as if she—and everything from before the trip to Dodgson—were beginning to fade.

"It's fine," said Alice. It seemed so much easier, so much better to say that—instead of bothering her with the burdensome details of Alice's arrival and departure, or worrying her with a report of how the Great Man had quit. The institute had become a place without enough teachers, or classes, or kids. But Alice was afraid to tell Aunt Esmé what the situation was. She was afraid to find out that Aunt Esmé might not care enough to change her plans.

"Are you having a good time?" said Aunt Esmé.

"Yeah," said Alice.

"Are the kids all right? Make any friends yet?"

"Yes," said Alice. "I made two."

"Cool. What are their names?"

"Faith and Hope," said Alice. She wished she could say many more things to Aunt Esmé. But Alice was hindered by the black plastic instrument against her ear—a cool, smooth object, not a person.

"There's a guy I talked to, too," said Alice. She waited.

"A guy?" Aunt Esmé comprehended the situation in a flash. "May I remind you, Alice, that you're eleven?" she said.

Alice smiled at Aunt Esmé's old, reassuring line. She felt as if she hadn't heard her say that in a long time, in many years. But then her half sister chortled on, in a new, encouraging tone. "A *guy*," she said, emphasizing the word quite differently. "And you've only been there a day! Fast worker. Just like your aunt, huh? *You.*"

That wasn't the response Alice had hoped for somehow. She wanted to tell Aunt Esmé the rest: that J.D. wasn't a boy her age who had just finished grade school, but a grown man with graying temples, that *a guy* was, in fact, Aunt Esmé's drug dealer, and that Faith and Hope were the only other people she'd seen on the compound. She wanted to tell Aunt Esmé that she wasn't sure whether to go or stay.

"Are you homesick already?" said Aunt Esmé, sensing some vague problem.

"Yes, I am," said Alice.

"You'll get used to it in a few days. I'm sure you'll make other friends, too. What are the counselors like?"

"Fine," said Alice.

"What have you done so far? Have you taken any swimming lessons?"

"I got my feet wet," Alice lied.

"Good for you. Without that stupid inflatable pillow, too. I told you you don't need it."

Alice felt a lump forming in her throat.

"I'm sorry I wasn't able to bring you down to Port Authority the other day, Al, like I said I would," said Aunt Esmé.

"That's all right," said Alice softly.

"You won't mention my trip to Dean, Alice, will you?" said Aunt Esmé. Alice heard a trace of anxiety in her voice.

"No," she said.

"You might not even want to bother telling him that I sent you away to camp, right?"

"Right," said Alice. "Why bother?"

"If you do tell Dean about the Balthus Institute, Alice, you might want to say that I drove you there or something. Not that you took a cab by yourself, or went on that short little bus ride on your own."

"No bus trip," Alice agreed.

"And that I, maybe, stayed up in North Carolina too, you know. Right nearby, say. At my friend J.D.'s house. To supervise you," said Aunt Esmé.

"Sure," said Alice. Her stomach muscles had begun to quiver. She couldn't bear to hear the mention of those two letters—J and D—not in this conversation, not coming from Aunt Esmé. "You were up here with me," Alice said. "For three weeks." She wondered how different, or how much the same, things might be if this were true. She wondered whether Aunt Esmé really was just J.D.'s good customer. She wondered if Aunt Esmé knew that Alice had stolen each of her boyfriends, accidentally, one by one.

"Are you pissed off at me, Al?" said Aunt Esmé.

"Kind of," Alice said.

"It was my last chance to see Crash until he goes on tour this fall." She said this in a fake voice. Baby talk.

"It was your last chance to see me, too," Alice said.

"What do you mean? I see you every day! I live in the same house with you, don't I?"

Alice wasn't even sure what she'd meant. "Okay," she said, picking at a scab on her knee. "Is Persephone there?"

"Persephone? Sure she is. She's being treated like royalty here at the Beverly Hills Hotel, Alice. She's in the . . . uh . . . the special dog yard."

"Can I talk to her?"

"It's a little hard to get to, Alice. She's fine."

"All right," said Alice. "See you."

"Be good."

"You too," said Alice. "Goodbye." She set the receiver down. Alice sat on the steel seat in the phone booth for a moment, feeling inexplicably sad. She wondered if anyone would notice if she died. It occurred to her that this desire to make someone you loved notice you might be what had led Dean to Saint Joseph's Hospital. As she sat with her knees drawn up on the metal seat, she opened and closed the door to the phone booth, watching the hinges. The folding doors, with their two separate glass panels, seemed, as she pulled the handle, to split in two. Then, when she shut the door, they came together again.

One, two. One, two. One, two, Alice thought. Alice and Rain. Dean and Rain. Separate and apart. Maybe that's what it meant to be grown, Alice thought. Dr. Fineman said he thought that the Fineman Study girls were growing quickly—because they needed to. He'd said there was a relationship between physical maturity and the social and psychological environment. He'd asked her questions from a list, each one followed by five ovals. As Alice had responded, he'd filled one of the ovals in with a pencil mark, like on the standardized tests Alice took at school. She couldn't remember the questions anymore, only that Dr. Fineman had wanted to know about Alice's mother and father. He'd used words like "mad" and "sad," and had asked Alice to tell him what her feelings were. Her feelings had always struck Alice as too personal to be shared with anyone, certainly not with a bespectacled man in a white lab coat. But Alice had tried to tell him about the feeling, of fear and apprehension, which had seized hold of her after Rain left and Alice had watched helplessly while, day by day, her deformities had grown.

The fear descended again as she stared out the window on to the deserted compound. The only inhabitants she could see, on the balding brown soccer field below, were birds. Shiny black starlings pecked at the overgrown grass, hunting for bugs and worms. Alice wanted breakfast, too. She'd fallen asleep without eating anything but the crackers. The constricting sensation in her stomach and chest was one she remembered. This was just how it had been those first few weeks after Rain had gone away. She'd felt this tightness in her gut. It became unbearable at night, when Alice had heard her parents' arguments replay themselves. She remembered her mother's brittle manner, and her father's shouting.

"I know what you did on Christmas Day," Dean had said in a bitter voice. "While your daughter and I waited for you to get home. You didn't go to any children's hospital to give *toys* to poor kids, did you?"

"No," said Rain. "I didn't."

"You met that idiot, Gnoo, right under my nose, at the Carlyle."

"His name is Knut," said Rain dispassionately.

"The two of you gold-digging wastrels fucked, and I was the one who paid the Visa bill. You dumb cow. Slut. You screwed him on Christmas, didn't you? On my money."

Loud voices, escalating. The sound of a fist pounding a table. Silverware clattering. Crash, went a glass. Alice had seen it from the landing on the stairs, the crystal glass that had belonged to her grandmother—flying through the air. Shattering against the sideboard where they kept the dishes. The soaring shards glittering beneath the chandelier that hung from the dining room ceiling. Rain putting her face in her hands. And then the sound—a weak lost kitten, a low, degrading mew. And then the ambulance, its red revolving light. And the ugly thick uneven stitches, sticking up like black bristles on her mother's smooth pale face. And the hands, without their nail polish, forlorn and pitiful, like the hands of someone ill. The pills in their amber vials with their typed labels from the pharmacy. The round mirror with its handle decorated with a painting of cherry blossoms—the same mirror Aunt Esmé would use later, for her cocaine. Rain keeping the cherry blossom mirror by her bed, and looking into it every few minutes, waiting for something—a healing up, a change. Not a large scar, really, just a cut below her eye.

Alice flipped through the pages of her spiral notebook until she got to the one with Rabbit's phone number on it.

"Two. Dollars. And. Sixty. Cents. Please," said the mechanical female voice after she'd dialed.

One by one, she inserted quarters into the slot. She heard the phone ringing, so far away. She imagined Rabbit in his tenement apartment, with its smell of cat urine, and the flat beige couch, the warped wooden floors, the chipped plaster, and the cigarette burns in the curtains.

"Hello," said a voice. Gruff, gravelly.

"Rabbit?"

"Who is this?"

"This is Alice. Don't you recognize me?"

Alice heard the sound the phone made when people pressed their palm against it so you couldn't hear them talk. It always puzzled her that anyone did that. It was so rude and obvious. Her pulse pounded fiercely.

"This is his brother, Mark."

"Hello," said Alice. "May I please speak to Rabbit?"

Again, the fuzzy, muffling sound.

"Yes?" said Rabbit, a minute later.

"Is my hamster okay?" said Alice.

"Alice, is that you?" said Rabbit. "The little guy's all right."

"Can me and Charlie Chaplin come over and stay with you for a while?" she blurted out. "If I go back to New York now?"

Dead silence. "Stay? What do you mean?" said Rabbit.

"I'm in North Carolina," said Alice. "I'm at camp."

"Uh-huh," he said. "Esmé told me. What's the problem?"

The hardness in his voice made Alice think he was playing a game with her, one that she was rapidly losing. She needed Rabbit to be her friend, but she wasn't supposed to admit it.

"Never mind," said Alice. "Bye. I'll be fine."

"Are you sure?" said Rabbit.

Alice hung up the telephone. She blinked back tears. Nervously, she ran her fingers along the metal strip, at the corner of the phone booth, which was bolted to the panes of glass. Seven numbers were etched into the plate of steel. She stuck her thumbnail inside the scratched white numerals, in between the cracks. Beneath them were two letters. J.D.

Alice picked up one of the quarters and slipped it into the coin slot. Without thinking about it, on an impulse, she dialed the number.

"This is J.D.," answered the nasal, breathy tenor that she remembered from yesterday. He spoke in an unusual cadence, almost faltering, not steady. This is. Pause. J.D. Pause. Alice listened.

"Can I help you?" he said.

She had a sinking sensation that he knew who she was, even though she hadn't told him. Alice breathed.

She heard J.D., on his end of the line, breathing, too.

"Hay-lo," he said in a singsong voice, playful and odd, the sort of voice Alice imagined a farmer might use to call a straying farm animal—a mule, a cow, a goat.

"Hay-lo, hay-lo," he said again, turning it into a little song.

He sighed, deeply. He waited. "So long, then," he said. "Whoever you are."

There was a short silence, then, as if he were waiting to make certain that his caller wouldn't speak. Then Alice heard a click, and the dial tone.

When she stood up, her knees were shaking. She walked out onto the soccer field, with the feeling that she'd made an irrevocable mistake.

The Swinger's Grin

On Sunday morning, Alice went on a picnic with Faith, Hope, and a teacher named Fitzy. She took some photographs of the desolate campus, standing by the window in her room. The Polaroids came out badly. The camera couldn't take long-distance shots, and she needed color film. The wildflowers in the garden looked like smears. Giving up, Alice burst out of the dorm, throwing herself against the heavy double doors and springing out into the daylight. She ran away from the compound, across the flat top of Goat Hill and down the other side. Blades of grass, still covered with dew, pelted her shins. She pretended to be a sprint runner, building up her speed. She'd packed away the platform sandals and the dress, exchanging them for shorts, a T-shirt, and sneakers. She took great wide leaps and imagined she was an astronaut on the moon, bounding and flying she went, away from the sculptures and the houses, past the scabbed wooden sign that said BALTHUS. She could do whatever she pleased. Fitzy said they should use the time for independent study, keeping a visual diary and making their own drawings. Classes didn't start until Monday, the next morning.

Alice ran down one slope and up another. The farther she went from the institute grounds, the happier she was. She was in the country. She was Alice. She was F-I-N-E, fine. She ran across the main road, not even stopping to look for oncoming traffic. She was a long-distance champion, a sprint racer, fast enough to outdistance any car. She scrambled up another incline. When she reached a wooded area, she slowed to a jog. She picked her way gingerly through the rocks and roots along the hiking path. Alice walked for a long time without once looking back. When she felt that she was no longer near the Balthus property but deep into the Blue Ridge Nature Preserve, she threw her tote bag to the ground. In one motion, hardly breaking her gait, Alice wrapped her arms around a craggy oak. She found holds for her fingers and her feet, and began to climb it. She caught the limb above her head and pulled herself onto it. It was an ideal tree. She could climb it without hesitating, without thinking. The course was exquisitely clear, as if it had been marked for her. Each indentation in the bark seemed to have been carved just for her fingers, and as soon as she needed a place to hang on to, she immediately found one. The branches were perfectly proportioned, each one located within reach of the next one. There were never any of those bald spots that, in tree climbing, left Alice breathless and stranded. She knew exactly what to do and where to go. It was as if the old oak had been waiting for Alice. High up in its leafy network of branches, she imagined the tree was a gargantuan arm. Its branches were the fingers of a hand that had been extended to Alice in welcome. When she'd climbed as high as she wanted to go, she found a spot to lean against the trunk. She stretched her legs out in front of her, as if she were

Rain sitting on the chaise lounge back home, and crossed them at the ankles. Looking down didn't bother her. She admired the view.

From her perch twenty feet above ground level, a mile away from the institute, Alice could see things she hadn't seen before. The campgrounds appeared minuscule and insignificant. Beyond the treetops, the institute was merely a disordered heap of cubes. From here, it was impossible to tell that the dormitories were empty, the basement floorboards rotting, the paint peeling. Up in the oak, the Little Studio appeared to be made by children out of Lincoln Logs. The green land around it turned slowly into a downward sloping hill, nestled in the curl of the black road.

She clambered further upward, easily, putting one hand over the other and using the branches like the rungs of a ladder. The thick rubber soles of her sneakers gave her purchase on the rough bark. It was a fine feeling, to be mobile and agile, to be a wild animal in the forest—a girl on the loose, no longer confined, no longer earthbound. Alice counted the branches as she passed them, taking pride in how high she could climb.

She was gazing up at the pattern of leaves and branches, imagining that they were chasing one another as they fluttered against each other in the wind, and wondering if she should pull some off for her collage, when she heard footsteps. A twig snapped. Through the greenery, far below, a figure came into view. It was white and blue. The sight of these two colors—the contrast of the blue against the white—set off a physical reaction in Alice's bowels. A shirt. A pair of mirrored sunglasses. A pair of bell-bottoms. A series of agonized, clutching sensations took hold of her. They emanated from deep within her internal organs, at the very core of Alice.

"J.D.!" she called out.

He looked up.

Alice, regretting that she'd said anything, stayed perfectly still. But it was too late, because now he was lifting his arms over his head, like a racer crossing the finish line. With both hands, he waved.

"Hey!" he said, and flashed the swinger's grin.

"Hey," said Alice.

"Hello up there," he said.

"Hello down there," said Alice.

"I thought it was you," said J.D. "Leaping across the road back there. Didn't you see me?"

"Nope." Alice's conversational abilities had deserted her. She began to move, restlessly, on her branch, dangling her legs, kicking the bark, like a toddler in a high chair.

"Careful up there," said J.D. "You're much too high, in my opinion. But what the hell do I know?"

Alice didn't respond.

"How's the air up there?" he said. He didn't shout, although Alice was quite far away from him. His voice was carried on the wind. It was a high, almost feminine voice. Again, she noticed his off-kilter cadence, his tone rising and falling, stopping and going. He talked through his nose, and paused between words in unlikely places. It reminded her of Neil Kruger, a seventh grader at the Fieldwood School who stuttered. Maybe J.D. had a stutter, too, or had once had one.

"Would you. Mind if. I join. You?" he asked in his wobbly way.

"You're too big," Alice shouted. "There isn't room for you."

J.D. patted the bark at the base of the tree with his hands. "I think it ought to hold me," he said.

Even though she was nervous and confused about seeing him, Alice felt irritated. Like most grown-ups, J.D. obviously didn't know how to play. The unwritten rule of tree climbing was that each climber scaled a tree of his or her own. The idea was to climb as high as you could, and to be free to pick whatever route you selected. Two climbers in one tree was unacceptable. It meant competition for the best path to the top, for the best toe-holds, for the best handholds, for the best branches. It wasn't the done thing. Alice had gotten there first: the tree was hers. Alice felt that by asking if he could climb up her tree, J.D. had made a glaring error of judgment. Looking down at him from her leafy perch, she thought slightly less of him. It was just the sort of mistake that adults often made when they tried to play with kids who were less than half their age. But then, Alice remembered, she wasn't sure she was a kid anymore.

"Am I welcome?" said J.D. "Can I climb up?"

Alice thought it over, sorting through the various conflicting impulses she felt toward him. "Okay," she said magnanimously. "You can." As J.D. began to hoist himself up, Alice glanced down at her watch. Tick tick, it went. Mickey Mouse was pointing in some incomprehensible direction, like the Scarecrow in *The Wizard of Oz*. Alice squinted at it, but she found she couldn't tell the time. Both of Mickey's hands were pointing down. He looked as if he were trying to tie his shoelace. Yet as the metal watch flashed in the reflected sunlight, Alice couldn't see the numbers on it. For a moment, they seemed to have disappeared. In their place, she thought, were letters. Four of them, one for each direction. N for north; S for south; W for west; and E for east. The watch was turning into a compass. The tick-ticking was turning into words.

"Which way?" it said. "Which way?"

Alice scolded herself. Of course she didn't have a talking watch. Of course there were no letters. She was getting herself all worked up for nothing. A cloud passed overhead, and she could see it was an ordinary watch again, with numbers on it where they were supposed to be. She was only upset because J.D. was there. He didn't know, she reminded herself, that she'd called him on the telephone. He couldn't know that, because Alice hadn't told him.

She waited in the tree, listening to the ticking and pretending to herself that the watch hadn't spoken.

J.D. had grabbed hold of the trunk and begun to ascend. The oak shook whenever he moved. Alice glanced down warily, but she couldn't see him, only the interlacing branches.

"You're up pretty high," said his voice, with its stopping-starting pattern. "I'm not sure I can climb as high as you can. Could you come down and meet me in the middle?"

"I don't think so," said Alice dubiously. His manners were poor, she noted. If he wanted to climb her tree, she couldn't stop him. But to suggest she give up her excellent vantage point, the spot she'd won—the special seat in the forked branches which the Great Oak had held out and offered to Alice specifically— that was impossible. A boy her own age would have known better.

Alice caught a glimpse of J.D.'s arms and legs through the bright leaves and dark wood. He was making progress—steady but slow. She had to admit he had a fairly effective tree-climbing technique, considering his advanced age. He wasn't as assured as she was, though. It was taking him a long time to climb, to get high up off the ground. As he got closer to her, Alice's perch swayed slightly from side to side. Her grip on the bark tightened. She looked at the earth below and realized, for the first time, that it was a long way down.

Through the leaves, J.D.'s face appeared. His head was turned upward and she saw only his mouth. The thin, liver-colored lips were pulled back over the shining white teeth. He was grinning. The rest of his face emerged, tan against the green.

Easing himself down on Alice's branch like a tightrope walker, he bent his knees and bowed his back, teetering precariously a moment before he straddled the branch. Facing her, he sat with his back against the thick trunk. "How's it going, Alice?" he said, hanging on to a branch overhead for support.

"I'm fine," said Alice.

"I thought you were gone. Decided to stick around?"

"Just until my aunt gets back," said Alice.

Pushing the leaves out of his way, J.D. took a look around. Alice looked, too. Beyond the campus, she saw a handful of scattered houses on square green patches of lawn. The landscape was dotted with bright threads and shining jewels. These were creeks and streams, lakes and ponds.

"I don't think anybody can see us up here," said J.D. "Do you?"

"Probably not," said Alice.

He began to unbutton his shirt. The two white halves of the garment parted to reveal his bare chest. When he got to the fourth button from the top, J.D. pulled out one of the black cords that he wore he around his neck. At the end of it was a leather pouch. He took something from inside it. It was a wooden pipe, similar to the one in Aunt Esmé's toy chest on Sixty-seventh Street. He emptied the pouch into his hand and filled the bowl up with bits of curled dry leaves. He took pinches of it, the way Ethyl had done when using spices in the kitchen, holding the crumbled scraps of plant between his thumb and index finger.

"You want some?" he asked.

"No, thanks," said Alice.

"You sure? It's good."

"That's okay."

J.D. took a pack of matches out from the pouch. He lit the

pipe and began to puff on it. "In case no one's told you," he said after a few moments, "I'm the institute's connection. I supply the entire Dodgson community, up as far as Asheville. I don't cover Asheville itself. That's Bruce Johnson's territory. But I've been making some headway into Glass County lately."

"You sell pot?" Alice asked.

"Herb, yeah. Pills and potions. Acid. Peyote. Whatever you want, I got. But I gather you're not into that scene. Not yet." Looking at Alice thoughtfully, he continued smoking.

"I already told you that," said Alice.

"Am I corrupting you?" he asked in his high voice.

"Not really," said Alice. She didn't know the word "corrupting."

"I don't mean to. I was just explaining who I am. I'm not pushing. Well, I am. Obviously. But not right this instant."

"Okay," said Alice.

"How old are you anyway?" he said.

"Sixteen and a half."

"Yeah. Sure. Why does that sound way, way—but way—too good to be true?" The grin came out again, and with it, the sharp dimples. Something happened to Alice whenever he grinned. She wanted to hold her hand to her eyes, or to show him a crucifix, as if he were a vampire.

"Maybe," Alice said, "because it isn't true?"

"May*be*," said J.D. He didn't ask her to tell him her actual age, though.

He continued to smoke his dope, now and then pulling a bit of the weed out of his mouth. "This is played," he said after a few minutes. He peered into the bowl of the pipe. "Finished." He knocked it against the tree trunk.

"Finished," Alice repeated.

"I hate to tell you this," he said, "but if you're going to spend your time up here in Dodgson, about ninety-eight percent of your acquaintances are going to be junkies. The other ten percent will be acid heads. Know what I'm saying?"

"Sure," said Alice. "That's how it is at home, in the Dollhouse."

"The Dollhouse. Isn't that the topless joint in Raleigh?"

"No," said Alice, annoyed. "It's not a topless joint in Raleigh. It's a room. It's my aunt's room. Inside a private townhouse. Where we live."

He made a face. "Well then. My, my, Alice. Excuse *me*."

"It's just a person's room inside their house," Alice said more reasonably.

"Anyway, Alice. As I was saying. If you're not a dope fiend, babe, this really isn't the place for you. It's complete decadence, Dodgson is. Sure, one or two of the kids can paint. But there's never been enough structure or supervision. It's become a wasteland now that the Great Man's retired. The whole operation is a dumping ground for unwanted brats."

An unpleasant sensation washed over Alice. "What do you mean?" she said.

"I didn't mean *you*, honey. You don't strike me that way somehow. But if this isn't up your alley, I swear to God, kid, you ought to call the old man and have him send you home."

"The old man?" said Alice, thinking he was talking about Mr. Balthus.

"Your dad," said J.D.

"I can't call him," Alice said. "I told you the other day, when we met. Don't you remember?"

J.D. pointed to his forehead, as he'd done when she'd arrived. "Short-term memory," he said. "I don't got none."

"I told you," Alice repeated. "He's in the nuthouse."

"That's too bad," said J.D. His eyes searched her face. "Really, hon. I'm sorry to hear that. What happened?"

"My mother left," said Alice.

"Oh. There I go, putting my foot in my mouth again. You're a kind of orphan, then. Kind of an abandoned kid yourself."

"No I'm not," said Alice quickly.

"I didn't intend to insult you," said J.D. "I don't really know how to have a polite conversation, Alice. That's why I do this for a living. I can't function in normal adult society. Drug dealers are losers. Don't let anyone tell you different. Whenever I interact with the Real World—which is to say, with women, with people, with human beings, instead of with pills, powders, junkies, and cash—I fuck up. Frequently. Which is all my long-winded way of trying to say that I'm sorry if I hurt your feelings just now. When I called you an orphan. Did I?"

"I don't know," said Alice. "I don't like to talk about it."

"I didn't mean to pry. But, if you don't want to stay here any longer, do you have someplace else to go?"

"I could go home," Alice said.

"You could. Is anybody there?"

"Usually, there's my Aunt Esmé. And Ethyl, sometimes."

"Aunt Esmé and Ethyl," J.D. said slowly. "Aunt Esmé and Ethyl. You know, Alice, I'm telling you honestly. I think I'm going to get you fucked up at Balthus. Whereas this Ethyl and this Aunt Esmé, on the other hand, would do you a world of good. Now maybe I'm giving myself too much credit here. And if I did fuck you up, in the broadest sense of that word, I can assure you it wouldn't be intentional. My aim, as ever, is to amuse. Are you following me?"

"No," Alice admitted.

"I'm what's known, historically, as a bad influence. On the

young. And you—being sixteen and a *half*," he emphasized the number, lingering on it. "Definitely. Fall. Into that category." As he spoke, J.D. crept forward, laying one hand over the other on the branch and pulling himself closer to Alice.

"Don't you?" he said.

"Don't I what?"

"Fall into that category?" he said.

Alice shook her head no. At the same time, she began to move away from him. She started to scoot backward, inch by inch.

"Hey," he said. "Don't do that, baby."

Alice didn't listen. She continued to advance toward the outer leaves, where the branch was more slender.

"Just tell me to get lost," said J.D. "If you want to be rid of me. I'll go away. It's that simple, Alice. It isn't necessary to break your neck, or run away. Just say: Shoo, J.D. Shoo." He cleared his throat and ran his hands through his hair.

She regarded him closely. She was trying to make up her mind about something, something she couldn't put her finger on. It had to do with whether he was good or bad, truthful or lying. But she herself, she remembered, was a liar. She wondered whether people could be two opposite things at the same time.

"What I would like to say," said J.D., "is that if you tell me to go away, I will. You know?"

"Sort of," said Alice.

"And if you *don't* tell me to get lost, I'll probably hang around and bug you, Alice. And corrupt you. And stuff. I'm playing fair, I think, by explaining this to you. Do you get that?"

"Yes," said Alice. Whatever was bad about him, she found him honest. "I don't want to get rid of you," she said.

"Oh," said J.D. He sounded surprised. "Uh-oh. I didn't think of that. Well, we're fucked then. Aren't we?" He scratched his chin. "I wasn't counting on your liking *me*," he added.

"Does that make it bad?" asked Alice, who felt they were trying together to avoid badness somehow.

"I really don't know, honey. I long ago lost the ability to distinguish right from wrong. Ah, Alice. Alice."

"What?"

"Nothing. I just like the sound of your name." He ran his hand along the bark. "Yeah, this spells trouble," he said.

"What does?"

"You and me. And me and you," he said. "I feel obligated, at this point, strictly in an advisory capacity, to let you know that I find you achingly attractive. So what I'm doing here, I feel, Alice, is the right thing. I'm alerting you. Babe, see, this is a warning. Climb down the tree, man. And get your ass the fuck home. Because once you cross that line, sister, you can't go back."

"Okay," said Alice. "I'll go."

They both sat there, though.

"Of course," said J.D, "there *is* another side to the argument. Which I haven't laid out for you. Would you like to hear it?"

"No."

"You might not have enough information yet," he said.

"I don't want anything," said Alice.

"Can't I play the devil's advocate?"

"What's the devil's advocate?"

"It's, uh, a game. See. Here's how it goes. It goes: on the one hand, and on the other. On the other hand, of course, Alice, you could stay. You could take a toke of my smoke. Which isn't a wise course, not at all. But it may well be the more interesting one. For *me*, that is, Alice. For me. I'm generally concerned primarily with myself, you see. But I do think about my fellow human be-ings. From time to time."

J.D. reached for the pouch around his neck and shook it at Alice. She was reminded of her dog, Persephone. When Alice had a new ball or a chewy toy for Persephone, she'd hold it up in the air and wave it at her in just that way.

"What do you say?" said J.D. "Can I interest you in any of this?"

Alice shrugged.

J.D. began to move forward on the branch. He put both hands in front of him, as Alice would often do in her gymnastics classes when she was on the balance beam in the gymnasium at the Fieldwood School. Lifting himself up, he approached Alice, inch by inch, walking on his hands, swinging himself forward, like an ape. He settled himself down a half a foot away from the crook of the tree that was holding Alice. He gave the bark di-rectly ahead of him a tap.

Tap. Tap tap.

Alice froze at the sound.

"Come sit here with me," he said. His gray eyes had caught the leaves. Turning color, like a chameleon, they'd become a gray-ish green.

Alice hesitated.

"It's up to you," said J.D. "If you don't want any, I'll just have a second bowl. Suit yourself."

Alice watched him go through the series of motions a second time—bringing out the pouch, opening it up, reaching in for the brown dried leaves, placing them inside the pipe.

"It can't damage you, you know," he offered casually, concen-trating on what he was doing and looking down at the pipe rather than at Alice. "It's perfectly natural. I grow some of my best product right here, though this gold, which I import from Colombia, is my personal favorite."

Alice maneuvered herself off of her Y-shaped seat and sat down across from J.D.

He drew still nearer. "Why hello there," he whispered when they were only a few inches apart. He leaned in closer, conspiratorially. With their heads together, Alice thought they formed a private club, for just the two of them.

"Hello," Alice whispered back.

"How charming of you to join me," he said in a fake French accent. He fluttered his long black lashes. "To zhare a bowl wiss you, Mademoiselle Aleesse"—he kissed his fingertips—"would be an honor." Again, Alice studied him—searching for a sign of the creepy, the unsavory. But he was only a guy with tangled hair, and an inviting smile that transformed his homely, pockmarked face. He smiled now.

Alice found herself smiling back at him.

"First of all," he said, taking a lock of her hair between his fingers. "Let's get the hair out of your eyes." Carefully, as if he might ruin something fragile, he tucked her hair behind her left ear, as he had on the day they met. He smoothed it down with his fingertips. Then he did the same thing on the other side. He stared at her mouth.

"Now pucker up," he said.

Alice pursed her lips.

"Open wide, please," he said, bringing the pipe to her mouth. With a sinking heart, Alice noticed that his instructions were the same as those she received on her regular visits to Dr. Fineman's office. She felt a heavy sense of disillusionment. She kept her mouth closed.

"I'd thought," said J.D., "that this was your choice. Remember?" He took the pipe away and stared at her contemplatively. "You don't *have* to," he pointed out. "You get the right of refusal. The magic word is no."

"Okay," said Alice.

"Okay, what? Okay, no? Or okay, yes?"

"Yes," said Alice.

"Remember this moment," said J.D., "when you're older. Promise me?"

"All right," said Alice.

"Repeat after me: J.D. never made me do anything."

"J.D. didn't make me," said Alice softly. She felt stupid, but she said it anyway.

"I did it because *I wanted to*," he said. "Say that. Whatever I did with him. It wasn't because of J.D. It was because of Alice, because of *me*."

"It was me," said Alice.

"You, Alice, have the power to control your own decisions and your own life."

"You, Alice, have the—"

"No, *you*."

"I, Alice—"

"I have the power, because I'm a free fucking human being, baby. And the Buddha is benevolent. He sees all. He accepts all. And he doesn't give a rat's ass whether or not I'm freaking sixteen."

Alice didn't feel up to saying all that. She smiled again, but only faintly. She felt left out. J.D. was talking to himself rather than her.

He made a dismissive motion with his hand. "You've got the general idea, I think," he said.

Alice nodded.

"J.D.," he said, "is a gentleman. A nice corrupter. He doesn't force anything on anyone."

"All right," said Alice a little crossly. She wished he'd stop talking in that strained, showy way.

"Say it please, Alice."

"Thanks? That's *it?*"

Alice wrapped her arms around her waist and hugged herself tightly.

J.D. pointed to his cheek. "Over here," he said. "Right here. Kiss the frog, young princess. You won't be sorry. Just a tiny little kiss is all I ask. Please? Plant one on me."

Alice darted forward and gave him a quick kiss on the cheek.

"That's better," he said.

Alice's limbs were shaking.

"You sure you're all right, sweetheart? You're all shook up, aren't you?"

Alice said she wasn't.

"Sure you are. You were scared. I don't blame you."

"I wasn't scared," Alice offered righteously.

"Okay, you weren't. *I* was scared. Courageous Alice who flies through trees, you have my undying admiration."

"Thanks," said Alice.

"Come sit down a minute, anyway, and catch your breath. Come sit over here with me."

Alice sat beside him. He put his arm around her. It hung around the back of her neck like a weight. But it felt sturdy, also, and reassuring. She couldn't help but feel glad that such a person existed, a man who would catch her when she fell from trees, a man who wore rings with skulls and nymphs on them, a man who talked of fantastic things. He'd relinquished Alice's shoulder and had started crawling through the weeds. He picked up a shining object—the ring. But instead of letting Alice have it, he put it inside the pocket of his jeans.

"Would you like to take a stroll with me?" he said, not looking at her. "We'll get something to eat."

"I'm not hungry," said Alice. "I need to leave."

"Can I walk you back to camp?" He was turned away from

her, facing the Balthus Institute. He was looking down the hill, squinting.

"I'll be okay," said Alice, "on my own."

"Use 'em and lose 'em. Is that it?" he said.

"Yes," said Alice. "I guess."

He looked down, raking the dirt with his fingers. "Everything we talked about today, me and you. You know." He shot her a glance. "That's just between us chickens."

"I know," said Alice, and she did—because of Aunt Esmé, who had also insisted that Alice shouldn't tell anyone. The whole trip to Dodgson was shrouded in secrecy. She remembered, with a twinge of shame, the way she'd drawn J.D.'s hand toward her, that she'd said yes instead of no, cradling it to her chest and putting it inside her mouth—salty and metallic-tasting—a foreign object that didn't belong. She could never tell anyone. It wasn't so much because of what she'd thought or felt about J.D. as because of what she'd already done, taking his middle finger between her lips and rolling it like a gumdrop along her tongue.

"Well then. It was a pleasure turning you on, my friend," said J.D., tipping an imaginary hat to her. "I look forward to doing it again someday." He ambled away, through the nature preserve, back toward Goat Hill, and to the road that Alice thought led to town. As he reached the bottom of the incline, he turned and blew her a kiss. Alice raised her hand for a second. Then, thinking better of it, she put it back down.

Clarence

On Monday morning, Alice clutched her camera as she walked under the portico of the white clapboard building. Her sneakers squeaked on the tiles. The White House lobby reeked of shellac, glue, modeling clay, and paint. Sculptures, in miniature, were arranged inside a glass case. Scientific-looking diagrams were drawn on light green graph paper, posted on the back wall. Notes and measurements were printed neatly in black ink. After the display cases of student art projects, Alice passed three vacant classrooms. Each was furnished with wooden worktables, easels, and shelves containing art supplies. She slowed her steps as she approached the lecture hall. The lights were off. If a class had taken place there that morning, she was already too late. It had ended.

The long, narrow room was spacious and simple. The floors were made of wide pine planks. A wheezy ceiling fan spun unsteadily, rustling a sheaf of papers. On a table by a radiator, a small container of milk sat, opened, with a plastic straw still inside it. A paper plate held a leftover jelly donut. Like a tracker hunting down an elusive herd of animals, Alice picked it up and squeezed. It felt squishy. She bit into it, testing to see how long it might have been lying around. It was stale. She set it back down on the tray, leaving her teeth marks in the powdered sugar topping. Now the donut had two ridges in it, where her incisors had been. Her bite was shaped like a half-moon.

Alice unfolded the note she'd been clasping in her fist. "Go to the lecture hall" was all it said, without explaining why she should go or when. The letters had been heavily penciled, as if the message were an important one. It was printed on a scrap of lined notebook paper, now damp from Alice's perspiration. She'd discovered it lying on the floor of her dorm room. Though the note was unsigned, Hope must have slipped it under her door earlier that morning. Alice wished Hope had waited for her, but her new friends weren't always friendly. She only saw Hope and Faith at mealtimes. They kept talking about a competition and a deadline.

It was the first day of classes. Alice had been at the institute all weekend, but the winding paths still took her to buildings she'd never seen before. To find her way, Alice had to consult a laminated map of the campus, with a red arrow that told her YOU ARE HERE. She'd made a rough copy of the map in her sketchbook. The institute owned three hundred acres of woods and farmland. The grounds were like a maze.

The windows of the lecture hall looked down onto the parched lawn and a double row of sycamores. A lone student was traipsing across the field carrying an easel. Alice was about to go outside to ask him where the first class was being held, but something in his posture stopped her. The boy's hair was shaved close to his head, and he marched like a marine. She removed her Polaroid from its case, took aim, and snapped a photograph. She blew on the dark square, watching the portions that changed color. The photo was dusky: the suggestion of a striped shirt, the blurred traces of someone passing through a field. At the sound of approaching footsteps, she slipped the slick photo into her tote bag. She heard the distinct sound of jingle bells. A young man about Rabbit's age walked into the room. The tunic he was wearing looked like a dress. It came down to his ankles; he wore a pair of trousers underneath. His long braids were interwoven with seashells. As he moved, each seashell clinked musically against its neighbor. Two gold bracelets jangled on his wrist. He didn't look at Alice. His face was drawn and tense.

"Is this where the first class is meeting?" Alice asked.

The young man had picked up a clipboard from the desk. He took a pen from his leather shoulder bag and began to write with it.

"Hello?" said Alice, who was beginning to think she was invisible.

He held up one finger. "Give me a moment," he said. He wore a diamond stud in one earlobe. His skin was the color of butterscotch. "Which class were you looking for?" he asked her finally.

"I'm supposed to go to the lecture hall," Alice told him. "My friend Hope told me to take a class with a sculptor. She has a funny name. Nobo?"

"You must be talking about Odette Noko." His lips formed a series of perfect ovals. "Odette. No. Ko." He was almost shouting. He spoke pedantically, as if Alice were a two-year-old.

"Odette Noko," said Alice. "Where is she?"

"By now you ought to be familiar with Noko's impact on abstract sculpture. Otherwise you'll never get anywhere." He unclipped the papers, straightened them, and rapped them on the desk.

"I'm trying to take her class."

"She's on the committee," he said. "Odette Noko is a major artist. Her sculptures are extremely important."

"Could you just tell me where her class is meeting, maybe?" said Alice. Getting basic information out of him was challenging.

"On Tuesdays and Thursdays," he said. "She gives critiques." He removed a notebook from his satchel. He thumbed through it.

"But today is Monday," Alice said. "Isn't it?"

"I suppose so. Her seminar begins half an hour from now, if you absolutely must know. It isn't here, obviously. There's no projector. Noko's seminar is always held inside the auditorium."

"Is that the place made out of glass bricks and concrete?"

"Don't ask *me*."

Determined to find out where the class was meeting, Alice crossed the room and stood beside him, holding out her map.

"Oh, all *right*," he said. "Happy now? It's there." He pressed the ball of his thumb on one of the squares that Alice had drawn on her map of the campus. His fingernails were manicured. He was wearing scented aftershave.

"There's no waiting list this summer," he added, "but if you're hoping to take one of Noko's courses, I strongly suggest you don't simply flounce in there. The procedure is that you request permission to attend. What we do here, when we want to take a class, is sign up for it. After all, this *is* the institute." He began to walk away, slinging his bag over his shoulder. He left the clipboard on the desk behind him.

The sheet on the clipboard was covered with numbers and

letters. "MWFɪɪTCELHNOKO," said the first entry in the first column. There was a blank space next to it.

"Come back! I don't know what this is," Alice called out. "Would you show me? I'm new here and my name is Alice."

He paused by the window. "I'm Clarence Cunningham," he said. "I don't have time." He hurried out of the classroom.

Alice ran after Clarence Cunningham. She caught up to him when he stopped to look at a carton filled with books in an open doorway. She pushed the clipboard toward him. "Please?" she said.

"What do I look like?" said Clarence, snatching it from her. "The baby-sitter? Figure it out yourself. I never assist the other pupils. Nev-er. I'll help you just this once. After that, you're on your own." He struck the top of the paper. "Monday, Tuesday, Wednesday," he said, indicating the first letter on the page. "This is the day of the week. This is the location. LS is the Little Studio. AUD is the auditorium. Got it?"

"Got it," said Alice.

"Take life drawing, why don't you?" He circled one of the selections on the form. "And both of Noko's courses, art history and criticism. How about 'Introduction to Design'? I see you've got a camera, so take 'Point and Shoot'—that's basic photography. And, let's see. A workshop. Watercolors." Without stopping to check these choices with Alice, he made more circles. "Alice— what was it again?" he said, starting to spell out her name on the form.

"Duncan."

"Here, give a thorough explanation." He passed her the clipboard and the pen.

"An explanation?"

"Don't be exasperating!" he said. "We've just discussed this.

Explain why you want to work with the painter, Mr. Fitzgerald, and the sculptor, Odette Noko!"

Glumly, Alice placed the clipboard on the floor and sat down in the hall. She wrote: "I want Noko and Fitzgerald. They teach the classes I should take."

"Now what?" said Alice.

"Now you leave the clipboard on the desk."

Alice was growing tired of these instructions, but she did as Clarence said. "Are we going to be in the same classes?" she asked.

"It's not your business," he said, turning the pages of a book. "We're on opposite teams, you and I."

"Is it the girls against the boys?" asked Alice, thinking of the kickball matches that her gym instructor had once organized.

"It's every man for himself," said Clarence. "We each operate in our own circle of hell, naturally."

"We do?" asked Alice.

"You bet your ass," said Clarence, blowing the dust off a book cover. "We're here to win TCE. We're not here to make friends, are we?"

"No?" said Alice. Faith and Hope had mentioned this TCE thing, too. Alice kept meaning to ask what it was.

"No. If you make it in and you place first, your career as an artist will be launched. Even now the institute has clout. Balthus's reputation as an educator may have suffered. But he's an artist of some stature, and his word carries weight. If he singles out one student—a gifted student of high potential—that the committee members should watch out for . . ."

Alice waited, but he didn't finish the thought.

"You're a photographer?" said Clarence, noticing her camera.

"Not yet," said Alice. "Not really."

"I'm not an artist of any kind, myself," said Clarence. "And I have no intention of becoming one. I'm an Anti-Artist. I employ paint, but I don't paint with it. I make Anti-Paintings."

"Ah," said Alice, trying to remember what she'd learned about matter and antimatter from an episode of *Star Trek*.

"I want my work to question the relationship between race and power," said Clarence. "As a gay black male, I'm an outsider. You're a female in a man's world. To infiltrate the system, we need to succeed on our own terms. Would you agree? That we're subversives?"

"Oh, sure," said Alice. "Sure I do."

He'd put the books down, and as they talked, they'd begun to meander toward the exit. When they reached the vestibule, Clarence said, "I'll see you in Noko's class in half an hour. I won't speak to you again."

"Why not?" Alice asked.

"I can't afford to encourage the competition, Alice. I need to win. My grandmother invested her life savings in my education. She sent me to Rice Academy in Massachusetts, an exclusive boys' boarding school. She was hoping I'd be a senator someday."

They had come to the front porch. A hornets' nest, shaped like a pear, buzzed beneath the portico's eaves. "Only one of us can take first prize," Clarence said, turning to her. "Good luck to you, Alice Duncan." Off he went, down the stairs and across the lawn. His robe was fluttering around his ankles; his seashells and bracelets were jingling. Alice seized the Polaroid and framed a photograph of Clarence Cunningham in motion. The scent of aftershave trailed behind him.

Noko

Odette Noko was a tiny person, no taller than four feet. She wore her thick orange hair cut short, tousled and tufted. She'd tied it with a red fringed scarf. The tassels shook while she spoke. She waved her arm in a wide arc, like the conductor of an imaginary orchestra. "Think about intention," Noko said into the microphone. "Think about context." She stood behind the slide projector, gesticulating. "Art is a language. Investigate the way the piece shapes space. Does it intrude? Amuse? Disturb or threaten?" She had a throaty smoker's voice and a French accent. Her manner was theatrical. She spoke loudly, and with passion.

With a click, a new slide appeared on the screen. It showed two cubes, placed on a pedestal, made from flattened cars. The smashed frames were arranged in layers, like a piece of pastry.

"Nineteen sixty-two," said Odette Noko, "*Snake Eyes*. This piece, by Marcus Langley, won first place at TCE. A former

Balthus student, Langley is of course a well-known sculptor now. By the time he was a senior in high school, he had established his signature motifs. The title evokes a pair of rolling dice, games of chance, and gambling. The work is suggestive of fallibility and waste. The colors—red, white, and blue—are associative. We think of red blood and blue veins. We think of patriotism. The brand-new car. The American dream."

Listening to the lecture, Alice felt a tingling sensation along her spine. Even more than the sound of Odette Noko's words, she liked the intensity behind them. It was evident, from the way Noko carried herself, that she was a person of grandeur and intelligence. Though she was well into her seventies, her face was unlined. Her figure was lithe, her movements youthful. She was ageless. Hope had said that Noko was the only good instructor left at the institute. She was famous for using materials no one had ever used before. The courses Alice had signed up for were "How We Look: Views of Art Across the Centuries" and "Critic and Creator." There weren't many students enrolled in either.

That afternoon, Noko was delivering her lecture to Alice, Hope, Faith, Clarence, an instructor, and two other guys Alice hadn't met. One boy had his feet up on the seat in front of him. His boots were encrusted with purple glitter. Another boy sat cross-legged in the center aisle. He had on horn-rimmed glasses and a beret. Fitzy, the drawing instructor, had taken a seat near the window. He was resting his head against the wall, softly snoring. In the back, a heavyset woman was tape-recording the lecture. Her gray hair looked like a mop. Odette Noko had introduced her as Dr. Muir. She lived in a house on institute property. Dr. Muir was the curator of the Balthus Collection—a group of paintings, photographs, and sculptures that were stored in the library basement. Between Dr. Muir and Mr. Fitzgerald, Alice had counted forty rows of empty seats.

In the past, Noko had told them, the institute had been so popular that four students had to share each dorm room. There'd been sleeping bags in the hallways. There'd been pup tents on the lawn. There'd been roasted marshmallows over campfires and a surprise performance by John Cage. In the old days, the auditorium had been filled with artists, scholars, beatnik spiritualists, political radicals, and argumentative intellectuals.

The auditorium had been built in the late 1950s. Its cream-colored concrete walls were no longer terribly clean. Its bland beige carpeting was lined with soot. The seats were shaped like ice cream scoops. They were padded, and they swiveled. Built into one arm of each seat was a plug for earphones, but there were no earphones anymore. A folding desk, like the tray on an airplane, was concealed in the other arm. Alice had set her sketchbook down on the desktop, and she'd turned on the reading lamp. The slide show was in progress. A steady stream of light connected the slide projector to the screen. A new slide had just clicked into place: a photograph of a sand-colored canvas. It was spotted, ripped, and torn.

"Look closely at this collage," said Noko, sweeping down the aisle, trailing the microphone cord behind her. Her all-red outfit looked suspiciously like silk pajamas. "It is sculptural," she said. "Tactile. Layer by layer, Vincente Collini added thickness, form, and shape, building up the canvas. If you are working in two dimensions, I suggest you try to do the same. Don't take baby steps. Make leaps. Move back and forth between media—even if your mastery is quite rudimentary. Sculptors, pick up a brush. Painters, borrow a camera. I have selected slides that may help you to branch out, to widen your visual vocabulary. Right now I would like you to make another list of observations. Note the technique. Note whether the style is Futurist, Constructivist, Expressionist, and so forth, but do not limit yourself to categories.

No one will look at this paper but you and I. Stop when I tell you to. The title at the top of your page should be *Slide Five*."

Alice heard the sound of pages being turned, and the scratching of pencil on paper. The few students in the auditorium had already started on their lists. Since the slide show had begun, Alice had felt she was the slowest, and that she was already falling behind. Turning to a clean page, she wrote her observations down.

"This artist," Alice wrote, "didn't try to make a pattern. The painting just has drops on it that could have gotten there by accident or fallen from the sky. Instead of shapes, these are stains."

Alice didn't see Odette Noko come up behind her until she felt the sculptor's sleeve lightly brush her arm. Out of the corner of her eye, she caught a flash of red. Noko paused and continued past her. The sculptor was winding her way through each row, looking over the students' shoulders.

"Stop," Noko said to the class. "Please pass these first six observations up to me." She gestured toward the screen, casting a shadow with her pointer. "Collini's is a harrowing work," she said. "He served in World War II. He turned to art, late in life, for relief. He suffered from insomnia, and was haunted by his memories of devastation. As you may have noted, Collini's material is gauze bandage. It is weathered and aged. The holes in the fabric bring to mind flesh wounds. This is an example of the persistence of the human figure, in various guises, into the twentieth century. Here, it inhabits the most abstract work of art."

Though the other students tore out their sheets of paper and brought them up to the desk in front of the blackboard, Alice remained in her seat. Removing the pages from her sketchbook, she surreptitiously stuffed them into her tote bag. She studied Collini's collage carefully. With its hidden message about the war, it made her think of a poem written in invisible ink.

"Now we go back in time," said Noko. "To *Venus of Urbino*. Painted in the middle of the sixteenth century by Titian. An oil painting, in the academic tradition. A list of observations please. What are the differences and similarities between Titian, the classicist, and Collini, the modernist? Contemplate the changes that took place over five hundred years. I am timing you. This is not an exam. All that is required is a verbal sketch, an improvisation. You may also wish to draw. This is a surrealist exercise to help your interpretative skills develop, to train your creative mind to be uncensored and adventuresome. You have three minutes."

Alice felt as if she were in a race. Sketchbook in hand, she looked at the screen. On it was the image of a naked woman. Curled on her side on a litter of pillows, she was rosy and plump. The skin above her knees was dimpled. She held a bunch of green grapes in one small hand. A black-and-white puppy lay at her feet. In the background was a garden where a woman in a long dress and an apron was washing linen in a bucket.

"This painting is like a photograph," Alice wrote. "It shows a place. The collage is a picture of a feeling the artist had on the inside."

"Stop," said Odette. "Compare what you just saw to this one. Manet's *Olympia*. Nineteenth century. Remember: in viewing art, the true subject is the self. Our interpretation of a work is a reflection, an externalization, of our inner life. Begin."

On the screen was another nude, a painting. The brushstrokes were visible, almost sloppy, instead of smooth. The woman looked less like an airbrushed poster, more like a blemished human being. The colors of the painting were cheerful— royal blue, ochre, crimson.

"The woman is looking out of the painting straight at me," Alice wrote. "She isn't perfect. She has thick black lines around her body like a cartoon. This isn't trying to be real."

"Hand your observations to me," said Noko, weaving in and out of the rows of seats as she walked along the corridor. While Noko waited, Alice had to tear the page out and hand it to the sculptor. She hadn't even had a chance to number her observations. She hoped the exercise was to encourage them to learn to see, as Noko had promised them. She hoped it hadn't been a test.

"And finally," said Noko, "I will behave like an egotist. I will show you one of my own recent works. It is here at the institute, part of the Balthus Collection. It is open for viewing, if any of you would like to see it."

Alice sat up straighter when the slide came into view. It glimmered like a jewel. Abstract, organic, Noko's sculpture looked like pomegranate seeds, or a geode after it had been split open. Thousands of glistening protuberances lined the walls of an eerie, formless cavern. It gleamed, lit from inside. The thing on the screen—whatever it was—Alice recognized it.

"As you may be aware," said Noko, "most sculptors aim for permanence. They select materials to last for an eternity. Marble, stone, and bronze are traditional. My own work, by contrast, is flimsy. My sculptures are whimsical, not magnificent. They are only temporary. I prefer to make them out of latex. They are designed like us. To disintegrate." She switched on the lights. On the screen, the image of her sculpture faded to white.

"That's all for today. Please be sure to schedule some time to work independently in the Little Studio," said Noko while the students put away their notebooks and sketch pads. "Use new materials. Try new approaches. If you are satisfied with your work, this is a sign. It will stagnate. Be restless. Move on."

As the students filed out through the double doors, Alice headed toward the side exit. When she passed a display of hand-made art books behind a glass case, she pulled her observations on slides five and six out of her tote bag. She threw them in the wire-mesh wastebasket.

Outside, rain clouds had gathered high above the tops of the tallest pine trees. The air was close and humid. It was almost two o'clock. Alice scanned the horizon for Hope or Faith, but there was no sign of them. She directed her steps to the other side of the campus. The library was inside a cottage near the old duck pond at the bottom of the hill. It closed at two-thirty. She wanted to read books about art history so she'd follow the next lecture more easily. She had to hurry.

"Duncan?" called a woman's voice.

Afraid she might have done something wrong, Alice pretended not to hear. She quickened her pace.

"Duncan!"

Alice spun around. The sculptor was calling her.

"Why did you throw this out?" said Odette Noko. Her eyebrows were orange, to match her hair. Her face was chalky, like the top of the sugar donut. But beneath the coating of powder was a strong face.

"I didn't want you to read it," Alice explained. "It isn't any good."

"You're mistaken," said the sculptor, handing the discarded pages to Alice. No longer crumpled in a ball, she'd opened them and smoothed them.

Speechless, Alice jammed the papers under the back cover of her sketchbook.

"You have something to say," said the sculptor. "Do not be silenced." The mellifluous French voice was stern.

Alice could only mumble, bashfully, in return.

"I'd like you to view the Balthus Collection this afternoon,"

Noko said. "Bring your sketchbook. I expect you to keep a record of your impressions. You must learn to take your hunger for art seriously. I was impressed by your application, Duncan. You have a good eye."

"I never sent one," Alice stammered.

"What nonsense," said Noko. "I review every portfolio. Applications for this session were due months ago. They had to be postmarked by January 5th."

"But I never heard of the institute until last week," said Alice.

"You must have. I've seen twenty-four slides of your collages. A gentleman sent in a personal letter about your character, together with your application."

"A gentleman?" said Alice.

"If I recall," said Noko, "he had the name of a small animal."

"Not Rabbit."

"Rabbit, yes. He described the genteel poverty. The history of mental illness. The neglect." She fluttered one white hand, adorned with an ornate gold and ruby ring. "Your financial need made you eligible for a full scholarship," she said.

"It did?" asked Alice, feeling more pleased with every second, and more miserable. The description sounded right. So Rabbit and Odette knew what she felt. They'd noticed her.

"The family situation is ultimately of little consequence," said Noko, shielding her eyes and gazing up at the clouds. "I admitted you to the program because I anticipate that you will become an artist. At this early stage, you talented, soulful girls are easily distracted. And derailed. Do not disappoint me, Duncan. Your thoughts are a resource. Don't give them to the garbagemen who cart our trash in their trucks each Monday. I advise you not to throw your ideas away. They have value. Make use of them." With a toss of her flaming orange hair, the sculptor turned. She glided uphill, noiseless in her black ballet slippers.

The Queen

Alice trudged up Goat Hill carrying her new collage inside a plastic bag. She walked past the twisted metal structures in the Butterfly and Sculpture Garden, between the slabs of carved basalt, and along the dirt path that led to the Little Studio. The door was ajar, but no one was inside. Alice stood at the front of the room. Beside her was a raised platform built of plywood. It held three easels and a single chair. On Wednesdays and Fridays, this was where the model posed, half undressed, for life drawing class. It was early on Thursday morning. The chair was empty. The Little Studio was still.

Overhead, a cardboard mask swung from a thread, attached to the ceiling. Two Mexican papier-mâché skulls swayed on a mobile made from a wire hanger. Alice carefully uncovered her collage. She set the thirty-by-thirty square of posterboard on one of the easels on the platform. The students displayed their work here twice a week, on Tuesday and Thursday. In a few moments,

Noko would begin her critique. So far, no one but Alice had arrived.

Alice took a seat near the center of the one-room log cabin. It smelled of sweet perfume. The lavender bushes outside were in bloom. They bordered the small patio that Alice could see from the window to her left. Beyond it was an expanse of trees and open countryside, sloping downward toward the highway. The window to Alice's right looked out onto the campus. It framed a view of the sculptures on Goat Hill, posted in the grass like sentinels. Some were tall, metallic, and bulky, while others, draped like hanging moss between fragile, twiglike structures, appeared to be part of the natural landscape. Just outside the White House, Alice could see four doll-sized people moving uphill along the dirt road: Odette Noko, with her crown of flaming orange hair; Hope and Faith, with their hair in pigtails, and Clarence, who was wheeling his latest Anti-Painting up the hill inside a handcart. It was unnerving to watch the four of them growing nearer. In a few minutes, Alice's collage, which she'd worked on all week, would no longer belong to her. It would be theirs to criticize.

She resisted the temptation to close the shutters. Every few seconds, she glanced down at her watch. According to Mickey Mouse, the time was 9:17. She'd been at the Balthus Institute for twelve days. The critique was scheduled to begin at 9 a.m., but only Alice was punctual. Hope, Faith, and Odette were often twenty minutes late.

Alice opened her sketchbook to a blank page and stared outside at the pines. A red-breasted oriole perched on the cracked, discolored birdbath on the patio. Hopping down, it pecked at a clump of weeds that grew between the bricks. Without looking at her paper, Alice began to sketch. Odette had said they should practice drawing in this strange, sightless manner, being sure never to glance down at their drawing. They were instructed to pay close attention to surfaces and textures, focusing only on an intense, meditative way of seeing. The exercise was called a contour sketch. Holding her pencil at an angle, feeling her way along the pimply surface of the paper, Alice drew the plump oriole in ample curls. Its flight became a soft ripple, a vibration of graphite against paper. The sound of trilling sparrows up in the boughs were wisps and zigzags. "The first abstract artists made sounds into shapes, feelings into colors," Odette had said in her last seminar as she showed them slides.

"To understand abstraction," Odette had told the nearly empty auditorium in the White House, "one must not look *for* anything. One should not look *at* anything. One must instead look *with*."

All of this remained tantalizing to Alice, who wanted to become an artist more than ever. She wanted to be like Odette Noko, with her red lipstick and her gold hoop earrings. Odette had been commissioned to build two large sculptures in Munich and in Venice. She'd had a one-woman exhibition at the Museum of Modern Art.

Alice glanced down at what she'd sketched. Her paper was a messy nest of scribbles. She tore the sheet of paper out of her sketchbook. She was about to crumple it up when she remembered Odette's advice: "Save everything." As she tucked the sketch back into her folder, the studio door flung open. Hope entered first, head held high, shoulders back. She paused by the platform and removed an eight-by-ten black-and-white photograph from her portfolio. It was a portrait of a soldier, seen in profile, aiming a rifle. He had a petite, elfin face with an upturned nose. The strap of his helmet was unbuckled. He lay on a cliff while a sandstorm swirled around him. Alice had seen the model Hope and Faith used. They kept him on the drawing table in the studio. He was two inches tall, colored green from head to foot, and made of plastic. Hope took the photographs, and Faith built the miniature sets. Each of their photographs had the name "Paul" in its title. Their older brother, Paul, had never returned from Vietnam.

Hope placed the photograph on the easel next to Alice's. She looked at Alice's collage. After a few seconds, she walked to the door to assist Clarence, who was hauling the handcart over the front step. Hope lifted one side of Clarence's irregularly shaped wooden panel, walking backward. Clarence held the other end. They carried Clarence's Anti-Painting across the floor of the log cabin like a pair of furniture movers. Its bright splashes of paint dominated the room. Alice looked from Hope's photograph to Clarence's painted panel. No one would have guessed that either piece was the work of a teenager. Alice's collage looked as amateurish as a schoolgirl's homework in comparison.

Hope and Faith now took their places on the windowsill. They sat face to face, on either side of the picture window, like bookends. Clarence sat in a chair at the side of the room. He gave Alice a secret nod. She nodded back. Since that first day, they hadn't spoken.

"Art is rude," said Odette Noko, flicking the corner of Alice's collage with a blood red fingernail. "To be an artist, one must announce: Screw you. I don't give a fuck. To hell with it. Damn you. Utterly." Spoken in her husky voice and refined French accent, the curses sounded elegant.

Hope and Faith continued drawing one another while Odette was speaking. They held their sketchbooks balanced on their knees. They were as oblivious to her criticism as they were to her praise. That morning, Odette Noko had suggested the twins were repeating themselves. They shouldn't get stuck in one place, she'd advised. They ought to venture into new territory. She'd said Clarence's piece was provocative. She applauded his experimentation with taboo subjects and found materials. Clarence had painted an American flag. Instead of red oil paint, he'd used cow's blood from a local butcher. He'd turned the flag's rust and white stripes into prison bars. Behind the bars, Clarence had silkscreened the brown, smiling face of Aunt Jemima. When Odette turned the painting on its side, the bars of Aunt Jemima's cell spelled the word NIGGER in long thin white lettering.

Clarence had compressed his lips together while Odette Noko praised him. Alice thought he'd looked pleased. He rarely participated in class, unless he liked something.

It was Alice's turn now. Odette was studying her collage, taking notes on the stack of index cards she always carried in her breast pocket. Maybe the collage was good. Maybe it was bad. Alice no longer knew for certain which was which. Moments passed, unbearably, in silence as Odette circled the platform, cocking her head first to one side and then to another. The fluffy peaks of her hair looked like plumes. She took one step forward and one step back, circling the easel like a large inquisitive bird.

Odette called Alice's collages "dreamscapes." This one showed a man in a tuxedo adrift in a sea of crimson poppies. He had no face. Alice had replaced his head with a hand from a jewelry advertisement. A slender wrist grew from the man's white collar, sprouting five tapered female fingers like the hydra Alice had once seen under a microscope in science class. Two feet away from Alice's collage was an unfinished canvas by Fitzy (also known as Roy T. Fitzgerald), the instructor who taught their life drawing class. His blurry painting reminded Alice of a heavy fog. It was colorless, like smoke. Staring at it, she began to see vaporous figures lurking in the mist. Fitzy had been a prominent artist in the late 1950s. He called his paintings "monozones," and had made them with acrylic paint, straight from the tube—no mixing—and an ordinary kitchen sponge. He'd recently completed monozone number 189. They looked as if they were all one color, but they weren't. He was a minimalist. He wanted people to think when they looked at his paintings. He wanted them to use their imaginations.

Next to Fitzy's painting, Odette had taped three snapshots of her own work in progress. Alice had seen it, in person, in Odette's private studio. It was a magical thing: a group of forty gossamer cylinders. Like grown-ups at a cocktail party, they were arranged in five disorderly groups. They appeared to be soft and floppy, but the material was hard as a rock when Odette had allowed Alice to touch it. Translucent, the color of a tooth or a fingernail, the cylinders were made of fiberglass. They'd been battered into different shapes, like crinkled paper bags. Alice had never encountered anything like Noko's sculptures. In them, she'd seen a bank of reeds, ruffled by the wind—and a handful of cigarette butts in an ashtray. When Odette had explained that her sculpture was an extension of her skin, that her own skin was her art, the little hairs on Alice's forearms had stood on end.

"Duncan's piece engages us immediately," Odette said now, tiptoeing across the floorboards in her black ballet slippers. "She has made a collage—a composite—not simply by combining specific visual images but by intermixing historical epochs, movements, schools of thought, and approaches. Duncan is paying homage to Pop Art's flatness, here"—she pointed at the flower—"while exploring the realist's illusion, here, of depth." She indicated the silhouettes of cliffs that Alice had made, in the background, out of black crepe paper.

Alice tried to write these complimentary comments down. The only words she caught, however, were "depth," "illusion," and "collage."

"She's created a sense of perspective in the traditional manner," Odette continued, "as you all learned to do in Fitzy's drawing class: employing the vanishing point. It's been done quite well. But it's not accurate. She has skewed the image, in order to disorient the viewer. To startle us. To create unease. I particularly like the way Duncan plays with proportion. It recalls the early collage of Bearden, who often mixed these small and large figures together in the same piece. Congratulations, Duncan. Your composition is developing, and your colors are almost luminous here. You've made effective use, too, of negative space. For an evolving young artist, this is really very fine."

Alice glanced across the room at Clarence. He was looking at her collage. "I am good," Alice wrote in large letters in her sketch pad. She underlined this four times.

"Look, Noko," said Hope, shutting her drawing pad and capping her pen, "your critique is off. I take issue with it."

"Do you?" said Odette. Her orange eyebrows flew up toward her hair.

"Yes. The collage isn't strong at all. The reason you're comparing Duncan's work to Romare Bearden is this. It's derivative. It's imitative. She's not doing art. She's copying."

Alice propped her elbow on the easel in front of her, covering her face with her hand.

"Duncan's collages always look like you've already seen them someplace else," said Faith. "She cuts her images out of mainstream commercial magazines. You can tell exactly where the photos come from. I'd say the guy in the tux is from *Cosmopoli-*

tan. The flowers are from a travel ad. And the hand with the diamond ring on it is from *Vogue*. Duncan, am I right?"

Alice swiveled in her chair to address them. But Faith and Hope didn't wait for her to speak.

"Unless it's done intentionally, to make a comment, like a Lichtenstein, you shouldn't be able to trace a picture's origins," said Faith. "To make an integrated whole out of assorted pieces. That's the definition of collage."

"What textbook is this written in?" said Odette. "You say she can't do this, she can't do that. Why not?"

"Because, Noko," said Hope, "it isn't a fully realized work. What Duncan's doing doesn't signify as American art. It's just a footnote to Europe. It's reheated Dalí. It's lukewarm stuff from sixty years ago. Collage itself is obsolete."

"Is art like a piece of cheese, then?" asked Odette. "Must it have a date stamped on its plastic package? An idea is fine one decade. Then it goes stale the next?"

"I'd say so," said Hope. The muscles in her neck looked taut, Alice thought, as if she were in a state of alertness.

"After Duchamp," said Odette, "who can issue such stuffy pronouncements? In Warhol's wake, surely we can no longer make secure distinctions. Commercial art, fine art, low art. There is no difference. Duncan has successfully subsumed these found images into a fully realized work. Yes, I see a bit of Magritte, here"—she pointed to the collage—"in these men in their dark suits. I see a bit of Dalí there, in the juxtapositions. She's built a statement with these. Contextualized. Referential. And entirely her own."

The Little Studio was hushed. "I have made a statement of my own," Alice wrote in her drawing pad. She could hear the impossibly loud scratching of her pencil on the paper.

"Tell me something, Alice," said Odette, taking a folding

chair and sitting down. Her feet, in their black slippers, didn't reach the ground. She made an adjustment to her scarf. "Do you have a project under way for the Two Carolinas art festival?"

"Yes, I do," Alice lied. Her voice was squeaky. It reverberated in the large space all around her. Alice had finally learned what the letters TCE stood for: Two Carolinas Exhibition. Odette had discussed the Two Carolinas Exhibition project with them days ago, but Alice hadn't even begun. She'd only made some sketches in her studio. Art students in North and South Carolina summer camps, high schools, community colleges, and art schools would all submit entries to the competition. Held at Blue Mountain College, near Asheville, the festival was open to the public. Each year, a professional art dealer was invited to judge the event. The winning piece would be included in a group show at the Blue Mountain College Gallery.

"I'm glad to hear that, Duncan," said Odette, removing her own photographs from the easel, one by one, and sliding them back into her zippered portfolio. "Because I think you've got a chance to win first prize."

The Sisterhood

Alice didn't go to dinner on Thursday night. She stayed in her studio and planned a new life. She'd win the blue ribbon at the Two Carolinas competition. Dean's agent would sell her collages in every gallery on Madison Avenue. Odette Noko would take her to Japan and France. Rain would take her to Rome and Morocco. Alice would dress in silk pajamas and black motorcycle boots. She'd ring her eyes with eyeliner. On her head, she'd wear a spangled scarf, like the one Odette Noko had. Crash Omaha would attempt to buy all of her collages, for his own private collection, but Alice would have a strict talk with her agent. No collages for Crash Omaha! Out of the question! She simply would not allow it! Her collages would be enshrined in glass, lit by dozens of colored Christmas lights, and framed in fourteen-karat gold. They'd be displayed—protected by a velvet rope—in the Cathedral of Notre Dame, in Paris. A crowd of admirers pressed close to them. Priests blessed them with holy water. Nuns prostrated themselves before the saintly collages of Alice Duncan and fainted from the sheer joy of witnessing her remarkable, her miraculous, her God-given talent. Women in fur coats, men in navy blazers, and girls from the Fieldwood School knelt and wept before the sight of Alice's collages. Hope and Faith begged Alice, who was the greatest child prodigy in history, to be their best friend.

But Alice couldn't win the prize because, in reality, she didn't even have a project. The floor of Studio A was littered with rejected sketches. She hadn't eaten since the morning critique in the Little Studio. She had no appetite. The thought of the deserted dining room, with its putty-colored walls and its ammonia smell, was disheartening. Each night, as she walked by the art library, past the sign for the café, she'd see a pail filled with dirty water. It sat on the janitor's cart, beside the mop and broom. There was never a sign that any janitor had been there at all, just the pail.

Once inside the café, she'd always see a covered tray on the steel table. When she lifted the lid, she'd find noodles or rice, a sauce, and a brownish stew. Next to that would be a bowl of limp lettuce and a pitcher of gooey salad dressing. Arranged on a platter in a geometric pattern—like the assignments with colored shapes made out of construction paper that Fitzy gave in his Thursday design course—would be chunks of Swiss cheese (sickly yellow) alternating with strips of American cheese (bright orange). They'd be emitting beads of oil, as if perspiring. The café's sole occupant would be Mary, the obese cook in her hairnet and apron, who read Harlequin romances in the office behind the kitchen. Faith and Hope never ate there, nor did Fitzy and Odette. The twins took some bread and cheese, wrapped it in a paper napkin, and went away. The instructors drove to a restaurant in Cool Spring.

Alice stayed in Studio A, drawing in her sketch pad. Through the sliding glass doors that let out onto the soccer field, two windows were lit up, near the bend in the road, on the second floor of the White House. That was Odette and Fitzy painting and sculpting in their own studios. Moths hovered above the outdoor lamps, casting flickering shadows on the curtain with their beating wings. Now and then, Alice heard the mournful call of an owl or the telltale squeak of a bat. The girls' dormitory was still. The institute's weekly marathon had begun. From Thursday evening through Sunday afternoon, the students and instructors retired to their own studios, hiding away for hours at a stretch, often skipping Friday classes. They emerged at midday to grab the sandwiches Mary left out in a wicker basket on the front porch of the White House. There were only nine days left before they had to submit their projects to the Carolinas festival. The previous weekend, Alice hadn't seen a trace of Hope, Faith, Fitzy, or Odette. She'd finally run into Odette on Sunday evening, when she'd gone to look at the monarch butterflies. With their orange-and-black wings, they sailed over Goat Hill every day at sunset, like kites. They came to the butterfly bushes, purple shrubs the Great Man had planted near the sculptures to attract them.

Alice was sitting at her desk after midnight, eating Ritz crackers with grape jelly, when a knock came at her door.

"Are you in there, Duncan?" said a high, girlish voice. "We're here to see you."

When she opened the door, she found Faith and Hope in the hallway dressed in matching white T-shirts and white jeans. Faith had a portfolio strapped over her shoulder. Hope held a stack of art books in her suntanned arms.

"Hi," said Alice, remembering how mean they'd been in the Little Studio. She still yearned to belong to their exclusive clique, to be accepted by them.

"Faith and I have been talking about you," said Hope.

"You have?" said Alice.

"For a few minutes at dinner in that godforsaken café. Mary made some sort of casserole. You didn't miss much, Duncan, trust me. We discussed your case."

"My case?" said Alice, stepping back from the door. She forced a smile.

"Yes. May we?" With regal grandeur, Hope paraded in and plunged herself into the chair by the sliding doors, throwing her two long legs over its arm. The skin on her calves was the color of taffy. It contrasted dramatically with the hem 'of her bleached jeans. She wore white sneakers without socks. Instead of shoelaces, she'd threaded a satin ribbon through the grommets.

Hope picked up the spiral notebook, filled with unlined drawing paper, that Alice had left open on her desk. She began to leaf through it, wearily. Her expression was balanced between mild interest and supreme boredom. "Duncan, we're here to analyze the nature of your work. It's nothing personal. Faith and I flatly disagree with Odette's assessment. Your collages show very little promise."

"Anyone can have an opinion," said Alice quietly.

"You may or may not be aware," Hope said, slowly turning Alice's sketchbook around and holding it a few inches away, "that your collages are decorative. Ornamental. Pretty. Faith and I make it our policy to despise anything that's merely beautiful."

Alice looked down at the quilt coverlet on the cot. It was embroidered with clear acrylic threads. She pulled at one of them. It was coming loose. "I just try to make the collages the best that I can do them," she said, her voice steady. She tried to imitate Hope, to keep her face from showing what she felt.

"Pretty things," Faith said, "are bourgeois. You may as well sell picturesque watercolors of farmhouses."

"What do you do want me to do, then?" Alice asked. She undid one of the stitches.

Hope leaned forward, hands on her knees. "Stop being such a goody-goody."

"Stop being so timid and innocuous," said Faith. "Your collages are too tight. Too tentative. Everything is cramped."

Hope drew a box in the air around her head. "Break out of that restrictive frame you put everything in," she told Alice. "Your instincts are all right. But you're thinking small instead of big. You ought to be doing installations. Environments. Performance art. Fully realized, three-dimensional creations."

"No one is going to give a fuck about some kid who glues scraps of paper to laminated posterboard," Faith said.

Alice didn't know how to respond to any of this. They seemed to be helping her and attacking her at the same time.

"We thought you'd benefit from our advice and guidance," said Faith. "We could give you some tips on your project for the Carolinas festival."

"At this rate, you'll never come up with a decent project on your own," said Hope. "Not until you've been formally inducted."

"In," said Alice, "in what?"

"Inducted into the Sisterhood," said Hope. "In order to win the competition you have to join."

"Join how?" Alice asked.

"I can't reveal that information, Duncan," said Hope. "First, we've got to determine if you're Sisterhood material. Don't we, Faith?"

"We do," said Faith.

"And neither of us is convinced that you are," said Hope.

"What usually convinces you?" Alice asked.

"There's a couple things you have to do, Duncan," said Hope. "I've written them down here. They're challenges. Each of them is a dare."

"A quest, you might almost say," said Faith.

"On this paper," Hope said, removing a scroll of white paper from the portfolio, "I've written down two tasks. You have to complete both of them to our satisfaction before Faith and I will even consider inducting you."

"May I read them?" Alice asked.

"No, Duncan, that's just it. You may not," said Hope.

"Out of the question," said Faith.

"You have to first agree to participate in the quest," Hope said.

"How can I," Alice said, "if you won't tell me anything?"

"See that?" Hope said. "There you go again. Nothing's impossible. You're trapped in that literal, logical mind-set. There aren't any restrictions except the ones you set yourself. You ought to know that. An artist's job is to defy the rules."

"Okay," said Alice, "I'll do it."

"Excellent," said Hope. "I told you, sis," she said. "She has some possibility."

"We'll see," said Faith.

"The first task you need to perform," said Hope, "is this. You need to go to the twenty-four-hour liquor store over in Cool Spring. And you need to buy us a half-gallon of red wine."

"I can't," Alice said, trying to remember what Aunt Esmé had said was the "drinking age." "I'm not twenty-one."

"No problem," said Faith. "It's easy. You look older than we do."

"You'll wear those shoes you had on when you first got here," said Hope. "And the makeup."

Alice began to hunt around the room for the high-heeled platform sandals that made her as tall as an Amazon. She found them beneath the bed.

"This is decent," Faith said. She held up Alice's sketchbook. It was open to the page where, earlier that night, Alice had compulsively drawn pictures of J.D.'s finger. Drafting the same image again and again, she'd arranged five of the fingers in a pattern, each one shaped like a starfish, forming eight stars made of human hands. Each finger, with detailed knuckles, nails, and veins, had taken her a long time to draw.

"What do you say, Hope?" said Faith.

Hope looked at it for a moment. "It might have been decent, but it isn't. Like everything Duncan does. She tries hard. But she always misses."

"Not to worry, Duncan," said Faith. "If you do what we say, your creative vision will solidify and you'll improve. You need to drop that sugar-and-spice routine. Remember this: art is never nice."

"Get ready," said Hope. "Put on some makeup. Fix your hair. You'll never pass for twenty-one looking like that." Grabbing Alice, she ran her hand, roughly, through her hair. "Don't you ever comb these golden locks of yours? Duncan has great golden locks, sis. Doesn't she?"

"She does," said Faith.

"I'm inclined to take a photograph of you, Duncan. Throw me that hairbrush, would you, Faith? I saw she had one there, on top of the dresser."

Faith rifled through Alice's belongings. She flung the hairbrush to Hope, who caught it with one hand.

"It's like a rat's nest," said Hope, pulling on Alice's hair. She began to brush it. "Make yourself useful, sis. Aren't there any thingies over there?"

"What sort of thingies?" said Faith.

"Rubber bands," said Hope. "Barrettes. Beautiful stuff I can stick into Alice's beautiful, beautiful hair."

The way she said "beautiful" made it sound like a curse.

"Thingies," Faith repeated. She stood on Alice's desk and rummaged through the objects on the dresser.

"They're in the top drawer," Alice said, not at all certain that she ought to be cooperating.

"Get them," Hope commanded.

Alice's unreliable heart was surging forward, as it had done in the tree with J.D. Her pulse had lost its regularity. Instead of keeping a steady beat, it throbbed and it leapt. Soon she would collapse on the floor and be dead of a heart attack.

"All she's got in here are socks," said Faith, looking through one of Alice's drawers. "And panties." She held a pair of Alice's socks in one hand, a pair of her white cotton underwear in the other.

Hope made a face. "You know, Duncan, I used to wear stuff like *that* when I was a little kid. For a visual artist, you lack style."

"Maybe I've got my own style," Alice said, remembering that she was going to win the prize. She allowed herself, momentarily, to be fortified by Odette Noko's critique.

"You can say that again, Duncan," said Faith. "Here we go. Hair barrettes. Bingo." She pulled the cap off Aunt Esmé's lipstick and opened and closed the clasp of a hair barrette. These small actions made Alice unaccountably angry, as if Faith had crashed through her window and gone through her possessions while she was out.

"Leave my stuff alone, please," said Alice. No one listened.

"Throw that over here, would you, sis?" said Hope.

Faith threw things, one by one.

Hope dropped most of them. They rained down on the carpeting around their feet. "Pick it up," she said to Alice.

Alice did.

"Hold it for me," said Hope.

Alice held the lipstick, the lip gloss, and the eye shadow while Hope pulled on her hair. She had three hairpins in her mouth. "I desperately need a glass of wine," she said, keeping her lips together to hold the pins there. "Don't squirm so much, Duncan. Let's get this makeover of yours finished with." She stabbed Alice's scalp with a bobby pin.

"Ow," said Alice.

Hope stepped in front of Alice to survey her handiwork. "I've done it. Does Duncan look incredible like this, Faith, or what?"

"Duncan looks all right," Faith allowed.

"Now for the final touch," said Hope, brandishing the lip gloss.

Alice stood stiffly while the small, soft thumb—so different from the tough skin that belonged to J.D.—ran over her mouth, slicking it with lip gloss. She'd felt she'd entered a huge pinball machine. Helpless, she could only roll along the tracks, responding to the pushes and the pulls, the bells and the thwacks. Alice didn't know how to stop the mechanism. Hope was the paddle. Alice was the ball.

A Good Shot

That ought to work," said Hope. "Faith, give me that, would you?" She pointed at Alice's desk.

"Give you what?" said Faith.

"That Polaroid camera. I'll take a shot of her."

"Please don't throw the camera, Faith," Alice said, jolted out of the pinball daydream.

Faith hopped down from the desk and gave the camera to Hope.

"Say cheese, Duncan," she said, pointing it at her.

Alice looked at the camera. A light flashed. The Polaroid ejected a black square of emulsion-coated paper. The three of them huddled together, watching it become a photograph of a tall, curvaceous, glamorous lady. She had a painted face.

Six Hundred Men

Gnats swarmed in a moving cloud around the lamp that lit the path. As high as the pine tree, it was taller than a giraffe, with a long bent neck. A single bulb splashed light on the soccer field. Alice couldn't see the stones underfoot, but she could feel them beneath the cork soles of Aunt Esmé's sandals. A few paces ahead of her, Faith's pigtails bounced against her shoulders. The platinum stripe in Hope's hair glimmered in the moonlight. A chorus of crickets whistled.

Alice held her wrist out in front of her and tried to read her watch. The lines and dots glowed pale green. Four minutes had passed since they'd left the dorm. Faith and Hope hadn't spoken.

They'd come to a shed, at the edge of the campus, which served as a garage. Beneath a corrugated tin roof, Alice saw a VW Bug, painted with wild, cheerful swirls, and Odette Noko's convertible. Beside it were Mary's pickup truck and a black sedan Alice supposed must belong to Mr. Balthus, though she'd never seen him. The girls' Honda motorbikes, one red, one white, had curved black leather seats. They were parked side by side, their wheels turned outward, handlebars and headlights gleaming.

Faith took the red Honda, wheeling it out of the small space without turning the motor on. Hope took the white one. "Get on the back, Duncan," she said, straddling it.

Alice climbed aboard. The engine thrummed under her. She turned to look at the campus, but it had been swallowed by the night. Like an abstract painting, the institute had been reduced to its most elemental components: a winding line and a few flickering sparks. Pale dots, in a mass of darkness.

They were hurtling forward into nowhere. Cars raced by, roaring as they approached, then fading down the highway. Beside them was emptiness, nothing but the road moving beneath them and the trees' ragged outline. Shapeless black forms leapt up and down against the night sky. The strip of asphalt beneath the headlights was in a constant state of flux, its painted white stripe unfurling like a paper streamer at a birthday party. A truck rattled past. The sound of its thundering wheels made Alice tighten her grip. The wind caught the tip of Hope's ponytail, like a paintbrush, snapping it back and forth over Alice's cheek.

They parked their bikes outside a shopping mall. The twins waited in the lot while Alice combed the mazelike aisles of Trudy's 24-Hour Liquor Shop. Like the Dewey decimal system which organized the library at Fieldwood, the store was arranged according to a special code. Bottle upon bottle of elixirs were on display, of different hues: the burgundy of grapes, the purple of eggplant, amber and pink, clear glass, and opaque. After wandering through rows of vessels, sleek and slender, squat and small, Alice stumbled across a case of inexpensive wine. Tucking a half-gallon jug in the crook of her arm, she strolled up to the cash register. Holding her head high, she tried to behave as if purchasing alcohol was an errand she performed daily. A line had formed at the counter, with a teenage boy, an old lady, and a grim couple. No one spoke. A middle-aged woman sat on a stool, taking customers' money, giving them their change. She had light brown curly hair, false eyelashes, and a mole above her lip. Her tight leopard-print shirt dipped low at the collar.

Alice handed her a crumpled ten-dollar bill.

"TGIF," said the woman in a Southern drawl, ringing up the purchase on the cash register. She winked at Alice. "Have a good weekend now, baby. Next in line?"

The photography studio was in a converted barn at the edge of an apple orchard, several miles away from the campus. Four spotlights were arranged inside it, on the floor. Bits of straw floated through the air, filling it with the scent of freshly cut hay. A dozen bales of hay, each the size of a suitcase, were stacked in a pyramid. Hope, Faith, and Alice lay on their stomachs at the top, surveying the miniature battlefield Faith had built for the toy soldiers below. She'd made a war-torn city out of sand, potting soil, and shoe boxes. Hope and Faith had a collection of six hundred plastic army men, the sort that were sold in toy stores in mesh bags. They cost, Hope said, $1.99 for a hundred. After their first solo exhibition, they'd invested in a complete set—not just troops but an arsenal of weapons and equipment. The deluxe military package came with twelve tanks, two cannons, four jeeps, ten machine guns, eight trucks, two jets, two warplanes, two missiles, a dozen land mines, and a dozen hand grenades. The soldiers, two inches high in their combat boots and helmets, manned a series of trenches that Faith had tunneled into the dirt floor of the barn. Looking through Hope's viewfinder, Alice could see the commanding soldier. He surveyed the battle from a mountain made of potting soil. Several more armed men were stationed in the mouth of a cave made from a half-buried coffee mug. They were lobbing hand grenades at a group of green army men which were splattered with red paint. Some were missing arms or legs. Hope said she'd removed them with an X-Acto blade. The severed limbs lay in a jumble, "offstage," on the outskirts of the miniature set. The twins had built a cemetery for the dead. Tombstones, made from white pebbles, marked the graves. Next to the graveyard was a cathedral, made of a box of Cheerios and two cylindrical containers of oatmeal. The town was made of cardboard, and Faith had painted the façades of the little houses (it was what Odette Noko called trompe l'oeil) to look like brick, wood, and stone. There were window boxes, filled with diminutive real flowers, on the window ledges, and the walls were covered with real baby ivy. One shoe box had been smashed, leaving behind only the wreckage—doll-sized furniture, books and food, and scraps of wallpaper and cardboard. A bomb from the twins' war had detonated.

To bring the army men to life in her photographs, Hope said she'd used a sophisticated backlighting technique that had once been used by Expressionist filmmakers in Berlin in the 1930s. The Great Man had taught it to her during her first summer at the institute. She kept her camera slightly out of focus so that the men wouldn't appear to be plastic, but to be human. Odette Noko had said that some of the twins' grainy black-and-white pictures mimicked the photographs of Vietnam taken by war correspondents and photojournalists and printed in newspapers. Others were copies of drawings made by German soldiers, artists, who had fought in World War II. They were shots of men firing their guns, nursing their wounds, and being blown to bits by explosives.

Shining a flashlight at the war zone, Hope raised the jug of wine to her lips and took a swig. She consulted the scroll of paper that contained Alice's fate.

"Take a look at this, Duncan," she said. "We've made a map for you." Hope retraced the lines she'd drawn in crayon, pointing at them with a stick of hay.

"That's the apple grove," she said, "right outside. Walk directly ahead, using that telephone pole by the old cow pasture, where the wire fence is, as your landmark. I'll give you my flashlight."

"How far away is it?" asked Alice.

"It's not far," said Faith.

"How long will it take me to walk there?" Alice asked.

"Not long," said Hope.

"At the far end of the orchard, you'll come to a meadow," said Faith. "Walk across it. There's an abandoned house. It's vacant. The hinge on the back door is broken. It's open."

"On behalf of the Sisterhood," said Hope, "we dare you to go inside. There's furniture and toys. Dishes and plates. They're covered with an inch of dust. Everything is just the way he left it."

"Who left it?" Alice asked.

"An old man. He used to live there."

"What happened to him?" said Alice.

"Nothing. He left, that's all. He had bad luck. He moved out in a hurry because . . . um. Because he believed in voodoo. Some voodoo person told him the house was hexed. So the old man got his ass in gear and moved away."

"*Is* the house hexed?" Alice asked.

"Don't be absurd," said Hope disdainfully. "You're not superstitious, are you, Duncan? I've already explained to you it's empty."

"I'm not going inside a voodoo house," Alice said.

173

"Honestly, Duncan," said Hope, "you sound perfectly idiotic. Anyone would think that you're a dumb little ten-year-old. It has nothing to do with voodoo. There are some cool antique toys that the Sisterhood wants out of there. We'd like to feature one of them in our next series of photos. There's a wooden puppet, in the back room, lying on a chair. I want you to take it. And bring it to me. That, Duncan, is the requirement for the Sisterhood. If you want to join up and be our sister, you have to do it."

"What if someone else has moved into the voodoo house?" Alice asked, peering out onto the orchard through a gash in the wooden barn wall. The gnarled trunks of the apple trees looked like witches' claws.

"Stop calling it that," said Faith. "Voodoo is nonsense. The only thing that's alive in there is a rat or two," said Faith.

Live rats didn't sound so great to Alice. Neither did dead ones. She worried about the way Faith had said this. The only thing alive. Maybe, Alice thought, something dead was in the house. "I don't know about this," said Alice.

"Just go," said Hope.

It was a dare. Alice had done dares before. The key was not to dwell on them, but to do them rapidly so she wouldn't lose her nerve. Alice began to climb back down the hay fort. The straw prickled her palms and soles. She'd left her platform sandals at the bottom of the pyramid.

"Duncan?" Hope said.

"What?"

Hope's fine-boned face appeared at the top of the pyramid, lit from beneath. She was a vision, Alice thought, of breathtaking beauty. The shadows that played above her shoulders turned, for a second, into great black wings.

"Take this," the Angel of Hope said, handing the flashlight down to Alice. "I know you can do it, sis," she said.

I know you can do it, my sis, my sis, my sis, ran the happy song that played, for many minutes afterward, in Alice's head. The beam of light swung around, lighting up dark corners of the barn—the peaked roof with its hayloft, the golden yellow straw, and the missing wooden planks in the barn's walls. No rat, no voodoo or dead spirit could deter her now. Hope had called her "sis." For a while, everything was wonderful.

Outside, darkness enveloped Alice. Beyond the flashlight's cone of brightness, the countryside was an all-black painting. It reminded Alice of a slide Odette Noko had shown, in the auditorium, during the last seminar. The black canvas had seemed babyish to Alice, but Odette had said the painter who'd made it was a master of modernism. He was stripping art to its essentials in order to help people see clearly. Alice wished she could see clearly now. Old tires and beer bottles were scattered over the deserted orchard, lit only by a starving sliver of a moon. The clouds floated in front of it, one after the other, unreeling themselves like a silvery sliding screen. The grass underfoot felt brittle. Apple trees reached their twisted branches toward her. Yet the night was soft, like a shawl that had wrapped itself around the earth. Alice charged ahead, walking fast. She said "Go, go, go," "Do it, do it, do it," and "Sis, my sis, my sis," under her breath.

According to her watch, seven minutes passed before the beam from Alice's flashlight fell on a wooden fence. It tilted at a sharp right angle. Alice walked further, and the fence changed shape. Now it tilted sharply to the left, as if it had been blown from side to side in a hurricane. Where the two slanting sides met, the wood had splintered. An animal's white tail flicked back and forth, but it was only an old rag tied to a post. It flapped in the summer breeze.

Alice was standing inside a front yard. In the beam of the flashlight, she saw a pile of firewood. An empty picture frame leaned against a garbage can. A sewing machine, a lampshade, and a roll of chicken wire were laid out like items in a tag sale. She walked closer. Alice saw a front porch with scabrous floorboards and a shingled house with broken shutters. Looking up, she thought she saw a gabled roof, and a curtain that fluttered in an attic window.

Alice cupped the flashlight in her hand, covering the bulb. Her fingers turned bright red, like the hot coals in a barbecue pit, and a thin stream of light escaped from between them. Creeping by the shingles on the side of the house, she passed a row of shrubs with pink blossoms, and a flowering hydrangea. The back door hung from its hinges.

Alice took the stairs two at a time. The screen door shrieked as she opened it. She stood still, listening. She heard a distant creaking. But only the wind sighed, and a scrap of newspaper fluttered on the grass. You can do this, sis, she told herself. She stepped inside, her bare feet coming into contact with smooth linoleum. It smelled faintly medicinal, like a cashmere sweater stored in mothballs for the winter. The shine of stainless steel, the white metal box of a refrigerator, told her she was in a kitchen. Three ceramic jars sat on a shelf beside a cookbook. A kettle was on the stove. A bouquet of dried roses hung on the wall, upside down. The person who had lived here had fled, Alice thought, leaving everything in place, like the inhabitants of Pompeii in ancient Rome. She felt a drumming in her rib cage as she remembered the photograph she'd seen in an encyclopedia. The people who didn't run fast enough had been turned into statues, writhing on the ground, burned by molten lava, buried alive.

She heard a muffled scratching. Alice gasped. Something rushed past her foot. There, scurrying along the sideboard, was a white mouse. It was only a small rodent, with shaking whiskers and a slithering tail. It stopped to nibble at some crumbs. Aiming the beam of light at the table, Alice saw a cardboard box of crackers had been left open. It was red. The brand was Ritz.

Alice trained her flashlight on the mouse. He whisked down a corridor, running over an Oriental rug. It was russet brown, with a pattern of black diamonds and curlicues. Alice followed the white mouse. She arrived at a low wall, covered with wainscoting like the walls of her studio in the dormitory. Mounted on the wooden paneling was a framed black-and-white photograph. At first glance, Alice thought it was a portrait of a young girl, seated at the foot of a staircase. But it wasn't human. It was a marionette. The girl puppet had met with a gruesome fate. Its arms had fallen off. They sat in the foreground of the photograph. Thick black strings were attached to them, extending from the two nails that protruded out of the heel of its hands. The puppet sat, helplessly, staring at her own missing limbs. She had delicate features, with large eyes that slanted upward, and a pair of pillowy, pouting lips. She wore a hair ribbon, tied in an enormous pointy bow. It stuck up out of her head like cat's ears. Her face was bumpy, as if she'd been pulled out of a fire. Two spheres, the size of cantaloupes, sprouted from her chest. They weren't breasts, Alice saw, recoiling, but buttocks. The marionette had been dismembered, turned inside out and upside down. Her body parts were jumbled. One of her puppet legs had been amputated above the knee. The hollow stump gaped open. A crudely tied rope held her other leg in place. On her one remaining foot, she wore a single patent leather Mary Jane and a white anklet.

Alice turned away. Her flashlight fell on a well-appointed room. An abstract painting, in a gilt frame, hung over the mantel of a fireplace. A circular rug, pink and green, covered the floor.

Alice saw a polished wooden table, an armchair, and a couch. Two rocking chairs sat in front of the window. With their backs turned to Alice, they faced the glass. One chair was large. One chair was small. Beside each of the rocking chairs was a wooden easel, shaped like the letter A. One easel was large. One easel was small.

Alice reached out to the miniature rocking chair. Her hand touched something woolly. She turned the chair around. There sat the puppet in her anklets and her Mary Janes. She was four feet tall. The skin on her face was gray and lumpy. Her features were unfinished, unpainted, like a mask. On her head was a wig of luxuriant blond hair, so lifelike that it felt human to Alice's touch. She was dressed in a white pinafore, and she wore a necklace made of pearls. Whoever had taken her apart had put her back together again. Alice took the puppet in her arms and cradled it, like a baby.

She heard a whirring sound, followed by a click. Another whir. Another click.

An electric wheelchair with a man in it rolled into the room.

Alice let out a shriek and backed up against the window, clutching at her throat like a heroine in a monster movie. She brandished her flashlight, shining it at the old man. His shock of white hair was combed back from his face, which was as brown and wrinkled as a nut. He was emaciated. But his fierce black eyes glared at her with vitality.

"I'm sorry, sir," Alice stammered. "This is the wrong house."

He said nothing.

"Let me go, sir," she said. "I didn't mean it. I didn't think anybody lived here. I . . . I beg your pardon."

She thought his head had tipped forward, ever so slightly, as if bowing to her.

She crossed one leg in front of the other and, without knowing why, she curtsied.

A gurgle came from the throat of the ancient man.

"Sir, my name is Alice," she said.

He blinked.

"I'm really only eleven," she confided. "But I lied. I told people that I'm sixteen and a half."

The elderly gentleman had a plaid fringed blanket tucked over his lap. He was dressed in a silk smoking jacket with wide black lapels. He watched her, with his piercing gaze, in silence.

"They said no one lived here," she went on. "I was supposed to take the puppet. My Aunt Esmé sent me to the institute and went to California with a punk rocker."

The eyes were upon her, all-seeing, all-knowing, all-forgiving.

"Are you God?" Alice asked.

He frowned.

"God," whispered Alice, "I sucked someone's finger."

His chin dipped down toward his chest.

"Can't you speak, God, sir?" Alice said wonderingly.

His wrinkled head moved a half an inch to the left.

"No?" said Alice.

His wrinkled head moved a half an inch to the right.

Alice looked down at the puppet in her arms, and back to the old man. "Can't you move, God, sir?" she said, not able to meet his eyes while she asked him this.

She let out another short scream as the wheelchair spurred forward, stopping only a foot away from her. Now she saw the liver spots on his cheeks, the puckered pouches beneath his intelligent eyes, the richly embroidered brocade of his jacket, the ascot at his neck, the cleanly shaven face. His long, bony hands rested on either arm of the electric wheelchair. Embedded in the metal were three round buttons, one red, one green, and one blue. The old man's thumb rested on the control panel. Alice watched as his thumb flittered. When he hit the blue button, the wheelchair rolled itself a few inches backward. His eyes stayed on her face.

"You can't walk or talk anymore," Alice said, the words slipping out before she could stop them.

He blinked.

"God, you're broken," she said. "God, you're sick."

His gaze fell to his plaid blanket.

"You tore your puppet apart, didn't you?" said Alice. "And then you tried to fix it."

His eyes searched hers.

"You don't take good care of your toys, God," Alice said. "So I'm going to have to take the puppet away from you." Standing at his side, Alice touched the old man's shoulder. His shoulder blades were sharp.

"Is it okay with you?" she asked.

He scanned her face.

She put her hand at the back of his head. It was warm, like a new egg. She ran her fingers through his thinning hair. She patted him, rubbing his hair the wrong way, mussing it. When she was done rearranging his hair, the fine white strands stood on end.

The corner of his mouth curled upward, in a half-smile.

"Thank you," whispered Alice.

As he stared at her, immobile, his hand jerked on the controls. He pressed the blue button. The electric wheelchair rolled backward, down the hallway, with a whir and a click, disappearing into the dark room behind the staircase where it must have come from.

The Pool of Tears

t was a test, wasn't it!" Alice shouted as she burst into the photography studio, waving the puppet aloft like a trophy. "I
passed the test!" Alice said.

No one answered. The barn was dark.

Alice aimed the flashlight at the corners of the cavernous,
drafty space, shining it at the bales of hay, a metal rake, a flat tray
filled with plantings and seeds. "Hey, sis!" she called. "I did it!
Someone lived in the house. He looked a lot like God. But I took
the puppet anyway!"

"Say cheese," said a voice.

There was a burst of light. In it, Alice saw Hope and Faith
standing at the top of the pyramid. The Angel of Hope was holding a camera. The flashbulb flared, the shutter clicked, and the
dark returned.

Alice heard a peal of laughter.

"You dumb shit," said the Angel of Hope. "Tomorrow morning, I'm going to show this photograph to your beloved Odette Noko. I wonder what she'll think of her precious teacher's pet when she sees what you did. You ripped off the Great Man."

Alice stopped moving.

"Didn't you see the Miró, the Ernst?" said the Angel of Hope's voice, closer now. "He's got famous paintings on the wall. Didn't you recognize his photograph? It's from the *Games of the Puppet* series, a minor surrealist masterpiece. You idiot. You're holding it in your hands."

Alice shined her flashlight on the marionette. Its head hung forward, loosely, from its neck. Its blond wig was gone, having fallen off in transit.

"Do you have any idea what that surrealist object is worth, stupid?" said Faith. "It's priceless. It was manufactured in 1932, according to the Great Man's precise design. He's supposed to donate it to a major art museum in Paris. Wait until they hear about this. Noko will throw you out. You'll get sent to reform school. You'll be a juvenile delinquent for your whole life."

"Birdbrain," said the Angel of Hope. "You'll never win the prize. Not ever. Not now."

Alice dropped the puppet on the ground. She sprang out the door, running as fast as she could. Her bare feet pounded against the grass, and against the bare earth. She ran while a cramp pinched her side, she ran while she was wheezing. She gulped for breath and continued at a jog. On and on Alice went, uphill and down, through the woods and over the fields. After a while, the muscles in her legs stopped hurting and the perspiration on her forehead and stomach began to dry. She kept hiking until it seemed she had been moving forever and had never been any-place. By the time she saw the outline of a tree before her, Alice had grown numb. The sky had turned the color of an unripe peach. The sun had begun peering over the mountains when

Alice's burning feet finally hit the flat hard surface that she recognized as asphalt.

Alice was traipsing along the side of the road. Her feet stung from the impact. When she reached a crossroads, she saw a car coming toward her. Quite deliberately—yet consciously gauging how far away the car was—she ran across the road, making it to the other side only instants before the car reached her. It passed, honking furiously. Breathless, elated by a euphoric, death-defying mania, Alice waited by the bushes until she saw another car looming in the distance. As it approached, she dashed to the other side of the road a second time, taunting the traffic, daring it to miss her. She turned around in time to see the red-faced driver shake his fist at her.

"Imbecile!" he shouted. "Get off the road!"

Alice turned her back, ignoring him. Her chest heaved up and down. She concentrated all her attention on the horizon, where the next car would arrive for a new game of Russian roulette. She was delirious, dizzy with the certainty that she would play in traffic until it killed her. She'd run back and forth all morning, all afternoon. And the Angel of Hope and Faith, her ex-friends, would find the Giant Alice lying in a ditch by the side of the road. Then they'd feel bad, and so would Odette Noko, and Fitzy, and Dean, and Aunt Esmé, and Rain if she ever found out. Everyone would realize, at last, the damage they'd done. She would let a speeding automobile hit her to show them all how unloved she was.

She was so overwrought that she hardly heard the car door slamming behind her. When she glanced over her shoulder, she saw the red-faced man marching toward her. Alice froze. The depth and magnitude of her stupidity began to dawn on her.

"What the fuck is the matter with you, huh?" said the man when he was a few feet away. His arms were outstretched, flailing around. Alice could see, from the way his hands sliced through the air, that he wanted to hit her.

"Are you trying to get yourself killed?" shouted the man, scowling and furious. "Get the hell off the road. Do you hear me?"

A stranger's rage brought Alice to her senses. "I'm sorry," she said in a small voice.

"Where's your mother while you're out here playing in traffic like a Mongoloid? I could have run you over, flat as a pancake. You think this is funny? Somebody ought to smack you."

Alice turned her back on him.

"Don't you walk away from me," he said.

Alice marched along the side of the road. The asphalt slammed against her feet. She had absolutely no idea where she was going.

The road stretched out ahead of her, a bleak path of boredom and monotony. Mickey Mouse had faltered. The watch had stopped. She didn't know what time it was, or how long she'd been walking.

The sun was now a flat white disc, ringed in flame, caught low in the branches of a tree. Once, a car had slowed as it approached her. It had honked. "Need a ride?" shouted the driver. Alice had ignored it, staring ahead like a zombie. Slowly but steadily, Alice was getting lost. She couldn't return to the institute. She couldn't bear to be thrown out of the program by Odette. Every time she took an arbitrary turn and wandered down a new road, she decreased her chances of retracing her steps and successfully finding her way. Her feet felt raw. Her stomach growled. She was crying, and she'd been crying for a while. It was not a normal kind of crying, more like a spilling. She didn't sob, but tears streamed down her face. They made her vision blurry, turning the trees on either side of her into a shimmering sea of green. When she heard another car approach from behind her, Alice turned her head away.

"Hey," said a voice.

Alice kept walking.

"Hey, you," it called again.

Alice held her head high and marched forward to nowhere.

"Girl in a tree," said the voice—nasal, faltering, breathy. "Remember me?" There sat J.D., in the driver's seat, with his ratty ponytail. His mirrored sunglasses were perched on top of his head. His gray eyes were wide with what Alice thought was empathy.

"Hi, J.D.," Alice said, her voice high and thin.

"Hi, baby," said J.D. "How ya been?" He spoke to her as if they were old friends. He didn't tell her to get off the road or demand to know why she was miles away from the institute on her own.

"I'm okay," said Alice. For one confusing, tumultuous moment, she was overjoyed to see him. More than anything in the world, she wanted to rush to J.D.—as if she were his, his lost girl, his stray dog, his pet—and throw her arms around his neck. She resisted this impulse more out of embarrassment than mistrust. With J.D. waiting for her in the car, her isolation vanished. Somebody wanted her after all. She was flooded with a warmth for him so powerful she was unable to suppress it. It poured out of her eyes, and rolled down her shirtfront, until she thought she'd drown in a pool of tears.

"Can I give you a lift someplace, honey?" said J.D.

Alice shielded her face with her hand, hoping he wouldn't see that she was crying. She didn't want to show J.D. how she felt. Her heart was racing, her palms were sweating, and she was still battling the urge to fling herself at him, to kiss him everywhere, to beg him to adopt her.

"What's this?" said J.D., letting his motor idle. "You're not talking to me?"

J.D.'s Volkswagen continued to keep pace with her. "Well, I'll tell you what, princess," he said. "We could have this conversation much more easily if you got in the seat beside me."

Alice didn't reply.

He continued driving alongside her at a snail's pace. "You need a lift? Or do you prefer just walking along?" he said.

"I prefer just walking along," Alice said. She was reluctant to get in his car for a reason she couldn't pinpoint. Aunt Esmé had told her not to accept rides from strangers, though Alice had never entirely grasped the nature of the menace behind this warning. But despite her delight at seeing him, some self-protective instinct made her hesitate.

"Oh come on in," he coaxed. "I won't bite you."

Alice continued walking, eyeing him sidelong.

"Where is it that you're going exactly?" he said.

"No place," said Alice. She began to find it strange that he hadn't mentioned her tears. A typical adult, she thought, would have wanted to know what she was doing in the middle of nowhere, barefoot, and what was wrong. J.D. seemed more concerned, somehow, with the present—with the very instant that the two of them now found themselves in.

"Well, baby, I can get you to no place in particular in two minutes flat." He flashed her his sly, seductive grin.

"I don't need a ride, thank you," Alice said as the car crawled along beside her. J.D. leaned out of the driver's window, looking up at her.

"How come you have a circus car?" she asked him, narrowing her eyes.

"Have I got a circus car?"

"Yes," she said, studying the bubble-shaped roof of the old car and the brightly painted graffiti. Next to a peeling, bedraggled peace symbol was the word LOVE.

"What's a circus car, sweetheart?" said J.D. He drove along, seemingly perfectly content to conduct this conversation in this odd way, with Alice milling by the road and he inside his automobile.

"Like those little cars that twenty clowns climb out of," Alice said.

"I don't see any clowns in here," he told her, looking around the car's interior.

"It's so small," Alice pointed out. She'd seen Volkswagen Beetles before. Rabbit had owned one, briefly, before he'd violated a parking regulation and it had been towed away. Rabbit's Beetle had been such an old model that the rusted chassis, as soon as it was attached to the tow truck, had broken clean in two. Alice, privately, thought these dinky little cars were dumb. They looked like a child's plaything, no different from the electric cars that FAO Schwarz advertised in its catalogue.

"Is *that* why you won't join me? My car's not big enough for you?" said J.D. Again, he gave her that knowing, insinuating smile.

"I guess," said Alice, at a loss to explain her reservations.

"I know it looks like a piece of crap, princess. But the Beetle's better than you think."

Alice didn't respond. She watched him open the door to the passenger seat. He continued to drive that way, creeping along, with the door open.

"Save your strength, it's hot out," he said. "Wherever you're going, baby, I'll get you there eventually." He wiggled his eyebrows like Groucho Marx.

"No, thanks," Alice said, more firmly. She squinted at him, shielding her eyes against the sun. "I'm not really going anywhere," she said.

"You're rambling around?" he asked.

"I'm rambling," she agreed.

"Did you know your feet are bleeding?"

"What?" said Alice.

"You got your feet all cut up. Come sit down and let me help," he said.

Alice glanced down at her feet. They had undergone a metamorphosis. No longer the clean ivory feet of a city girl, they'd tanned a light golden brown. They were covered with dirt. And what J.D. had said was right. She must have cut them while she was running. Lines of vermilion liquid ran up between her toes. The ankle of her left foot was bleeding. The red looked shocking and surreal under the blue sky, beside the greenery. Alice stared down at it, mesmerized as she often was by the sight of blood, and the incredible fact that this unlikely substance was always circulating through her veins, unseen but plentiful, a complicated plumbing system hidden inside her.

"Does it hurt?" J.D. asked.

"No," Alice told him, though now that he'd alerted her to the injury, it was beginning to.

"Why don't you stop a minute and I'll stop too," he suggested. "We can get this problem taken care of. How's that?" He steered the car off the road and parked it beneath the shade of a pine tree.

Alice approached him. He'd opened the VW's glove compartment and was rummaging around inside it. Peering in, Alice saw half a dozen plastic baggies. Each one was tied with a rubber band. Like the kind Aunt Esmé kept in her toy chest back home, they were lined up neatly in a row.

"I know I've got some friggin' Band-Aids in here someplace," he muttered. "For just such occasions. You never do know, sweetie, when you're going to run into a Princess Alice. A girl with a boo-boo. A fawn whose hoof is lame."

"You never know," Alice agreed.

"Aha." He shot her a glance. "Found 'em. Park your tootsies over here." Swiveling toward her, J.D. spread his legs open into a wide V. They were clad in tight faded jeans. They looked large and engulfing. The sight of them alarmed her. She didn't move.

He held up a box of Band-Aids and rattled it. "*Alice in Wonderland*," he said. "Just for you."

"What is?" Alice said.

"These Band-Aids, babe. That's what it says on the package."

Alice leaned forward and studied the Band-Aid box. "Those aren't *Alice in Wonderland* Band-Aids," she told him sternly.

"Aren't they?" He looked down at it, surprised. "I thought they were. Okay, I stand corrected. *Snow White and the Seven Dwarfs*. Whatever."

"I just use regular Band-Aids," Alice said disdainfully. "The Band-Aids with cartoons on them are for babies."

"You think? You mean, not only is my car too small but my Band-Aid collection is unacceptable?"

"Yes," said Alice.

He crossed his legs. "Well, you know, Princess Alice, the point of this wasn't to make a fashion statement, or to separate the women from the girls—as it were—or the girls from the babies."

"What do you mean?" asked Alice suspiciously.

"The point of giving you a Band-Aid was because you cut your foot. I didn't realize, Alice, that the type of bandage was going to be so very deeply important to you."

"It isn't," Alice admitted.

"Well then, give it here." He made a cup out of his hands and held it out toward Alice, near his knee.

Alice lifted her foot up and placed it, gingerly, inside his hands.

"What a foot," he said. "Is that a foot or what? Look at this arch. You've got a high arch there, Princess Alice. Yes you do."

"Is that good?"

"Good? You kidding me? You *bet* it's good. A high arch is a, ah, it's a mark of distinction." He'd placed her foot on his thigh and begun fiddling with a white plastic container. It was the size and shape of a lunch box. A bright red cross was stamped across it, in the center.

Alice watched, apprehensively, as J.D. removed a bottle from the first aid kit.

"Is that disinfectant?" she asked. It was a small glass bottle, like the kind Alice remembered Rain and Dean used to bring home when they'd gone someplace on an airplane.

"Actually, Alice, it's gin."

"Gin?"

"Gin, yeah." He looked down at it inquiringly, as if the bottle might speak for itself. "I don't remember where it came from. It should do the trick, though, in this situation. But it might sting." Unscrewing the cap, he handed it to Alice.

She took it, puzzled.

"Drink me, Princess Alice," he urged. "Drink me." He spoke in a girlish falsetto, pretending—Alice figured—to be the bottle of gin talking.

"Aren't you supposed to sterilize cuts?" she said accusingly. He obviously had never taken care of anybody, she thought. A baby-sitter, a mother, an aunt, or a father would never have handed her a bottle of gin. "You have to clean it," she reminded him, since he seemed inept at this essential element of child care.

"I am, honey. But you better fortify yourself first."

"For what?"

"It may hurt. No. Let me be completely honest with you. Not may. Will."

Alice delicately removed her foot from J.D.'s lap. "I don't want to then," she said. "Don't you have any of that disinfectant that doesn't sting? The cream?"

"Ah, the cream that doesn't sting," he said. "I wish I *did* have that. Doesn't everyone? They haven't invented that cream yet, Alice. Have they?"

"Ethyl buys it at Falk Drugstore, on 112th and Broadway," Alice said, frowning. "At home."

"A Hundred and Twelfth and Broadway. Is that where you come from?"

"That's near Ethyl's house," she explained. Alice peeled, nervously, at the edge of the label on the liquor bottle. The shiny paper was black and gold.

"My old school is around there, you know," said J.D.

"It is?" Alice brightened. The thought of J.D. being near her in the fall made her happy. She coughed, feeling exposed by her own enthusiasm.

"The school I went to once," he said. "I dropped out a decade ago."

"Oh," said Alice, disappointed.

"Well, not exactly. No," he answered, though she hadn't asked him anything. He looked at her. "Why is it that in your presence, I feel compelled to confess? I didn't drop out, Alice. They kicked me."

"Kicked you where?" Alice asked.

"They kicked me out of college."

"What for?"

"For writing Latin, baby. For writing Latin phrases on the wall."

"I thought they'd probably want you to write Latin when you're in college," Alice said.

"I thought so too, Alice. I thought so too. But that was a few years ago, and Columbia University wasn't ready for me. I'll bet students write the same thing on the wall every day there now. And no one bothers them. That's how it goes, Princess Alice, when you're a trailblazer."

"A trailblazer?" Alice said.

"Someone who does stuff before the rest of the crowd. Someone who's ahead of his time." He pointed at the gin. "Someone like me, sweetheart, who doesn't believe you have to be twenty-one to take a shot of that. Why *should* you be? You're a human being, aren't you? It's your *mouth*, isn't it? It's your stomach. It's your *right* to put whatever the fuck you want to in it. Excuse my language. Including, if it pleases you, a drop of gin."

Alice tipped back the bottle and took a minuscule sip. She made a face. "It's gross," she said.

"Have you never had gin before?"

She shook her head.

He touched her elbow. "Have some more, baby. It's an acquired taste."

"That's what my aunt says about Led Zeppelin. I don't like it." She tried to give it back to him.

He pushed her hand away. "You will. Trust me."

"It tastes bad. It tastes like medicine."

"It is," he said.

"I don't need any medicine. There's nothing wrong with me."

"You've got me there, Alice. That's absolutely true. I'm the lovesick fool here. Not you." He stared at Alice with his cool gray eyes. Alice felt a surprising impulse to reach out and feel his eyelashes with the tip of her finger. They looked appealing to her, like thick satin fringe.

"You drink it then," she told him.

"Don't mind if I do. You go first, though."

"I'll have some, and you'll have some too," Alice bargained.

"Excellent plan."

She took another sip.

"You can do better than that," he advised. "Take a nice big long swig of it."

Alice held her nose between her thumb and index finger, as she did when Ethyl made her drink particularly heinous cough medicines. "Yuck," she said.

"See?" He pointed to the bottle. "I recognize a potential convert when I see one, Alice. You complained. You kicked and screamed. You protested, Alice. And then—see what happened?"

"What?"

"You downed half the bottle."

"I did?" said Alice.

"Just about." He took the bottle from her, and as he did, he ran his hand along Alice's fingers. He stroked them slowly. Even when his hand was gone, his touch lingered. Alice looked down at her skin in surprise. She felt as if the two hands—his and hers—had been communicating on their own, speaking in a private language, like two lovebirds she'd once seen perching with their heads together.

"You starting to feel it now?" said J.D.

"To feel what?" said Alice.

A smile appeared on one side of his face. "The gin," he said. "The gin."

"A little," Alice admitted. "Yes." A warmth was spreading over her. It was like having the sun shine on her back, except the heat began in her chest. She felt lightheaded, as she had when she'd smoked J.D.'s pot.

"Are you ready now?" said J.D.

"For what?"

"To be cleansed. Not that you're in need of cleansing, really. But you did screw your feet up there a little, sweetheart." He touched her calf, like a shoe store clerk, and lifted her leg, drawing it toward him and placing it on his bony kneecap. Alice, standing in front of him, steadied herself. She held on to the door.

"Whatever you do, Princess Alice, please don't *scream*. Because, see, if you scream, state troopers will materialize from out of nowhere. They'll think I'm molesting you. And kidnapping you. And everything. And they'll drag me off in chains, Alice, and arrest me."

"No they won't," said Alice. "You're lying."

"I wish I were. I wish."

"Why would I scream, anyway? You're just going to pour that on my foot, right?" said Alice.

"That's right. And I've warned you, it'll probably hurt. I wish there were a way to get the job done without some pain. But I don't know how to do that, I'm afraid."

"Just pour on a little," Alice instructed.

"Yes ma'am."

"I'll tell you when to stop," she said.

"A fine plan, Alice. Very fair." He tilted the bottle, and a drop fell on her foot.

"Ouch," said Alice.

"How was that?"

"It stings."

"A lot?"

"Kind of," Alice said.

"Shall I continue?"

"Isn't that enough already?" she asked.

"Enough already. I suppose." He stooped down and looked at the cut on her foot closely. "It might be. I can't say this is a meticulous job I've done here, Alice. It's what you'd call quick and sloppy."

"Could you just put the Band-Aid on it? Or give it to me, and I will," said Alice.

He handed her the strip of adhesive and gauze, which he'd torn out of its rectangular packet. Alice pressed it carefully down on her ankle.

"I pronounce you cured," he said. "My condition, however, is more critical. Alas. It's worsened considerably."

"What condition?" said Alice, testing her foot out, stamping it on the ground to see how sore it was.

"Being in love," he said, "with you."

Alice didn't look at him. "Since when?" she asked after a minute.

"Who can say? I think, probably, since the first second I laid eyes on you."

"Don't act stupid," Alice warned him.

"I'll try not to," he said.

Alice had put her bandaged foot on the running board of the Volkswagen, and now she could feel J.D.'s leg beside hers. She could feel the warmth of his body through his jeans. It was only their two calves that were touching—a small space on their skins. But where their limbs made physical contact, beside the driver's seat of J.D.'s car, Alice felt as if she'd been fused to him. She imagined that if she allowed other parts of herself to touch him, those too would become attached to him. The two of them would be stuck together just the way her G.I. Joe and Barbie doll had been once, many years earlier, when Alice had conducted an experiment upon them with a stick of Krazy Glue.

The Underworld

J. D. let his hand drop, gently, like a falling leaf, onto her leg. Now his fingers were resting quietly on her inner thigh. "How can I convince you?" he said.

She kept her foot up on the running board, as if it were a step. "Of what?" she said, still not moving away from the hand, but paying studious attention to what it was doing. It was only lying there, peacefully. J.D.'s hand at rest alongside her crotch. It seemed to have gotten there on its own, without him—by chance.

"That I'll treat you right," he said.

"But when I met you . . ." Alice began.

"When you met me. Yes?"

"You said I should leave so that you didn't . . ." She paused, trying to pronounce the word he'd used. "Corrupt me," she concluded.

"I wish you wouldn't listen to me, Alice. I'm full of shit most of the time."

"Were you full of shit just now when you said that you were nice?"

"Probably." He took his hand away from her thigh. Alice couldn't tell if she was glad or sorry that she could no longer feel his touch. His fingers had given her a melting feeling, which she liked.

Backing away from her, further into the car, he put his arms up over his head and stretched.

Alice had stepped down from the running board. She half wanted to do the thing he'd spoken of, the corruption, whatever that was. Fidgeting, she gathered her hair into her hand. She began to separate it, carefully, combing it out with her fingers until she had three thick blond cords. She focused all her concentration on braiding her hair. Casually, as if it were an afterthought, she said, "Do you want to be my boyfriend?"

"Why, Alice," said J.D., "how forward of you."

Alice stole a glance at him to see if he was joking.

"Of course," he said in a different voice. "I'd like that. I'm glad you asked." He bit his lip. Alice had the feeling that he was playing a joke on her, or that he was only saying he'd be her boyfriend because he felt sorry for her.

"Do you mean it for real?" she asked him.

"I do," he said.

Having popped the question, Alice wasn't certain how to proceed. The hesitant, cautious, warning feeling hadn't gone away. She wasn't sure it ever would, not even if she drew him toward her, commandingly, as if she were Rabbit and J.D. were Alice. Not even if he led her hand to the fly of his jeans, pressing down hard on her fingers the way Rabbit had done. There was some gap between Alice and J.D.—a discomfort, an imbalance, a fundamental inequality. She knew the problem. J.D. was a grown-up. Alice regarded this as a surmountable barrier. She searched for a means to get to know him better, to feel he really was her boyfriend, despite his advanced age.

"Are you old?" she asked him, to try to calculate how far apart they were, in time.

"Are you?" he countered.

"You already asked me that."

"And when I asked you," he said, "what did you say?"

"That I'm . . . sixteen and a half," said Alice.

"Well then, Princess Alice. I'm . . . sixteen and a half, too," J.D. said.

"Then why do you have those long gray hairs on your head? Why do you have those bags and wrinkles around your eyes?"

"My *God*, Alice. Do I? How unsightly. How unseemly of me."

Alice leaned in close and touched his face.

J.D.'s nose twitched like a dog's nose—a quivering, a testing of the currents of air around it, a sensing of the dangers and the possibilities. He closed his eyes.

Alice explored his face with her fingertips, letting them run down his cheeks and tapping at them very lightly, pretending that her fingertips were rain.

"That feels nice," J.D. whispered.

"Why are you whispering?" Alice whispered back.

"So as not to disturb you," he whispered. "So that you won't stop."

"Stop what?" Alice asked.

"Touching me that way."

Alice did the rain thing again, since he seemed to like it. It pleased her to do things that people liked, as long as their requests struck her as reasonable. Rabbit was unreasonable. Maybe

J.D., being an adult instead of a teenager, would have a better sense of dignity and self-control, two qualities that Alice valued.

"I like the way you smell," Alice told him.

"I like the way you smell, too," J.D. said, still whispering, still with his eyes closed.

Alice sniffed his hair. It had a complex odor, not like Alice's braid, which contained the single scent of herbal shampoo. J.D.'s hair smelled of the outdoors and the indoors—of wind and marijuana, of sweat, of soil, of moss, of leaves, of bodies, of incense, and of breath. She put her own cheek against his. It was stubbly and rough. She continued to run her hand along his face. The wrinkles were as thin as strands of cotton thread. They radiated from the outer corners of his eyes, white against his suntanned skin, like starfish.

J.D. shifted his position on the seat of his car. He opened his legs up again, like a scissors. This time, Alice stood fearlessly between them. She knew that within the space of a few seconds his legs would begin moving. Inevitably, they would close in on either side of her, like a gate. This knowledge came to her intuitively. Much later on, it would seem especially terrible to her—that she had been complicitous, that she had known such things. Slowly, as if she had made it happen by thinking about it, J.D.'s open legs began to close. They reminded Alice of the jaws, in the film about flowers, on a Venus flytrap.

"Hello," he said amiably when she was inside his grip. It was the way he'd greeted her up in the tree that day. This made Alice think that being close to her turned J.D. into a whole other person.

"Hello," she told him. To her own surprise, Alice put her arms around his neck.

"Fancy meeting a girl like you in a place like this," he said. She could feel him squeezing her with his leg muscles.

"Does everyone really call you J.D.?" Alice asked, drawing back to look at his face. Now her own hand had dropped, like a falling leaf, onto J.D.'s knee. He covered it with his own. He didn't answer her question. Alice flipped her hand over and clasped his. Now they were holding hands. Alice's mind went blank. For a long time, for forever, she couldn't think. They're holding hands, said a disembodied voice in her head, a voice that made no judgment, a voice that was observing and narrating. She felt a chaotic fluttering in her stomach, and a tingling at the back of her thighs, her lower back, and her neck. More words floated through her brain. She thought of good and evil. She felt a curious combination—about the hand-holding—of triumph and revulsion. There was something wrong with it, doing this with a grown man. Alice knew that. The feeling passed.

J.D.'s palms were clammy. They hadn't been sweaty before. They'd started sweating all of a sudden. At this, Alice was deeply dismayed. How disappointing that J.D., who seemed so superior to Rabbit in every other way, could have the same moist, babyish palms that Rabbit had. It was a real failing on J.D.'s part, Alice felt. She noted it. Then she forgave him.

Alice tried to pull away. He released his hold on her and let her go. He made a barely audible noise in the back of his throat. She watched his Adam's apple leap up and down. He swallowed. Alice wondered if it would be J.D., instead of her, who might burst into tears. She could see that she'd upset or flustered him, just as he'd upset or flustered her. So she touched his face again, to steady him, smoothing down the hair on his right temple. His hair felt heavy and slightly greasy. He was looking at Alice's breasts the way boys and men so often did. It was a greedy, fierce expression, alert and predatory. This was why they were both ruffled and upset. The trouble began with Alice, with THE BREASTS. An image came to her, of her breasts turning into shiny red apples. One by one, she would feed these apples to him. She shivered, first repulsed and then delighted by this vision. She couldn't tell whose thought it had been—J.D.'s or her own. She felt herself gradually losing hold of something, her own sensible nature, her own self. Her breasts, her hands, her arms—all parts of her were whispering. Her essential being, her very Aliceness, was quietly drifting far away. She heard the urgings of their limbs to entwine. It was bad, she thought, to be able to hear it. She wasn't sure what either of them would do. Her gaze fell on their two hands—hers small and fair, his large and tanned. A long time passed with nobody speaking, except for the burning words that weren't said aloud.

"Well?" said Alice, keeping her voice level and matter-of-fact.

"Well, what, baby?" said J.D.

"I asked you if your name really is J.D. It's too short. I feel silly calling you by letters."

"You can call me whatever you like. Call me Rover, for all I care."

"Rover," said Alice, "is a dog's name. Do you want to be my boyfriend? Or my dog."

"I think Rover would be entirely appropriate, at least while I'm drooling. Don't you?"

"I don't know," said Alice.

"Then call me Jay."

"Is that what your girlfriends call you?" Alice said in a businesslike tone. It was peculiar, Alice thought, this bossy new way she was talking to him. She needed to feel she was in charge of things.

"Nah. Usually they call me Hey You Big Fucking Jerk. Which *you* won't do. Will you?"

"No, I won't," Alice said.

"Promise?"

"I promise."

"So what would you like to do, Princess Alice?" J.D. asked. "Now that we're boyfriend and girlfriend. Or do I look a gift horse in the mouth if I ask you that?"

Alice couldn't say. She wondered what a gift horse was.

"How about we go to the lake together and go swimming?" said J.D.

"I can't swim," said Alice.

"No?"

"No, and I don't have my bathing suit," Alice pointed out. Their hands were swinging back and forth, like a pendulum. The pendulum of Alice and J.D. oscillated this way and that, toward the car window to the steering wheel and back again. "We could go back and get it," she said. "Except . . ." She thought about Odette Noko and the trouble with the puppet, and the twins.

"I don't think we should do that," said J.D.

"Why not?"

"Someone might get the wrong idea if they saw us together."

The wrong idea. The term disturbed her. "It's a secret then?" Alice asked.

"Yes."

"Everyone's always keeping me a secret," Alice observed, thinking of Rabbit.

"Everyone? Really? I had no idea, Alice, that you were such the 'it' girl."

"What's the 'it' girl?"

"The gal about town. How many boyfriends do you have?"

"None," Alice said. "Just one guy that's a secret."

"One guy, meaning me?"

"One *other* one," said Alice.

"I see. Thanks for telling me, Alice." She hadn't been able to look at him for quite some time now. She stole a glance at his face. His expression was sulky.

"He's a *boy*," she said consolingly. "It's only Rabbit."

"Only Rabbit. Only!"

"Should I tell him to stop it?" Alice asked.

"I'd like that. Is it too much to ask?"

"I'm leaving in a few days," Alice reminded him. "I can tell Rabbit to stop it when I get back."

"You do that. Can I drive you to the lake now, little girl-friend? For a swim."

"I don't know how to float," Alice said. "I haven't got my in-flatable pillow. And like I told you, I haven't got my swimsuit."

"I'll teach you. Floating's very easy."

"I tried it, but I sink."

"Preposterous. Impossible. No one sinks. Water is buoyant. You don't have to do a thing. You just lie there. I can teach you to float like that." He snapped his fingers. "Once you know how to float, there's nothing to swimming."

"I used to be able to," Alice confided.

"To swim?"

"Yeah."

"You forgot?"

"I stopped swimming because of sharks," said Alice.

"So then you *do* know how to swim."

"I knew before, but now I don't."

"Hmmm, that's weird, little girlfriend. I've never heard of that. Usually, once you learn to swim, you don't forget."

Alice shrugged. "I had nightmares about this great white shark, and then I didn't like swimming anymore."

"That's a pity," J.D. said. "Nightmares should never stop you from doing things you want to in real life."

"I have the nightmare while I'm awake," Alice explained. "Whenever I go to the swimming hour at the pool on Ninety-second Street. I try to swim, but I keep thinking about the shark. That it's coming to get me. And then I can't."

"There aren't any sharks in a swimming pool, honey."

Alice rolled her eyes. "I know that," she said. "I see a great white in my head, and I can't swim when I see him. Sometimes I just see the fin, coming up out of the water and moving toward me. He's hungry."

"What if I told you that he's not a dangerous shark at all, but a gentle one?" said J.D. "A friendly shark who doesn't do anybody any harm? Certainly not you, at least."

Alice put her hands on her hips. "I wouldn't believe you," she said.

"Come on. We'll drive over to the lake, and we'll see." J.D. gave her hand a squeeze.

"I'm not supposed to get inside of strangers' cars," Alice pointed out.

"Ah," said J.D. "Now there's your source."

"My source?"

"The source of your nightmares. Who can blame you? They contain a grain or two of truth. It's what you're taught—to fear. Take me, for example. A man with a car. A man with a fin—you might say—and appetites. Do *I* look like a stranger?"

Alice, playing with his fingers, thought about this. "I'm not sure. You might be," she said.

"How can I be your boyfriend and a stranger at the same time?"

"I think you can, probably."

Bending down, he kissed the back of Alice's hand. "I think so too," he said. "I think you're smart not to get inside strange boyfriends' cars. I wouldn't want to be the one to interfere with all this wise practical training that you've had. I'll lock the car and we'll walk over there. How's that?"

"All right," Alice agreed.

"See? I knew we could work this thing out between us, little girlfriend. I'm a reasonable guy. And I'm willing to make compromises. Doesn't that sound fair?"

"I guess," she said dubiously. When he'd spoken just now, she'd been looking at his throat. There was a bump there, the Adam's apple, which had been continuously leaping up and down. Since she'd begun speaking with him in his car, J.D. had kept on swallowing. He seemed nervous about coming out and asking Alice for what he wanted. Of course, it was a drub J.D. was angling for, Alice felt. But instead of kissing her and unzipping himself, as Rabbit did, he was getting her to talk about other things while the drub was on his mind. It would be easier just to drag J.D. off into the woods with her for a second and give him one.

"Why don't you take these, baby? So your feet don't bother you," said J.D. He handed her a pair of flip-flops that he'd taken from the floor of his car.

"Who do these belong to?" Alice asked as she put them on.

"They're Faith's, princess. I'm sure she wouldn't mind. She'd let you borrow them." He picked up a zippered duffel bag and carried it with him.

"Is Faith your girlfriend, too?" asked Alice.

"We're just buddies, me and Faith. Faith and I are pals." They began to walk, hand in hand, into the forest. Faith's rubber sandals made a flapping sound as they hit against the soles of Alice's feet. J.D., in sneakers, moved along more quietly. They walked for a while in silence. The ground was covered with magnolia blossoms, which had turned brown. It smelled like perfume. They emerged in a clearing, where two crows were hopping around a tree stump. Alice could see the faint outline of a path leading down a hill among the stones and grass. It was a worn trail, made on the ground from people's feet tramping along, each one walking in just the same place, in just the same direction.

"The lake's that way," said J.D., sticking out his thumb. "But if we head in this direction, over where those trees are, we'll wind up in a better spot. It's always empty there, and we can be alone."

Alice didn't respond. He'd taken his mirrored sunglasses out of the breast pocket of his denim jacket and put them on. They made him look remote and aloof, as if he had on a mask.

"Would you rather go to the popular spot, baby?" he said. "There's a beach. Where all the kids hang out."

"Maybe."

"I leave it entirely up to you, Alice. I'm like putty in your hands. Your wish is my command. You tell me where we ought to go. I'll take you."

"You don't have to pretend like that," said Alice softly.

"Pretend what?" J.D. let his sunglasses fall down onto the bridge of his nose. He peered at her from over the rims.

"Look, I know what you want, okay?" said Alice.

"You do?"

"Yeah. I know why you keep saying we should go swimming in private. I'm not completely stupid."

"Perish the thought, Princess Alice. It never crossed my mind that you were stupid. Not even a little bit."

"You might as well just ask me," she said. "You don't have to sneak."

"Do I seem sneaky to you?"

"Kind of."

"You don't approve of sneakiness?" he said.

"Not really."

"You're a smart girl, aren't you?

"Not especially. I flunked the . . ." Alice had begun to tell him that she'd failed at school, getting D's and F's in most of her subjects in the sixth grade. But then she remembered that she'd told him she was sixteen. If J.D. was sneaky, she was sneaky too.

"Flunked the what?" asked J.D.

"Nothing," Alice told him. "If you want a drub you should just ask me for one."

"A drub?"

"A D-rub."

"Forgive me. I'm afraid I don't know what a D-rub is."

"A dick rub," Alice said. "You never heard of that?" Though she'd never known what it was until Rabbit had shown her, Alice had assumed all boys did.

"I can't say that I've heard it called that. But now that you've explained . . . Well, sure. I know from dick rubs." He put his hand on top of her head and twisted it, as if Alice's head were a jar. As he turned his hand, she was forced to move her neck. "Alice, look at me a sec," he said.

She stared into the reflective mirrors that covered his eyes. She saw her own face inside the chrome. Her features, distorted by the lenses, were skinny and elongated in the middle. Her forehead and her jaw fanned out on either side. She looked like an hourglass with a pair of eyes, a nose, and a mouth drawn on it.

"Is that what you think this is all about, baby? A dick rub?" he said.

Alice nodded.

"According to you, I'm trying to pull you over to the dark side of the woods to make you jerk me off?"

"Probably," Alice ventured.

"Princess Alice. A mere sixteen. Or thereabouts. And already so cynical?"

"I guess," she said.

"Do you think I'd be so selfish, little girlfriend? Honestly. What kind of rube do you take me for? You hurt my feelings."

The conversation left Alice somewhat mystified. But she soldiered on, determined to get to the bottom of it. "When you said you'd be my boyfriend," she said, "wasn't it a dick rub? Isn't it a dick rub that you wanted?"

"Oh, Alice. O ye of little faith. I wouldn't turn a dick rub down, dear. But no, it wasn't what I wanted."

They were headed away from the path—toward the place he'd told her was deserted, where no one went, where they could be private. He'd made such a fuss over telling her that they didn't have to go there that Alice didn't see the point in objecting now. He wasn't sneaking, she thought. She'd told him not to sneak. She'd asked if he wanted what Rabbit had wanted, and now they were openly discussing it. Alice had the sense that things were fair between her and J.D.—frank, mature, and aboveboard. The more they talked about sexual matters, the more Alice felt that J.D. wasn't perverted. Speaking about it, under a clear blue sky, had the effect of making J.D. seem trustworthy. They'd come to a shaded area, filled with tall leafy trees. J.D. took off his sunglasses and put them inside the front pocket of his jacket. He looked at Alice carefully.

"Look, I know you're not of age," he said. "It doesn't bother me."

"Of age?" she echoed. She'd never heard the expression.

"You're just a kid, sweetheart. It's perfectly obvious. You talk a nice game, but you're an innocent."

"I'm not innocent," Alice protested.

J.D.'s dimple appeared in his left cheek. He gave her a ghost of his radiant big smile. "It's all right," he said. "It isn't a bad thing to be."

"I'm not, though."

It had gotten cloudy and overcast, Alice thought. But when she looked up, the sun was still out. They were in a dark spot, dense with vegetation. Alice felt herself get cold.

"Alice, Alice," he said. "You don't need to lie to me."

"I'm not," she said. Her voice had fallen to a whisper. There was something in his expression that she hadn't seen before—a gleam in his eyes, a tone in his voice. She didn't like it.

"I've been around the block and back, kiddo. I know a virgin when I see one."

Alice had stopped breathing. The word "virgin" sounded menacing and frightful. It was the way he'd said it, caressing the phrase as if it contained a hidden pearl. She'd heard him hold on to the syllables in his mouth the way he held in the smoke from dope.

"It's a nice place to be, baby. You don't have to act like you're not there. You don't have to be somebody else with me, Alice. You be you."

Alice didn't feel it was a nice place—not the place she was standing in with J.D., alone in a glade, where she couldn't see or hear anyone for miles around.

"I *am* being me," she told him steadily. She looked him in the eye. "I'm not the age I said."

His face changed, the half-smile turning dark and mean. "I know that, babe," he said. "I ran into Hope and Faith at Hanson's Diner the day we met. Alice *Cale* was with them. They told me that you're Alice Duncan."

Alice couldn't account for the sickening sensation that filled her intestines, the feeling that she was guilty of a crime.

"You're Dean's kid. Esmé's sister. Aren't you?"

She hung her head without answering, ashamed of both of them.

"I'm not pissed off at you, Alice Duncan," he said. "Maybe I should be. But I do know why you lied."

Alice was speechless.

"Do *you* know why?" he asked.

"Why what?" said Alice.

"Why you lied to me."

Alice's fear rose. "No," she said.

"I think you do know, little girlfriend."

Alice didn't want to be his little girlfriend anymore.

"And the real you is, what? Fess up. Fifteen?" he said.

Alice glanced around the grove of trees, searching for one that might be suitable for climbing. She felt a need, all at once, to be up off the ground, in a higher place—away from J.D.

"Fourteen?" J.D. said. She felt as if he were offering her something and lowering the price bit by bit.

"Fourteen," Alice chose.

"I think you know," he said. "I think we both know why you're here."

"Let's go to the lake now," Alice told him loudly.

J.D. walked over to a patch of green grass under the shade of a tree. He lay down on his side, propping himself up on one elbow. His long legs were sprawled out like a pair of plastic Pick Up sticks. His posture was stubborn and defiant. It was as if, now that Alice had expressed a desire to go to the lake, he was demonstrating that he wouldn't listen, he wouldn't go.

"Love doesn't have a number on it, does it?" he asked.

"I don't know," Alice told him. She didn't like what was happening to her voice. It was getting higher and higher. She had that same sensation that she'd had when she first arrived at the Balthus compound—that she was shrinking. In another moment, Alice thought, she'd start to cry again. She felt humiliated by being tearful so often, and by so often acting like a coward.

This was not how she wished to be. She wished to be strong and fearless.

"The squares might give a shit," he said. "But not me. Why should it make any difference? I say: Alice, *try everything once.* We're all pleasure seekers. We live so damn briefly. You'll grow old real fast, believe me."

She heard anger in his voice. She couldn't tell whether it was directed against her or something else.

"Come here to me, baby," he said in this same angry way. He patted the grass next to him.

Alice didn't move. "Why should I?" she asked.

"Because, sweetheart, this is the end of the road."

"No it isn't."

"It is for us. I don't know where we are. I'm afraid, Alice, that we're lost."

"No we're not."

"I don't have any idea which way to go. So come over here and help me figure it out."

Alice pointed ahead. "You said the lake was near here," she said accusingly. Her voice was shrill.

"I must have taken a wrong turn someplace. I don't know how to find it. I'm sorry, Alice."

"Are you telling the truth?" she said. "Or are you pretending?"

"I honestly don't know where we are. Or where we're going."

"I don't like this," Alice told him.

"It's okay. We'll find it. Relax. Let's just lie down here a minute."

"Why should we lie down? What about the lake? What about swimming?"

But J.D. just reclined on his back. "Come over here with me," he said, directing the question to the sky. He was taking a cigarette out of his shirt pocket, putting it between his lips. Alice watched in silence while he lit it.

"You see, I knew it," Alice told him, bitterly. She strode toward him, sat down a few feet away, and crossed her arms over her chest.

"Knew what?" The smoke billowed like a sail in front of him.

"You just want a drub," said Alice.

"You're wrong." He kept talking to the space above his head. "I told you. What I'm interested in is love."

"You do want a drub," Alice whispered. "You *do*. You're a pervy creep. I should have realized that. It's pretty obvious."

"I just want to lie in the grass for a while with you. Is that a problem?"

"Well, you might ask *me* if I want to," Alice said.

"Would you like to lie in the grass with me, Alice-who-wishes-she-was-sixteen-for-reasons-I-can-guess?"

"No, I wouldn't. I would like to go swimming. Now."

J.D. sighed. He looked up, arching his neck. "What made me think this was going to be easy?" he said to the trees.

"What was?" Alice asked.

"Beating the enemy. The enemy inside."

"What enemy?" she said.

"Our inner Victorian. The struggle, Alice, against centuries of repression. The fight to trust our natural instincts and free ourselves."

"That has nothing to do with *me*," Alice told him.

He took off his sunglasses. His eyelashes fluttered. "Doesn't it?" he said.

"No," said Alice. "It doesn't.'

"I want to set you free, baby. Won't you let me?"

"I don't need to be set free," Alice insisted. "It's only now. It's only now that I feel stuck."

J.D. blinked several times in rapid succession. "Right now you mean?" he asked, astonished. "You feel stuck here with me? You feel cornered?"

"Yes," said Alice.

"My apologies, little girlfriend."

"I'm not your little girlfriend," she said. "I want to go home. Don't call me that anymore."

J.D. rolled over onto his stomach, closer to Alice. She wanted to move away from him, but found she was immobilized. He stroked her ankle with his thumb. "Poor Alice," he said with a smile. "I think I've terrified you."

She didn't respond.

"You don't mind if I smoke a jay before our swimming lesson, do you?" He continued smiling and smiling. He seemed to enjoy Alice's discomfort. She refused to let him see her fear, to let him see her suffer, to let him win.

"Yeah," said Alice, "I do mind. I want to get out of here. I don't want to go swimming."

"Aw, princess. Don't be that way."

"I'm not a princess." She was starting to dislike him more and more.

"One short swim and then I'll return you. Unharmed," he said.

Alice didn't like the idea of herself as a piece of equipment— a raft or an inflatable inner tube—to be borrowed and "returned, unharmed."

"I don't want to swim anymore," she told him.

"Please?" he said.

Why was he—his eyes and his pleading tone—so hard to resist? So easily, so effortlessly, J.D. wore her down. "Then I want to go to the shore of the lake, where there are other people," she insisted, though she knew that she'd already given in.

"Can I ask you a personal question?" he said.

Alice shrugged.

"Do you think I'd rape you?" he said. He said it in an even, contemplative tone as if the question puzzled him.

The word "rape," like the words "virgin" and "love," hit Alice with the force of a blow. She felt she and J.D. were engaged in an invisible battle, and that the psychic violence between them had escalated. Alice looked in his eyes. The word hurt.

"I mean it," he said. "Is that what you think of me?"

Alice's throat felt parched. "I don't know," she said.

"You don't need to be afraid of me," he said. "Don't you believe that I'm your boyfriend? Could a real boyfriend ever rape you?"

Alice thought this over. "I don't know what it means," she admitted. This was true. She thought of "rape" as a four-letter word, not much different from the other ones she'd heard adults use. In Dean's studio, she'd seen the photograph of a statue. It was called *The Rape of Persephone*. It was sculpted by someone hundreds of years ago, Dean said, and it was an "exquisite work." A muscular man lifted Persephone up, holding her high in his arms. Persephone twisted her torso, trying to escape, to struggle. Where the man grasped her thigh, his thumb pressed into her skin. Like real flesh, Dean had said admiringly. Even the tear on Persephone's white cheek looked real, a droplet of white stone. That was what Alice knew of rape, that Persephone was so white and beautiful they'd named a dog after her.

"It means fucking a girl when she doesn't want you to," J.D. explained.

Alice thought about this for a minute. "No," she said. "I don't think you'd do that."

"Neither do I," he agreed. There was something extremely bizarre, Alice thought, about the conversation. It was as if J.D. didn't know himself, and had turned to a girl for guidance.

Four-Letter Word

Alice sat on the grass eyeing J.D. warily and thinking about the meaning of the word "rape." She tried not to guess why he'd introduced this term in the first place, flashing it like a concealed knife, then studying her reaction to see what she would do. Does this scare you? he'd asked. Are you afraid of me? Whatever trust she'd had in him had vanished. She felt he'd broken the rules—the delicate, fragile set of rules which had been established between them.

Different sets of rules were operating, Alice ruminated. There were rules that said a man J.D.'s age shouldn't talk of "love" and "rape" to an eleven-year-old girl. Those rules had been created by other people, not by Alice and J.D. Alice could bear the breaking of those other people's rules. But certain rules, still more sacred to her, had been broken by J.D. This other private set of rules didn't have much to do with violating a law, something general and abstract. It had to do with trespassing over a single human being. It had to do with violating Alice. Do you think I'd rape you? he had asked. He'd tossed it out as if it were a trivial matter, as if he'd said, Do you think it's going to rain? He'd said this thing to her which was, the more she thought about it, a really very terrible, a very ugly thing. He'd presented it to Alice, who knew so little, as if she might adjudicate the matter better than he could himself. Maybe, Alice thought, neither of them knew the meaning of the word.

Alice took an inventory of what she knew about sex. There were the rudimentary terms, the school yard rumors, and the textbook diagrams. She'd observed the transparent plastic model, in the American Museum of Natural History, of a naked woman. She recalled half-learned lessons about the human reproductive system. She'd seen an illustration someplace of an egg—round, vast, unassailable, as big and weighty as the moon. It had been surrounded by dozens of infinitesimal spermatozoa, which wagged their tails in a desperate effort to wriggle through. They needed to cross the egg's borders, to go inside. This, then, was sex, thought Alice. A breaking and an entering. A writhing and a pushing. Hammering and flailing to wear down the resistance of the stolid, the large, the sturdy, the sober egg. There were other surreal pictures in Alice's mind, connected to the highly implausible stories she'd been told by friends. Outlandish fictions about the human body, its portals, its capacities, its desires, and its functions. There were lurid, distasteful, sinister details that Alice believed had been fabricated by eighth- and ninth-grade girls who often discussed four-letter words during recess.

"What are you thinking about, Alice?" said J.D.

She'd been so absorbed by her contemplation of rape—its mysteries and its implications—that she'd almost forgotten about J.D. She started at the sound of his voice—high-pitched and innocuous, with its funny little irregular rhythm, and that way he had of speaking through his nose. He was still wearing his sunglasses. Alice wondered if these, too—like the R word, like J.D.'s inviting smile—were an instrument of deception. When he had them on, J.D. could see Alice. He could look at her and observe her. But Alice could not watch him back.

"You've been sitting there so quietly, sweetheart," he said. "I was wondering what you're thinking about."

Alice took off her flip-flops and probed the Band-Aid on her foot. It was made of shiny white adhesive, and decorated with Disney characters. These were printed in bright primary colors—Snow White, with her jet hair and her red lips; Sleepy, with his blue cap; and Sneezy, with his pointed elf shoes.

"Won't you tell me?" J.D. urged.

Alice could tell from his manner that J.D. was repentant, that he felt bad for having scared her, that he was going to start acting nicely again, instead of beastly. She'd learned, in the very short time they'd been acquainted, that J.D. was a mercurial personality. He was an unstable person who never behaved consistently, who always changed. Now he was playing dumb, Alice decided. Because there was no point in asking her what she was thinking about. He must know. She was thinking about rape. And he had made her think about it. He had planted the seed of it, the idea, in her mind.

"I'm thinking that you're turning out to be a jerk," Alice told him.

"Really?" J.D. asked. He looked surprised. He sounded wounded.

"Yes," said Alice. "You're a jerk."

"Can't a guy get lost in the woods for a minute without being a jerk?" he asked.

"You're not lost. And you know it," she told him.

"Okay, okay. You're right. So sue me."

"You shouldn't make things up," Alice said, frowning. "If you know where the lake is, say so. I don't like people playing head games with me, or trying to scare me." Alice had borrowed the term "head games" from Aunt Esmé.

"I *do* know where the lake is," said J.D. He pointed left. "It's about a quarter of a mile that way. You want to go to the lake, Alice? Follow that path. See it?"

Alice looked.

"It's even marked," said J.D. "See the white paint on the bark of the tree?"

"Uh-huh," said Alice.

"You can go by yourself. Or I'll take you. Or you can just chill out and quit being so paranoid and hang out here for a while with me."

"You should apologize," Alice noted.

"I apologize. I shouldn't have pretended I was lost. I had this crazy thought, to be honest. I had this crazy thought . . ." He trailed off.

Alice wasn't sure she wanted to hear the crazy thought. She feared it might be another four-letter word.

"I had this stupid idea, Alice," he said, "that here in this glade, I might seduce you."

Alice spelled the word in her mind, as she would have during a spelling bee. Seduce. S-E-D-U-C-E. Six letters. "That *was* stupid," Alice agreed.

"It was, wasn't it?" he said.

"Yes, it was." After a moment, Alice added, "But I don't know what that is, exactly."

"You never heard of a seduction?"

"I don't think so." F-U-C-K, thought Alice. Four letters. R-A-P-E. Four letters. L-O-V-E. Four letters. They might have been the same words, Alice believed, or different words in the same category. They might belong to each other as, in her natural history textbook, a species belonged to a genus.

"You're precocious in some ways," said J.D. "But backward in others. How can that be?"

Alice felt a desperate, dangerous urge to confide in him, even as she distrusted, even as she disliked him. She wanted to tell J.D. all about her child's brain being grafted onto her womanly figure. She wanted to tell him that she had just completed the sixth grade, and that she was one of the Fineman Study girls. "I'm a freak," was all Alice said.

"How so?"

"I'm just . . . I'm bigger. Tall, I mean. I'm always the tallest girl at school."

"That's not especially freaky."

"There are other things," Alice said.

"You're creating an aura of mystery?"

"What?" she said.

"What are these other freaky things? You want some of this, by the way?" He was filling the bowl of his pipe with pot.

Alice shook her head no.

"Well, the truth, Alice," he said, "is that it's been on my mind for some time. The seduction of Princess Alice."

Alice waited for him to explain. He didn't. The new word—a word she'd heard before, but whose subtleties escaped her—floated in the air, like the smoke from J.D.'s pipe, between them.

"Would you tell me what it is, please?" Alice asked. She said it harshly, hurriedly, as if she were in an alien land hearing a foreign tongue being spoken and struggling to communicate. She could not make her own choices known if she didn't know what the choices were. He was thinking about "seducing" her. If the term meant nothing, how could she say no?

Again, J.D. patted the grass next to him. "Can't I get you to come over here? You feel so far away. Sit down beside me, Princess Alice. Let's talk about it."

"I don't want to," Alice said.

"Peace," he told her, lifting his index and ring fingers up together, the way Rain's friends had done before the soldiers came back from the war. "Please. We'll smoke the peace pipe together. We'll call a truce."

Leaving the sandals by themselves in the long grass, Alice walked over to him. She sat down at a safe distance, three feet away. The time when she'd held him close, when she'd put her arm around his neck and sniffed his hair and made rain on his face with her fingers—that seemed long ago. So much had altered between them since then. Yet nothing had happened, really, Alice assured herself. Nothing had happened at all. But it wasn't the same as before. There was another feeling in the air between them. The thought crossed Alice's mind that J.D. was her enemy.

"Seduction, Alice, means to lure," he said. "To tempt. To lead astray. To persuade someone to do something they didn't think they'd want to."

Alice looked down at the ground beside her. A ladybug, with its red shell and jaunty black polka dots, was clambering along in the grass. It opened its translucent inner wings, and its hard outer wings. It perched at the tip of a green blade, which bent under its weight. Off it dove into the air, and made a whirring sound as it flew away.

"Should I settle for a drub then?" J.D. said.

Alice glanced up. He was flashing his smile. "No one offered you one," she said.

"It was just a thought," he told her, standing. His shadow fell across her. "Just a thought," he repeated. "And not a good one." J.D. kicked Alice's knee, very lightly, with his sneaker. "Let's go swimming, okay?" he said. "Let's go jump in the lake." Slinging the bag over his shoulder, he turned and walked, away from Alice, down the dirt path. He didn't wait to see whether she was following him.

His back was turned. Alice was free. What she should do now, she thought, was flee.

Alice looked around the wooded glade. Ahead of her, she heard J.D.'s sneakers rustling in the undergrowth on the path. He was getting farther and farther away. She was not entirely sure if she could find the way back to the main road by herself. Running away from J.D. might be hazardous, because she didn't know where she was going, or how to get out of the woods, back to the road, or how to get from the road to anywhere. She was torn between two perils: the unknown wilderness and J.D. She reasoned that the wilderness was safer. It was people who were menacing, not trees or bears. It was men.

By now J.D. was easily a hundred feet ahead of her. She was losing sight of him. If she left now, if she returned to the institute, she'd be rebuked by Odette Noko, scolded, and expelled. But she could take the next bus home. The encounter with J.D. would be over. It would soon become a forgotten incident.

Alice tried to envision her life, in which things continued more or less as planned, as expected. She saw herself striding through the high grass and the trees, finding the road, walking along it. Then she saw herself holding her thumb out as she stood on the shoulder of the road, hitching a ride back to the institute. If she could find a gas station or a 7-Eleven someplace, she could even call the local police station and tell them she'd gotten lost.

One of these choices was the right one. One of these choices would present itself to Alice as the thing she should do, as the thing she would do. Escaping from J.D., the paradoxes of J.D.— his threats and his lures, his criminal charm—that was the key.

Escape was the best possible action, the best possible decision. J.D. was peculiar. It was time to stop hanging out with him. She'd been flirting with disaster since she'd met him. How easy it was, she thought, to leave J.D.

Alice glanced at her watch. It had stopped and started again. It said that eight minutes had passed. A breeze rustled through the grass. The cicadas were humming in the high trees around her. A woodpecker, someplace, made his distinctive rap against a tree trunk. Alice looked first one way and then the other. Behind her was the path that led to the lake. Ahead of her was open space, no path at all, just a hope that if she put one foot in front of the other, it would lead her back to New York City. Alice planned it all out—her walk to the road, her discovery of the gas station, her contacting the police, her delivery to the bus station, her return home.

And then she did the opposite. She let her feet take her wherever they led, and she went wherever they wanted her to go.

On the Rocks

t took Alice about twenty minutes to reach the lake. The brush and the trees went right up to the shore, and at first she didn't see anyone there. Low to the ground, half hidden by the clusters of yellow reeds that grew up out of the water, she glimpsed J.D. He was lying on a flat rock, naked, propped up on his elbows. He had a sandwich in one hand. In his other hand, he held a book. As she approached, she could make out the black words printed on the white cover. It was the one Stuart and Rabbit liked, the one about good and evil. He set the book down and cupped his chin inside his hands. Alice stopped walking. It seemed to her as she looked at J.D., without him knowing she was there, that he was an entirely different person than she'd thought he was. Seen from the back, he looked almost like a girl. He had a narrow, willowy waist and long thin legs. The man who had tossed out that word, "rape," now appeared to be boyish and vulnerable. Standing on the path watching J.D. as he thumbed through the pages, Alice felt sorry for him. How thin he was. How greedily he gulped his sandwich down. How sad he looked, alone.

"Hey," Alice called, walking up to him.

J.D. started in surprise. "Hey," he said. They stared at one another for a few moments, settling something. "Sit down," he said. "Have some lunch."

Alice climbed on the rocks. She was ravenous.

"There's a jar of peanut butter in my bag, and a loaf of bread," said J.D. "Help yourself." He went back to reading.

He'd left his clothing on the rock. His jeans and his faded green T-shirt were folded, and his green-and-white-striped Adidas sneakers were beside them. Alice found the jar of peanut butter in his duffel bag. She opened the lid, scooped some onto her finger, and began to eat it.

J.D. rolled over onto his back and put his arms behind his head. His armpits were black and bushy. From between his legs, out of a nest of hair, his penis was a purplish red, and swollen. It looked unrelated to the rest of him, Alice thought, like one of the plastic attachments—nose, ear, hand—that belonged to Mr. Potato Head. It extended into the air improbably, like a ruler. It was many things at once, Alice thought, regarding it observantly. It was impressive yet clownish. It was a threat, a joke, an exclamation point, a question mark. There was nothing to do in its presence, finally, except to quietly take notice.

J.D. seemed blissfully unaware of his penis and its shock value. He sprawled there, looking at her lazily, as if the tumor that sprouted from him was nothing much. He was completely unself-conscious about it. The penis wasn't a defect, apparently. J.D. wasn't ashamed of it, as Alice was ashamed by her enormous deformed breasts. Of his comfort with himself, Alice was envious. She wondered what made him proud to display his body, while Alice since the age of eight had only wanted to shrink from those who stared at hers. For a while, she pondered this, lost in thought, absorbed by the unknowable riddles of masculinity. Then Alice went back to eating her peanut butter. She certainly wasn't getting anywhere near that thing, she decided. She wouldn't have any idea how to approach it—giving a drub to a penis like that. She doubted she could even get her hand around it. It was nearly the width of the peanut butter jar, Alice marveled with a kind of appalled glee. She looked up at it again. She looked back down at the peanut butter jar. She was sizing the thing up—like a naturalist on safari, observing exotic foreign animals. She was calculating, measuring. Well, no, it wasn't nearly as large as that. But it was an abomination, Alice decided, just the same. The giant penis and the Giant Alice, she thought. Excess was what they had in common. There was too much of both of them.

Then again, Alice admitted to herself, she didn't have anything to fairly compare J.D.'s penis to, except for Rabbit's and Crash Omaha's, neither of which she'd properly examined. She'd felt them, but she hadn't seen them. In both cases, Alice had closed her eyes. To the best of her knowledge, J.D.'s dick was atrocious. Alice made a special effort not to laugh at it, so as not to hurt his feelings. Laughter was welling up inside her chest, though. It wasn't because she was amused. It was a response to being startled by the penis, an alternative to being frightened.

Absently, J.D. let his hand fall from behind his head to his crotch. He gave it one hard twist, as if he were wringing a small neck. "Take off your clothes," he said.

Alice's laughter came bursting forth. She didn't speak, but only made this raw, raucous cackling sound.

"This is a nudist colony," said J.D. "And everybody here has to get naked. If you want to eat my peanut butter, you have to get undressed." He wasn't smiling.

Alice set down the jar of Skippy's on the rock beside her.

J.D. rolled onto his side, propping himself up on his left elbow. His penis was larger, more engorged. Alice thought it might grow, larger and larger, until it socked her in the stomach right where she sat, about five feet away from J.D. Once, a boy in the Fieldwood School—named Allen Jamison—had drawn a cartoon of himself in which his own penis had done that, springing forth in endless coils that stretched out like a Slinky. In the drawing, the sharply pointed tip of Allen Jamison's dick had pierced the torso of a cartoon girl. Alice had sat next to this Allen Jamison person in the fifth grade. He had passed the drawing over to her, sliding it along the school desk. He had helpfully labeled the male figure "Allen Jamison" and the female figure "Alice is my bitch," with the four words running together so that they became one new one, Aliceismybitch. She'd taken a close look at it and then had passed the drawing back.

"I made that for you," Allen Jamison had said. "Do you like it?" His eyes had flashed with an emotion Alice couldn't read, and didn't share.

"It's all right, I guess," Alice had said politely. She hadn't been sure what the etiquette was. She hadn't wanted to be rude to him. There under the leaves, by the lake, with the naked J.D., Alice felt the same uncertain, inexpressible anger. Layered just beneath her outrage was curiosity, sympathy, and skepticism. J.D. was a bully, as Allen Jamison had been a bully. She willed herself not to cower from him.

"You already ate some, Alice. Didn't you." J.D. said. It was one of those phrases uttered by J.D. that should have been a question but was not one. It was a statement. It was a sentence.

Words came to Alice's mind that made no sense. Fuzzily, she thought: J.D., don't arrest me. Let me be.

She had some peanut butter left over on her finger. She wiped it off now, on the rim of the jar. She put the lid back on and closed it tightly. She pushed the jar far away from herself, and then still further away. There was a mouthful of peanut butter on her tongue. She leaned forward and spit it out. The slimy caramel-colored gob fell to the dirt, below the rock that Alice sat on. She looked at J.D.'s face. She was disturbed, even enraged, by what he'd said. She was disturbed, even enraged, by his tyranny, his dominance, his bullying. She sat up taller. She held her head high, bristling.

"I was just kidding," he said with a small, cruel smile. "You shouldn't take everything so seriously."

The air had cooled and the sun was warm on Alice's back. A fly with a green head and red eyes alighted on her arm. It tickled her skin. Her pulse galloped. She swatted the red-eyed fly away.

"You're not funny," Alice said.

"Skinny-dipping prevents tan lines," said J.D. "I like a dark, smooth, even tan, hon." He wiggled his rear end at her. "How about you?"

"No," Alice said. It was a cosmic no—loud and large. No, Alice thought, to your dark, smooth, even tan. To hell with you. To hell with everything.

"Aw, come on, Alice, don't be sore at me. Don't be a prude."

"I'm not a *prude*," Alice said. It was the same term Aunt Esmé goaded her with. Alice was annoyed.

"I promise not to attack you or whatever," said J.D. offhand. "I just want to see what you look like without your clothes." He stood up. Alice watched his movements, arrogant and easy, like a king. He began walking toward her. Alice turned her head. She kept her eyes fixed on the ground. She saw only his feet now, and his legs, up to his knees. The tanned bare feet came to a stop about a yard away from Alice. They planted themselves in the grass, turned outward slightly, a pace apart.

"I was only playing around with you, baby," he said. "I'd never . . ." He didn't finish the sentence. "Don't you know that?" he asked.

Alice wouldn't look at him. She felt he should have stayed where he was and not come any closer, not when he was naked.

"There's nothing to feel weird about, hon," he said. "The human physique is beautiful. The only reason people wear clothes is because they've yielded to convention."

"What is convention?" Alice asked, still keeping her gaze lowered.

"It's Mind Control Central. It's the part of us that refuses to take a risk. Its favorite words are 'no' and 'don't.' It says: 'I won't,' and not 'I will.' "

Alice thought this over. She raised her chin and scanned his nudity. She weighed his words against his naked presence. She could see the musculature of his frame, the taut sinews of his arms and neck, the pattern of dark hair, like an upside down triangle, on his chest. It became more sparse on his belly, forming an arrow under his navel that pointed down to his crotch. Seen in close-up, the penis was not sleek, as she thought, but exposed and frail. It looked pink and private, like the litter of blind, hairless newborn hamsters Alice had taken Charlie Chaplin from, at her friend Skye's house. Her own private parts might look like hairless hamsters, also, like J.D.'s, if they'd been turned inside out. The penis was a spectacle. Seeing it was like bearing witness to someone's internal organs in the act of slipping out—like seeing a large intestine manifest itself unexpectedly, in public. Despite what he said about the beauty of the body, Alice felt this display of J.D.'s was lewd, improper. Before taking one's clothes off, she thought, one ought to ask permission. How much more considerate it would have been if he'd said: "Alice, if I undressed, would you mind?" But he hadn't. He regarded his nudity as a right, it seemed. Alice suspected him, too, of wanting to surprise her. It was a preemptive strike.

"What are you thinking *now*?" said J.D. with a crafty look in his eye. He grinned his grin. The cleft in his cheek appeared, and the wrinkles around his eyes grew more pronounced. His radiant smile lit things up, and Alice had the extraordinary thought that J.D.'s dimple was edible, that she could taste it, like candy. She disowned the thought as quickly as she had it. It must have been planted in her mind by J.D., she felt. It seemed too foreign and unwelcome for Alice to have arrived at on her own. Alice became wary of him. J.D. was an alien being, like an extraterrestrial, she decided. She would have to be careful around him. He possessed secret powers.

"What's going on behind those pretty peepers of yours?" J.D. asked. "You're looking right through me, babe. For five minutes, you've been staring at me like the Mona Lisa. Like the Sphinx."

"Nothing," said Alice.

Alice watched, inexplicably mesmerized, as he ran his hand along his arm, his chest, his shoulder. Alice found herself studying the movements as if she'd never seen a hand before. Such tanned skin. Such long fingers. Such well-shaped fingernails, like small shovels, she thought, the kind she'd had, long ago, in the sandbox, where the nursery school kids brought their plastic dump trucks and their plastic pails. Each fingertip was squared off at the ends, shaped just so. She would remember precisely when it was that these hands struck her as breathtakingly beautiful.

"Can I touch you?" J.D. asked. He'd waited patiently, diabolically, until she'd heard the words "beautiful hands," until she'd had the treacherous thought. He didn't seem to be addressing her, however. He was looking down at his duffel bag. For a moment, she thought he was talking to it. She wondered if the bag would open, like a mouth, and speak to him. Yes, J.D., it would say, *you may touch me*. But Alice didn't think she said that out loud. She kept the confused thoughts to herself.

"I'd like to, Alice," he said. "Please." This was a *please*, like so much of J.D.'s language, that lacked a question mark. It wasn't an inquiry but a demand.

"I want to," he said.

A long moment passed.

I want you to, Alice's evil mind thought, but only a sputtering noise came out. It was her new, choked voice, the sound of a girl getting strangled.

"Come here," said J.D. "Let's."

Alice could only shake her head no. The word was gone.

"Why not, baby? Are you shy of me?" he asked.

She shook her head.

"Another time, maybe?" he said.

She shook her head no a third time.

He folded his arms and stared at her, sizing her up, diagnosing her internal struggle. Alice couldn't look him in the face, but the expression she saw out of the corner of her eye reminded her of Dr. Fineman.

"Is it because you're not used to seeing me like this?"

Alice nodded no once more.

"I can't help you if you won't tell me what the situation is," he said.

I never asked you to help me, Alice thought. What kind of help is this? She wanted to say this to him but she couldn't.

J.D. took one of the shirts out of the bag and tied it around his waist. It covered only his rear end and was, Alice felt, a pointless gesture in the direction of getting dressed. He reached for his aviator glasses, which were sitting on the rock beside his book, and put them on. Disappearing behind them, he lay back down, as he had been, except now he was beside Alice. He folded his arms behind his head. He lay there staring at the drifting clouds, and his mirrored lenses reflected them. He was just as Alice had once envisioned him, except the sun was out and there were no stars.

It was then that Alice began to imagine J.D. as one of the people in her collages, a man without eyes. He had, instead, windows in his head. She saw gaps in his skull, openings, and through the windows in J.D.'s face Alice saw the trees, the clouds, a bird, the world.

"May I look at you at least?" he said.

Alice didn't move. She didn't speak.

"Do you want to take your clothes off?" said J.D. "Or should I undress you?" The reflective sunglasses made him look like a robot. He reached toward her, and Alice saw the terrible and the beautiful: the sinuous hand that she'd unwillingly admired. His fingers trembled.

"Come here to me," he said.

Alice took his hand. Standing, she looked down at J.D. where he lay on the ground. Now he led her closer, guiding her into position. She drew nearer still, until her sandals were on the rock right beside his freckled shoulder. He was looking up her skirt.

"Yes," he said. "Like that."

Alice lifted her shirt over her head and pulled it off. She let it fall in a heap, on the rock.

"So pretty," J.D. said.

Unhooking her white cotton bra, Alice flung it to the ground. The deformity of her round breasts stood out, revealed.

"Man," said J.D., "that's awesome."

Alice let herself be awesome. It felt the same as being deformed.

"What's up with the peep show?" he said. "Aren't you going to let me see the rest?"

She tried to unbutton her skirt, but she found that something had seized hold of her hands, a muscle spasm or a cramp. She fumbled. Her hands weren't working. They wouldn't cooperate. They didn't want to take Alice's skirt off for her.

"May I?" said J.D. He reached up and undid the button. He pulled the zipper down. Alice watched his eyeless face. His throat convulsed, as if he were thirsty. As before, the prominent Adam's apple leapt up like he'd swallowed a toad.

Alice started to take off her skirt, but J.D. stopped her, tapping on her hand. "Do it slowly," he said, tap-tapping like the woodpecker's beak. The tap felt like an assault—insistent, bossy. J.D. was in charge now. Alice had lost command of her ship. She'd surrendered to whatever it was, and she wasn't even sure how it had happened. She felt herself turning into a puppet, a performer. She was filled with a kind of hatred for him. Yet now she did exactly as he said. She slid the skirt down slowly. It crumpled as the starchy fabric moved against her legs, down her bony knees, over her shins, and onto J.D.'s head. The skirt covered him like a fallen parachute. His ghastly, lovely hands appeared against the fabric. For a moment, he stretched the skirt over his face. Through the loose weave, Alice could see the outline of J.D.'s aviator glasses. She could see his features. His nose was a pointed triangle, his brow was a straight line, and the circular indentation below the triangle was his open mouth. Two semicircles that didn't meet: these were his lips. This was a map of a man. This was J.D.'s geometry.

He pulled the skirt away from his face. She watched his chest rise and sink, just like the Adam's apple. "And your panties," he said.

Alice started to take them off, no longer knowing who was talking and who was listening, who was ordering and who was doing.

Again he tapped her hand. "Wait, hon," he said. "I *told* you. Slow, baby. Do everything real slow."

Alice waited. It was too late to be infuriated by the tapping. They were in it together. They were conspirators. Alice was implicated. He said it; she did it. She thought it; it happened. She hitched her thumbs into the elastic waistband of the white cotton underwear and drew it down.

J.D. sucked at the air. "Yes, Alice," he said, with his s's in a whispered hiss.

She let the underpants fall to her ankles and stepped out of them. J.D. fingered the sad, collapsed pile of cotton idly as he watched her. "Would you spread your legs?" he said.

Alice shook her head no. She'd be too naked, then, too exposed.

He brushed the toes of her right foot with his hand. "Put your foot here," he said, trying to move it.

Alice held her ground.

"Step over here," he said. "I want to see you. Step over me." His fingers were stroking the top of her foot, directing her. She couldn't say no to him. She gave in. She gave up. Forever and forever.

Forever after, Alice hated herself for it. She placed her foot where he wanted it to be. She stood with her legs apart, trying not to look down. She couldn't confront the eyeless face of J.D., which was now immediately under her.

"I have to go home now," Alice whispered.

He held on to each of her ankles. "I'll take you home, Alice. You don't go anywhere," he said. "Not now. Stay here."

Avoiding the sight of him, she looked up at a large white bird, on the other side of the lake, as it sailed across the air and settled in a tree.

"I just want to look at you," he said. "Would you open it up for me?"

At it, at you, you're it. Alice felt her face get hot, ashamed that she knew what he wanted, everything he wanted, what he meant. She was filled with a sharper certainty that she was a freak of nature, a hideous monstrosity. Her knowledge seemed perverse. She did as he asked. She was horrible now, and so was he. She looked up into the sky and tried not to think. She could feel what he was doing underneath her, giving himself a drub, the movements of his elbow slow and steady, then jerky and fast. She moved away, ever so slightly, so that the skin of his arm made no more contact with her leg. But still she sensed the vibrations from him.

"Don't touch me," she whispered to the leaves.

He breathed. "Okay," he said.

Alice stole a glance at him. She saw the tugging movement of his hand on his own skin.

"I'll be right with you, Alice," he said beneath her. "Give me just a minute, hon." His tone was perfectly ordinary. He might have been excusing himself while he stepped away, for a few seconds, to answer the telephone.

Alice looked away, quickly, and squinted up into the sun. On the ground underneath her, J.D. was watching, watching the small part of Alice, between her legs. Watching, watching something that wasn't Alice but a twin sister, a demon daughter. The "it" girl, body.

Alice Underwater

She could tell when he was done with it. His breathing pattern had changed into a burst of soft, rapid snorting. There was a cluster of these barely audible huffs and puffs, like the exhalations Alice made sometimes when she was crying. Then he was quiet. The low regular sound he'd made, a faint whoosh of skin on skin, stopped abruptly. Now there was none of the vibrating motion Alice had detected near her right ankle, where J.D.'s elbow was. What he had been doing was over. Finally, sure that he was finished, Alice looked at him. He was using his T-shirt to mop off his thigh. It was like seeing someone blow his nose into a handkerchief. The substance he was cleaning off himself looked like rubber cement. For the first time since she'd been doing the things she knew she shouldn't have been doing with him, Alice felt nauseated. The wet gunk on J.D.'s T-shirt was evidence of disease, depravity.

J.D. sighed contentedly. "Don't you feel good now?" he said.

Alice stepped over his head and hugged herself. Glancing down, she was relieved to see he was looking at her face now. During the moments that had passed while he had observed it so intently, her vulva had become a strange sort of rival, as if she'd grown a second head which was prettier and more interesting than she was.

"I don't know," said Alice. It wasn't as hard to talk now.

"Don't you feel nice and free," said J.D.

"I guess."

"Feeling good is good, Alice. Do you know what I'm saying, baby?"

"Not really."

He looked down to the twin, between her legs. "Feel good," he instructed her. "Just concentrate on that. Would you do that for me? Let's forget everything else."

Alice thought about this. It didn't make much sense to her. What she was thinking about was: feeling sick, feeling excited, feeling disgusting. She was thinking about leaving, staying, getting back home, getting lost, losing herself, losing Alice, being torn in two, head and heart, reservations and curiosity, by this man who talked to vulvas, J.D. But she didn't know how to explain all this to him. He was obviously older than sixteen, but in many respects, Alice felt, he was ignorant. He'd made things sound simple. Things weren't simple. Things were complicated.

J.D. caught her eye. "Thanks, Alice," he said. "That was hot."

Despite his earnest tone, Alice was doubtful that what had just occurred had been normal or okay. He kept acting like it was, though. Gradually, tentatively, Alice succumbed to his vision of their world. She felt too inexperienced to judge J.D.'s actions on her own. He behaved so naturally that, aside from the small whispering anxious voice that told her not to trust him, she began to accept him. In fact, after J.D. had finished communing with her vulva in that way, she felt more at ease. Some gathering storm had passed.

Now Alice tried to sort out her own feelings from J.D.'s, and found she couldn't do it. J.D. was stretching himself out on the rock, luxuriating in the sun like a cat. He was relaxed. She wasn't. But because he felt good, Alice felt good too.

He removed the mirrored lenses through which Alice had seen herself exposed. His eyes were laughing, happy. "That was real altruistic of you, to do that striptease for me, Alice."

"Yeah," she agreed, wondering what altruistic was.

"I'll bet you don't do that for that guy Rabbit. Do you?" he said.

"No. I haven't," Alice said. She was sure Rabbit would never want her to do that.

He patted her knee. "Sit down a sec. Talk to me."

Alice stepped back over his rib cage—the bridge of flesh that she'd somehow crossed. She sat down beside him, with her legs and torso facing away from him, curling them beneath her so that he couldn't see the private places anymore. She felt that whatever had been closed and personal on her body was now more vulnerable, more open. She had the curious sensation that she had given something away to J.D. and that she couldn't take it back.

"I didn't freak you out just now, did I?" he said, reading her mind as he was apparently able to do now, scanning her eyes, her face.

Alice shrugged.

"I mean, you know all about that shit. Right?" he said.

Alice bit her lips.

J.D. leaned back, basking in the sunlight. He reached for the pipe and the pot, taking them out of his duffel bag. "Just what is it you do with this Rabbit, anyway?" he said. "Want a hit, Alice?"

Alice shook her head.

"Are you sure you're not freaked out?" said J.D.

"No," said Alice. She picked at an old scab on her elbow.

"Is all this new to you or something?"

Alice shrugged and nodded yes at the same time.

"I don't get you, doll. There's something about you that eludes me. You mean to say you never did this sort of thing? I thought you gave your boyfriend hand jobs or something. That was what you said."

"I kept all my clothes on," Alice explained. She continued worrying the scab, peeling the corner of it back, trying to make it hurt, to make it bleed.

"Quit doing that," said J.D. "That's disgusting."

Alice started for a second. "You're the one that was gross," she said.

"You thought it was disgusting, what *I* did?" said J.D. His voice was cross and challenging.

Alice plucked at the tiny blond hairs on her forearm.

"You did, didn't you?" J.D. said. "Alice, I'm disappointed in you. You're still young. But already they got to you. They turned you off. They spooked you. They taught you to fear it, to hate it. The sheer raw power of your own humanity. Of your desire. Of your sex."

Alice examined her beauty marks. She saw she was getting freckles near her shoulder, just like J.D.'s. It must be the sun that made them, unless they were marks of badness.

"Are you even listening?" said J.D. He sounded upset.

"Who are They?" Alice asked.

"Who are who?" said J.D.

She took her braid in her hands and pulled the elastic off. "You said They got to me. They taught me. Who are They?"

"The moral mafia, that's who."

Alice began to take her braid apart. She loosened the plaits with her fingertips and felt her long hair cascade down her back. "What is the moral mafia? I don't know what those words mean." Her voice was queer and quavering. It was scratchy, as if she'd contracted laryngitis.

"It's the Suits, baby. The government. The drones. The nine-to-fivers with their houses in the suburbs and their poor fascistic desk jobs."

"Why don't you like them?" said Alice's small tremulous voice. She loathed J.D. She liked him. She despised herself.

"I told you why," he said pedantically, as if she'd forgotten her lesson. "They're robbing you of your freedom. Every day. Stealing it away. Yours and mine, baby."

"How are they robbing me?" Alice asked.

J.D. clamped his hand to his forehead. "Shit, Alice. They get everybody brainwashed, man. Okay? They get everybody walking the same walk, talking the same talk, moving in this march, left, right, left. This mindless lockstep. They're afraid of pleasure and spontaneity. They're repressive. They steal the life force—the thrill of it—away from folks. Like vampires. Slurp." He pantomimed a vampire. "Suck your joie de vivre. Right out of you."

Alice watched him.

J.D. flushed. "Forget it. You want to go swimming, then?" he said.

"I told you about a million times that I can't." The small voice was angry.

"And I told *you* I'd teach you to float. It's easy. Come with me," he said, taking her firmly by the hand.

Alice went with him, loathing herself for it.

They had to walk through long slithering reeds that tickled her skin. Underfoot, the mud was warm and slimy. To Alice, it didn't feel like mud. It felt unspeakable. It felt obscene. She imagined that it was whispering to her to lie down in it. Come to me, the mud said, come to me Alice, like J.D. She kept going, through the mud, past it, and into the cool water. It grew colder as they walked out further, first up to Alice's knees, then to her hips, then to her waist. Her naked skin beneath the water had turned a yellowish green.

"Stop," she said.

J.D.'s grip on her hand was tight. For a terrible moment, she feared that he would pull her out deeper, and that he'd drown her.

"See any sharks yet?" he said.

He looked less menacing in the water. He was just a person, Alice saw. He had a slightly concave chest, decorated with coils of scraggly hair. He had bony knees and bony elbows.

"I'm scared," said Alice, and wondered why it was so easy to admit this to him now, when she hadn't been able to say it before.

"Scared of the water," he asked, "or still scared of me?"

Alice didn't answer.

"Look, this is simple. Watch me." He fell backward, into the water, holding his nose. He made a huge splash. Alice yelped.

He splashed some more. She splashed him back. He grabbed her by the waist and pulled her in. I'm having fun, she thought. She threw her head back, gasping. She began thinking about sharks again, the ones that dwelled at the bottom of the sea, lurking there, feeding off whatever scraps they could find. She was in up to her chin. The fun faded. The fear surrounded her. Every inch of her skin felt unprotected, endangered. She paddled toward the shore, panicked.

When she reached the plateau where she could stand, J.D. swam up to her. "How can I convince you that this is no big deal?" he said.

"You can't," said Alice.

He touched her hipbone. "We'll take it easy. We'll both do it. We'll lie back." He was crouching in the low water.

Alligator, Alice thought. Crocodile. Lizard. "An alligator," she said aloud.

"What?" said J.D. His fingers skimmed the surface of the water, making ripples. The circles expanded, spreading across the pond.

"Nothing," Alice said. She thought: Large teeth.

"I can show you this in three feet of water," he said. "I can show you how to float. Do what I'm doing."

Alice imitated him. Now she was an alligator lizard shark, lolling in the shallows, too.

"Stretch your legs out in front of you, Alice," he said. "Support yourself on your hands."

She kicked her legs toward the shore. Her fingers slid into the mud. She let them slide into slime.

"What you're doing now is floating," said J.D. "Do you see how the water is supporting you? Do you see how you're completely weightless? It's like being on the moon."

Alice nodded.

"Lie back, baby. Lie all the way back. Put your head in the water, too."

It felt cold on the back of her scalp. She looked at the sun, lower in the sky now, the same sun she'd always looked at, the same sun she'd seen when she'd been standing on the rock and J.D. had been looking up her skirt.

"Now all you have to do is this. Watch," he said.

She turned to see him.

He lifted his arms, stretching them far out on either side of his body, keeping his legs together, toes pointed, like Christ being crucified on His cross.

Alice tried to do it, but she immediately felt herself begin to sink. "I can't," she said. "I can't."

Swimming to her, J.D. put his hand underneath the small of her back. "You're psyching yourself out, Alice," he said in a reasonable tone. The voice of reason. "Let me hold you. You're trying too hard. Take it easy."

Alice could feel him lifting her up, keeping her from drowning.

"You're *trying* to do something," he said. "Don't, hon. Don't do anything. Do nothing." His voice got softer and softer. "Shhh. Close your eyes. Relax."

Alice obeyed. She felt his other hand cup the back of her head. She liked the feeling of floating and being held.

"Don't let go," she said.

"Okay, babe. Okay."

The water rocked her, gently, this way and that.

"Keep your arms way, way out. Stretch your legs out in front of you, honey. Now you're floating nice and high."

The air was cool on her stomach and on her breasts. She was halfway in the water, and halfway out of it, like a leaf drifting along. She kept her eyes closed as J.D. moved his hand lower, running it along her bottom.

"Does this feel good or bad?" he said.

"Good," Alice said.

"See? You're floating."

Alice felt something happen to her breathing, and to her heart. J.D.'s hand had come up, like a sea serpent, between her legs.

"It's all right," he said. "You stay still, Alice. I want you to do *nothing*. I want you to float."

There wasn't any water in her nose, but Alice made a noise as if she might start to choke. She didn't open her eyes. She allowed J.D. to steer her floating body. She rose, and sank, and rose. The callused fingers were touching her in the place she'd told him not to. She stiffened and relaxed, relaxed and stiffened. She froze, appalled. She melted, appalled. She let him. He was embracing her now in the span of his arms. One hand supported her shoulders. The other hand fondled her. He floated her toward him. "That's it," he said, near to her head. Calm. Cool. Her instructor. Her swimming coach. "Now you get it." He kissed her mouth. "Don't you get it, Alice, now?"

Alice nodded.

"See," said the swimming coach, the voice of authority. "What this is about, baby," he said, "is going with the flow. Letting it happen. Not being uptight. Loosening up. Feeling it. Doing it. Not fighting things." She felt his scratchy stubble on her left breast, and then the scorching lips that closed around her nipple. His other hand had stopped its investigation of her person, of her innards. How cold and lonely they felt, at once, without him there. When he put his hand back, she welcomed its return, tightening her legs.

"That's good, Alice," said the voice, deepening, softening. "That's so good. Isn't it? Say yes."

"Yes," Alice said.

"Does your boyfriend make you feel like this?"

"No," Alice said.

"Do you do this for yourself?"

In the water, Alice rolled her head from one side to the other. She never had.

"I want you to. I want you to do this. Do this, Alice, just like this. Do you feel this?"

Alice nodded.

"Say yes."

"Yes," she said. It came out high-pitched and sharp.

"You're going to do this," he explained, "because this feels good. And when you do this, baby, you're going to think of me. Of *me*. You hear? You think of me. Every time. Always of me."

Alice nodded.

"Say yes, sweetheart. I like to hear you say yes."

"Yes," said Alice.

"I'm going to show you the best feeling that you'll ever know. And you're going to remember me, always, and you'll always love me. Because the first guy who does this, babe, is the one who blows your mind."

Alice looked up at J.D. The expression on his face was ugly. His eyes were slits. She half expected that he was going to push her head underneath the water until she drowned. He spoke of love, but he hated her. He'd gotten love and hate confused. Alice could see that plainly now, in his eyes, his face, his lips. She began to churn in the water, kicking her legs and paddling with her arms, swimming away from him, deeper into the water.

"No, baby," he said. "Don't run away."

She tried to stand. The water came up above her neck, over her mouth. Her feet had found the muddy bottom of the lake. She kept her chin tilted upward so she could breathe. He'd followed her, swimming to her. They were face to face, J.D. with his back to the shore.

"There's nothing to fear," he said. "It felt good. You said so yourself. You need to go with that."

Alice pushed up off the rocks on the lake's bottom and propelled herself forward. The water swirled as she thrashed her legs. She moved sideways like a crab. If she could keep on swimming without sinking, she might be able to reach the other side of the lake and climb out. She focused on a pine tree on the opposite shore.

J.D. was beside her. He mirrored her, also moving like a crab, also swimming sideways. "I'm doing you a favor, actually," he said. "You'll thank me in about five minutes. You'll beg me to do it again, man. Because love is the best thing you'll ever get in your life, Alice. I've got a whole lot of love to give you."

Alice, doing the dog paddle, turned away from him and looked longingly at the shore. She was running out of breath. "J.D.?" she said.

"What, honey?"

"Are you going to kill me?" She kept her eyes on her target— the clump of weeds, the tall tree, the place she could run to, safe on the shore of the lake, where she could walk, and run, and breathe.

J.D.'s eyes widened. "*Kill* you? Alice. Christ. You've got me all wrong, kiddo. Oh my God, Alice. Jesus, honey. I don't want to *hurt* you. What made you think that?"

"You won't let me get away," she said, gasping for breath. "You're like the devil from *The Exorcist*, the one who made Linda Blair bad, the one who gets inside her."

"Wow," said J.D. For a moment, he was silent. "Alice." He sounded genuinely stunned by her remarks.

"Please don't kill me, J.D.," Alice said.

"Sweetheart, no one's going to harm a hair on your head. Let's get this straight between us, okay? The only reason you're here today is because *you* want to be. Own that, okay? Claim that. Take possession, Alice, of your want. Say: I want to be with J.D."

"If you make me say it, it doesn't mean anything," Alice said. She'd swallowed some water. She was spluttering, treading water.

"And the reason you *want* to be here," he said, "is because you need this feeling, Alice. This special feeling that I very much would like for you to have. This feeling is something I'd like to *give* you. As an *offering*, babe. As a *present*. Maybe you haven't tried it yet, Alice, so you're weirding out. The way you should think of it is, it's a *gift*. See? A nice thing. A real good thing. Can you do that for me?"

"Okay," said Alice, because it was easier to say okay.

Tall enough to stand, he reached his arms out to her. Alice swam into them. She let herself be carried, wrapping her arms and legs around him, like the girl he wore on his silver ring. She felt his muscles moving underneath her limbs, her skin.

"You cold?" he said.

"Yes," said Alice.

"You're shivering."

Alice listened to her teeth chattering.

"You were swimming on your own, see?" he said. "Now would you float one more time, please? For me. Let's try it once again."

Alice looked from the shore to J.D. and back again. She clung to him.

"Hey, princess," said J.D., hugging her back, "you tried to wriggle away, didn't you?" He patted her head affectionately.

"Yes," said Alice.

"But you want to be with me. Am I right or what? You already love me a little bit. Don't you?"

"Yes," said Alice. "You're right."

"Here's my hand underneath your ass. Now you lie back, baby. I'll support you. You float for me."

Alice stretched her arms out as J.D. had done, and let herself be the dry leaf adrift on a river, an aimless human boat.

"Good," said J.D. "You have something pleasant in store for

you, kiddo. And if I were in your shoes I wouldn't turn it down. This is good shit I'm offering you." As he talked to her, he steered her into the reeds in the shallows, at the far end of the lake. He pushed. Alice floated. Ahead of her was a weeping willow with long flowing fronds like hair. The branches bore small white flowers, like ribbons. They formed the skeleton of an umbrella that extended out into the pond. The thin, dangling branches dipped into the water, creating a loose curtain between the lake and the land. J.D. parted the curtain with one hand. He floated Alice through it. Inside, the two of them were hidden from view. Alice wondered if J.D. brought other girls to this hiding place. The weeping willow had made a cave for him, at once out in the open yet secret, an outdoor lair.

Alice kept floating. She was waiting for it, whatever it was. He kissed her brusquely, his fingers rubbing at her, coaxing her, his hands on her thighs, pulling her legs apart. She felt a melting liquid silk, a sensation that was utterly alien. With a start, she saw the soft hot feeling was being made by J.D.'s tongue.

"Like that?" he asked, looking up.

Alice no longer knew anything. She said nothing.

"How about another taste of honey. Open wide," he said. "You do it. You show me that you want this. You spread your legs for me."

Alice did.

The warmth permeated her entire being. Alice thought she would forget to breathe, or accidentally swallow water until she choked to death. She needed something to hang on to. She needed someone to explain. She needed to lie down on the ground, in the ground, someplace solid, underground. She ceased to think, and was transported to no place and to nothing. It lasted only a short time, this ecstatic nothing, and then it ended.

"Ah," said J.D., lifting his head from between her legs and standing. "Aha! Now you *do* get it. Don't you get it now, little girlfriend?"

Alice nodded. He was right. Whatever he was doing, the wet kiss on her, it was absolutely evil, and she'd liked it.

He led her toward the shore. He lay back against the muddy riverbank. The water flowed over his pale thighs. He pulled Alice toward him and sat her on his lap. Behind her, he rested his cheek against her back. His hand squeezed her waist, kneading at it. He nuzzled her with his nose and forehead. He bit the back of her neck with his teeth, not hard, pretending to chew on her. The feeling of being bitten gave Alice goose bumps. His teeth remained on her skin, keeping her in place, as if Alice were a rat that Persephone had captured in the backyard by the fence where the garbage can was, on Sixty-seventh Street.

"Has anybody ever given you an orgasm?" he asked when he'd stopped biting. His fingers stroked her other deformity, petting the thing which children in the locker room at the Ninety-second Street Y didn't have, the coarse pubic hair.

"I don't know," Alice said.

"In that case, they haven't," he said. "If they did, you'd know it. I want to."

Alice didn't answer.

"Do you know what it is?" he said. "You don't. Do you?"

She remembered Rabbit's derogatory tone of voice when he'd accused her of not knowing anything, not what a drub was or how to give one. She said nothing.

"You can't possibly be in your first year of high school, or whatever it is," he waved his hand dismissively, "and not know that. Can you? What are you, Alice? In kindergarten?"

Alice's heart began its frantic rhythmic beating. All this attention to her deformities, to her age. It seemed to her he kept changing and rearranging her, placing her first in high school as a sixteen-year-old, then in junior high school, and now, sarcastically, in kindergarten. Alice herself wasn't sure where she belonged. "I *do* know," she lied. "I know everything."

"Let's see," said J.D., probing her with his thumb. "Let's see how much you know about it." His voice was derisive and superior, but his fingers were intoxicating. A disturbing tremor passed through all of Alice, an involuntary shaking which continued and escalated until the self that had been Alice became disrupted, fragmented. She let out a gasp of surprise and pushed herself up against his hand.

"Ha," he said. "Aha, Alice."

Alice didn't care if he was laughing at her expense, or if he'd won the unspoken contest of wills between them. The sensation he made with his fingers was sublime. Adroitly, as if well-rehearsed, well-practiced, he rearranged their two bodies, lying Alice down on the muddy shore, lifting her legs up and placing them on his shoulders. Alice had no muscles and no bones. She was meat. J.D. crouched like a jackal in front of his prey, and Alice was now an eager victim. She began to fall away, to dissipate, to break apart. He was licking at it. Not at it. At *her*. She was dissolving. She was splintering. When the voluptuous, forbidden kiss had ended—this miracle, this abomination—Alice felt herself changed. She was in pieces. She was erased. While J.D. sat back on his haunches—victorious—grinning his grin, Alice stayed precariously poised between two worlds, teetering over an abyss that felt like heaven.

"Not yet," said J.D., smiling. "It gets better when you wait." He helped Alice to her feet. He put his arm around her—most kindly, most considerately, most gallantly—and led her out of the water. Her knees were rubbery. The feelings she had for J.D. didn't feel like her own. She'd turned into something feral, a wild girl, hungry for this food, this drink, this feast that belonged on the grown-ups' banquet table. He led her out past the rocks, into the woods. Lying between the brambles and the scrub grass, they traded places. It was Alice who became predatory, a hunter wanting to feed. She threw herself upon him, wriggling against him—the demon Alice—nibbling on his grown man's mouth, desperate to get more of the terrible miracle feeling.

"That's right," he said, offering her his hand. "You do like it. You do." What happened between them would never feel, to Alice, like J.D.'s doing. It would seem for many years afterward as if she'd raped herself.

One Pill Makes You Smaller

The sun crept closer to the treetops on the hillside, slowly leaching away the light. Alice and J.D. sat side by side. His hand—unmoving—rested between her legs. Their backs were against the trunk of a tree. Alice was uncomfortable. The bark, the leaves, the cold ground, it all made her itch everywhere. And yet these other sensations faded into the back of her consciousness. Her essence had relocated itself to the spot that J.D. had ceased to touch. This was all that mattered: this spot. This was all she amounted to: this need. To continue the fondling, Alice would do anything.

"Would you like to come back home with me now?" said J.D. His voice was much changed. It was deeper, richer, more confident. The game was over. Finished. He was the victor, and she the conquest. He was right, and she was wrong. She was weak and he was strong. She'd wanted it, just as he'd said. Alice was vanquished, a toy, a doll, a puppet in J.D.'s possession.

Alice nodded yes, she would go with him anywhere to get the feeling, she'd go to the ends of the earth, she'd jump off a cliff, she'd go anywhere to be with him.

"Have you ever wondered why the sea and the sky are both blue?" J.D. asked her idly. They were sitting inside his moving car. Alice had crossed her legs tightly, to contain the feeling, to contain the damage, to keep the feeling going forever and ever, to allow herself to wait for him to start again. He didn't touch her in the car. She wasn't looking at him anymore. She was staring out the window, at many of the sights she'd seen when she'd first arrived—shaggy stalks of corn; a silo in an open field of green; a herd of brown cattle; a flock of sheep; a rocky creek; a glimpse of a winding stream waving in and out of the landscape.

"Hey, Fifteen," J.D. punched her softly on the shoulder. "You with me, kiddo? You listening?"

"No," Alice admitted. Strangely enough, she was no longer interested in J.D. He had become irrelevant in comparison to her sexual discovery. J.D. had now become a means to an end.

"No, you're not listening?" he said. "Or no, you've never pondered that particular question. The question of blue."

"I don't know," said Alice listlessly. She shifted her weight and glanced at him. She wished he'd pull over somewhere and get it done with—do it—create her and destroy her with the godforsaken feeling. She wanted him to shut up. She could not imagine how he could speak about such matters when all she could think about was his hands, his lips, his tongue.

"It's because they're part of the same cosmos, baby," he said, eyeing her in the mirror. He drew a sketch, in the space in front of him, with one pointed finger in the air. It was the same finger that had been up inside her at the lake, the same finger that had left a hole in Alice. "See," he said, oblivious to the urgency of her monstrous new need, "this is water"—he stabbed the air—"and this is sky." He stabbed it again. "And up in the sky, the water nymph rules. There's no difference between them, sky and river. They're all one thing. Everything is. When you figure that out, man, you reach nirvana."

"What's one thing?" Alice asked, frowning.

"The water nymph I was telling you about, up in that tree, sister. The other day. Before you were my girlfriend," he said. How astonishing, Alice thought, that there had been such a time. Now she was imprisoned by J.D. and his calculated, expert caresses.

"The nymph," said Alice. "Yes."

"You wanted to wear my ring. Remember?" He was smiling lopsidedly. He looked giddy over having won Alice rather easily. Noticing this smugness and self-satisfaction, Alice found that she hated him completely. She despised him. But she still wanted to do the thing and feel the feeling.

"Yes," she said. "So?"

"What the water nymph does, see, is she rules places that we can't go to during our normal, straight, uptight, regular waking life. You know?"

"No," said Alice. "I don't." He wasn't handsome. He was a nerd. She saw that now, with perfect clarity. He was a loser who sold drugs because he couldn't do anything else. He was a depraved person who devoured girls.

"In that special state, doll, that's when the revelation comes. That it's all one. Sky and sea. Good and evil. Male and female. Have you, in high school, studied Jung?"

"I'm not in high school," said Alice.

"Oh. Well, you ought to check it out sometime. You'd see what I'm driving at. The idea of the supreme unity of all things reappears again and again, honey." He seemed excited. "In every culture. In every religion. In every dream."

Alice, bored, began to fidget. She pulled at the zipper of J.D.'s duffel bag. It sat beside her on the car seat. Open. Close. Open. Close. She yawned, not bothering to cover her mouth. It was taking forever, this car ride to her ruin, and he was blathering on about nonsense. Ruin me already, Alice thought. Ruin me now.

"See, Alice, language chops things up and divides them artificially. Ever read Wittgenstein?" He glanced at her.

She shook her head.

"Guess not. Well, see, Alice, there are some things that can't be expressed. Like my feelings for you, for instance. In a sense, you might say that words refer to *this* world. When you're trying to talk about the Other World, that realm of dreams and water nymphs, of spirits, that realm that lies beyond this one . . ." He trailed off, and the hand that had touched her so memorably moved back and forth, near the windshield.

"All you can do, really," he said, "is what I'm doing now. Point *toward* the fucker, Alice. Make a road sign. Make a diagram."

Alice shrugged.

"Okay," said J.D., "look." He took his sunglasses out of the pocket of the denim shirt he'd put them in when they'd dried off and gotten dressed at the lake. He held them out toward her.

Alice took them.

"Take a look, Alice. Look closely at yourself in those."

Alice peered into the shiny silver surface. Her face, reflected back at her, was goofy and distorted, as it had been ever since she'd first seen J.D. There was the bulbous forehead, the small pointed chin, the enormous eyes. "So?" Alice asked, glancing over at him.

"Through the looking glass, Alice, is a place where false dualities are exposed. There's an intersection between the two worlds—sane and insane, dream and reality, dead and living. Did you glimpse that space, princess, when you got love? When we smoked?" He sounded enthusiastic.

Alice didn't know what he was talking about. "I don't think so," she said quietly.

"By the way, does anyone know where you are?" said J.D. They had come to the end of a long, empty road and had driven over a small bridge. He'd taken a sharp left, and was now driving alongside a narrow brook with a steep embankment covered with wildflowers. As far as Alice could see, ahead of her and behind, and to the left and to the right, there was nothing but open countryside. She wondered where it was that J.D. lived, and where it was that they were going.

"Yes," said Alice. "Faith and Hope know."

"I thought you told them you were going back to New York City."

"I never said that," Alice said quickly. Her heart was drumming at a faster pace now. She turned around and looked out the back window. "Where are we going?" she asked in a panicky voice.

"Don't you trust me by *now*, kiddo?" He tapped her on her kneecap. Tap. Tap tap.

Alice moved her knee away.

"I've said to you all the time," he said, "that the *last* thing I'd want to do is hurt you, or upset you, or do anything that you wouldn't like. Haven't I?" He slammed his foot down on the pedal. With a screech, the car came to halt on the dirt road.

Alice felt vomit rise up in her throat. She was going to throw up now.

"You have to learn not to doubt me," said J.D. "You don't want to be here? No problemo, baby. Just fucking say so. If you want me to take you back, I'll take you back. If you want me to drive you home to New York, Alice, I will do that."

Alice couldn't account for the blend of helpfulness and cruelty in his voice, of anger and affection. She looked down at the floor of the car.

"Baby," said J.D., "I know this has been a big day for you. I know you've made some tough decisions, Alice. And I know, incidentally, that you've told some whoppers, sweetheart. You've told me some huge—major—fucking lies."

Alice swallowed. In her ears, it sounded as loud as an ocean tide.

"I know everything about you," J.D. said. "So don't think that you fool me."

Alice tried not to whine. "You're frightening me," she said. "Please stop it." She was far more distressed now than at any time before.

"I'm not doing anything," he said. "You're doing it to yourself. You're *making* this feeling. This fear. It's an illusion. If you'd stop worrying so much and just do what I told you—let go, sweetheart—you wouldn't keep getting all spooked and uptight and freaked out, okay? Everything is fine. It's important that you finally fucking get this already, Alice," he said. "The choice is *yours*. It's all about what *you* want. It's all about what *you* tell *me* to do."

Alice pressed her thumb to her pulse, hoping she didn't have one. If she could only have a heart attack, he'd have to stop.

"It's important to me," he said, "that I do what you want me to. If I've been mistaken here, Alice, I apologize. It's that simple. I'll take you back, just like I said I would. I'll take you wherever you want to go. I'd appreciate it if you didn't mention what we did together at the lake, because that shit could get me into some serious trouble. I know you like me, Alice. I think you might even love me a little already, like you said you did. All I am is a sensual man. I only give pleasure. And I know that you wouldn't want me to get locked up under some draconian penal code they created to deny desire. I'd be thrown together with a bunch of really *seriously* malevolent thugs like murderers. Thugs who'd kill a man for loving a girl like you. You wouldn't want that. Would you?"

Alice shook her head no. She only comprehended half of what he said, but she didn't want to be responsible for sending J.D. to prison. The thought of it made her feel sick to her stomach again. She pressed her hand to her lips to fend off another bout of nausea.

Now he took her hand in his and massaged her fingertips, pressing down, moving along toward her knuckles. He touched her hand as if it belonged to him, as if her hand was his own. "It would mean a lot to me if you wouldn't ever tell anybody," he said. "What I did—people will tell you it was wrong. But you know better. Your heart knows what it loves, Alice, and what is right."

Alice lurched toward the car door. She opened it just in time to lean outside and vomit onto the ground. She retched for a long time. She heard J.D. get out of the car, his footsteps walking around the fender and then toward her. His bare feet and jeans came into view. She couldn't see anything above his knees, because she had to keep her head down to continue vomiting. She felt his hands in her hair, gathering it carefully together and holding it away from her face. When she was finished, tears were streaming down her cheeks.

"Poor baby," he said. "You take it easy."

Alice lay back on the seat, overwhelmed. She couldn't care about any of this anymore. She was trembling again, turning into a bowl of Jell-O, quivering everywhere.

"Do you want me to take you home? To your home, honey?" He said this with genuine concern, Alice thought. And yet he had kidnapped her in some way, too, and made her his captive. This was part of her confusion: his considerate manner, his odd charm. He made the offer. He asked her nicely.

Alice heard herself saying, "I don't know."

"We're only about ten minutes away, honey," said J.D. "We'll drive over to my place, and I promise I'll let you alone. If you're not feeling well, sweetheart, you can just lie down. On your own."

Alice made a small movement with her hand. It might have been a yes. She wasn't sure then, or later. She wasn't sure what kept her quiet, or why, instead of protesting, she tended to try to figure out what J.D. wanted—her friend, enemy, boyfriend, stranger. Over and over again, all that day, Alice would figure it out and she'd give in.

Ten minutes later, they pulled up in front of an old stone farm-house on an expanse of untended land. Two of the windows had been replaced with sheets of plastic. A dirt path led up to the front entrance, where the bright red wooden door appeared to have been painted recently. The color clashed dramatically with the pale sandy stone and the gently sloping green hills in the background. It didn't look like a haunted devil's house, as Alice had feared it might. But it seemed to lack something. It had a temporary quality, as if it had been unused for a long time. There were no curtains hanging, only white sheets tacked against three of the windows, and no sign of habitation or activity. No tire swing in the tree in the yard; no lawn mower by the garage; no basketball hoop in the driveway; no decorative urn planted with flowers; no metal mailbox nailed to a post, as there were in the other houses Alice had seen in North Carolina. From the out-side, it looked empty.

"Is this your house?" Alice asked.

"You bet," said J.D. Lazily, he placed a friendly hand on the back of her head. "You feeling better?" he asked.

"A little," Alice admitted. Her doubt and confusion would come and go, and come back again. She didn't trust J.D., but she . . . She didn't like him, but she . . . No. It couldn't be explained.

"Maybe you were nervous?" he said.

"Maybe," Alice said.

"Shall we?" said J.D.

Alice got out of the car, convinced that she was watching her own actions from someplace outside herself. Her own limbs felt weak and useless, appendages which only through great effort could be moved. She followed J.D. up the pathway, searching the shape of his back—the wide shoulders, the trim waist, the faded jeans slung low—for clues. Her heart began again to rattle, ricocheting off the inner walls of her chest cavity. It no longer felt like she had a heart at all, but a black rubber Super Ball. Its movements were frantic and unpredictable. She pressed her hand to her chest, hoping to quiet it. Alice was torn about what to do, what not to do. She imagined her body being cut apart into three pieces, a head, a torso, and a pair of legs. Alice's legs would run inside J.D.'s house. Her round head would roll away, down the road, back to the bus station, and away from Dodgson to her own home. Yet even after Alice's head had left the scene of the crime, her torso would stay seated outside J.D.'s house, on his front stoop. It would remain there like a birdcage that contained the twittering heart of Alice, waiting patiently while her legs went inside with J.D.

As Alice stood on the steps, J.D. fumbled with his keys. She stared at the shiny new red paint along the doorframe. The paint shimmered and trembled, as Alice had shimmered and trembled at the lake. It took Alice a few seconds to discover that what made the paint tremble was a tear. She flung it away, rubbing her eyes with the back of her hand, impatiently. But new tears formed, welling up on her lower lashes. Overhead, the gathering clouds shook. When she gazed at the tiny white wildflowers and weeds near the doorsill, growing in a broken green plastic bucket, they rippled. She was becoming a jar brimming with water. She was full of lake.

"Here we are," said J.D. as they stepped down five cement stairs to get to the subterranean first floor. He opened the door. Alice walked over a faded doormat that spelled LOVE. The four letters were split apart into two groups, LO on the top line and VE on the bottom line. The V was crooked. Alice stared down at it, though she'd seen the same LOVE sign before, in posters and on coffee mugs.

"You coming or what?" he said.

She followed him.

Drink Me, Eat Me

The first thing Alice noticed when she crossed the threshold was the dim blue light. After a second or two, her eyes adjusted to the dusk, and she saw that they'd entered a cool, low-ceilinged room. It had the damp underground feeling of a basement. In one corner was a potbellied stove and, beside it, a rough brick fireplace filled with charred logs. The only furniture was a long table and three mismatched metal chairs, dented and splattered with white paint. A heel of bread sat on the table, wrapped in plastic. From somewhere nearby, she heard a distinct rustling and a fluttering. She imagined for a second that there were real angels nearby, invisible ones she couldn't see, watching over her and beating their white wings.

J.D. was leading the way past the central room with the table and the stove. Alice intended to follow, but she didn't. When he got to a beaded curtain that had been hung from the rafters, J.D. stopped. "Change your mind?" he said.

Avoiding his eyes, Alice looked down. The floor was made of wide beams. It was scarred and warped with age, and there were missing pieces in between the floorboards. Light spilled across the room where the wall met the floor, and colored diamond patterns danced: the reflection of the glass beads from the curtain. Sunshine came in one of the dusty, dirt-speckled windows.

"Alice," J.D. said.

He looked dwarfed, as if she were staring at him through the lens of her camera.

"Do you feel sick again?" he asked.

She watched the distant figure of J.D. walk down the hallway, growing bigger as he got closer. Even when he was near her, he seemed very far away—and Alice felt far away from both of them, from J.D. and from herself.

"Alice," he said again. He stood immediately in front of her now. He tilted his head to the side. He leaned in to kiss her. He reached around her and rubbed her back, pressing into the indentations of her spine with his fingertips. Alice imagined that each one of his fingertips contained a mouth, and that they could speak to her. They sang soothing little songs. She took one step forward, closer to J.D.

"Are you going to stay here in the front hall?" he asked. "Or are you going to come inside?"

"I'll come inside," said Alice in the high breathless voice that she had never heard before that day, and didn't recognize as her own.

J.D. put his hands on her shoulder, steering her, pushing her, down the hall. "Honestly," he said, "You're such a nervous Nellie. I told you I wouldn't hassle you, baby, didn't I? You just lie down and take a rest. You feel okay?"

"I guess," said Alice.

They entered a second room with a circular star-burst design hand-painted on the furthermost wall, stretching from one window to the other. There was a grandfather clock in one corner and a mirror in a wooden frame in another. A battered armchair sat next to a wide, round bed. It was covered with a fuzzy blue fabric that looked like fake suede. A red-and-white-checked tablecloth was heaped between the windows, covering something. She heard a noise above her. Looking up, she saw that this room was where the fluttering sound had been coming from. There was a hole in the roof, and a pair of swallows had built a nest in there. They were perched up on the thick wooden ceiling beam. One lifted its wings and flew along it, setting himself down next to the other bird. They were slim and brown. Alice found their presence comforting. She could see the scraps of twigs and leaves stuck into the missing plaster where the two swallows had built a nest.

"I named them Hope and Faith," said J.D., gesturing toward the birds. "After the twins. It's mainly Hope, the little one, who eats from my hand. Faith is more suspicious."

Alice peered at a piece of darkening sky, visible through the broken ceiling.

"Faith's a male," said J.D. "I didn't realize they were a pair, but in the spring there were speckled eggs in that nest up there. I nearly broke my neck climbing up to take a look at it on the fucking ladder. Excuse my French, Alice."

"They had baby birds?" Alice asked.

J.D. looked sad. "They did. They didn't make it, though. The eggs never hatched."

"Oh," said Alice, disappointed.

"But Faith and Hope will have some more, I'm sure. They're both tame now. Watch." He threw his duffel bag onto a card table by the door, searched through it, and took out a package of sunflower seeds. He made a high-pitched cawing sound, trying to get the swallows' attention. Then he slipped three of the seeds between his lips. He strode into the center of the room and threw his head back. With a great flapping of feathers, the bird nearest the window swooped down from the rafters. It hovered over J.D.'s head and flew away again, alighting on the wooden beam just where it had been. But now it lowered its head and began pecking at something on the wood. It had been hard for Alice to see what had happened in the confusion of movement and feathers. Now J.D. had only two seeds in his mouth.

"Did she take it from you?" Alice asked, incredulous.

"Sure she did. Why shouldn't she?"

He poured more of the sunflower seeds into his palm and held it out toward the swallows. The second one, up on the beam, flew down and landed on his open hands. It opened its beak. Alice watched as it pecked at the seeds.

"He's biting you," said Alice.

"Naw," said J.D. "This is Hope. She's my best pal. She's playing hard to get. She's flirting with me, Alice. Just like you did."

Alice was sure she had never flirted with J.D. or played hard to get. The comment gave her a wrenching feeling in her abdomen. She wondered what else was warped and backward in the way J.D. perceived her.

"How did you get the birds to do that? To eat out of your hand?" was all Alice said.

"It took me the better part of a year, honey. I'd just get high and sit down on the floor here. They start to get used to you. As long as you become part of the furniture—like a rock. And don't move."

The swallow had returned to its roost. "Would she take the seeds from *me*?" Alice asked.

"I'm not sure, baby. They don't really know you yet. You can try, though. Here." He emptied the package into Alice's hands, which she held cupped together. She offered the seeds to the swallows. They ignored her.

"You have to wait," he said.

Alice craned her neck to see the birds, sorry that they didn't want to be fed by her.

"Why don't you sit down on the floor?" J.D. suggested. "Let me see if I can find you something to sit on. I'll bring you a pillow." He walked away.

"Come here, birdies," Alice whispered. "Come here." She wanted them to be near her. She wondered if this wanting to be close was a feeling that was familiar to J.D. He must be lonely, she thought, to sit inside a run-down house for hours, getting high and feeding seeds to birds.

J.D. had returned with a square pillow. It was purple, with little bits of mirror sewn all over it, like on the Indian shirt Aunt Esmé had. He set it down. Alice knelt on it, still gazing up at the birds.

"You feel fine now," said J.D. "Don't you?"

Alice hesitated. It was better for J.D. to think she was sick. That way she wouldn't have to take her clothes off again. She didn't want to anymore. The new sensation, though powerful, had disappeared. It was, she thought, like dew on the blades of grass, that feeling. It came and then it went. She almost felt like herself again.

"Can I offer you something to drink?" said J.D.

"Yes, please," said Alice.

"What can I get you?"

"Whatever you have," said Alice. She thought he wouldn't have much. Maybe water.

"How about a Long Island iced tea?"

"All right," Alice said, listening to the way her voice echoed against the walls in the unfinished house, and to the sound of J.D.'s footsteps as he walked away.

Alice looked around the room, able to see it differently now that J.D. was gone. Against one wall was a desk. It held some old books, a stack of postcards, a string of beads, and a saucer filled with keys. Faith and Hope were both perched on the plaster ledge made by the gap in the ceiling. One after another, they pitched forward and flew out. The room was empty now. She stooped down to the floor and picked up the sunflower seeds from where she'd dropped them. She began to eat them, nervously. As she cracked the shells between her teeth, she pulled at the checked tablecloth, revealing what lay beneath. Under it was a statue made of clay. Like the figurine on J.D.'s ring, it was in the shape of a girl. At its feet were three small tangerines, but the skin had hardened and buckled. Beside them was a bouquet of wildflowers, but the petals had withered and dried. There was an incense stand at the base of the idol.

The birds returned, twittering, as Alice collapsed onto the bed. She realized instantly that the mattress contained not stuffing but liquid. It undulated, responding to her weight, enfolding her like a living thing. It was a water bed. The fabric felt spongy to the touch. Alice sank down into it, setting off a wave on either side of her. The bed made the faint glug-glugging sound of someone drinking.

Her hand fell on a table, low to the ground, next to the bed. It contained an assortment of objects that struck her as mysterious—a stack of cards, facedown, were tied with a fraying scrap of fabric. An image of an Egyptian goddess was printed on the back. Next to the cards, four miniature ceramic bowls stood in a row. The first bowl held crushed dried roses, their frail petals turning up at the edges and lined with a tracery of veins. The second bowl held three white candies, discs that looked like throat lozenges. The third held a cube of sugar. The fourth held slices of some kind of food. It looked like homemade potato chips. Alice took one of these and nibbled at it. The chip tasted foul. She put it back, covering it with the others so that the small bite she'd taken out of it wouldn't be detected. She reached for one of the white candies and put it in her mouth. It was even more bitter than the chip. It tasted horrid. Alice looked around for a place to spit it out. Rising from the bed, she began to open the screen on the window so she could spit into the grass below. Because it tasted like an aspirin, she realized, too late, that she'd eaten one of J.D.'s pills. It was dissolving on her tongue, an acrid flavor that made her wrinkle her nose and gag. She'd maneuvered the window, which rattled in its frame, a few inches up, but it got stuck. She heard J.D. approaching from behind her. Her stomach lurched and heaved with apprehension. Not wanting to get caught stealing, Alice closed the window and swallowed the pill.

"Iced tea. Here you go," said J.D., presenting Alice with a beautiful old-fashioned glass, like the ones her mother had kept locked inside a cabinet. It was heavy, made of crystal, and it had a crosshatched pattern cut into its surface.

"Thanks," said Alice, taking care to keep her lips close together so he couldn't see the remains of the bitter pill on her tongue. She took the glass from him. An ice cube clinked against the side as she tilted it up to her mouth and drained it. The pill had left a chalky texture in her mouth. She drank quickly to wash it down. She'd nearly finished it when she realized that she wasn't drinking tea at all, but a cocktail made of alcohol.

J.D. watched her with a bemused expression on his face. "Wow," he said. "Take it easy, Alice."

Like a child who has finished a glass of milk, Alice thrust out the glass toward him. She meant for him to take it away.

"Want another one?" he said, raising his eyebrows.

Alice shook her head no. "Just water," she said in a raspy voice. "Please."

"You got it." He bit his lips the way he did, Alice thought, when he was trying not to smile. "One glass of water for the lady, coming up."

He left the room. "This is an old, old house, Alice," he called to her as he walked away. "From back in the 1700s, right around the time of the American Revolution. No one gives a fuck around here, baby. It's an historic landmark and worth a bundle. But I bought it for a song."

His voice faded. He was at a safe distance. Alice raced back to the shelf where she'd found the white pill and grabbed the cube of sugar. She took a bite of it to chase away the disgusting bitter taste left by the pill and the alcohol. When she heard J.D. returning, she shoved the rest of the sweet sugar cube in her mouth and ate it.

He entered the room carrying a stack of LPs tucked under his arm, and a glass of water, which he handed to Alice. She gulped it down while J.D. turned on the phonograph and put the record on. "Do you like Zep?" he asked.

"No," said Alice. "I hate it." Her heart sank. Was there no escape from the perpetual Led Zeppelin?

The weird screeching, wailing music came into the room, playing through two oblong speakers at either end of the doorway. J.D. set the album down on top of one of them. Alice saw the jacket she had once pondered—the one that showed a picture of naked little girls, each one with hair the color of the sun. Many things had happened to Alice since she had last seen them. Yet they were clambering over their pile of jagged rocks, trying to get somewhere, as always. She sat down on the bed and studied the image, listening to the music. Behind her, J.D. strolled along the edge of the room, adjusting the white sheets that hung from the window frames. A heavy blanket, nailed to the top sill, had been tied back with a scrap of rope. He untied it, and the blanket covered the window, casting the room into darkness. He repeated this action at the second window. The last rays of the setting sun had been dancing on the floor. They disappeared. There was hardly any light in the room at all, just a narrow streak of it around the corners of the windows. She didn't ask J.D. why he wanted it that way—dark and secret, so no one could see in, so they couldn't see each other. She knew.

She heard a scratching noise and turned to see J.D. lighting a long match—almost as long as his arm—which he'd taken from a tin canister. He lit the incense, and the candles. "Alice?" he said. The sound echoed oddly. All. Is. All. His. His. His.

"Yeah?" she said.

Through the Looking Glass

She could see his face behind her, in the glass. J.D. had placed his hands on her shoulders, and had turned Alice around so that she faced the mirror. It was speckled with age, shaped like an elongated oval. It rested on a stand, carved of dark wood, in the shape of an animal's feet. Each of the four paws had toes and claws that might have belonged to a giant lion. The flame of the candle flickered, reflected in the glass. She saw two hands on her two hips—as if he were about to lead her in a dance. There was an insistent buzzing in her veins. She thought something was gnawing at her insides, threading through her organs, worms crawling in her brain. She was going to explode any minute if she couldn't get rid of them. At the same time, a languor was spreading through her. Alice was stricken with the anxiety that in the places the worms had chewed, her limbs were rotting. It was just what happened when caterpillars came and devoured plants. The sawing, chewing sound continued in her chest, and it moved up into her head. As it passed, the melting feeling washed over her, outward, into each of her limbs. She was all mixed up. J.D. was kissing her shoulders. Alice didn't know how to tell him to stop. She'd changed her mind. She wanted to turn back, but there was no place to go. There was only the two of them, reflected in the mirror. Her face, and his, stared at her. Her dark eyes, his gray. Two fiends. Two freaks. Two ghouls. She was becoming two-dimensional. Unreal. A cartoon. Flat. Now she would be trapped inside the looking glass. Across the water. Over the border.

Easily, casually, J.D. cupped her left breast under his palm. It was trapped now, too, like a fly caught beneath a saucer. Alice was afraid she might start gasping. She should not gasp. It was of overwhelming importance, now that she was frightened of everything, that J.D. not notice. Only by appearing strong and brave could Alice stay calm, proud, and victorious. She would have liked an excuse to leave, but without one, she wouldn't run and hide. The worms were chewing, but Alice was going to tough it out.

"Little Alice," sighed J.D., manipulating her breast with dry, thick fingers. "You're not really fifteen." He spoke in the flat declarative which, since Alice had met him, he'd used. It left her no room to argue.

"Are you," he said. An accusation.

Alice anxiously gauged his expression in the mirror. The stakes felt high. Everything seemed to rest upon her answer.

"No, I'm not," she said. Her voice was unsure. Wavering. Childlike.

"Tell me. How old are you? Really." He ran his thumb down between her breasts, toward her stomach. He hooked it inside her navel, like a plug.

She didn't say anything. Too many different reactions floated through her. She couldn't begin to sort them out. She felt ashamed.

"It's okay," J.D. said. He pressed inward, gently, with his thumb. "Okay?"

Okay, okay. J.D. always said that. But was it? No.

"You can tell me," he said, wiggling his thumb.

Alice made a vague gesture of helplessness. She raised her hands, then let them fall back down again.

"I *said* it's okay," he said almost crossly. "What are you afraid of?"

"I'm not afraid," insisted Alice.

"Do you think I'll get mad at you?" He drew her toward him. Now his hand was on her forehead, hot and flat. She rested, reluctantly, against his chest. The girl in the mirror looked awkward and uncomfortable. She regarded Alice with half-slit eyes.

"Yes," said Alice. "I think you will."

"I won't. Do I seem mad to you now?" To prove how less-than-angry he was, he bent down and kissed her cheek, softly, tenderly.

"Yes," said Alice. "Yes, you do seem mad."

"I do?"

"Yes." She was no longer very sure what the word meant. Any of the words. Softness. Tenderness. Those two, also, were certainly in question. She hardly knew what she was saying. The most pressing matter, for some reason, was to do it—whatever it was—and to do it quickly. Then he'd stop asking her questions, disguised as commands, and he'd stop giving her instructions while pretending to be asking things. It was getting too hard to understand, like the night she'd tried to read Aunt Esmé's calculus textbook. Too many signs and symbols, arrows and numbers, everything foreign, adult, and difficult. Alice heard herself say, "I don't understand."

In the mirror, J.D.'s face had changed. His jaw protruded. His lips had tightened. "You said I seemed angry, which I'm not. So stop imagining things. All right?"

"Yes," whispered Alice. "Yes, yes. Okay?" She was going to start crying any minute. Everything felt wrong. Something ugly was now happening. It was the same ugliness she'd sensed on the rocks when he'd told her to undress, the same ugliness she'd felt when he'd talked to her in a low insinuating tone at the lake, when she'd tried to run from him.

In the mirror, the suntanned hand stroked Alice's cheek. It brushed a tear away. "This isn't scary," he repeated. "See?"

Alice nodded. They both were lying now. He was saying it wasn't scary in the room between them because it was.

"There's nothing to feel guilty about," said J.D. And, again, Alice sensed they both knew this wasn't true. He was scared, and he was guilty, and so was she.

"I want what you want," he said. "I know why you lied to me about your age." He patted the top of her head. "All right?" he urged.

"All right," said Alice falsely.

"We want to be together. That's what we want. Right?"

"Uh-huh. Right," Alice answered quickly. Was it so? She had to choose. Right or not right? Forward or back? Stay here or go? Alice didn't know the right answer. She didn't know. She didn't know the meanings, even, of the words. Tender. Stay. Gentle. Go. Angry right. Guilty no. Everything jumbled up in a web, all leading up to the same thing. One answer only. She felt herself collapsing under pressure. She'd done that throughout the sixth grade, too, anytime she had to take a test. The worst was multiple choice, when all the choices began to look the same. In the end, she'd panic. It was happening, just like that reading comprehension test she'd failed at the end of the sixth grade—even though she was good at reading, she really was. She'd failed it anyway. Her brains deserted her. They bailed. She'd taken any available answer just to get one, any one, just to finish it, no decision, no reason, no thinking, just to Go and Stay and Yes and Do. It was because time was running out and the clock was ticking, she could hear it on her wrist. Mickey Mouse keeping track, urging her forward, click click, tick tick, click click. And the grandfather clock in the corner, too, was counting, its pendulum swinging back and forth. And counting most rapidly of all was the ticker within, the pounding of her heart—or J.D.'s heart, which was which, who was who, Alice couldn't tell. Me, Alice. What I want. Or you. And me. And you. Yes was probably the best answer. Of course it was. When in doubt, pick yes. Like on Aunt Esmé's record by the Beatles. "Yes is the answer," that's what it said. Never say no. No was square. No was wrong and yes was right. Yes was easiest. And wasn't the easiest the best? Alice had grave doubts, unexpressed. She was frozen solid. Stuck inside the ice mirror, the flat reflecting pond. But yes, the clock said, yes, said J.D., heart beating, yes, said Alice, he and she, me and you, us and them, yes, yes.

"What are you, then, fourteen?"

Alice moved her head a fraction. No more speech.

"Thirteen?"

She flinched. No mouth with which to speak.

"Alice, baby, are you thirteen?" His tone was incredulous. There was a smirk on his face of disbelief. Menacing. Leering. Alice wasn't sure that it quite qualified as smiling. She wasn't sure what smiling meant, or what it was.

"Thirteen," picked Alice, in a frog's croak of a voice, electing the number arbitrarily. A number, a word. Count to thirteen, ready, set, go.

"Really?"

"Yes."

"Thirteen is a nice age," he said. "Alice, thirteen's just right." He nuzzled her cheek. Her hair. "Don't be frightened, doll," he said. "We won't turn on the lights."

This comment made no sense. Nothing did. Everything, in and out, around and about, was about to collapse. The light was nice. Usually, Alice was afraid of the dark. If they didn't want the lights on, it could only be to get away from the mirror, to hide away, to keep it secret, its secret yes.

Alice gulped and a gurgling noise escaped her. Still she felt no mouth in her face, no words in her mind, no tongue, no head, no throat. She remembered in the woods how J.D. had said, This isn't a good idea. If it hadn't been good then, why was it good now? If only she could bring herself to whisper that: Not a good idea, J.D. To remind him.

Alice wanted to say: I'm not a woman. I'm a girl. But her tongue was tied, she couldn't.

"Then you haven't done this yet, I guess. If you're thirteen."

"Yah."

"You have?"

"Um," said Alice.

"You're getting all nervous for nothing baby. I told you to relax."

Relax, Alice commanded herself. You nervous nothing. Relax! But the more she tried, the worse she felt.

J.D. massaged her shoulders. She liked the feeling, but in the mirror his hands looked like two tarantulas.

"It doesn't matter, Alice, what age you are. Okay? Relax. I've got love for you anyway."

Alice felt she was being taught an equation she couldn't grasp. She was supposed to have finished the lesson by now. There was no more time to work out the problem. They'd moved on to the final test. He took her hand in his and pressed it earnestly. For a black moment, Alice's hand was gone. She couldn't feel. Alice had the uncanny conviction that she was not entirely present, that she was not part of the conversation, not even in the room. He was talking, but not to her. He was talking to the image in the mirror. To himself.

In the looking glass, J.D. flashed himself a grin. "It's a turn-on," he said, "to be honest."

The girl in the mirror turned her head away, into J.D.'s shirt. She felt safe there. She could hide for a while. She could feel his breath, tickling the hairs on the back of her neck. She moved away from the sensation. It irritated her. It felt stupid and annoying. No, it wasn't safe to be near him. She hated everything. What a fool, what an imbecile, he seemed. In the mirror, his lips were pursed as if he were about to play a flute. His instrument was Alice. She felt the stream of air come out of his mouth, again and again, onto the back of her ears. He was blowing on her.

"Stop it," Alice said. It was the only time that she objected, the only time in J.D.'s basement that she summoned the conviction to say no.

"Shhh," he said, ignoring her, using his hands—all over her face—to rub her complaints away. "Shhh. I promise. Nothing will happen that you don't like. It's all good. It's all all right."

They stayed still, suspended in motion.

"Listen," J.D. told her after a moment. "My love's speaking. Don't talk." Alice listened. She felt him press himself against her backside, as Rabbit had done once. She heard absolutely nothing but the deafening sound of silence.

Flight

Alice was floating, belly up. A majestic bird was poised above her. Its wings were stretched from east to west, concealing the sun from view. The bird was a swan. The bird was as big as the world. It pecked her apart, eating her from the inside out, until there were only drops of Alice left, rolling, gathering, and breaking. Someone screamed, not Alice. Alice was a rising mist. Alice was a fine dispersion, scattered.

Alice in Bed

When she was Alice again, or what was left of Alice, she was lying in J.D.'s bedroom on J.D.'s water bed. The bed was covered in artificial suede, soft to the touch, and it was blue. The room was silent except for the sound of wind chimes in the backyard, dangling from a tree. Alice could see into the garden through the open back door, the small white wildflowers which dotted the grass. Alice was sore between her legs, but she felt completely safe and secure. It was the same feeling she'd had whenever she'd been violently ill with the stomach flu, when the sickness had finally passed. A storm had occurred in her brain. She'd been injured in some way, but she sensed these events were now a part of history, finished, past. Whatever the calamity had been, it was over.

J.D. padded into the room. He was wearing a pair of loose white pajama bottoms. "How you feelin', kiddo?" he said.

Alice turned away from him and looked up at the rafters. The room was dusk now, and she could see stars and planets, made of yellow phosphorescent stickers that had been pasted on the ceiling. The birds were gone.

J.D. crouched down at the side of her bed, squatting on his haunches. "Jesus, Alice," he said, "do you think you could have told me?"

Alice didn't move, but her eyes turned toward him. She could not speak.

"I had no idea you were tripping your brains out until you lost your grip and flipped completely out," he said. "Next time you decide to drop acid, babe, I'd be grateful if you'd tell me."

Alice whispered something that made no sense.

J.D. stared at her. "Look, babe. You're okay. Okay?"

It was an order. Alice had to be okay now, whether she was or wasn't. She glanced down, bewildered, at her limbs. Her inner thighs were encrusted with rust, like the metal chains that held the swings in the playground in Central Park. J.D. patted her leg reassuringly. "Fuck, Alice," he said. "I didn't know. It's not my fault. You should have told me."

"Ssss," Alice said, "ree. Sorry." There was an echo inside her. A space had been carved out in her innards, she believed. She felt hollow.

"Sorry? No, no, babe. You don't have to be sorry. Shut up with that, would you? I'm not asking you to apologize."

He was asking for something, though. Alice wondered what he wanted. She thought he probably wanted her to go home. She closed her eyes. How tired she felt, and how heavy. How exhausting it was, she thought, to play this part that was expected of her, of a girl, an Alice.

"How was I supposed to know?" said J.D. "How?"

"Shhh," said Alice with her eyes closed. He was giving her a headache. All his accusations. All his unanswerable questions. All his fears.

"See, Alice," he continued, "I thought we were on the same wavelength, kiddo. I thought you were right there all along, you know, with me. I was high, and I didn't realize how off your fucking gourd you were, sweetheart. You do know that, right? By the time it hit me that you were on some bum trip, I'd gotten kind of carried away, I guess."

So many words. Alice didn't care about them. Only one number mattered. She opened her eyes and said this number. Alice said: "Eleven."

J.D.'s face didn't register the information. Then he said, "Eleven what?"

Alice put her hand to her heart. "Leven," she said. "Leven."

"E-leven?" said J.D.

She nodded yes.

"You're kidding, right?" he said.

"Eleven," she said again. The word didn't come out normally. Her mouth wasn't functioning. She spoke the way Claire James in the tenth-grade special education class spoke. Claire James was deaf.

"Are you telling me that I just popped the cherry of an eleven-year-old?" he said. J.D. stood up and backed away from the water bed. "If you're fucking with me, Alice. Don't. Okay?" he said.

She didn't answer. Her capacity for speech was limited. For the moment, it was gone.

"What the fuck is your problem?" said J.D. "Are you trying to screw me up here? This is bullshit. Did you lie to me?"

Alice grabbed the pillow that was beside her and smothered her face with it. It smelled of sweat, the waxy oils from human hair, shampoo, semen, and musk—odors that she would forever afterward identify with J.D. She pushed the pillow hard against her mouth and nose, suffocating herself, not wanting to be this Alice.

J.D. tore the pillow out of her hands. "Christ," he said. "Please don't do this to me. You're fine. You're fine now. Hear me?"

Alice bit down on the inside of her mouth and kept biting until she felt a warm liquid and tasted blood.

"Get up, sweetheart," said J.D.

Alice ignored him.

"Get the fuck up out of my bed, baby. If you tell anybody about this, I'm dead. Do you hear me, Alice? *I am dead.*" He took her by the shoulder and shook. "This is no joke, Alice," he said. "Knock it off. There's absolutely nothing the matter with you."

Alice growled at him, a low guttural noise from the back of her throat.

"This is fucking terrific," said J.D., walking away and standing in front of the clay statue on the table between the windows. "I've already got a prison record for dealing. Now I'm a child molester? What the hell were you thinking?"

"Aggh," said Alice.

"You don't look like any eleven-year-old I've ever seen," he said.

"Ahh ah," said Alice. She rolled over onto her stomach, the water sloshing inside its fake suede casing. She pressed her forehead into it and did something that was like crying. She felt the water inside the bed roll as J.D. sat at the foot of it. She felt his hand on her arm. "I'm sorry I got angry," he said.

Alice lay perfectly still. J.D. spoke to her with his fingertips, stroking the back of her neck, rubbing her shoulder blades. She shrugged her shoulders and moved closer to the wall, hoping to shake him off. He stopped touching her at last.

She felt the waves inside the water rock her and heard J.D. lying down beside her. "Come here a minute," he said. "Don't shut me out like that, sweetheart, don't push me away."

Alice felt wrong and bad at every turn. Whatever he did, whatever she did, all of it was wrong. If she turned her back on him, that was bad. If she no longer cared about him, or herself, or what either of them did or said, that was bad. If she pretended to be sixteen, that was wrong, but it was no good being eleven, either. He was lying down, putting his arm around her. She stared down at his forearm, next to the chipped yellow wall. It had prominent blue veins and dark hair down to his wrists.

"You're not tripping," he said. "You came down late last night, and you were fine. You slept for sixteen hours. You've been at my place all night, all day. Today is fucking Saturday, Alice. You can't still be tripping. Can you?"

Alice studied his fingernails. They were wide and flat. The one on his thumb was uneven, as if he'd chewed on it or it had gotten broken. Each of his nails had a line of brown beneath it. His hands were dirty. It took Alice a moment to see that the dirt was her own blood, which had dried.

"Are you listening to me or what?" said J.D.

Alice nodded. She stared at the chipped piece of plaster on the wall. It became a blank screen and on this blank screen she watched a movie. What she saw was a scene that was now preserved, indelibly, in her memory. It had taken place on the water bed, Alice remembered.

"Listen, baby," she remembered he had said, "I've got to tell you, if you're going to lie there all stiff and rigid, honey pie, you're not going to have fun. What can I do to help? How can we loosen you up, Alice, and relax you?"

Alice had stayed where she was. She'd been perched on the edge of the bed. The space around her had begun subtly shifting. The room had been shrinking and expanding. Everything she saw had a pulsating halo of light around it. Nothing would stay still. The world was in a turbulent, dizzying state of motion. Objects that had been solid were fragmenting and splitting. Whatever she looked at fell away, broke apart into bits of light. She had nothing to grab on to. Even her hand, when she brought it to her face, swirled into orbit and became a thousand shooting stars, a thousand atoms. A chasm had opened up between her, with her incoherent exploding thoughts, and J.D. He spoke to her from the planet that she'd left. She struggled to stay near it, not to drift into outer space too far.

"Hmm?" he said to her, in the past. What past? That night. That Friday. "Isn't there anything I can do?" He'd made a patter with his fingertips on the small of her back. "Shall I give you a massage?" he'd offered.

Alice had lost language. She had neither the capacity for the one she'd known, in words, or for the new language of the body which J.D., that day, had been speaking. She heard a noise escape from her lips. It was nothing human.

"We should do this on the floor. Come down here," J.D. said.

But Alice couldn't move.

"Alice, what's up with you? Come on over here, honey."

She could not.

He pulled her to him clumsily—half lifting her, half dragging her. The bed lurched like a ship beneath them. "Earth to Alice," he said, looking at her eyes.

"Sick," Alice managed. She was not sure what she'd said, or what it meant.

J.D. switched on the lamp. It had a red fringed shade, and it cast a glowing red light. The room turned into a chamber of the heart. Alice listened to the crashing thunder of her pulse. With each heartbeat, J.D.'s room contracted and expanded.

"Wooh," said Alice.

He leaned in closer. "Are you on something, baby?" he asked. "Your pupils are completely dilated." His face was changing. It had become white and flat, like a paper moon.

"Oh," said Alice, to warn him. He was no longer a man, but a cardboard figment.

"You're tripping?" he asked.

Alice scanned his features, uncomprehending.

"Did you take stuff from me—from my bag?"

"Show," she told him.

"The sugar?" said the moon.

"Shoe," she agreed.

"Oh. The sugar!" he told her in a voice full of treacle and false cheer. Even in her condition, Alice had heard the fear behind it. "Okay!" he said. "It's okay. Just lie down here, baby, and I'll turn some music on. Don't worry about anything."

But on her private planet, there was no sun or oxygen. And Alice was very worried. Worry had become a geographical place, and a monolithic condition. She was worry personified.

Three thousand years had passed since Alice's deflowering. J.D. was rocking her like a baby, crooning nonsensically to her, telling her little stories, jokes, and rhymes. "You're coming down," he said again and again, wishing it so. "You're coming in for a nice soft landing."

When had this happened? This holding, this crooning, and this rocking? Alice didn't know. Now there was time and it was passing.

"Scary," said Alice.

"I'm sorry, Alice. Really I am. That was a bum trip you had." He patted her all over, the security guard patting down the suspect, the doctor checking for broken bones. "You're all sweaty. You sweat buckets. You want a bath, Alice? You want something to eat? You want some eggs? Some orange juice?"

"J.D.," said Alice to remind herself who he was.

"Alice," said J.D.

But the edges had been blurred—the fine line crossed that distinguishes all things: he, she, we, me, you. Alice couldn't quite tell who she was, or what.

J.D. seemed to sense her confusion. "Me, J.D," he said, thumping his chest with his fist, pretending to be a caveman. "You, Alice," he said, patting her stomach lightly.

Alice, who had been hallucinating for hours, fell asleep.

"This will help. This will make you feel better. This will be nice," promised J.D.

They were in the dreary bathroom, with its mildew smell and its stained floral wallpaper. Alice was climbing into the bath. The shades were drawn. Night had fallen, maybe many of them. For all Alice knew, days or years had passed since she'd left her house on Sixty-seventh Street, when she'd ridden in a yellow taxicab. She drifted in and out of reality.

"Is this a church?" asked Alice.

"Sure, it's a church," said J.D.

She thought it was a church because there was water—holy water?—in the white porcelain tub, and there were white candles in foil saucers. She sat down in the church. J.D. soaped her back, singing along with the music that played, a hollow sound, from down the hallway.

"You are my flower, you are my power, you are my woman who knows," he chanted.

"Are you back, Alice?" he said. "Anybody home? Not yet? Don't worry. It's fine. Fine, fine, fine. You'll be all right. All right? *All* right." He was trying to convince her, to convince both of them. But Alice could tell that he was worried. Something was wrong. It wasn't going to be all right again.

"How much of that cube of sugar did you eat?" he asked in a nonchalant tone.

"Half," said Alice, barely remembering.

"Just one half. Right, baby?"

"I think so," Alice told him.

The hours lengthened. Alice stayed in her bath. J.D. went in and out of the room. Now when he saw her, he looked at her strangely. Long, sad, guilty looks. "How's it going?" he asked each time, checking. "You all right?" he'd say repeatedly, tickling her neck as if she were a little kid. He didn't call her princess or little girlfriend anymore. Alice paid attention to him for a moment or two, and then she lost track. On the wallpaper, in the flickering candlelight, she had a great deal to amuse her. She had winged fairy friends who danced and whispered; she had animated griffins, goblins, and cartoons to watch; she had displays of light and color to attend to. Outside, dawn was breaking. Alice listened to the songs of birds. They were singing especially for her, and Alice understood them.

Voices softly speaking, rising and falling, from down the hall. They were arguing. Night had turned to morning, and morning had turned to day. Maybe many of them, one after another. Alice didn't know.

"You don't take a tripped-out kid to the fucking hospital," said He.

"Who are you concerned about?" said She. "That girl? Or yourself?"

"I'm concerned about Alice. Of course I'm concerned about fucking Alice. She's been tripping for three days."

"We've got to take her. Her sister called up at the institute. A girl named Esmé."

"I've spoken to her sister."

"What are you going to do about Noko?"

"I've spoken to Odette. I said I was her uncle."

"Jay, I have to tell her at some point."

"Tell her what? Tell who? Back me up, Faith. Please? I need you."

"I said the Duncan girl went on a camping trip with Hope. And she came down with a mild case of food poisoning. Jesus, Jay. Don't fuck around with this. We've got to get her back to New York. Otherwise her sister will call the state police."

"Why would she do that?"

"Because she happens to be flying back to New York City tomorrow morning, that's why. I said Alice would be there. Look, I don't want to be mixed up with this crap of yours, Jay. I don't have a good feeling."

"She never told me she was fucking eleven, all right? I thought she was fifteen, fourteen."

"Oh well. That ought to explain everything. Why not try telling that to the cops?"

"Go screw yourself. You know what I mean."

"Jay, I want to believe you."

"What is it that you think? Huh? Go on, Faith. Tell me. Say it."

"I don't know what to think of you. You take a child in your car, you give a child acid."

"I didn't give her anything. She took it from me. And I've

told you four million times, Faith. She fooled you too. Just look at her. She's as tall as I am, practically. I had no fucking idea she was a little fucking kid."

"Stop swearing at me. I'm not the one who did anything."

There was the sound of heavy footsteps, and something slamming on a table.

"Someone ought to lock you up, really," she said. "You have no control over yourself. You have no judgment. You just do whatever you want, you act on impulse, you never think twice, Jay. You just take an action."

"What action would you suggest I take now?"

"I told you. Do the right thing for once. Take that child to the hospital."

"Quit calling her a child!"

"That's what she is."

"She's Alice. All right? You make me sound like some kind of criminal. I feel bad enough as it is."

"So we just won't do anything? To help prevent you, Jay, from feeling worse?"

"She's not some little kid. She's Alice. She's a person. She's my friend. Okay?"

"No, it *isn't* okay. You'd better deal with that. It's been more than seventy-two hours. She isn't coming down."

"She is. She's going to."

"She took a hit of the strongest acid you've ever dealt."

"Not one. Just a half."

"But you counted. I was standing right here and you said a cube was missing."

Alice heard a sniffling sound. The He was crying. It filled her with foreboding.

Bad-bad, bad-bad, bad-bad, went her heart. She could hear her blood pounding in her temples, or she thought she could.

Bu-buh, bu-buh, bu-buh. Alice stood up, in the badness, frightened.

"You said we'd take her to the emergency room if she wasn't coherent in seventy-two hours. Well? In another fifteen minutes, Jay, it'll be seventy-four. I'm counting. I'm not waiting for you anymore."

"Let's wait. Another hour. Please. We'll wait. She'll be fine. She's better already."

"The last time you went in there, she didn't even recognize you. She's a babbling idiot."

"She isn't. She isn't. She's Alice. She's a—"

"She's a what?"

"She'll be strong."

"Is that something that you've tested lately? An eleven-year-old's strength?"

"Shut up with that. I've explained. I've explained!"

"You can't just keep her soaking in there, you know, like a pet turtle, in your bathtub. It isn't good for her."

"She likes it in there. In the bath, in the candlelight, she does all right. Listening to *Houses of the Holy*. She likes that. She seems perfectly happy. She's good in there. She's calm."

"She's wasted. Gone."

"I didn't hurt her. Not at all. I would never—"

"You'd never what? I was thirteen. Or have you forgotten all of that?"

"You came to *me*. It wasn't *my* idea to get together with you."

"That's funny, I thought there was a law. Statutory rape is—what? Around three to five years in the state of North Carolina."

"Thanks for the info. You looked it up, or you checked in with the police department, or what? You're turning on me now? Is that it? Turning me in?"

"I'm just informing you."

"But she lied to me. Can't you understand?"

"Did you bother asking her if she was out of grade school?"

"It never in my wildest dreams occurred to me."

"Time's up now, Jay. I'm making the call."

"I need to talk to Alice first."

"Forget it. I'm calling."

"I'll be right back."

Alice heard footsteps. A minute later, the door to her candlelit shrine opened.

"Hey, baby," murmured J.D., nodding in Alice's direction. He shut the door behind him. He knelt down before the toilet bowl and vomited. When he'd finished heaving, he wrapped his arms around the porcelain seat, as if the cold white tile had become something soft and comforting, like a stuffed animal.

"I'm in deep shit," he said. "They're gonna cut my balls off. I'm gonna fry."

"Jay," said Alice.

"Yeah, baby?" He didn't turn around.

"The water's cold."

He stayed still for another moment. Then he crawled across the floor toward her and sat beside the tub, dangling his fingers in the water.

"You want to get out of there or what?" he said. "You've been sitting in that tub forever. You're getting all waterlogged and wrinkled." He grabbed her hand and examined it.

"I feel okay now," Alice said.

J.D. kept looking at her hand. He blinked. His nostrils quivered in that way that she remembered—like a rabbit. Sniffing. Testing, to see which way the wind was blowing. "Are you?" he said with his head bowed. "Are you really, Alice?"

"Yes."

"Thank the fucking Lord," he said. He looked up at the ceiling. "You're sure?"

"Yeah."

"Absolutely one hundred percent fine?"

"Fine. Yes. I am."

He dangled his hand over the rim of the tub, back in the tepid bath again. Under the surface of the water, Alice's fingers swam like minnows to greet his. The two sets of fingertips nosed against each other, like pairs of kissing fishes.

"He and she," said Alice. "You and me."

"Are you really all right?" he said, frowning. "You still sound off."

"All right," she said. The objects in the room had a glow around them. She could hear a whispering coming from underneath the sink. But she didn't like to see J.D. getting upset over her. She would pretend to be fine, she decided. Alice dried herself off with a thin, scratchy towel and began to walk into the bedroom. She walked slowly, with the feeling that her feet weren't touching the ground. She kept her hand against the wall, as she'd once clung to the edges of the pool on Ninety-second Street when she was swimming.

"You sure you're fine?" J.D. said, following after her.

"I'm fine."

Her clothes were not where she'd left them. J.D. had folded them and put them on top of his dresser, with his own things. Alice took them down. "Would you please leave?" she said.

J.D.'s eyes widened in surprise. "Sure," he said, and walked out.

Alice got dressed as quickly as she could. Everything felt complicated and difficult. Unfolding her shirt. Getting on her bra. Putting the shirt over her head. She couldn't find her shoes. Then she remembered that she'd been barefoot, and she found the rubber sandals sticking out from underneath the dresser. She put them on. The Band-Aid on her ankle was gone, but the skin was sore. She felt pain between her legs, too. She had no clear memory of what she and J.D. had done, only the pressure of his body flattening hers down on the rolling water bed, and the sawing sensation, the certainty that she was being cut apart with knives. That, and the grimacing, wincing faces J.D. had made, working and working, from over her. It had taken a long time.

"Alice," said Faith, gravely, when Alice—at last—had made it to the front room. She'd had to walk like an old woman, inch by inch. "How do you feel?"

"I feel better," Alice said. She could see her own belongings— her knapsack, her tote bag, and her Polaroid, sitting on J.D.'s floor. Faith had brought them over.

"Should I call your aunt?" said Faith. "Alice, should I—"

"No," said Alice, cutting her off. "I'm fine."

"Should I call the police?" said Faith.

"Why?"

"Because . . . I was worrying about you."

"What would the police do?"

"Arrest me," said J.D. He was sitting on the floor holding out sunflower seeds to the birds. Alice couldn't see them. They were high up in the rafters.

"They'd talk to you," said Faith. Her voice was low and, to Alice, ghastly.

"Don't call anybody," she said. "Don't!"

"Okay," said Faith. "Alice, I won't."

"I want to go home. Take me home."

"May I just check first, Alice? To be sure that you're okay?"

J.D. threw the sunflower seeds down. They scattered across the floor. "For God's sake, what's the matter with you?" he said. "Are you crazy?"

"I want to check her, Jay."

"Check her for what? Why treat her like a felon? Can't you see she's tired and scared? Can't you leave her alone? Leave her alone. She wants to go back. Take her. Take her home."

"I'd like to be sure, Jay," said Faith.

One of the quivering tremors that had been bothering Alice intermittently passed through her. It began in her spine and traveled up her neck, then down her arm. She straightened her back, hoping that the shaking wasn't visible.

"Fuck that shit," said J.D. "She had a bad trip. It's over now. She's fine. You're fine, aren't you, Alice?" His eyes burned, pleading with her.

"Yeah, I am," said Alice. "What day is today? Is it July? Is it August yet?"

"No. Not yet," said J.D., the desperate eyes saying something more, something different. "It's Sunday, July 27th. You'll go back to your aunt now. We'll get you back home just fine. There's plenty of time. They'll be expecting you."

But Faith was walking toward her. Alice backed away. Faith reached out and put a hand on Alice's shoulder. "It'll only take a moment," she said. "Let's do it over here."

"Don't you dare touch her," said J.D.

Faith stared at him, her mouth opened slightly.

"If you touch her, you're dead, Faith. If you touch Alice, I'll kill you."

"You're out of your mind," she said.

"Just please leave Alice alone."

"You did it," said Faith. She turned from J.D. to Alice. Alice felt her face turn hot, the truth-telling rush of blood, a tide of crimson. It was Alice's fault, and it was all going to come out now.

"You did, didn't you?" said Faith.

And then no one said anything. Alice hung her head, burning at the stake. Burning.

"I don't know what Alice was even doing at your house in the first place," said Faith. "Alice, why did you come over? How did you get here? Why did J.D. bring you here?"

"I was upset when you and the dark angel played a trick on me," said Alice. "I ran away and I got lost. J.D. found me and we drove here."

"The angel?" said Faith.

"Hope, I mean," said Alice quickly.

Faith's eyes moved back and forth, back and forth. First she looked at Alice. Then she looked at J.D.. She was studying them. "Did he get you drunk?" said Faith. "Did he give you a quaalude?"

"No," said Alice. "He was downstairs when I took them."

"Why would you do that, Alice?"

Alice shrugged.

"I've got to go," said J.D. "Would you drive her home, please?"

"Where are you going?" said Faith.

"I have to be someplace."

"Which is? Where?"

"There's someplace I need to be. Let it go, Faith. Let it be."

Alice watched, with a pang, as he took a jacket from a peg on the wall. He shrugged it on and lifted up his hand, waving at them. "Bye, girls. Alice, you take care." He strode out the door, leaving it open. For the last time, Alice looked at him. She thought he would turn back to see her once more, to say something once more to her with the sky gray ocean of his eyes, but no, he didn't. She heard the car door open and then slam shut.

She heard him start the ignition. He turned the motor on and, without Alice—without Alice—he drove away.

"What happened at J.D's house?" Faith said.

Alice was lying, bundled under a blanket, in the backseat. It was dark. They had been driving for a long time. The only light came from passing cars, headlights that shone brightly and then vanished. They had reached a tollbooth, and were about to cross a bridge. Alice was afraid as they drew up to the uniformed woman who stood high up in a plastic box. She was afraid they'd pull her out of the car and charge her, and arrest her.

"Nothing," said Alice. She gathered the blanket more closely around her.

"Did he do anything to you?" Faith handed some money to the attendant. The long wooden bar that blocked their path was raised to let them pass. Alice breathed a sigh of relief. She wouldn't be arrested this time.

"Like what?" she asked, playing dumb.

"Anything. Anything at all," said Faith. Down the black road—following that bright white line—the car went.

"He fed the birds," said Alice. "He showed me how to feed them but they didn't like me to be near them. They didn't let me."

"How are you feeling now?" said Faith.

Alice watched Faith's face in the mirror. "I'm feeling fine," she said.

"Why did you do what you did, Alice? You didn't have to run away."

"I don't know."

"What made you take shit out of J.D.'s stash?"

"Aunt Esmé and her friends are always doing it all the time," Alice said. "I just wanted to try it."

"Acid's not a game, Alice. You don't just steal some and take it on a whim."

"I know," said Alice.

"Would you do me a favor and not tell your aunt that you were tripping?"

"Okay, I won't," Alice said. She was making a list in her mind, counting on her fingers all the things she couldn't tell anyone, all her secrets.

"Alice?"

"Yes?"

"Are you certain about this?"

"About what?"

"That nothing happened."

"Yes," said Alice. "Yes. Yes, yes. Okay? I'm sure."

Faith didn't ask her anything more. She turned the car radio on. Alice listened attentively. She understood all of it now—the shrieks and the wails, the bass and the percussion, the chase, the challenge, the hunt, and the surrender. This, then, was rock and roll.

"What time is it?" Alice asked. She wrapped her fingers around her wrist. She felt nothing there. She'd forgotten her watch. She'd forgotten Mickey Mouse.

"It's about three o'clock on Monday morning," said Faith, stifling a yawn.

According to the grandfather clock in J.D.'s room, it had been seven o'clock at night when she'd left. Eight and a half hours after Alice had walked down the overgrown path that led away from J.D.'s house, she arrived at the front steps of 202 East Sixty-seventh Street. Faith crashed on the couch. Alice found a wedge of Jarlsberg cheese in the refrigerator, and a stale seeded roll in the bread basket. She took them with her to bed. Faith left early the next morning, quietly letting herself out of the house.

Alice was still lying there, curled up in the fetal position, the next afternoon when Aunt Esmé came home.

"How's it going?" said Aunt Esmé, striding into Alice's room. She had cut her hair short and dyed it green. "You feeling better?"

"I have an upset stomach," Alice lied.

"I heard. How was camp?"

"It was fun," said Alice. "How was Crash?"

"Fantastic."

"Where's Persephone?" said Alice.

Aunt Esmé walked over to the shelf where Alice kept her collection of miniature porcelain animals—porcelain squirrels, hedgehogs, dogs, cats, and frogs. She began picking each one up and putting it back down again.

"Where's Persephone?" asked Alice again.

"She's in California."

Alice said nothing.

"Oh, Alice, I'm really sorry . . ." Aunt Esmé began.

"It doesn't matter," said Alice, turning away to face the wall.

"I'm sure she's having the best time, Alice. We went for a hike, Crash and I, in this beautiful redwood forest. And Persephone was just so happy when she saw a groundhog. She began chasing it and somehow, I'm not sure how it happened. Somehow she broke loose and got away from me. She'll be a wild dog now, Alice. I think she'll really have a better life in California. Don't you?"

"Sure," said Alice. She wondered whether Persephone was alive.

For hours, she stayed in bed.

"Hey," said Rabbit from the doorway. The long shadows on the wall meant it was afternoon.

"Hey," said Alice.

Stuart and Rabbit tramped upstairs and down, raiding the re-frigerator, getting high, opening the windows to get rid of the smell, and playing the stereo at top volume. Everything was just as usual. When she heard the melodies from *Houses of the Holy*, Alice listened for a moment. Then she covered her ears with her pillow.

The telephone began to ring at odd hours of the night. It rang once or twice, then stopped. It took Alice two more days—during which she stayed in her room, staring at the ceiling—before she decided she should answer it. When she was sure that everyone else was asleep, Alice took a blanket and pillow downstairs and slept on the couch. When the phone rang again, she picked up the receiver reflexively, before she'd even opened her eyes.

"Hello?" Alice whispered.

No one answered.

"Hello?" she repeated. She heard breathing on the other end of the line.

"I know it's you," said Alice. She listened to him breathing. Alice breathed back. They breathed together, a duet of sighs.

"I'm sorry," Alice whispered. "I'm sorry that I lied."

Silence. After a moment, the phone went dead.

Alice walked over to Charlie Chaplin's cage. She gathered him into her hands, and held him and petted him for a long time. Opening the back door, she set the hamster down on the ground. He sniffed the air for a moment. Then he made a mad dash to-ward the rhododendron bushes, skirting around behind them, and running through the pebbles in the flower beds. He paused, his ears pulled back, listening.

"Bye," said Alice. She closed the door.

A Visible Woman

Alice had curled up in the armchair in her room. She spent most of her time there, looking out the window. The bamboo blinds were drawn. Like a bandit in hiding, she peered through an opening between the slats. A dachshund was trotting eastward on Sixty-seventh Street, pulling the man who held his leash. A woman in a poncho took a toddler by the hand. Two boys in navy blue school uniforms rode their bikes down the block. Most days, this small patch of the city—the cars, dogs, and pedestrians that passed—was all Alice saw of New York.

Alice pulled her blanket around her shoulders. The late September air was cool and mild. She'd already missed three weeks of school. Her old teachers at Fieldwood weren't expecting Alice; they thought she was starting the seventh grade at I.S. 70. Her new teachers at I.S. 70 hadn't missed her, either; she wasn't in their records. She'd never enrolled. It was as if she didn't entirely exist. Aunt Esmé kept reminding Alice that the situation couldn't last forever. Eventually, the Board of Education would catch on. They'd send a truant officer to hunt Alice down, as they'd done once with Aunt Esmé. In the meantime, however, the days rolled along. No one called to ask why Alice was not in class. Dean was still in Connecticut; Aunt Esmé visited him by herself. Alice didn't know whether Esmé had told Dean that his younger daughter hadn't left the house since July. Sometimes, Alice called Dean to say hi. She'd discovered that they could talk about modern photography, Diane Arbus and Edward Steichen. To cheer Alice up, Aunt Esmé often brought home stacks of art books from the public library. Alice looked at the pictures, reading a few of the slim bound books each week.

There had been dank, humid afternoons in August when Alice had rarely exited her room. Aunt Esmé had visited her as if she, like Dean, were a patient in the hospital. She'd sat on the suede footstool in front of Alice's chair. She'd tried to get Alice to eat, offering her Pop-Tarts and greasy slices of pizza. Once, she'd taken both of Alice's hands in hers.

"I made an appointment for you to see Dr. Fineman," Aunt Esmé had said.

But the date of the appointment had come and gone.

In July and August, Alice had tried to go outside. The instant she'd set foot on the sidewalk, a doorman from the apartment building across the street had begun to laugh. A bag lady pushing a cart full of trash had taken one look at Alice and spat in the gutter. Alice had felt her face turn red. She'd forced herself to count to one hundred, slowly, to prove that she could withstand the menace. Beneath the wide-open sky, she'd felt condemned, diminished. The traffic lamp across the street became an unfriendly red eye, winking. Her skin became transparent. Bones, muscle, tissue, circulation system, reproductive organs, and digestive tract: everything rotten was exposed.

It was already evening, that mild September day, when Alice rose from her chair. She showered and dressed. Downstairs, inside the laundry room, she poured detergent into the washing machine. She threw a load of clothes in and turned it on. She was sorting through a pile of clean laundry when something tumbled out of the pocket of her skirt. It rolled across the floor, hit the edge of the rug, and fell on its side with a clink. Alice knelt down to look at it. It was the silver ring that she'd taken from J.D.'s dresser. When she'd gotten out of the bathtub at his house in North Carolina that night, it had been sitting on top of her neatly folded clothes, waiting for her. All that seemed long ago.

Alice cupped J.D.'s ring in her palm. The little silver woman, made of metal, was shiny and unbreakable. Alice carried the ring to her bathroom and set it down on the sink. She tore off all the paper that she'd taped to the mirrored medicine cabinet. In August, Alice had gone on a systematic campaign against mirrors, walking from room to room, covering every reflective surface in the house. Aunt Esmé had said it was refreshing to be free of vanity: she'd been going to lectures at NYU about Eastern philosophy. Now, for the first time in weeks, Alice confronted herself—her wan, worn, sickly face. She slipped the ring on. Nothing happened. Alice didn't feel any different. But in the mirror, her hand began to change. It became more shapely, womanly, and capable. Fingers that were not quite hers picked up the hairbrush. They brushed Alice's hair, they ran through Alice's blond curls.

A hand that was not quite Alice's opened the door to the medicine cabinet. It touched things that were not quite real. It probed the bottle of aspirin and the jar of calamine lotion, the packet of scented soaps, the cough syrup. It grazed the vial full of orange-and-yellow capsules, a prescription for tetracycline that Dr. Fineman had given her when she'd had an ear infection last year. Her hand made contact with the blade of the scissors, hard, sharp, and pointed like the metal figurine. The girl who was not quite Alice took them off the shelf.

"Agh!" said Rabbit when Alice walked into the kitchen. "What have you done?" He pressed his arm against his brow.

"Move it," said Alice. "You're in my way." She'd tied the tails of her shirt high up on her rib cage, showing off her belly button. She was wearing a pair of Aunt Esmé's bell-bottoms—torn and tight.

"Did *you* do this?" he said, staring at her, agape. "I hope you didn't pay a professional. Alice, it's much too short. They butchered you. I can see your scalp, angel face. You looked like you're molting. You have bald spots."

"I didn't like the weight around my neck," Alice said. She opened the refrigerator and stood in front of it, scanning its shelves. "I feel lighter."

"You couldn't have just worn it up or something? Shit, Alice. Your hair was your crowning glory. This is drastic."

"So?" Alice said. She picked up a carton of milk and checked the date. "This," she said, "has been here since September 14th." Taking aim, she chucked the carton in the sink. Some of it spilled on the floor. It smelled rancid.

"Bunny," she said, "get a sponge and clean that up."

"Bunny?" Rabbit wrinkled his nose. "Since when am I *Bunny*?"

"Since now." She opened the fruit and vegetable bin. Someone had left a stick of butter and a jar of jam in it, next to a withered tangerine. Alice unscrewed the lid of the jam jar. She stuck her middle finger in. The jam felt gelatinous and sticky. "Clean it up *now*," she said to Rabbit, stirring the goo around.

Rabbit just gawked at her.

Imitating him, Alice gawked back. She opened her mouth, let her tongue hang out, and crossed her eyes.

"Excuse me, Alice," he said, "but what *is* your problem? You on the rag?"

"Eat me, fuckface," said Alice coolly.

Rabbit covered his ears with his hands. "Gads, girl. Where did you learn to talk like that?"

"Where do you think?"

"Come on," said Rabbit. "Don't be that way. For a change, try being nice to me." He grabbed a blue dishrag and tossed it on the puddle of sour milk. Stepping on it with his basketball sneaker, Rabbit swirled the wet towel around on the floor with his heel.

Alice slammed the refrigerator door and leaned against it. The metal was cold against her bare back. She could feel the motor running. Minute vibrations were coursing up to the surface from somewhere deep inside it. Alice put her finger in her mouth. She licked the jam off. She glanced at Rabbit.

"What are you looking at?" she said.

"Nothing." He straddled a stool. He picked up a box of Froot Loops. He leaned forward, his shimmering dark hair falling like a black sheet across his face. He was reading the printing on the back of the box. He frowned in concentration, as if that particular cereal box was especially engrossing.

Alice hopped up on the kitchen counter and sat down, swinging her legs against the cabinet doors. She kicked them, hard, with her bare heels. She'd been living in the same house all her life, but she'd never done what the rest of them did. She'd never climbed up on the kitchen counter. She'd never kicked the cabinet doors with her dirty feet, or swung her long, long legs. From way up there, the room looked smaller. Down in the corner, near the shelf that held the toaster and coffee mug, was Rabbit. The elastic waistband of his underwear was showing. He had a hole in his shirt. She could see the acne on his back.

"Do I *have* to be called Bunny?" he said, still examining the cereal box.

"Yes," said Alice.

"That's an old alcoholic Wasp name, isn't it? It belongs to some guy who summers in Cape Cod and plays bridge. He's wearing tasseled loafers."

"And now it's all yours," said Alice.

"What if I don't want it?" said Rabbit.

"It's yours anyway."

"Who says it's up to you?"

"Because it is."

"What, you're the queen of the universe now, Alice? Is that it?"

"Yeah, Bunny. I am." She was rummaging through one of the cabinets. She took a half-full package of corn chips down from the highest shelf. She opened the bag and sniffed it. "I am now the queen of the universe," she said, taking a test bite. "You have to do exactly what I say." She took another bite, crunching the salty corn chip loudly. She'd lost weight over the summer. She was starving.

"Is that so?" Rabbit opened the file of index cards beside the cookie jar. They contained recipes. He began flipping through them.

"Yup, Bunny. I'm the queen and you're not. That's the way it is."

He folded his arms over his chest. "I don't believe you," he said.

Alice drew her knees up and wrapped her arms around them. "What would you do if I told you I was hungry?" she said. "If I told you to go to the deli on the corner and buy me a chicken salad sandwich with lettuce and tomato, and a bag of potato chips . . . would you?"

"No, I'd tell you to go fuck off, probably," said Rabbit. He shot her a glance. "But you never know. Try me."

"Go to the deli on the corner and buy me a chicken salad sandwich with lettuce and tomato," said Alice.

"Why should I?"

Alice shrugged. "Because . . . it would make me feel good," she said.

Two bright beady eyes assessed her. "Just what's the matter with you, anyway? Esmé said you had mononucleosis, and have to stay home from school in bed."

"Oh, that," said Alice, sounding bored. "I'm playing hooky."

"Then if there's nothing wrong with you, why don't you go get your sandwich yourself?"

Alice wavered. "I'm not sure if I can."

Nobody spoke. Alice imagined they all knew what had happened. The whole world knew but the world avoided certain questions.

"All right," said Rabbit, putting an end to his investigation. "I'll get it for you."

He took his floppy cap from the coat rack. "What kind of bread would you like, your highness?" he said, turning.

"A roll."

"Mayo?" said Rabbit.

"No."

"Anything to drink?"

"Get me a Dr Pepper," said Alice.

"I'll be right back, kiddo. Don't go anywhere." He headed east on Sixty-seventh Street, wearing denim, legs bowed like a cowboy's. After he'd gone, Alice stood in the sunlight for a long while, in the open door.

They were lying, legs entangled, in front of the old black-and-white television set. They were on the rug in her room watching *Star Trek*. Behind the TV, by the open window, ten Polaroid photographs hung from a clothesline, attached with clothespins. They were pictures of Rabbit. When she'd posed him, Alice had covered his eyes with geraniums from the pots in the backyard. She'd covered his genitals with wilted purple petunias. She'd covered his mouth with lipstick.

"Bunny?" she said.

"Yeah?" He held her hand.

"Go get the scissors from the medicine cabinet."

Rabbit's chin jerked up suddenly, as if he'd heard a loud noise. "Enough with the orders, baby. It was just a game." His voice was strained.

"Get them," Alice insisted.

"Oh no," he said, sensing what she wanted from him. "Oh no you don't."

"Do it," she said.

She watched Rabbit set down his can of beer. He stood up and shuffled out of the room, his white athletic socks sliding along the parquet floor. He was doing as she'd told him to. She'd given the orders to Rabbit, just as she'd given the orders to J.D. He was her robot. Press this button, he kneels. Press that button, he bows. It was all up to Alice. She made suggestions, she had ideas, and other people followed them. She'd never lost control.

"What now?" said Rabbit.

"Come over here."

He skated, on his socks, across the bedroom floor. He handed her the scissors.

"Turn around," she told him.

"You're *not* going to cut my hair," he said.

"You'll let me," Alice said. "Say yes."

When she gathered up his silken black hair into a thick rope, he didn't run away. He let her play with it, weighing it, sifting it through her lovely, grown-up fingers, holding it in her lovely, grown-up hand. It looked like a horse's tail.

"Say yes," she said. "Let me do what I want to."

"Okay," said Rabbit after a time. "Fuck it. It's too long anyway. Shoot."

The hair was plentiful. She'd have to press down on the handle to cut it. Alice opened the scissors. As the jaws of stainless steel began, with a squeak, to close, she could feel Rabbit's muscles stiffen. His face was contorted, as if he were afraid she'd hurt him.

"This is how much you love me," she said, her voice flat and unemotional. "Isn't it?"

Epilogue

"Quit moving, Bun," said Alice. "Keep your neck and shoulders out of the frame. I just want your head in this one."

"I feel like the star of a grade B movie," said Rabbit, reaching—for the tenth time—for the hand mirror. He held it close to his face and admired himself. She'd dressed him up in a costume. She'd used her own shorn blond hair to make him a crude curly wig. With painted pouted lips and two spots of color on his face, Rabbit looked a little like a marionette.

"Hurry up," said Alice. "Get back in place."

"We've been doing this for an hour, Alice. I've got a cramp in my left leg."

"Just one more minute," Alice said. She took another look at him through the viewfinder. Her Nikon was set up on its aluminum tripod. "You're okay for now," she said. Under the heat of the two lamps she'd set on either side of the basement stairs,

Rabbit had begun to perspire. The pink circles she'd penciled onto his cheeks were beginning, ever so slightly, to smear. His makeup was melting. She had to hurry, or else she'd need to reapply the whiteface. She should have used more of the powder. It was a fixative.

"Put the mirror down already," Alice said. "I haven't even shot half a roll yet. You keep goofing off, Bun. We're not finished."

If she ever did a series of stills again, she wouldn't use Rabbit. She'd use Stuart instead. He didn't squirm around or talk as much as Rabbit did. But she'd begun the project with Rabbit. There was no time to change models. The entry had to be postmarked by December 8.

"I'm not comfortable," Rabbit complained. "You've got me squeezed up against the wall, with my leg twisted at an inhuman angle."

"Get your foot out of my photo," Alice instructed. "It should look like it's been amputated. And keep your arms behind your back. You're a puppet, Bun. You're not supposed to have any."

"Th—th—that's my girlfriend, folks!" Rabbit said, doing his impression of Porky Pig while gazing upward at the ceiling. "Yes indeed. She's a deeply twisted little chick. Honestly, this is sick shit. Why me, Lord? Why do I put up with this?"

"If you'd just hold the pose, Bun. Please," said Alice. "Stop bouncing around like that. Look what you did. You're wrecking my entire composition." As Alice let go of the Nikon, it bounced softly between her breasts. Her wool sweater was scratchy against her naked skin. She often forgot to wear a bra or underwear, but she never went anywhere without her camera. She'd nearly gotten caught the day she shoplifted it. It hung from a leather strap around her neck. She wore it like a badge of honor.

Alice rearranged the objects on the stairs—the marionette's

missing leg on the floor, the fallen hair ribbon tied in a bow, the white lace anklet, the single black patent leather Mary Jane. She'd been so happy to find the old-fashioned Mary Janes that she'd actually paid for the shoes at the Salvation Army. On the basement stairs, she'd measured the distance between each of her stolen props and had marked their proper locations in chalk. Mr. Harris, her photography teacher at the YMCA, had told the students to be perfectionists. Whenever Alice was shooting photographs in the basement of her tenement apartment building on 108th Street, she was meticulous. She kept her art and photography supplies in perfect order. She had turned her closet into a darkroom. But Dean said the bedroom, which she shared with Esmé, was a health hazard. She'd stopped cleaning ever since the idea for the puppet series had come to her.

"I'm just sitting here, being a puppet. I didn't touch anything," Rabbit said.

"You must have, Bun. It isn't lining up. I had the marionette's arms and legs arranged just exactly how and where I wanted them." She should have given Rabbit a Valium so he'd stop whining and stay in his place. All she needed was five good shots of Rabbit and the puppet. She'd stolen the old wooden marionette from a junk shop in the Village. She'd traipsed all over the city, looking in every thrift store and antique shop, before she'd finally come across it. Her marionette wasn't identical to the one Balthus had used in his legendary series of surrealist photographs, but it was similar. She'd removed the puppet's head and had pried the pins out of its arms and legs—just as, forty years earlier, Balthus had done. She'd put the pieces of the puppet in the foreground. When she'd shown Mr. Harris sketches of the project, he'd suggested that Alice use a wide-angle lens. The puppet's limbs were in the foreground, scattered at the foot of the stairs. Looking at the finished photographs, it would be hard to tell which parts belonged to a lifeless puppet and which were a real boy's.

"Sorry, boss," said Rabbit.

Mercifully, Rabbit got back into position. Alice moved the puppet's broken hand a fraction of an inch. Between the thumb and forefinger of its wooden fingers, she'd glued a ransom note. She'd cut out letters from magazines and cemented them to a sheet of paper. "Want 2 see me alive?" the puppet's message said. Beneath that were ten digits.

212-895-2282. Alice's area code. Her phone number.

It was the autumn of 1978. *American Photo* magazine held a contest every season. As Alice had read, Hans Balthus was going to be the judge that winter. When he saw Alice's kidnapped puppet, he'd recognize it immediately—the lighting, the camera angles, and the composition. She'd copied the Great Man, shot for shot. It was a small contest, with a fifty-dollar prize. Alice planned to win it.